Kiandra Gold

Also by Hugh Capel and published by Ginninderra Press

Where the Dead Men Lie:
The Story of Barcroft Boake, Bush Poet of The Monaroi

Hugh Capel

Kiandra Gold

A Tale of Love, Murder, Bushrangers and Gold

Dedicated to the memory of Barcroft Henry Boake

Kiandra Gold: A Tale of Love, Murder, Bushrangers and Gold
ISBN 978 1 74027 234 6
Copyright © text Hugh Moore 2003
Cover design: Helen Walker

First published 2003
Reprinted 2016

GINNINDERRA PRESS
PO Box 3461 Port Adelaide 5015
www.ginninderrapress.com.au

Contents

Preface

At the height of the Kiandra rush in April 1860, ten thousand men and women were scouring the countryside in search of gold around Kiandra. Hundreds braved the winter snows and a substantial town sprouted from the mud and slush of the Snowy River diggings. Timber buildings – stores, banks and public houses – lined the streets.

Early in 1861 there was a second rush – to the nearby Thredbo/Crackenback diggings.

By the second winter, in 1861, only three hundred miners were left at Kiandra, and a few at Crackenback. The easy pickings had finished. But many fortunes had been made, and the gold kept coming for those who persevered.

This is a story about what happened during those brief but turbulent times. A story about the men and women who lived, loved and died in pursuit of their dreams, during Australia's highest gold rush.

It is also the tragic story of Kitty McCrae.

1

Four Mile Creek
Spring 1861

High in Australia's Snowy Mountains, the Eucumbene River cuts a deep valley for itself after leaving the Kiandra plains, making a broad sweep past its junction with Four Mile Creek before carving its way down through the mountains to Providence and Denison. In the 1860s, when this mountain torrent was called the Snowy River, the lower slopes facing Four Mile Creek were treeless and windswept, as they'd always been.

In the spring of 1861, not long after the last of the winter snows had melted, a young horseman came riding down the grassy spur opposite Four Mile Creek. His mount was a wiry beast, one of those mountain-bred horses favoured by the local stockmen, hardly fourteen hands high but with spirit and bearing in every step.

His hair was long, in the bush fashion; brown strands bleached by the sun. His hat tilted forward, shading his weathered face and the makings of a youthful beard. Despite his youth, he rode easily, surveying the scene ahead with the confidence of a man at home in his country.

It was mid-morning. Grey clouds scudded across the sky, an occasional patch of sunlight briefly lighting the wooded hilltops. Ahead, the rider could see a party of miners digging beside the river. Even at a distance, he recognised them as river men. He spotted their shelter tucked into the side of the hill, despite its camouflage. It was no new-chum's tent. The walls were stacked high with turf, and a thatch of grass and leaves was bound to its roof. These miners knew what the mountain weather could do, even in the warmer months.

A wisp of smoke from a smouldering campfire twisted this way and that in the gusty breeze. He caught the smell of burning eucalyptus before he could see it clearly. His horse smelt it too, and tossed her head, but she never faltered as she picked her way confidently through the rocks and scrub at the foot of the spur.

The noise of the river rushing and gurgling over the rocks, and the metallic clang of the miners' picks and shovels, drowned out the sound of the horse's hooves as the young rider approached the miners' camp. Only when he pulled up immediately in front of them did the men stop their work and look up.

At close quarters, he recognised the miners as Clarke's party. They had a river claim upstream from Kiandra township. He'd seen them working it last time he'd been through the town. They were a hardy lot, having seen out two Kiandra winters. He wondered why they were so far from their claim.

Old Clarke was the tallest in the party, and the most gaunt, with a long, grey-streaked beard that blew in the wind. The other two were younger, and stockily built. All were dressed in typical Kiandra digger style – warm woollen jumpers and thigh-high vulcanised rubber boots. The jumpers had started out blue or red but were now closer to the colour of the river mud. Their hats were battered, their beards and hair wild and matted. They were a fearsome-looking lot that a stranger would have approached with caution. The young rider knew them as God-fearing men, yet he also knew they were not to be trifled with.

Old Clarke leaned on his shovel and tipped his hat in greeting. 'Care to join us for a smoke?' he said.

'Sure,' said James.

'We may as well boil the billy. It's getting on. See to it, Harry, will you?' Clarke nodded in the direction of the youngest in the party.

James dismounted and tied his horse to a bush, next to some green feed. 'There you go, Jasmin,' he said, giving her a pat. He never did find out how she came by her strange name. 'How's the digging?' he asked.

'Fair to middling,' replied Clarke. 'Can't complain. So long as the weather holds.' He looked skywards as he spoke.

Harry fixed the billy. Some logs were pulled out of the woodpile, and they sat round the fire, upwind of the breeze. There was a bite in the air up here, even though it was well into spring below the mountains, down at

Cosgrove's Station. They held their weather-worn hands out towards the fire. It quickly got cold when a man stopped working.

'New claim?' queried James.

'Not really. We're near done here,' said Clarke.

He pulled out his pipe and a wad of tobacco and cut off a clump, offering some to James, who'd produced his own pipe. The others did the same. They lit up using twigs from the fire, then cradled their pipes in their hands as they leaned towards the warm coals.

'This is the last of the Snowy diggings for us,' said Clarke between puffs. 'We'll be off – soon as that pile of wash dirt's gone.' He gestured towards the large heap of freshly dug material beside the river, waiting to be washed for gold. 'We'll give Lambing Flat a go. Sounds like a steady diggings these days, where a party can make reasonable wages, without being bothered too much.' He paused to smoke. 'So long as that business with the Chinese stays settled. No doubt it will, with Commissioner Cloete in charge. Pity we lost him from Kiandra.' He spat into the fire. 'Hope it's not like here. With that – other commissioner.' He nearly swore, but checked himself.

His companions frowned darkly and shook their heads.

'Never mind, Cloete'll sort things out fairly, you can be sure,' he said. 'For the life of me, though, I don't know why the Celestials have come back. Kiandra's full of 'em now. They're all round our old claim – reworking the ground up and downstream where the others left off.'

'We only stayed this winter 'cause our claim was paying well,' said Harry. 'It's not a fit place for temperance men here, now.'

'No diggings is,' said Clarke. 'That's why you've got to stand up for what you believe in. You've got to have the courage of your convictions.'

'But when you can't respect the highest authority? What then?' said Harry. He didn't expect an answer. 'It's ungodly the things what's been going on here.'

Although he didn't share their religious persuasion, James knew what Harry meant.

The billy boiled. They put aside their pipes and cradled hot mugs of tea in their hands.

'That business with the sluicers, it still rankles,' said Clarke. 'At least you and young Davy stood by us. Pity he's left. There's not many left now, is there?' He stared pensively into the fire. 'You know, it's sad to be leaving this place. You sort of get settled, even if it's only a goldfield. There's been some good people here. And this mountain climate, you get used to it. It's got something going for it, despite the cold.'

'Dunno about that,' said Harry. He fixed them all a second mug of tea. Then they took out their pipes again.

'You getting good colour here?' asked James.

'Barely making wages,' was Clarke's reply.

James didn't press the point. He knew only too well you couldn't trust anyone on a goldfield. It didn't pay to be open about your earnings. Diggers who made a big splash about their takings were likely to be talking up the value of their claim for a sale, or had some other, non-straight reason.

'So where you heading now?' asked Clarke.

'Up to Four Mile,' said James. 'I'm back stock riding again. Given away the digging. The others from Cosgrove's have gone ahead. I'm on my way to meet 'em. They took a mob of bullocks up through Nine Mile. What we don't sell to the stores at Nine and Four Mile we'll graze up top, like we used to before the rush.'

'You won't find many diggers up there now,' said Clarke. 'What didn't leave before winter has gone to Lambing Flat. They tell me the Fletchers are still at Four Mile. They stayed through the winter. It would've been tough up there.'

'I was up there myself,' said James. 'It was tough.'

'Are you really giving away the digging?' asked Bob, who'd been silent till then.

'For the time being,' said James. 'Can't say it's for ever. It's hard to get it out of your blood.'

'That's for sure,' said Bob. He sat thinking.

They smoked a while longer.

'Never been to Four Mile this way before,' volunteered James. 'I was thinking I'd cross over there,' he said, pointing down the river. 'Then head up the creek.'

'You wouldn't have got across a few days back,' said Clarke. 'See – that's where the river was up to.' He pointed to the leaves and rubbish caught in the bushes next to them. 'It was a real Old Man Flood. We lost all our wash dirt, and some of our firewood. All gone – swept away in the night.'

'There was a body come down too,' said Harry.

'Poor fella. We couldn't reach him,' said Clarke. 'Reminded me of the first winter. We seen a few go by then, at our old claim.'

The mention of death gave them pause for thought. They puffed silently for a few minutes. Harry stoked the fire with a stick.

Old Clarke broke the silence. 'I'll give you some advice,' he said. 'I've never been to Four Mile that way, but starting out, you want to stick to the left, and stay high. The scrub's pretty thick elsewise, specially down at the creek. We've been over there collecting wood.'

'Thanks for the advice,' said James. 'And thanks for the tea. I guess I'd better be moving on.' He got up, dusted himself off and took his leave.

'May God be with you,' said Clarke.

They were good men, thought James. It would be sad if they never met again. It got him thinking that you didn't have to share a man's religion to count him as a friend.

He walked over to where he'd tethered Jasmin, unhitched her and swung himself up into the saddle. The tea had warmed him inside, and lifted his spirits.

He found an easy place to cross the river and urged Jasmin down the bank and into the rushing stream. It was a murky, muddy colour, carrying the spoils of countless upstream excavations. He remembered how it was two years ago, before the rush – then, the mountain streams were famed for their crystal clearness. Now the land was oozing mud from innumerable wounds. Upstream on the open Kiandra grasslands the valleys and hillsides were scarred with multiple cuts where the miners had ripped away the vegetation in search of the precious metal below. It would take years to heal, if ever.

On the far bank, James rode over mullock heaps and through scattered rocks before heading Jasmin into the dense scrub on the bank of Four Mile

Creek. She baulked at first. He had to give her a pat and say encouraging things. Tangled branches scraped at his legs as they pushed through. After crossing the creek, he headed up the slope to clear the worst of the scrub. Here, they picked their way through scattered snow gums clinging to the steep hillside, the tousled heads of the twisted old trees rustling in the breeze. It was rocky underfoot, with a cover of low bushes and clumpy grasses – slow, careful riding country, through the scrub. As the clouds cleared, the hillsides around sparkled and shimmered, the gum leaves glinting in the sun.

Below him, Four Mile Creek flowed swiftly in its deep, winding valley. Old Clarke was right about staying high. In the bottom of the valley the stream gurgled through a dense cover of trees and bushes. Occasionally he saw a flash of water through the bushes. Hearing the muffled roar of a waterfall, he rode low to take a closer look, watching as the water plunged into its rocky pool. Further on, he came on a second waterfall. Tethering Jasmin, he scrambled down the slippery bank.

There was magic in the air. A fairy rainbow shimmered in the misty spray. He felt the tiny droplets damp and cool on his face. Delicate little ferns clung to the undersides of the overhanging rocks. Waterfalls fascinated him. He was amazed this one had stayed untouched, so close to the diggings. He drew in the damp cool air and smelt the fresh aroma of the bush. Reluctantly, he climbed back through the scrub to untie Jasmin and resume his journey.

After a mile of winding through the trees and scratchy undergrowth on the steep hillside, the valley flattened out. From a rocky rise, ahead he could see the grassy clearings of the lower Four Mile flats.

Four Mile Creek rises in swamps and frost hollows near the top of the range. Its middle reaches, below the highest waterfall, flow through open snowgrass flats, before it plunges headlong into its deep cutting on its way to join the Eucumbene River.

He paused to take in the view. The sunny green flats contrasted starkly with the dark, low-set, forested hills that hemmed them in. Behind him was the tangled scrub of the valley gorge. It was like approaching a secret place.

Stock riding may not pay well, he thought, but it had its rewards. Where else could you be your own man, out in the bush like this? Where else would you be given your own horse, with the freedom to chase after wild brumbies in the mountain ranges? Riding in the bush gave him the chance to think. So many things had happened these last two years – good things, bad things. People and events from the past came tumbling into his head, all jumbled together. He saw the faces, he heard the voices.

He enjoyed being alone, but sometimes it was lonely, now they'd all gone. He still had the memories – memories of the hard work, of the friendships as they'd braved the cold winter nights together; memories of the mud, the slush and the ice, of nights huddled round the fire telling yarns. Catching himself, he remembered he had a mob of bullocks to meet. He'd better stop dreaming, and get on with riding. He needed to reach them before they left the Nine Mile trail.

He rode out of the trees and into the open grassy flats. Soon, signs of mining were evident. The wide banks of the creek were lined with scratchings and odd piles of disturbed rocks in amongst the tussock grasses, but there was no sign yet of any miners. The only diggers left were working much higher up the creek, beyond Commissioner's Gully, up past the highest waterfall.

He rode past a discarded pick and shovel, half hidden amongst the tussocks. He thought it strange. Perhaps they'd been thrown away in disgust, or more likely lost in the snow. He knew that many of the miners had buried their tools at the approach of the first winter, intending to come back. Most never did.

The wind suddenly dropped. His horse halted. He didn't know why. She pricked up her ears. It was a moment frozen in time. He listened. Without the rustle of the wind, the only sound was the quiet burbling of the creek. Suddenly, from behind the grassy hillside ahead, a squabbling flock of crows flew into the air, squawking, before quickly dropping out of sight again. Black birds of ill omen, he thought. Inexplicably, he felt a shudder down his spine.

He nudged Jasmin forward, following the creek around a gentle bend, till he came to a gully on his right. It was full of pits, and strewn with loose rocks and mullock heaps. Halfway up, the crows were perched around one of the mullock heaps, some on top, others to the side. As soon as they saw him, they flew into the air, like a guilty party caught in the act. Flapping their wings and squawking noisily, they made off up the valley.

On the spur of the moment, he swung his horse up the gully. He couldn't explain why. He felt an urge to see what the crows had been doing. It would probably be a dead wombat, or some other carrion.

Jasmin didn't seem keen.

'Come on, old girl,' he said, giving her a gentle nudge with his knees.

She moved forward reluctantly, tossing her head. The ground was boggy from a recent storm, and sticky with streams of overflow mud from the diggings.

As he approached the mullock heap, he could see its side had been partly washed away. On the far side of the mound, halfway up its eroded slope, he saw a human arm sticking out from the gravel and rocks.

'What the hell!' he exclaimed.

It was a grisly sight. The elbow and shoulder were all that were protruding – what was left of them. The crows had ripped the clothes and skin from the body, exposing the flesh and bones.

He jumped down onto the rocks. Jasmin shied, skipped away and trotted back down the gully. He swore at her, but decided to let her go – for the moment.

The recent rains had flooded past the mound, scouring a new channel in the middle of the gully, and washing away the rocks and gravel at the side of the mullock heap. This had exposed part of the body, allowing the crows to get at it. Scraps of cloth from the torn coat sleeve lay in the muddy channel beside the mound. Loose strands of flesh and sinew hung from the exposed bones.

James felt he was going to vomit, and turned away. Doubling up and squatting down, he held his stomach. He wasn't usually this squeamish. Dead bodies had never bothered him before. He felt annoyed with himself.

After a few minutes, he felt better and stood up. He saw Jasmin had reached the creek and was busy feeding. He turned back to look at the body again. The poor beggar, he thought. Then he started to wonder how the body had got there. It looked as though it had been dumped beside the mound, and rocks and gravel from the mound scraped over it. It was lying on its side, which was why the arm and shoulder had been exposed first. The cover hadn't been deep. This area had been deserted over winter, so the body could have been buried under the snow and ice until the recent thaw.

It was odd, he thought. There had been plenty of dead bodies at the diggings over the last couple of years – but why would anyone be buried in a mullock heap? It didn't look like an accidental death. It wasn't from a trench collapse, or anything like that. He hadn't fallen down a shaft, like some he knew. Why bury a fellow at the side of a mullock heap? Surely it wouldn't have been too much to dig a proper grave?

He began to wonder if there'd been foul play. I can't leave him like this, he thought. I'll have to do something – at least to keep the birds and animals away. He remembered the pick and shovel he'd seen further down the creek. Damn that horse, he thought. He needed to catch her first.

Jasmin was unimpressed at being taken away from her feed.

'You'll have plenty of time for that in a moment,' he told her as he mounted.

In a short while, he was back at the mullock heap with the pick and shovel. He left Jasmin at the creek, this time with the hobbles on. He didn't want any brumby stallions catching her scent and making off with her.

He knew it wouldn't be good enough just throwing some gravel over the body. The next storm would expose it again. He'd have to give it a decent cover. He started by digging a hole beside the body. His plan was to move the body into it, before covering it with a good layer of gravel and heavy rocks.

When he'd finished the hole, he began to dig around the body. He worked gingerly, as he still felt uneasy. He uncovered the bottom half first, then its back. It was remarkably well preserved. The poor fella had been buried boots and all. When he'd cleared the rocks from around its back, he could see matted blood amongst the dark, curly hair. It looked as if the digger had died from a wound to the back of his head – it had to be foul play, for sure. He moved to the side and tried to avoid looking at the body. It still disturbed him.

His digging undermined the body and it rolled backwards into the hole, face upwards. As it did so, he glanced down. Its pallid, dirt-stained face stared up at him with glazed eyes.

'Christ!' he yelled out loud. 'It's Davy!'

He dropped the shovel. Jumping backwards he slipped and fell in the mud. In a panic, he scrambled up the nearby bank, half crawling, half stumbling. He stood on the bank, holding himself round the chest, and shivering.

'Davy? But it can't be,' he said out loud. 'Davy's at Lambing Flat!'

Successive waves of emotion broke over him – first fear, then anger, then guilt. Fear that kept him glancing furtively and anxiously behind his back. Anger at the person who had done this – the low, murderous villain. Guilt that made him want to grab hold of Davy and shake him, to scream at him, 'I'm sorry. You've got to believe me, Davy. It wasn't my fault!'

He covered his eyes with his hands and turned his face away, unable to bear Davy's stare, or to look at his ripped and mangled arm.

'How could it be? How could it be?' he kept repeating to himself.

He sat down and held his head between his hands. He took off his hat. It made no difference. He put it back on again. He looked at his mud-stained hands. He turned them over and looked at the callused palms. A wave of guilt came over him again.

'But who could have done this?' he asked himself. He knew Davy had plenty of enemies. But why this? He didn't deserve to die. Not like this! What would he tell Kitty? What on earth could he tell Kitty now?

He looked again at Davy's dead stare. He couldn't take it. Clambering down the bank, he rescued the shovel from the mud. Holding it by the far end of the handle, he managed to lever the body onto its side so that it faced away from him. Lying like that in the hole, with the damaged arm underneath, Davy could have just been sleeping. James felt better. He stood back, well clear of the body, and leaned on the shovel. His arms and legs started to shake.

What now? It didn't take him long to decide. He had to cover the body. He didn't have all day. He still had to meet Clarrie and the bullocks up past Four Mile diggings.

All of a sudden he felt very thirsty. He ran stumbling down to the creek to Jasmin. Grabbing his water flask from the saddlebag, he drained it in one go. Then he unstrapped his roll from behind the saddle and took out a blanket. He carried it back to the mullock heap and placed it carefully over Davy.

He stood and looked at the forlorn bundle for a few minutes. Then he set to and spread a layer of gravel and rocks over the blanket, making sure it was well covered. He kept shovelling till there was a large mound over the body. To finish off, he stuck the pick by its handle into the top of the new mound. With bowed head, he stood silently over Davy's grave, and paid him his last respects.

After wiping a tear from his cheek, he turned his back on the grave and walked slowly down the gully to the main creek. Earlier in the day, he had everything to look forward to. Now his life had been turned upside down. Davy's death left a gaping hole. He felt so hollow – and so sad. For Davy to have been murdered was so unfair. Where was the justice in that? He felt an emptiness inside him that made every move an effort.

Battling against his instinct, he forced himself to go on. He had to catch Jasmin again. Once in the saddle, he rode up the creek towards the main diggings. They made good progress up the grassy valley. At the junction with Commissioner's Gully, he picked up the track from Kiandra. This climbed the spur to the left of the creek before disappearing into the trees. To his right, the valley narrowed before ending at the foot of the high waterfall. As he rode up the track, the trees closed in. On the higher slopes, the sturdy snow gums grew bent and twisted, whipped and buffeted by the fierce alpine winds. Amongst them stood jagged and splintered stumps, where miners desperate for winter firewood had hacked into the living trunks. Some of the trees had refused to die. Clusters of soft new shoots sprouted from their sides.

He suddenly felt cold – cold from the inside. The bush around was unreal and strange – cold, eerie and hostile – not friendly, as he usually found it. He struggled to ride on, every move needing an effort of will.

Jasmin seemed to sense something was wrong. She faltered and whinnied nervously.

The track led him to the upper Four Mile flats. Here, above the waterfall, the valley widened and the true high plains country began – a land of gentle, rolling contours, of low, snow gum-covered hills, open grassy clearings and shallow gullies. On these high slopes, the flats and gullies were carpeted with soft waterlogged sedges, spongy mosses and snow grass tussocks mixed in with the heath. That's how it was – where the miners hadn't been.

The cluster of weatherboard buildings at the Four Mile soon came into sight, surrounded by its field of diggings. All around, wherever there'd once been snow grass and marshes, now there were untidy piles of rocks and mounds of earth. The leftover burrowings of a multitude of men. No wonder the lower creek was murky with sediment.

These days, the diggings were all but deserted. So were many of the buildings. James rode straight towards the closest. Beside the front door, a tattered Eureka flag fluttered in the breeze. How much trouble that flag had caused!

The building looked empty. James rode round it, peering into the windows without dismounting. He had to find Eureka Jack. Had to tell him about Davy. Jack would know what to do, although he hardly expected to find him at home in the middle of the day. He glanced at the other buildings – they looked equally deserted. All he could see was a lonely-looking bullock tied to a post behind one of the stores. Wheeling his horse around, he set off across the diggings.

Jack's claim was in the next gully. Jasmin picked her way through the piles of discarded rubble and over the open water channels towards the claim. Memories flashed by. Here was where Davy had found the twelve-ounce nugget. Now he was crossing the German party's extended claim. To the side were the remains of their puddling machine. Over there was where the party from Maitland had their claim.

There was no sign of Jack at his claim.

'Damn,' said James. He stood up in his saddle and looked around. Further up the hillside he could see a wisp of smoke from a fire. It was coming from behind the high dam. He made for it. The weather was changing. Low clouds skimmed across the hills, just above the treetops. The wind was picking up. Occasional drops of rain blew into his face.

At the edge of the dam, he found the Fletcher brothers, Charly and Fred. They had their backs to the wind and were shovelling material from a large stockpile into a wooden water sluice.

'Hey there, fellas,' he shouted at them into the wind, jumping down from his horse.

They nodded acknowledgement, holding onto their hats as the wind buffeted them.

'You wouldn't have seen Old Jack? Recent, like – would you?' asked James.

''Fraid not,' said Charly. He told James that Jack had gone to Denison to get supplies and wasn't expected back till the next day.

'What about the mob from Cosgrove's? Any chance you seen them? Should've been a few dozen bullocks and a couple of stockmen. They should've been through this way by now,' said James. 'I need to be joining 'em.'

'They went by this morning,' said Fred. 'Said they were heading for Bullock Head Creek on the high track. We took one of the bullocks. You might've seen 'im tied up near our place. Thought we could do with some fresh meat. We told 'em there wasn't no one else around.'

'They won't have got too far,' said Charly.

James thanked them and said he'd best be on his way. He couldn't tell them about Davy – it just wouldn't come out. As he rode into the wind, he felt so empty and so sad. He didn't know if it was rain or tears he could feel damp on his cheeks.

2

Cooma
Spring 1859

'Hey, lad, give us a hand with those bellows, will you?' said Mr McNeill.

The speaker was a short stocky man, barrel-chested and brawny-armed under his long leather apron, with a thick ginger beard. Streams of sweat ran down the side of his face. Inside the blacksmith's workshop it was cooking up a furnace. A wall of heat radiated from the red-hot coals on the raised hearth.

James did as he was asked.

The workshop was a jumble of iron bars and implements – hanging from the big timber roof beams, stacked against the walls, and lying in untidy piles on the earthen floor. The smell of burning coke and scorched metal added to its interest. James liked watching the steam spurt up when the hot metal was plunged into the water cask. It was a good place to be in winter. In spring, with the outside temperatures rising, it wasn't so attractive. By summer, it was to be avoided at all costs.

'May as well make yourself useful if you're here,' said Mr McNeill. He had a twinkle in his eye. 'Don't s'pose it was me you come by to see, eh?'

James didn't reply. He kept pumping the bellows till the coals fairly seared with heat. He liked Sally's father, but experience told him it was best if he didn't say too much.

'Guess it's Sal you're lookin' for, eh? Don't worry, she can wait. I need a hand here. Pass me those tongs, will you?'

James passed the tongs.

Sally's father took a searing white metal bar from the fire. He held it on the anvil in the middle of the workshop and took to it with a heavy hammer. Red-hot sparks flew at every clang.

'That young fella of mine,' he said, grunting between blows. 'He's disappeared again. Never here when I need 'im. Hold that, will you?'

James didn't mind helping.

'Makes you doubt the wisdom of working with family.' The blacksmith belted the red-hot metal as if to teach it a lesson. 'You know, oft times a man and his son get on better when they're doing different jobs.'

James agreed. He was in trouble with his own father for his reluctance to learn the boot-making trade.

'I'd be happy to take you on. If it wouldn't be so quiet,' said Sally's father. 'You seem pretty handy with the tools.'

James said nothing. He had no ambition to become a blacksmith. But the compliment made him feel good.

Mr McNeill put a new iron bar into the fire. He stepped back and wiped his forehead with a rag as he waited for it to heat up. 'Sal was out looking for you this morning,' he said. He took the white-hot metal out of the fire and started belting it with his hammer, then stopped. 'Here – take this,' he said, handing James a hammer. 'We'll do this one together.'

They took turns belting the bar until it cooled down. Then the blacksmith thrust it back into the hot coals. After another session of hammering, and when it was flattened to his satisfaction, he plunged it into the water cask with a sharp hiss.

'That'll do,' he said. 'Let's have a break.'

They went outside and sat on a rough-hewn plank, balanced on two stumps, under a lean-to roof at the side of the forge.

Mr McNeill offered James tobacco for his pipe. 'You an' Sal,' he said. 'You two been spending a fair bit of time together, I seen.'

James nodded.

They lit their pipes and smoked for a while.

'Not sure how serious you two is.' He paused, searching for words. 'Well, if you want to know, you've got my support.' He looked James in the eyes. 'You're a good lad, from what I seen.'

James felt embarrassed. He didn't know what to say, or if he should say anything. He fiddled with his pipe. They smoked some more.

'You and Sal – you been doing some book learning, I know. But that don't give you a living, do it? I mean, you decided on a trade to follow yet?'

James thought for a while before answering. 'Not really. I was thinking I might do a bit of stock riding first.'

'That wouldn't hurt, I guess. You're still young. Just remember: a fella's got to make something of his life.'

James didn't reply. He was glad Sally's father left it at that.

They watched the draughthorse in the stall next to them – the blacksmith's next job. He shook his shaggy mane out of his eyes and munched his oats methodically, looking as if he didn't have a care in the world.

'They're a great breed, those Clydesdales,' said Mr McNeill. 'They've got the patience of Jove. There's more than a few other breeds could do with some of their patience. You'd know that, wouldn't you? Sal tells me you've been round horses a bit. She says you're a good horseman.'

James felt embarrassed again. 'I guess so,' he said.

Don't worry, I'll be right to shoe 'im meself,' said Mr McNeill, as if anticipating an offer from James. 'I'd be happy to shoe Clydesdales all day. You can nip round the back and see Sal now.'

'Thanks. I'd better,' said James, 'or she'll be wondering what's happened to me.'

The wooden cottage behind the workshop was well separated from the forge – for good reason. Plenty of buildings ended in a pile of char from the careless use of fire.

Sally's mother was propping the clothesline with a long forked pole. 'Sal!' she shouted when she saw James coming. 'Sal! James is here.'

'Good day, Mrs McNeill,' said James, touching his hat.

'Nice to see you,' she said. 'You've been helping at the forge, I see. Don't worry,' she laughed, 'I'm used to my men all covered in soot.' Her face came to life when she laughed. She had sparkling blue eyes and would have been pretty when young. Now her face was creased with the cares of a working life.

A little girl poked her head out from behind Mrs McNeill and made a face at James. James made a face back. The little scamp ran away, but not far. Returning, she gave him a big gap-toothed grin as she poked her head out from behind her mother's skirt.

'Don't do that,' chided her mother, as the little girl and her young brother started a tug of war over a sheet.

At this point, Sally arrived. She had a similar build and appearance to her mother, but without the ravages of time. They were both small, self-contained women, lightly built but shapely. James liked the way Sally walked. She had a spring in her step that made her soft bits move up and down in just the right way. He liked the way her light brown hair caught the sun when she wore it loose. Most of all he liked her smile. She was an attractive girl, without being beautiful. He remembered his uncle's advice. When taking a wife, first look at her mother. That's what you'll be living with in twenty years' time, his uncle had said. James looked at Sally's mother. It wouldn't be so bad, he thought, though he had no immediate intention of marrying.

'Why don't you two go for a walk?' said Mrs McNeill, with a knowing smile. 'Don't be late, though.'

'Yes, let's,' said Sally. She was keen to get away from her little brothers and sisters. They always made a nuisance of themselves when James was around, trying to steal his attention.

As soon as they were out of sight of the house, Sally surreptitiously slid her hand into James's. She didn't mind that his hand was dirty from the forge. She liked the rough feel of it.

James wasn't unaware. He enjoyed the warm softness of her little hand. He liked the little moves Sally made and didn't think of her as being too forward. That would have put him off.

For a while, they walked without speaking. They'd known each other long enough to feel comfortable just being together. Every now and then, Sally looked up at him, or he down at her. Their eyes would meet and they'd exchange a smile.

Their walk took them along a winding track up Nanny Goat Hill to one of their favourite places – a fallen log amongst the rocks, near the top of the hill, worn smooth from where they'd sat on it.

'Looks like I'll probably get that job at Cosgrove's,' said James.

'With the horses?' asked Sally.

'No. The summer grazing.'

'So you won't be at Adaminimi Station?'

'No. We'll be up the high country. At Gibson's Plains.'

'Will you be away for long?' said Sally. There was concern in her voice.

'I don't know for sure if I'm going yet,' said James. 'If I do, it'll be for the whole summer – probably till Easter.'

'I'm not certain I'd like that,' said Sally, looking at him apprehensively.

He was staring into the distance. 'They told me we'd be right for a visit home round Christmas,' he said, still gazing into the distance. 'It'll depend on someone coming up to take over. You can't leave the cattle alone up there.' He broke off a grass stalk and started to pick the seeds off it.

'Do you really have to go?' Sally was upset and could no longer hide her feelings.

'You know I have to, Sal. We've been through this before.'

'What about us?'

'It won't be for ever. I do care about you, Sal. But I can't live at home any more. I've got to get away. I feel like I'm trapped. I'm fed up, having to stitch leather. Father's always at me about taking up the boot-making trade permanently. Now we're done with schooling, I don't have an excuse any more.'

He finished shredding the grass stalk and picked another. 'You'd understand if you were in my position. Imagine if your father wanted you to be a boot-maker. Imagine stitching boots every day. Hell, Sal! I can't do it. I've got to get away. I've got to live.'

'I know, James. I s'pose I'm being selfish. But I can't help it.' She wiped her eyes. 'It upsets me that you'll be away so long. You understand that, don't you?'

'Yes, I do. But it won't be forever. We're still young, Sal. You might change your mind about me anyway. You might find another fella.'

'Don't say that, James. You promised me you wouldn't.'

'All right. But truly, Sal – you wouldn't want to end up like your mother before you'd lived, would you? With nothing but chores and little ones bleating all day long? We need to do something interesting before we settle down. At least *I* do.'

'It's fine for you. You're the one who's going off adventuring,' said Sally somewhat petulantly.

'I can't help it if I want some excitement in my life,' said James. 'I need it – I've got to have adventure. That's how I am. If you don't like that, I can't change it. Maybe you should look for someone else.' He immediately regretted the remark.

'That's not fair,' said Sally. 'And you know it.'

'All right,' he said. 'Sorry.'

She moved closer to him. James felt bad when they argued. To make amends, he put his arm round her and pulled her closer.

She put her head on his shoulder and snuggled up against him. 'You know how I feel about you,' she said. 'I know a girl shouldn't say that. But I don't care.'

He felt the warmth of her body beside him. They sat snuggled together on the log for a while without talking. He enjoyed smelling the sweet muskiness of her hair.

'Sometimes I think you expect too much from life,' said Sally quietly. 'I'd love to be rich or something. I'd love that it was different. But it's not going to happen. We can't expect to live more than ordinary lives – we're just ordinary people.'

James thought for a while. 'I guess I do expect more,' he said. 'I'm not ready to accept just being an ordinary person. I look around at the people here, in this place – at the people we know. I swear, surely there's got to be more to life than this.'

'You keep saying that,' said Sally. 'But what do you want? How do you want to live?'

'I don't know, I guess,' said James. 'I just feel there's got to be more than this.' He decided he'd better say no more. He wasn't ready to be tied down yet. Being trapped in marriage wouldn't be so different from being trapped by boot-making. But he wasn't going to tell Sally that.

He liked Sally. When he was ready to settle down, she might fit the bill. But that was a long way in the future. He was barely sixteen, and she was even younger. There was so much to see and do. He'd hardly been out of Cooma yet.

He could sense Sally's sadness.

'You do matter to me, Sal,' he said. 'Let's not talk about it any more.' He gave her a gentle squeeze.

It didn't make her feel better. She couldn't help thinking how unfair it was that men got the chance to have adventures while women were expected to wait meekly for them to return. If she had her way, she wasn't going to let that happen to her.

After they returned from their walk, James had to return to help his father, while Sally had to do her chores.

Over dinner that evening, Sally's father mentioned how James had helped him out at the forge. 'He's a useful lad. And dependable too,' he said, looking at his eldest boy.

The boy kept his head down and ignored the comment.

'I told James I'd noticed how Sal and 'im's been spending time together.'

Sally looked at her father darkly.

'Here, pass that bread,' he said. He bit off a big mouthful. When he'd half finished chewing he added, 'I told 'im that he had me support if he was serious 'bout Sal.'

'Dad!' said Sally angrily. 'How could you!' She jumped up from the table and ran from the room.

'Look what you've done!' said Mrs McNeill. 'You big galoot! Haven't you got any brains? The last thing Sal needs is you sticking your big clumsy oar in.'

'What have I done wrong?' said Sally's father. 'I was only trying to help. She needs to get married soon, and he'd be a good match. He seems a steady enough young lad.'

'That's not the point,' said Mrs McNeill. 'Can't you understand?' She looked exasperated. 'Boys need careful management. Any sign of a trap and they're off like a shot. How d'you think the lad'll feel now? It's enough to scare him clean away, what you said.'

'I never meant no harm,' said Mr McNeill. 'I thought you were keen for Sal to be married off soon. It's either that or we needs be looking round for a station for her soon.'

'I'm in two minds about that,' said Mrs McNeill. 'I don't know what I'd do about the house without her. But I'm worried by her wilful ways – it could put off a man. I thought the schooling would help, but it doesn't seem to have made much difference. At least James and her seem to get on well.'

'James an' Sal would make a good match.'

'Which is why you should stay right out of it,' said Mrs McNeill.

After the dishes were tidied away, Mrs McNeill went looking for Sally. She found her on the back veranda.

'What's the matter, dearie?' she asked. 'I've saved some dinner for you. Would you like it now?'

'No,' said Sally. 'I don't feel hungry.'

Her mother could see Sally was still upset. They got talking about James.

'Your father doesn't understand,' said Mrs McNeill. 'And he probably never will. He doesn't mean any harm, though.' She put her hand on Sally's arm.

'I shouldn't let it bother me,' said Sally. 'Oh, Mum, I'm so unhappy. James told me he's going away. You don't know how I feel.'

'There, there, dearie,' said Mrs McNeill, patting her daughter's arm. 'It's not the end of the world. How long will he be away?'

'All summer.'

'That's nothing. When your father was courting me – '

Sally cut her off. 'I don't want to hear that. I don't want to hear about you, or about any other people. What if he doesn't like me any more? What if he changes his mind?'

'Come, now,' said Mrs McNeill. 'There's no point in distressing yourself. You're getting all worked up over nothing. Time will fly. He'll be back in no time.'

'But summer is months and months.' Sally wiped her teary eyes. 'I'll miss him so much. And he doesn't seem to care. He says he cares, but then he tells me he's going away.'

Mrs McNeill kept trying to reassure her daughter, but without much success. 'Are you really sure he's the one for you?' she eventually asked.

'After all, he's the first boy who's been seriously interested in you, isn't he? You're both very young, you know.'

'If that's all you can say, just leave me alone,' snapped Sally.

'All right, then. I won't say any more. But you do need to be sure, you know.'

They sat in silence for a few minutes. Sally's eagerness in James's presence hadn't passed her mother's notice.

'I know you don't want to listen to my advice,' said her mother. 'But I will tell you one thing – you mustn't ever be forward with boys. Remember that. If there's nothing else you remember from me, remember that.'

'Come on, Mum. What do you think I'm going to do?' asked Sally.

'I'm not saying anything. I've said enough,' replied her mother. 'If you truly want James to marry you, you'll need to keep him at a distance. And you'll need to be patient.'

*

A week later, when James took his leave from Sally, the goodbyes were tearful. Even James had watery eyes. His farewell to his parents was much less emotional, though his mother did fuss a lot. His father was surprisingly friendly. He wished James well, and told him to make sure he profited from his experience.

James could see the main range on the horizon as he rode across the rolling hills from Cooma. The view lifted his spirits and gave him a thrill of excitement. He'd never been as far as the mountains before. He could even see patches of snow on the sides of the highest peaks.

Cosgrove's Adaminimi Station was a bustle of low, timber buildings set in a wide, open, grassy valley. The touch of early spring had greened the pastures sloping down to the Eucumbene River some three miles distant. Here the river wound its way across a broad, treeless flood plain of swampy tussock grass flats. It was a river of sandy beaches, whose mountain-fed waters flowed crystal clear on their way to Jindabine. To the west, beyond the sparse bush on the closest hills, rose the rugged slopes of the Snowy Mountain ranges.

The stockmen were mustering the herd for the start of the journey to the high country when James arrived at the station. Clarrie, the head stockman, was an old hand. He'd been taking stock to summer pasture in the high country for longer than anyone could remember. His word was law.

Cattle moaned, dogs barked and whips cracked. Clouds of dust hung about the stockyards, and the smell of leather and fresh dung filled the air. As the mob got under way, the seething mass of cattle constantly threatened to break out. Stock riders spurred their horses, wheeling in the strays. Dogs raced backwards and forwards around them, chasing the action.

The mob was a fair size – upwards of six hundred beasts, including a number brought in from outlying areas. The wild-eyed youngsters, less familiar with dogs, men and horses, were eager to put their keepers to the test. It took most of the morning before the frisky beasts had quietened down, and steady progress had been established.

At the end of the cavalcade came the packhorses, roped together and loaded with provisions and the stockmen's swags.

Clarrie would have liked a few more days for the herd to settle down. But if he delayed too long, others would take the best of the high country grazing. They'd already lost time, and possession was nine tenths of the law in the days before there were leases. He remembered how strangers from Victoria had occupied his hut one year – they were a mean-looking lot, and he'd had to pay them to move their stock.

Although this was a bigger mob than James had mustered before, he had the advantage of an experienced horse. Susie was a farewell gift from his father. She had belonged to one of his father's friends, an old stockman who'd taught James to ride. She hardly needed direction when the strays made a bolt for it, taking to the chase at the slightest touch.

The stockmen James fell in with included Dusty Bob, a grey-bearded bushman, who took James under his wing, and said he'd show him the ropes. Then there were the two Crow boys from Euecumbene Station. The Crows were off to the high country to look for brumbies, but had offered to give Clarrie a hand for some of the way. Bill Sweeney and James made up the numbers. James was the youngest. Sweeney wasn't much older than James, but was ten times more experienced, by his own reckoning. He was slightly built, but walked with a swagger, and spat and kicked the dirt a lot.

Clarrie's plan was to get the cattle in good condition on alpine summer feed as soon as possible. A buyer from Victoria was due to meet him at Gibson's Plains after Christmas. Then there was a prospect that some of the cattle might be taken to the Adelong and Victorian goldfields markets. The droving arrangements for the deal would need to be worked out. Clarrie told James and the others he might need them to help.

The route to the high country pastures took them upstream to William Russell's station at Denison and to Providence Flats. It was easy going at first, along the wide, grassy valley. As they approached the mountains, the hills closed in on them. The slopes beside them became steeper and stands of tall mountain ash filled the narrow gullies.

When they reached Russell's, Clarrie came to an arrangement with William Russell, and the stockmen ate at the station with the local hands. Cheeky young John Russell, the station owner's son, joined them. In the evening, around the fireplace, they got talking about gold.

'You figure on panning for gold when you're up the high country this time?' asked Harry, Russell's head stockman, a lanky, weather-beaten bushman.

'May do,' said Bob. 'There's a pan at the hut. We washed a few ounces of dust last year. Best not to say too much about it.'

'Is there really gold in the mountains?' asked James. He'd heard talk of it in Cooma, but there were different stories. His father told him not to believe everything he heard.

'Sure is,' replied Harry. 'There's plenty of gold in the mountains. Only question is whether it's payable.'

'What do you mean?' asked James.

'He means, can you make a living out of it? Does it pay as much as wages?' said Bob.

'Would there be that much up there?' asked James.

'That's the big question,' said Bob.

'There was a fella here the other week,' said Harry. 'He was on his way back from the Adelong diggings. He knocked back a few too many nobblers and made a nuisance of himself – but that's another story. Anyway, this fella reckoned there was lots of gold along the Tumut River and higher up, near Gibson's Plains. He said all the easy gold was finished at Adelong but he'd found a new El Dorado. We tried to get him to tell us where – but he went to sleep. When we woke him the next morning, he wouldn't talk about it. We threw him out.'

'There is gold up there,' blurted out young John Russell. 'I seen it myself.'

'What's that?' said Harry.

'It was before winter,' said John. 'I took Mr Pollock to where Father was working.'

'Was that David Pollock?' asked Harry.

'No. It was his father. It was Mr Robert Pollock,' said John. 'Father was with Mr Berrigan, Mr Black and Mr McClean. They were panning in the creek. Father and the others had two bags full of gold – I seen it. It was really something.'

'Funny that,' said Harry. 'Mr Russell never mentioned it to me.'

'Why would he?' said Clarrie. 'Could give you ideas. He'd want to keep you working here.'

'What happened then?' asked Bob.

'Mr Pollock was asking Father's permission to take the gold away for assay. He said he'd find out how valuable it was. Father wouldn't agree at first. They argued a bit. Then Father agreed and they all shook hands. Father gave him one of the bags.'

'How much was in the bags?' asked Clarrie.

'They wasn't big bags. About this much each,' said John, cupping one of his hands.

'I still wonder why I wasn't told,' said Harry.

'Do you know what Robert Pollock did with the gold?' asked Bob.

'I don't,' said John. 'Father said telling him was like shouting it from the rooftops. Some men came to talk to father about gold after that. They wanted Father to show them where he'd found the gold. But then it snowed and everyone left.'

'Are you sure you should be telling us this?' asked Clarrie.

'Yes, it's all right. Father said it's no secret now. But I'm not to tell anyone where he and the others found the gold.'

'Looks like we'd better take a gander ourselves,' said one of the Crow boys.

'I might come up and see how you're doing in a week or so,' said Harry.

With that, they turned in for the night.

After Russell's, the hard work began. Taking a mob of cattle up Alpine Creek was no picnic. Harry told them it would be best to go up through Boggy Plain, if they had to go that way at all. He didn't know why Clarrie was set on Alpine Creek. Heading up by Table Top and Happy Jack's would be much easier. Clarrie said that was the long way round. He might go that way if he had more time. But he knew the country and reckoned it was pretty open under the trees since the fires the summer before last.

'Did you bring the branding irons?' Clarrie asked as they were about to set off.

'Yes. They're on the last packhorse,' said Bob.

James asked Bob why. 'Aren't the cattle all freshly branded?'

'That they are,' said Bob. 'But you never know. We might find some as got left last summer. Or there might be some calves. Without a brand, it's near impossible to prove where a calf come from – or who its mother be. Up the high country there's cattle from all over, from Yass Plains to Tumut, as well as from the Monaro.' He gave James a wink. 'It's easy for them to get mixed up.'

The lower reaches of Alpine Creek flowed through clearings bordered by tall stands of mountain ash. Thick scrub lined the creek bed. The herd trampled through the undergrowth, crunching and cracking branches, spilling out amongst the tall trees on either side of the creek. It was easy to see where they'd gone, from the trail of trampled vegetation and boggy hoof prints. Clarrie scouted the way ahead. Sweeney covered the left side while the Crow boys took the right side. From the rear, where Bob and James were riding, it was hard to tell what was going on. Their job was to turn back bolters and make sure no stragglers got left behind.

Chasing strays through the undergrowth, dodging tree trunks and jumping over logs was tiring work. It also meant slow progress.

'It looks harder than it is,' said Bob. 'With these steep hills on either side, there's not much chance of a break-out. As long as we keep prodding from behind, they'll keep going up the main creek.'

Bob and James had paused at the edge of a marshy clearing. The grass was still damp from an overnight shower. Sunlight dappled through the trees, lighting up the occasional wattle and sparkling where it caught a wet leaf. James could smell crushed eucalyptus and the musty scent of trampled bark and leaves. Being in the bush was so much better than boot-making.

Clarrie ignored Harry's advice. Instead of following Alpine Creek to Boggy Plain, he drove the mob up the gully and over the ridge towards Rocky Plains. It was steep going, and he wouldn't have tried it without the Crow boys along to help.

They reached the top of the ridge just before nightfall. There, on the edge of the high country, they pitched camp. It was very dark that night. Low cloud blocked out the stars. The flickering light of the campfire cast eerie shadows around them. Out of the darkness came the sound of wild dogs howling, bristling the fur on the backs of their own dogs and making them growl. James wrapped himself in his coat as the cold night air descended, and moved closer to the warmth of the fire. He was glad Sweeney had drawn the short straw for first night watch. No one said too much. It had been a hard day in the saddle. They soon called it quits and wrapped themselves in their swags for the night.

James was the last to wake, though it was barely sunrise. He shook off the morning dew and rubbed his eyes. A quick mug of tea and a bite, and they were off to get the horses.

James could see they were on the edge of a wide valley. Rocky Plains was the start of the summer pastures they'd come to graze. Heath and lush snow grasses carpeted the valley floor, giving way to snow gum forest halfway up the hillsides. Granite boulders littered the hills amongst the trees and were strewn casually across the valley floor. The flats and gentle gullies were soggy with marshes, full of mosses and bogs. The horizon was a blue-grey vista of bush-clad mountain ranges.

The colours of the landscape were a subtle contrast of light browns, grey-greens and grey-blues. The sky was a sharp blue behind white puff clouds. This was living, thought James.

They took their time travelling through Rocky Plains, letting the cattle feed before moving on. The main river valley steepened again after Rocky Plains, so Clarrie sent the mob up the hillside and through a saddle to Gibson's Plains. As they came out of the tree line, high above the river, the view across Gibson's Plains was stunning.

It must be like this for eagles all the time, thought James. Way down below, the river snaked its way though a deep, grassy valley. Across the far side of the river you could see for miles as the valley turned into rolling grassy hills that reached right to the horizon. Mountain ridges framed it on either side, topped with snow gum forest like the trees they'd just been riding through – with sturdy grey trunks, slender white branches and drooping leaves designed to shed the snow.

He could see someone else's cattle dotted over the hillside on the far side of the river. Their own mob could see and smell the water, and hurried down the hillside towards the river.

Luckily, the river level was low. They let the mob cross slowly at the ford, giving the cattle and horses plenty of time to drink, then headed up the valley, so as to keep the herds apart. A stockman came riding across the slope to greet them. He spoke briefly to Clarrie before riding away again. It was one of the Mulligan brothers. Relations between the Mulligans and Clarrie had become strained recently – ever since last summer, when Clarrie had questioned the parentage of a few of the calves in the Mulligans' herd.

They kept the cattle moving, and over the far side of the hill they passed below a mob of sheep, grazing on the hillside just down from a hut at the head of a gully. The Pollock boys come here every year, said Bob. All the way from the Murray River, down in Victoria. Two men waved at them from the creek.

'That's Dan and Joe,' said Bob. 'Looks like they're panning.'

'Keep the stock moving,' said Clarrie, whistling to his dogs. 'We can catch up with them tomorrow, if we need to.'

Their own hut was a rough and ready slab and bark affair. It was tucked into the lee of an eastern-facing gully so as to catch the morning sun. There was barely room for them all inside.

'Don't like huts,' said Bob. 'I'll be sleeping outside.'

'Same for me,' said Sweeney.

The Crow boys had brought their own sheet of canvas for shelter.

'You'll all be grateful for the hut if it snows,' said Clarrie. 'At least it's got a fireplace.'

'Where's the pan?' asked Sweeney.

The pan was hidden under the wood pile at the side of the hut. There was only one, and no spade. Clarrie reminded Sweeney he'd been contracted to look after cattle, and not to search for gold. After some argument, Clarrie agreed they could all take turns panning for gold, so long as there were no problems with the cattle that needed attending to.

The Crow boys were soon to head off, so they took first turn. Sweeney was to be next. Being the youngest, James was to get last turn.

After their day of panning, the Crows returned to the hut and showed the others what they'd found. It wasn't a lot. But it was gold. James got a chance to touch it. He'd never seen gold before. It was so beautiful, the way it glinted in the firelight. He'd heard how men fought for this precious metal. Now he began to understand why.

James didn't get to take his turn at panning the following day. Early in the morning, just on daybreak, the cattle decided to take off. Something must have frightened them. They never did discover what. One moment the herd was feeding quietly, the next they were off at a bolt. The first James knew was when Sweeney grabbed him by the shoulder and shouted at him. By the time the men had saddled up, the cattle were almost out of sight, up the far end of Bullock Head Creek. The mob took off again up the grassy valley as soon as they saw the stockmen coming.

The Crows had left, so there were only the four of them. That should've been plenty to round up the mob, but it wasn't so easy. By the time they'd headed the cattle and brought them under control, they were near the headwaters of the creek, in a swampy clearing bordered by snow gums, almost on top of the mountain range.

'That's Victoria, over there,' said Bob, pointing beyond the ridge.

'Can we have a look?' asked James. Clarrie said they could. The cattle had settled down and were now feeding quietly. He and Bob stayed with the herd.

James and Sweeney rode to the crest of the rocky ridge, then along it to a vantage point. The trees and undergrowth were sparse on the top. The view was magnificent. In front of them, the ground fell away steeply. Series upon series of rugged, blue-tinged mountain ranges stretched away into the distance as far as the eye could see.

Suddenly, they saw the stallion. He was further along the ridge, on the far side of a grassy clearing. They could just see him through the trees. Sweeney motioned to James. They held their horses. They were downwind of him, and he hadn't seen them yet. Even from a distance, they could see he was a magnificent beast. He stood high and proud, his glossy coat deep brown, almost black, his tail arched. As they watched, he raised his head, pricked his ears and sniffed the air. Something had alerted him.

Sweeney spurred his horse down the ridge. James followed. They were always going to be too slow. At the first sound of the crack of a twig, the stallion bolted. There was no sign of him when they reached the clearing. Looking around, they found a horse trail and started to follow it. It led them in and out of the trees along the ridge for a few hundred yards. Then it plunged down a spur towards Victoria.

'Damn,' said Sweeney.

After a brief discussion, they agreed they'd better go back.

'What were you going to do if you caught up with him?' asked Clarrie, when they told the others their story.

'I've got a rope,' said Sweeney.

'You'd need more than a rope with a stallion like that,' said Clarrie. 'You'd need to set a horse trap.'

'I know that,' said Sweeney. 'I've caught brumbies before.'

'Sounds like the same stallion we saw last summer,' said Bob. 'I wonder where he goes in winter. When we seen him last year, he had his mares in tow.'

Sweeney was set on going after the stallion. He brooded about it as they herded the cattle back towards the hut. Eventually, Clarrie agreed to a deal. Sweeney and James would go after the stallion to see if they could find him and his mares. If they caught him – or any of his mares – they'd split the takings with Clarrie. If they couldn't catch the brumbies, they'd come back and get tools to build a set of horse yards. Then they'd set a trap and drive the brumbies into it.

'That stallion gotta be worth more than a few ounces of gold,' said Sweeney.

'You've got to find him first,' said Clarrie. 'Then you've got to catch him.' He was less sanguine than Sweeney about their chance of success. Still, he had nothing at risk, and stood to gain if they succeeded.

Sweeney and James set out early next morning with provisions. They picked up the trail where they'd left off the day before. This led them round the side of the mountain and through a series of gullies to a flat ridge crisscrossed with tracks. They'd already passed a number of side tracks, so it was difficult to know if they were on the right trail. Sweeney said it didn't matter, so long as they kept finding fresh horse droppings. There were piles of dung heaped high at some of the track crossings. This told them they were in a stallion's territory. They decided to follow the top of the ridge, as the main tracks seemed to go in that direction.

The ridge was lower than the main range. Tall mountain ash were the dominant trees. They rode along the track, winding in and out between the trees, ducking under low branches and brushing aside long hanging strands of bark. Every so often, by surprise and without apparent explanation, they'd find themselves in a grassy clearing. Horse trails led into and out of these from every direction.

As they followed a track into one of these clearings, they came upon the stallion. Then the chase was on.

The stallion was out of sight in seconds. This time they were closer. They saw the direction he went, and could hear him crashing through the bush ahead. They galloped hell for leather after him, risking life and limb – over fallen trees, through the undergrowth, ducking low-lying branches and dodging trees, till they lost him down the far side of the hill. They pulled up to listen. There was no sound to tell them which way he'd gone. By now, they'd gone past the end of the ridge and were on the steep side of a rocky spur, amongst stunted stringy bark trees and scratchy undergrowth.

Sweeney swore.

James agreed. 'What now?' he asked.

'We've come this far. We're not giving up now,' said Sweeney.

In front of them was a precipitous saddle and, beyond it, a sharp conical hill. Beside them was a deep, narrow valley.

'We're not going down there,' said Sweeney.

The way ahead didn't look promising either. They decided to head back the way they'd come.

From the top of the ridge, through the trees, they could see the hills falling away steeply in front of them.

'There might be some good flats down there,' said Sweeney. 'That could be where he's headed for. He had to be going somewhere.'

After a brief conference, they decided to head along a spur. Shortly, the trees on its steep side gave way to low-lying heath and scrubby wattles. They stopped and looked down into the valley below. To their right, the spur ended in a line of sheer cliffs, its rocks streaked in red and brown.

'Lucky we didn't go that way,' said Sweeney, pointing at the cliffs. 'What a view. Must be all of a thousand foot drop down there. Look,' he said, pointing downwards. 'Bet you that's where our stallion's gone. Looks like there's good flats down there.'

Below, half hidden beyond the folds of the hills, they could just see the beginning of what looked like sheltered grasslands.

It was a steep and dangerous descent to the valley. They rode through dry scrub, more trees, then heath again on the lower slopes, till they finally reached the bottom. Here, they were at the head of a grassy valley, beside a bubbling stream lined with tall mountain ash trees. Behind them was the heath-covered slope they'd descended. To their right were even more cliffs than they'd realised. Ahead, the valley widened out for a few miles, then the surrounding mountains closed in again, shutting off the river.

'This is some place,' said Sweeney.

'Certainly is,' said James.

'Let's see what's down the valley,' said Sweeney, urging his horse forward.

They rode over a rise then pulled up short. There was a small herd of cattle grazing on the river flats below.

'That's odd,' said Sweeney, looking puzzled. 'Why would there be cattle down here?'

They rode past the cattle, staying high and giving them a wide berth so as not to disturb them. Next they came to a gully on their left, where a creek tumbled out of a deep cleft in the mountains to join the main valley. Facing them, on the far side of the creek, was a sheer rocky slope, covered with native pines. Beyond it, the valley closed off. On the grassy river flats immediately below them, a dozen or so horses were grazing – not wild brumbies from the look of them. Some were even hobbled.

Before they had time to speculate, a bullet whistled over their heads, followed by the sharp crack of a rifle. For half an instant they looked at each other.

'Hell!' swore Sweeney. Then he yelled at James, 'Get out of here!'

Instinctively, they spurred their horses towards the nearest trees.

'Up the creek!' yelled Sweeney.

They had little choice. There was no cover the way they'd come. For a split second, the alternatives flashed across James's mind. They'd be sitting ducks on the open slope they'd come from. The only other way was back past the cliffs – and who knows where that might end?

The bush quickly turned into impassable scrub, so thick a dog couldn't bark in it, as Bob would say. But they'd made enough distance to draw breath. There was no sound of any pursuit.

'That was a close call,' said James.

Sweeney recovered his bravado. 'They was just warning us off,' he said. 'They only shot over our heads.'

'You think so?' said James, not entirely convinced. He could still feel his heart pounding.

'Sure. But it don't do to hang about,' said Sweeney. 'If we'd stayed, they'd have shown they meant business.'

Climbing back up the range wasn't easy. They gave up all thought of the brumby stallion. The bush was thick and the slopes were steep. It took them all the rest of that day, and most of the next, before they found their way back to their hut. It rained overnight, which put out their fire. James was very glad to see the others again.

When they told Clarrie and Bob what they'd seen, Clarrie didn't sound surprised. 'I didn't think you'd get that far,' he said. 'You found The Hollow – some call it Lob's Hole, others call it The Hollow. That's where the Mulligans hang out. Those horses you saw – they'd be stolen. I've never seen the place, but I've heard about it. A man'd do well to stay clear of there.'

'I won't be going back,' said James.

'You'd be wise not to let on what you seen, either,' said Clarrie. 'They're a bad lot, those Mulligans.' He paused to spit out some tobacco. 'You'd want to hope they didn't get a good look at you.'

'Don't the police know about it?' asked James.

'The traps?' said Clarrie, laughing. 'They're probably in on it!'

Sweeney laughed too, but in an unpleasant way that implied James was stupid.

3

Gibson's Plains
Spring 1859

The next few days it bucketed down rain, the sort that usually falls in the tropics. Sheets of water fell from the sky. There was no escape, everything got soaked. It was a devil of a job to keep the fire going. The rain put paid to panning.

'Look on the bright side,' said Clarrie. 'It ain't that cold. It ain't that windy. And the herd won't be goin' anywhere.'

The cattle turned their tails to the weather and stood together stoically. The dogs didn't take it so well. They went slinking around miserably, with their tails between their legs, cringing at the sound of each thunderclap.

It finally cleared. Bob and Sweeney each took a turn at panning. Neither found much gold.

'I told you so,' said Clarrie. 'There's more money in cattle.'

When it was James's turn, he rode over to the same place as the others – downstream from where they'd seen the Pollock brothers panning. After hobbling his horse, he walked through a carpet of alpine flowers to where the creek swirled through a series of sandy pools. Getting material to pan was easy. All he had to do was bend down and scoop it up from the creek bed.

He couldn't believe his luck! There was a nugget in his first panful. It was a tiny one, no bigger than his thumbnail – but it was gold! He leapt out of the creek. 'Eureka! Eureka!' he shouted, jumping up and down.

There was no one in sight. The Pollocks' sheep – hundreds of them – stared at him. He was so excited. He did a dance around the pan, clapping his hands over his head. Suddenly he felt foolish and stopped.

The rest of the day was an anticlimax. He only found a few more grains, and his whole day's takings were less than a thimbleful. It didn't bother him. He was happy. He enjoyed the mild weather, the clear bubbling stream, and the beautiful mountain scenery, thinking how great it was to be alive.

Back at the hut, he showed the others his nugget. They were impressed.

'Maybe there is payable gold,' said Bob.

Sweeney was jealous. He said it wasn't fair for James to find the nugget. He'd already panned the same spot and found nothing.

The good weather held for the next week, apart from occasional morning fogs and some light, misty rain. The cattle were easy to look after. The stockmen continued taking turns at panning. Even Clarrie joined in. No more nuggets were found, but each day of panning increased their stores of gold.

James kept his grains of gold wrapped in a cloth tucked into his swag. In the evenings, he took them out and watched them glitter in the firelight. He could hardly wait for his next turn, and the chance to find another nugget. In the meantime, he made plans. He decided that he'd turn the gold he'd found into a ring, and give it to Sally for Christmas. She'd love it. He thought of her and pictured her laughing smile. Thinking of her made him want to feel her warm body next to him again.

When James wasn't panning, he spent the day yarning with the others, helping to keep a weather eye on the cattle, and riding. It was an easy life. Galloping across the open grasslands was great sport, with his horse pounding under him and the wind in his face. He had to be careful, though. Snowgrass country was deceptive. The hillsides were generally firm, but the gullies and marshy flats were full of hidden holes that could snap a horse's leg. James learned the hard way. As he was chasing a stray calf, his horse took a dive and rolled head over tail. Luckily he was thrown clear, and the soft marsh cushioned his fall. Amazingly, his horse wasn't hurt either. The calf trotted back to its mother.

Bob saw it all. 'Great style,' he said, as he rode over to James. 'That's one of your lives gone.'

James was remounting, rather stiffly.

'Sometimes it's best to wait,' said Bob. 'That calf was never going far. You can spend a lot of time rushing round and still get the same result. You young fellas need to learn patience.'

James noticed that Bob always did things with an economy of effort, and rarely got excited – it was a long time since he'd been thrown from a horse.

Around the campfire at night, discussion turned to the merits of life in the bush. It was a tried and true topic amongst bushmen. Clarrie put the 'for' case: there was freedom in the bush. There was fresh mountain air, plenty of tucker and no crowds. When you were out droving, there were no worries about money. In any case, there was nothing to spend it on. Bob agreed. He added that there were no cheats or thieves, and no women to cause trouble. You could trust your mates in the bush. No one put the case for city living.

Clarrie and Bob told stories about the mountain stockmen, and of things that happened in the mountains in years gone past. They told of freak summer snowstorms, and of how in some years, caught by the early onset of winter, cattle and sheep had perished. They told how Dr Gibson, one of the first to graze the area, had given up on account of his massive stock losses, when hundreds of sheep and cattle had died in the snow.

'You don't have to believe this,' said Clarrie, 'but I swear it's a true story – my uncle told it to me.' He kicked a coal back into the fire. 'One year, the men were up here with a mob of cattle. It snowed early, and they had to get down the mountain in a big hurry. In the end, they had to leave a couple of bullocks behind.'

'What happened?' asked James.

Clarrie tapped his pipe on a rock to empty it, before continuing. 'The next year, when they came back, they found the lost animals. They was in a gully – near where they'd left 'em.' He paused to refill his pipe. 'Only problem, they was skeletons – twenty feet up – in the tops of the trees.'

'What happened?' asked James, puzzled.

'They was feeding on the tree leaves,' said Sweeney. 'That's how high the snow drifted,' he said pointedly, as if explaining the obvious to an idiot.

'Twenty feet sounds a bit high,' said Bob. 'But it does drift pretty deep.'

There were also tales of the blacks in those early days.

'The blacks called this place Giandarra,' said Clarrie. 'They'd come here each year to eat the moths up at Big Bogong. That's what they called that big fella mountain over past Table Top.'

'Haven't seen 'em last year or two,' said Bob. 'They used to make fires all through here. Then you'd see 'em coming back from the mountains all sleek and fat. Must've been something good in them moths. Always meant to try one.'

'Won't see me eating no damn moths,' said Sweeney, spitting into the fire with disgust.

'They roasted 'em in the coals first,' said Bob. 'We had a gin at the station what told me, before she went and died.'

James enjoyed life in the mountains. It was good to wake in the morning, even on foggy days. Shrouded in mist, there was a quiet mystery to the mountain bush. All was dank and wet. Tiny droplets glistened on the leaves of the phantom snow gums and on the low-lying heath, and trickled down the blades of the snow grasses. Dark shapes of cattle loomed out of nowhere as he rode through the fog, before vanishing again. All was peaceful and quiet in the mist.

Clouds were never far away. Some mornings, they skimmed just overhead, almost in reach. Other mornings, wisps of mist suddenly appeared from nowhere amongst the snow gums, only to disappear again as mysteriously as they'd come. The weather was never dull.

James got on well enough with his fellow stockmen – except for Sweeney. There were tensions between them from the start. James was an average build, but Sweeney was slighter and had a weedy look about him, despite being a few years older. He was no weakling, but his beard was not much thicker than a youth's. For whatever reason, he had a chip on his shoulder. He never had a good thing to say about anyone or anything. He even resented the time Bob spent explaining things to James.

Sweeney treated animals badly. He kicked the dogs and treated his horse roughly. 'It's only a bloody horse,' he said, after James had told him to go easy with the whip. It escalated from there, and they nearly came to blows before Bob intervened.

James and Bob were riding across a swampy creek when Bob said, 'I bet that looks just like a bog to you.'

'Sure does,' said James.

'And I bet the bush always looks the same to you, too,' said Bob.

'I s'pose,' said James.

'Stop, and we'll take a look.'

They dismounted.

'See this 'ere,' said Bob, pointing at the boggy vegetation around their feet. 'If you look closely, you can see all the different plants. There's more than a dozen – just in this square foot or so. There's even different kinds of grasses, if you look close, like. See the little flowers.' He stood up. 'It's sad. I don't know the names of any of 'em.' He bent down and picked a purple flower, twirling it between his thumb and finger. 'You remember that gin I was telling you about? The one that died?'

'Yes, I think so,' said James.

'She was a real lady – for a black girl. She knew the names of all the plants. She'd prattle on about 'em to me in 'er lingo – an' tell me what they was all good for. I never paid no notice.' He paused and looked thoughtful. 'Then she up an died.'

'What killed her?' asked James.

'Dunno, really,' said Bob. 'All the blacks was dying. Y'know, there's lots they knew about this country, and we'll never find out now.'

They remounted.

'I kinda liked that black girl,' said Bob, as they rode towards the hut. 'It was bad when she died.'

They rode some more before Bob spoke again. 'You needn't mention 'bout 'er to the others,' he said. 'Most don't think much of the blacks.'

As they hobbled their horses at their camp, Bob said, 'Remember what I told you 'bout the bush. You gotta take time to look. The bush can tell you a lot, if you know what to look for. Don't forget the moss on the south side of the rocks – you can use that when there's no sun to tell you direction.'

'I'll try,' said James. He decided he'd pay more attention to the bush in future.

*

Grice and party were the first prospectors to arrive. When James next rode over to the creek to go panning, he saw four wooden stakes sticking up amongst the snow grass and heath. There were three men working where he usually panned. Further up the hill, just below the tree line, he saw a tent. Four horses were tethered nearby.

He rode towards the men. It was early, but they'd been busy. A good-sized area beside the creek had been cleared of vegetation. One of the men was digging next to a mound of fresh dirt. The other two were standing in the creek panning.

The men looked up as he arrived. They were dressed more like gentlemen than stockmen. The two in the creek wore waistcoats. The man digging had rolled up his sleeves. All were wearing good-quality felt hats.

'Good day, young man,' said the man standing in the creek. He looked at the pan James was carrying. 'I see you're planning on doing some prospecting.'

'Yes,' said James.

'You'd be a local, would you?'

'I'm from Cosgrove's,' said James. 'We've got a mob of cattle over there.' He pointed to where he'd come from.

His horse showed an interest in feeding, so he dismounted and let her do so, but still held onto the reins.

'We should introduce ourselves,' said the man who'd been digging. 'I'm Mr Grice. My companions here are Mr Gillon and Mr Hayes.'

Each nodded at James in turn.

'We're on commission from Mr Wright. You'd know Mr Wright? Mr Wright from Queanbeyan?'

James knew of Mr Wright as a wealthy storekeeper. 'You're digging where we've been panning,' he blurted out.

'Would that be a registered claim?' asked Grice.

'What do you mean?'

'Where are your pegs?' said Mr Hayes. 'We never saw any pegs. You've got to put in the pegs. That's in the regulations.'

'I don't understand.'

'The goldfields regulations – you'd know about them, wouldn't you?'

said Hayes. 'You can't go round accusing people of claim jumping if you haven't followed the regulations.'

'Hold on a minute,' said Grice. 'He's only a lad. I don't think he knows about the prospecting business, do you?'

'No,' said James, quite confused. 'I don't know what you're talking about.'

'He probably hasn't even got a miner's right, have you?'

'What's that?' asked James.

'See?' said Grice, looking at the others. He turned to James again. 'The goldfields regulations set out the rules. They're the law for prospecting. You've got to follow them. If you don't do prospecting like the regulations say, then you're breaking the law.'

'What are these regulations?' asked James. He felt quite uneasy. 'I've never heard of them.'

'Here,' said Grice. 'I'll offer you a deal. You were planning on doing a day's prospecting, I take it?'

'Yes,' said James. 'We've been taking turns.'

'Here's the deal. You give us a hand today, and we'll say nothing about you not having a miner's right. In exchange, we'll show you how prospecting is done. I've got a copy of the regulations in the tent. I'll let you have a read of them. You can read, I take it?'

'Yes,' said James.

'What d'you say?'

'But what if I find some gold? I've already got some,' said James.

'It's not yours. By rights you should give it to the government,' said Hayes.

'All right,' said Grice. 'We know prospecting goes on outside the law. Just don't tell anyone you've done it. If you do a fair day's work with us, we'll give you a payment – in gold. How about it?'

James thought for a minute, then said, 'I'll do it.'

'Good, let's get started,' said Grice. 'You can start by digging here.'

James worked hard that day. Mostly he did digging. He was glad when they stopped to boil the billy. 'What brought you here looking for gold?' he asked.

'Mr Wright gave us a commission,' said Grice. 'He heard about the Pollocks. He wanted to find out if there was any truth in it.'

Grice and party knew their business. By the end of the day, they'd panned as much gold as James and the other stockmen had found in all the time they'd been there. They even found a few little nuggets.

'No question about it,' said Grice. 'There's a payable field here.'

Grice was true to his word. He showed James the goldfields regulations, and at the end of the day he gave James a portion of the gold they'd panned.

As James rode back to camp, Clarrie met him. He told James they'd be moving the mob next day. 'Young Alec McKeahnie came by this morning,' he said. 'He needs a few more head to make up his herd. He and his brother are taking a big mob down to Adelong and the Victorian goldfields. There's a buyer needs twelve hundred and he's only got eleven hundred. We'll make a move first light. I said we'd meet him further up the river. There's a long gully the other side of this hill with good feed in it. May as well move our mob over there at the same time.'

James then told the others how he'd met Grice and party and what they'd told him about the goldfields regulations.

Bob and Clarrie were unimpressed.

'Those regulations – they're only for when there's a declared goldfield,' said Bob. 'Who's to know if you find some gold? Are the traps going to be out searching everyone in the bush?'

'They were just having a lend of you,' said Clarrie.

Sweeney didn't say anything. He wasn't happy. His turn at panning would be delayed, and it would be further to ride to the creek.

Next morning, the wind was up and the cattle were tetchy. They were used to being left alone. It took some trouble to muster them and get them moving in the right direction. They had an inclination to charge off downstream. It needed some quick riding to cut them off and wheel them towards the higher ground.

By midday, the wind had eased. On the other side of the river, a couple of miles ahead, the McKeahnies' mob came in sight. Clarrie and Sweeney cut out the hundred beasts for the McKeahnies, leaving the rest of the herd with Bob and James. James watched as they drove the cattle across the river to meet Alec McKeahnie, who was waiting on the far side.

Just as Alec and his men were about to take delivery, the cattle changed their minds. Maybe they missed their companions, or perhaps they took fright at the McKeahnies' dogs. They bolted in panic back across the river.

In an instant, Alec McKeahnie spurred his horse after them, charging across the river without a trace of fear. He raced the cattle through the swampy river flats, splashing through pools and leaping over wombat holes. Single-handedly he outpaced them, turned them and brought them up short. The other stockmen weren't far behind. It was a fancy piece of riding – one of the best James had ever seen.

'That Alec McKeahnie sure can ride,' said Bob, clearly impressed. Coming from him, it was a real compliment.

After farewelling the McKeahnies, Clarrie and his stockmen drove their remaining cattle to the head of a long, grassy valley. They were now close to the top of the main range. A short ride to the top of the adjacent ridge, and they could see over the mountains to Victoria. There, just short of the ridgetop, they pitched camp in an eastern-facing gully. Although their camp was no more than a canvas awning strung between two trees, it was surprisingly sheltered.

'This should do us for a while,' said Clarrie, looking across the valley. 'There's plenty of feed for going on with.'

Sweeney didn't come back after his turn at panning. Clarrie was furious. When he returned a day later, Clarrie told him he wasn't going to get the pan again for a week. Sweeney looked very sullen, but said nothing. The weather closed in again after that. Rain fell intermittently for a day and a half. The awning leaked. Nerves started to get frayed.

On the third night, when James unwrapped his swag, he was sure there'd been more gold in his store. It was hard to tell. The little nugget was still there. Perhaps he was imagining that some was missing. He couldn't be absolutely certain. All the same, he was left with a vague feeling of uneasiness.

The next day, when James rode over to take his turn at prospecting, Grice and his party were gone. The pegs were still there and so was the tent. There had been much digging beside the creek, but there was no sign of the men. James started panning further down the creek, outside their claim, just to be certain. He found another little nugget and a fair sprinkling of gold dust.

When Bob returned from panning the following day, he said there were now half a dozen parties prospecting in Pollocks' Gully.

The following morning, there was no sign of Sweeney. Clarrie called him a string of names, none of which was complimentary.

Bob said he was sure some of his gold was missing.

Clarrie checked his own store and said the same. Then he became very angry. 'There's nothing lower than thieving off your mates,' he growled. 'If I catch up with that sneaky little piece of scum, I'll tan his hide till it comes off in strips.'

James believed he really meant it.

That night, James thought he heard noises. It was very dark. There was no moon, and the low clouds blocked out the stars. As he lay half-awake, he could hear the wind whistling through the treetops. It rustled the canvas awning and eddied past his head. He rolled over in his swag and turned his back to the draught. The dogs growled at something in the darkness, then went quiet.

'Where's that little calf?' said Clarrie. He was standing in the saddle, looking across at the cattle grazing. The morning sun cast long shadows across the valley. 'The one with the white blaze,' he said. 'It better not be what I'm thinking,' he added in a threatening tone.

'I can't see it,' said James. He knew the animal, as he'd had to chase it a few times.

'You'd reckon a fella wouldn't know if a beast or two was missing, but you get a sixth sense in this game,' said Clarrie. 'I got a feeling we're missing some cattle.' He was talking to himself as much as to James and Bob.

Clarrie then made them do a head count. As best as they could work out, there were three beasts missing. Bob said he'd also heard something in the night but, as the dogs went quiet, he'd dismissed it too.

'It's got to be that little mongrel,' said Clarrie. 'A stranger would've set the dogs off. I'm going after 'im. Bob, you stay here with the mob. James, you come with me. I'll need help driving the beasts back when we catch up with 'em. The bastard can't have got far.'

Clarrie said there was only one way thieves could've taken the cattle. It'd be up through the open head of the valley, over the saddle to Bullock Head Creek. He was certain the beasts were headed for the diggings at Pollocks' Gully. He said it wouldn't be possible to drive stock through the trees on a dark night. He was right. At the head of the valley, they found fresh cow dung.

There was no clear trail after that, so they followed Bullock Head Creek downstream. As they rode over the rise to Pollocks' Gully, the diggings came into view. It was a totally different sight from the quiet scene they'd left a few days ago. Strewn in confusion across the hillside were dozens of tents. Scattered amongst them, on either side of the creek, were mounds of earth, piles of rocks, ditches, holes and channels. Numbers of parties of men, stripped to their shirt sleeves, were digging, sluicing and panning in and around the creek and its various diversions, like a human ants' nest.

'Hell!' said James, wheeling his horse side-on.

'Jesus!' said Clarrie. He pulled back on his reins and stopped.

It wasn't long before Clarrie saw what he had come looking for. Close by, was a large tent, flying a green flag. In front of it, under a lean-to awning, was a rough-hewn slab sitting on timber stumps, with a collection of wares on it. On the near side of the tent, hanging from a pole frame, were three fresh-looking carcasses.

'Damn it!' said Clarrie. 'We're too late.' He rode over to the front of the tent and hailed the storekeeper. He didn't dismount.

Dan Pollock came out to meet him.

A doubt crossed Clarrie's mind. He didn't have a quarrel with Dan. 'Those fresh killings there,' he said, pointing to the carcasses hanging beside the tent. 'Where'd you get them from?'

'Why? What's it to you?' said Dan, suspiciously.

His brother Joe joined him from the back of the tent. He stood next to Dan with his arms folded.

'Three of my beasts got stolen last night,' said Clarrie.

'Nothing to do with us,' said Dan. 'Those ones there came from the Mulligans.'

'Where's the hides, then?' said Clarrie.

'They got 'em. They killed and skinned 'em for us,' said Joe.

'So where's the Mulligans now?'

'No idea,' said Dan.

'You want to sell some of your cattle to us?' asked Joe.

'Not now,' said Clarrie. 'Come on, let's go,' he said, gesturing to James.

'What do we do now?' asked James, when they'd ridden clear of the diggings.

'Nothing,' said Clarrie. 'Unless we can find the hides, it's pointless. They'll probably have the brands cut off by now anyway. The miserable mongrels. They've beaten us this time. May they rot in hell!' He was silent all the way back to their camp.

James could see he was fuming.

'Just as well we're not closer to the diggings,' Clarrie said when they'd dismounted. 'Or we'd likely have lost more.'

After this incident, Clarrie decided they'd better take their cattle further away from the diggings. First, they revisited their hut and collected everything of value that could be carried.

Next morning, with packhorses loaded, they set off with the mob. By evening, they were at the upper reaches of the Snowy River. There, they met a party of diggers. Around a common campfire, they boiled a billy and swapped stories. The men told how they'd come up from Tumut by way of Talbingo Mountain. They'd been at the Adelong diggings and heard about Kiandra and Irishtown.

'Irishtown?' queried Clarrie.

'Yes, that's on account of the Pollock brothers,' said one of the party. 'The diggings used to be their run. Now they've got the store there. It's down to them being Irishmen.'

'That's one story,' said another of the party. 'I've heard the commissioners are calling it Kiandra.'

'How's that? said his companion.

'I don't know. It's not a declared goldfield yet.'

The diggers wanted to know whether the field was paying well, where the best place for prospecting was, and all the questions diggers are interested in. The stockmen couldn't help them much. In the morning, each party went their separate way.

Over the next few weeks, wherever the stockmen took the mob they'd see parties of diggers. It was getting close to Christmas. The sun became fiercer and the flies more annoying. They lost a few more beasts, though they may just have strayed. James wanted the chance to go panning again, but they were always on the move.

Clarrie worried about the prior arrangements with the Victorian buyer, now that circumstances had changed so much. He left Bob and James in charge of the mob and rode back to the diggings to see what he could find out. He returned with good news, for James at least. He'd got word from Joe Cosgrove. Arrangements had been made to sell the herd to the Pollocks.

That's how James came to be in Kiandra before Christmas, with a cheque, a bag of gold, a horse and no commitments.

Clarrie and Bob decided to ride over to Tumut to take on another droving job. Bob said he'd prefer that to digging. He said he was too old to learn new tricks. In any case, he said he could get everything he needed in life from droving.

James was glad to be free.

Bob warned him to be careful. 'A new diggings ain't a safe place on yer own,' he said.

James said he needn't worry. His plan was to spend Christmas at home in Cooma. Then he'd return and try his luck at the diggings.

4

Kiandra Diggings
December 1859

James hardly recognised Pollocks' Gully. Hundreds of men were digging where weeks ago there'd only been a few dozen. The tent and shanty city strewn amongst the rubble of the diggings now spilled down the hillside towards the river. The more savvy miners had built their shelters higher up the slopes, close to the tree line and supplies of firewood. Those worried about theft and claim-jumping camped with their tools on their claims. The swarming activity of the men on the diggings was like a mass of bees over a broken hive. Men were coming and going in all directions. Camp fires were smoking. Mud was everywhere.

The Pollocks' wasn't the only store tent any more. Others lined the sides of the muddy track that wound its way through the diggings towards Russell's and Cooma. James tethered his horse to a rail beside one of the new tents. He had planned to inquire about tools and provisions, but thought he'd take a short walk first.

The place was so different, it was hard to work out where he'd been prospecting. The creek had been diverted into numerous channels and there were piles of rocks and dirt everywhere. Every few yards, he had to step around a pile of rocks or over a ditch.

James was detouring around a mullock heap when he heard a shout. Turning, he saw a digger throw his hat high into the air. It was caught by the wind and blown sideways, landing near James. The man kept shouting and dancing about. A crowd quickly gathered as diggers dropped their tools and ran over to him. James picked up the hat and walked over to see what had been the cause of the excitement.

'Look at that!' said an excited digger, as James squeezed his way through the crowd. 'That's got to be over twenty pounds! What a fortune!'

The man at the centre of attention kept on shouting. There was a look of absolute joy on his hairy face. He kept tossing a large gold nugget into the air, then catching it. It was huge! Two of his mates were trying to calm him down, without success. The onlookers were talking excitedly amongst themselves. James overheard someone saying the nugget had been found barely a foot below the surface, right where the finder was now standing.

When the excitement had died down slightly, James managed to get closer to the man. 'Here's your hat,' he said.

'Thanks, young fella,' said the man, clapping it on his head. He turned to the crowd. With a wide sweep of his arm that nearly took the heads off those closest, he shouted, 'The drinks are on me!' He turned to James. 'Come on, young fella,' he said. 'Let's go.' Thumping his arm around James's shoulders, he steered him in the direction of the store tents.

'Here, let me hold it,' asked a digger beside them.

The owner of the nugget reluctantly handed it over, but made sure he didn't let it out of his sight. The nugget was passed around the crowd as they walked and jigged to the store tents. The excitement was infectious. James got to hold it – though only for a moment – before it was grabbed out of his hands by someone else. If only he could find one like that. He'd never forget the look and the feel of it. So smooth, and yet so heavy. And what a beautiful colour.

The crowd headed for the nearest sly grog shop – at the rear of one of the store tents. The diggings were not yet a declared goldfield, so it was against the law to sell spirituous liquors. Such legal niceties never stopped anyone providing for the needs of diggers on a newly discovered field, and these diggings were no different. It only meant the sale of drink had to be carried out surreptitiously, with an eye out for the traps. The grog was kept separately so its ownership couldn't be easily proven, should this become an issue.

The sly grog tent was little more than a canvas awning propped up by poles. Under this temporary shelter, behind a roughly made counter of split timber, a keg of rum had been tapped. Word of the find had gone ahead of the party. Standing in front of the counter was the owner of the sly grog shop, a portly, balding man with grey mutton-chop whiskers and a wide, yellow-toothed smile. His bulging waistline was barely contained by a dirty waistcoat. The proprietor looked almost as happy as the owner of the nugget.

'Drinks all round! The rum's on me!' ordered the nugget owner. His name was Peter.

The proprietor had already anticipated the order, and had placed a row of nobblers on the counter. These were quickly taken up. The thirsty and the greedy knocked them back in a gulp and were quickly back for seconds.

'Keep it flowing,' said Peter. 'Who cares about money now? Put it on my account.' He stood the nugget on its end in the middle of the counter. 'Here. That's the place for it. Let everyone have a good look. No one's to touch it, now. You make sure of that, won't you?'

The proprietor beamed. He was more than happy to protect the nugget. It was his guarantee of payment.

James was handed a nobbler for a toast, and pressed to join the celebrations. This toast was quickly followed by another. James wasn't used to drinking and soon began to feel light-headed. The company was jovial. The talk was all about gold. There'd been some amazing finds already. Everyone knew of someone who'd struck it rich. The nugget on the table was only the most recent proof of the amazing riches just waiting to be found on these diggings.

'Mark my word – this field 'ere – it'll be the richest in the country yet,' said a tipsy digger, swaying as he spoke. 'You can forget about Bendigo and Ballarat. I been there. They was nothin' to this.'

'He's right,' said his mate. 'There's no gold left in Victoria – 'cept it's deep underground and needs tunnelling.'

'Or shaft sinking,' said another in the crowd.

'Same thing. It needs capital. There's no chance for the workin' man.'

'Aye, that be true.'

'You won't catch me workin' wages for some rich cove. If a man can't get it easy on the surface, like, it's time to try another rush.'

'Sure is,' said the digger next to James. ''Ere, take a look at this.' He fumbled in his pocket and produced a small cloth bundle. 'See what I found yesterday.' He unwrapped it to show a beautifully formed little nugget, about the size of his finger, glistening amongst the folds. 'That's nothing to the one up there,' he said, pointing to the big nugget on the counter. 'But it ain't such a bad find, eh?' He gave it to James to hold.

James was impressed, though he had to blink to see it properly.

His new companions did most of the talking. James asked them about tools and provisions.

He was advised in the strongest terms not to purchase anything at the diggings. 'You should see what those Pollocks are asking for a pick! Why, you could get ten of 'em anywhere else for that price!'

After more drinks than he could keep count of, James decided he'd better leave. He was worried about leaving his horse for so long.

The diggers pressed him to stay.

'We're just getting started,' said Peter. 'Come on, have another drink.'

James agreed to one last nobbler. After that, he insisted on going. He felt bad to be leaving such friendly company.

His horse gave him a long-suffering look when he unhitched her. After a couple of attempts, he managed to climb up into the saddle. He felt dizzy. Luckily, Susie seemed to know where to go. The world was swimming. The sky and the hills moved around disconcertingly.

'What the hell. It's a beautiful day,' he said to himself. He waved at the diggers coming the other way. 'Lots of gold!' he shouted cheerily as he rode past.

The trail to the diggings was now well marked with hoof prints and muddy dray tracks. Everyone was friendly. He greeted all the parties with a smile. It was great to be alive. The bush was beautiful. His horse was like an old friend. He felt goodwill to all and sundry.

The sun was warm. By the time he reached Rocky Plains, James was feeling rather tired, and somewhat hungry. He stopped for a bite of his oatcakes and a drink from the creek. Then he found a quiet shady spot, hobbled his horse and lay down for a rest. He immediately went to sleep.

It was afternoon when he woke up. A tribe of tiny ants had found his legs and were trying to get into his boots. His mouth tasted like leather. His head hurt.

After a long drink from the creek and some trouble catching his horse, he set off again. Once he was on the move, he started to feel better. He let Susie set her own pace. She decided walking was fast enough. Even so, it wasn't long before he was riding through the tall mountain ash trees beside Alpine Creek.

Suddenly, two horsemen came galloping along the track towards him. Before he realised what was happening, they'd dashed past, almost crashing into him. He only avoided a collision by quickly wheeling Susie sideways at the last minute. As the horsemen brushed past, he noticed they had muslin over their faces, as stockmen sometimes wore on dusty days. He thought this curious, as there was little dust around. Their hats were pulled low over their eyes, so he didn't get a good look at their faces.

He kept on riding till he came to a clearing. He was still wondering about the men when he heard a noise in the bush. He stopped to listen. He heard it again, this time clearly. It was a shout for help – from the far side of the creek. He urged his horse through the dense scrub beside the creek bed to where the noise had come from.

On the far side of the creek, he found two men. They were stark naked. Their hands were bound by leather thongs, which were tied to the branch of a tree above their heads. They looked most uncomfortable. Their pink flesh looked totally out of place in the bush.

The men were very glad to see him. James thought they looked so comical, especially the plump one, whose rolls of fat quivered as he wriggled against his bindings. It was all James could do not to laugh.

'Thank God you found us!' said the taller man. 'Our clothes are over there.' He nodded in the direction of the creek.

James quickly untied them. As soon as they were free, they stepped gingerly through the prickly undergrowth to where the robbers had thrown their clothes. Then they told James their story.

They'd set off from Russell's earlier in the day, on their way to the diggings. Just before a narrow bend in the track, they'd come across two men blocking the way – one man leaning over the other. He'd called on the riders to help him with his sick mate. But as soon as they'd dismounted, the man lying down had leapt up and pointed a pistol at them. His face was covered. His friend had then covered his own face – they didn't get a good look at him, because his back had been turned before. It had all happened so fast. The only thing they could say about the men was that they were definitely both colonials, as they had spoken with colonial accents.

The robbers had marched the men into the bush and tied them up, after making them take off their clothes. The men said they'd lost nearly everything. The villains had taken their horses. Their only good fortune was that one of them had managed to slip his wallet into the scrub as they crossed the creek.

'We're greatly indebted to you,' said the fat man, looking decidedly more comfortable now that he was dressed. 'I don't know how we can repay you. If you hadn't found us, who knows what might've happened – what with dark coming on. I should introduce myself. I'm Reginald. My companion is Walter.'

'They warned us at Russell's about bushrangers,' said Walter, 'but we didn't believe them.' He had the voice and bearing of an English gentleman. 'Perhaps one day we'll be able to repay you.'

'Don't worry,' said James. 'I guess you'd have done the same for me.'

Reginald found his wallet. It was only a bit damp. Their adventure hadn't put them off their plan to go to the diggings. They told James they'd return to Russell's, and re-equip themselves with horses and tools.

'We've heard such stories of gold, we couldn't give up now,' said Reginald.

James told them about the nugget he'd seen earlier that day. That confirmed their resolve to continue. Then he apologised that he couldn't offer them a ride to Russell's as he only had the one horse. The men said they'd be right as rain now. James promised to make sure a couple of billets were put aside for them at Russell's.

Back on the track to Russell's, James came upon two bullock drays, laden high with provisions, pulled up for the night. The bullockies had made their camp on the Kiandra side of the river and were squatting round a blazing fire. James could smell their cooking as he rode past. It reminded him that he hadn't eaten a decent meal all day. He suddenly felt very hungry.

Russell's was no longer just a cattle and sheep station. William Russell was an astute man. He saw the business opportunity as soon as prospectors started coming through in numbers, and quickly set himself up to cater for the new visitors. Since James last passed through, the builders had been busy. There were now a number of new slab huts, and some store tents had been put up.

As James rode up to the station buildings, John Russell was busy organising accommodation and meals for two parties of would-be diggers from Sydney. He quickly included James in his plans.

'A quick feed is all I'm after,' said James. 'I can still make it to Cosgrove's tonight.'

'You're right on time,' said John. 'The cook's just dishing up. Over there, in the big shed. Tell 'im I sent you.' He wouldn't hear of James paying.

James told him about the two men he'd found.

John laughed. 'Wait till I tell Father,' he said. 'We had bets those two'd come to grief. They were so *English*,' he said, mimicking their accent. 'They couldn't be told anything.'

James was the centre of attention at the meal. The parties on their way to the goldfield wanted to know all the hows and wherefores about the diggings. James told them about the nuggets he'd seen with his own eyes, and the stories he'd heard. They sat there so wide-eyed he could have told them anything. He didn't mention his own finds – an instinct stopped him.

After some hard riding, he made it to Cosgrove's that night. The following day he was back at home in Cooma, in time for Christmas.

*

'Look at that,' said James, throwing his bag of gold onto the middle of the kitchen table. His younger brothers and sisters were excited – till they learned it was not for them.

His mother looked at the nugget. 'Very nice,' she said.

His father grunted, before complaining that he couldn't get decent quality leather any more. 'I've got all these people waiting on work, and I can't get supplies.'

Dinner time ended with an eruption as his younger brother pursued a grievance against his little sister. His mother ineffectually tried to make peace. His father growled and left the room to have a smoke by himself.

James felt he'd stepped back into the past. So little had changed at home. His family weren't greatly interested in the world beyond Cooma. They were more interested in what was happening in the street next door than at Kiandra. When he tried telling them about his life in the bush – camping out, chasing cattle and panning for gold – the children listened for a while. But they were too young – he could tell they didn't really understand. His father asked how long it would be before he settled on a trade. James said he didn't know. His immediate plan was to return to the diggings.

The next day, James sold his gold dust and cashed his cheque. He was rich! With his new-found wealth, he paid his father for his horse, bought a new kettle for his mother and indulged himself by buying new clothes. He still had plenty left over to kit himself out for the goldfields, even after Christmas presents and the like.

Maggie, the storekeeper's daughter, gave him a wink as he walked into her father's store. James was taken by surprise. Maggie didn't usually notice him.

'I hear you've been at the goldfields,' she said, with a smile and a tilt of her head.

'Yes, I have,' he stuttered.

She was a pretty girl, with dark curly hair, long dark eyelashes and a cheeky, upturned nose. 'It's dreadfully dull now all the men have gone to the diggings,' she said. 'Why don't we go for a walk – and you can tell me what it's like.'

James was caught off guard. 'I'm not sure. You mean now?'

'Why not?' said Maggie. 'You're not busy, are you?'

'No, no,' said James. 'I guess not.'

As they strolled down the street, James told her about his adventures droving and prospecting.

'It sounds terribly exciting at the diggings,' she said. 'I do wish I could go.' She asked a few questions, but let him do most of the talking. She kept looking up at him with a winning smile.

He felt slightly awkward, but enjoyed her attention.

After they'd walked the length of the town she said, 'I'd better go back now, and help Father in the store.' As they parted, she smiled sweetly at him and thanked him for keeping her company. 'We must meet again,' she said.

James felt strangely disturbed after she'd gone. He didn't know what to make of it. Maggie hadn't previously shown any interest in him. Perhaps it was the new clothes, he wondered. He found it unsettling – though enjoyable.

Cooma being a small town, Sally soon heard news of his walk with Maggie. It upset her. 'Why would he be spending time with that girl?' she asked her mother. 'Maggie knows about James and me. Why would she do that? I never liked her anyway. She's such a flirt with men. I don't trust her one bit. She was always telling tales about me.'

'I don't know,' said Mrs McNeill. 'There might be an innocent explanation.'

'But why hasn't he come and told me?' said Sally.

'It only happened this morning,' said her mother. 'Sometimes you've got to trust people. I'm sure it'll be right.'

Sally wasn't reassured. She remembered how, for a joke, Maggie had told their friends that Sally had chickenpox, so they'd all avoided her. That was the sort of girl she was. She thought it funny when other people were upset. It was a different story when the tables were turned and she was being embarrassed. She wasn't the sort of person you could trust with confidences, either, and had a rightly deserved reputation as a gossip. Sally couldn't understand why men seemed so captivated by her.

When James visited Sally later in the afternoon, she waited to see if he would mention Maggie. He did. He said he'd taken a walk with her. Sally wanted to know why.

'She asked me to tell her about the diggings,' said James.

'Why did she want to know that?' asked Sally.

'I don't know,' said James. He sensed her concern. 'It's all right, nothing else happened. We just talked.'

'I'm not jealous,' said Sally. 'I was just wondering.' She tried to sound offhand, worried at the impression she might be giving.

'No need to worry,' said James. 'She was just being friendly, that's all.' He knew he wasn't being completely honest. He suspected there was something more to it. But why upset Sally?

Sally said nothing further, though she wasn't fully reassured.

'Here,' he said. 'Look what I've brought you for a present. Shut your eyes and hold out your hand.'

She did as he asked.

He took out the little nugget he'd found, and put the little shiny gold piece in the palm of her hand. 'You can open your eyes now.'

She was taken aback. 'Oh, James! Isn't it beautiful?' she cried. She hadn't expected anything like this from him. She tiptoed up and flung her arms around him, giving him a kiss on the cheek.

As her hair brushed against his face and he felt the soft, warm touch of her lips on his cheek it made him tingle. He loved the smell of her closeness.

'Thank you so much,' she said. All her worries about Maggie disappeared. James could be so nice, she thought.

They sat on the back veranda.

'You know,' said James. 'I was thinking – I might have the nugget made into a ring. But I wanted you to see it the way I found it, first.'

'It's lovely the way it is,' said Sally.

They sat together for a while. Sally snuggled up against him, feeling no need to say anything.

James had a further thought. 'We could still have it made into a ring,' he said. 'What say we have it turned into a ring if we ever decide to settle down together?'

'What are you saying?' asked Sally. 'I thought – ' She could feel her pulse rising.

'I'm not promising anything – or saying we ever will,' said James quickly. 'It's too early to know. I was only thinking it'd be nice if we ever did. Anyway, you might meet another fella.'

'James, don't start that again.'

'All right. But you know what I mean. Neither of us is ready for marriage yet. There're so many things we need to do. And we haven't got any money.'

'We don't need much money. I can work, too,' said Sally. 'I'll be helping out with the schooling in the New Year.'

'Maybe I'll strike it rich,' said James. 'I might find a big nugget – like the one I told you about. Don't laugh – it's possible. You should've been there. I saw it myself.'

'Could I come with you?' asked Sally.

'What? said James. 'To the diggings?'

'Yes,' said Sally. 'Why not? I'm not afraid of work.'

'No. It's not possible,' he replied. 'The diggings are no place for a girl.'

'Maybe you're right,' she said, suddenly realising her father would probably have a strong view on the matter. But she wasn't going to let that be the end of it. Just because her parents would be opposed wasn't sufficient reason to abandon the idea. There were lots of things they had views on that she disagreed with. She still went to church with them on Sundays, but she no longer believed everything the parson said.

Being able to read had opened her eyes to things her parents had no idea about. She could never take a position as a domestic servant. She was sure that's what they had in mind for her. Marrying James could be a way to escape to something new and different. In the meantime, she'd see if she could get some work teaching. That was the most promising alternative. Maybe she could become a governess. She'd already been asked to help tutor the doctor's children.

James spent Christmas Day with his family. Although he was keen to return to the diggings, he'd promised he'd spend time with Sally. This was hardly a chore. He managed to borrow a horse and a side-saddle so they could go riding together. Sally was delighted.

They rode to the far side of Mount Gladstone, where they could see for miles in all directions. After tethering their horses below a rocky outcrop, they sat and watched the view. The Monaro grasslands were a pale, dried-off summer brown. They stretched into the distance as rolling plains till they met the shimmering blue mountain ranges on the horizon. Thin cotton clouds stretched across the sky. The bush they'd ridden through was rugged, hungry country – scrawny, white-branched gum trees – and stands of bright green native pines where it was too rocky for other trees – with a sprinkling of native wild flowers amongst the scratchy undergrowth, dry and brittle in the summer heat.

James watched as Sally drank thirstily from the water bottle. Her wet lips hinted at something more.

'When will you be leaving?' she asked, trying to sound casual.

'In another day's time,' he replied.

'I'll miss you – a bit,' she said. 'Maybe you could write.' She tried to sound cheerful.

'I will,' said James. 'They deliver mail to Russell's now. I should be able to get a letter through.'

They talked some more, and Sally mentioned Maggie.

'I don't know why you keep going on about her,' said James. 'What am I to do? What do you want me to say to her? Do you want me to say, "Sally won't let me talk to you"?'

'Of course not. Don't be silly. I just don't know why she keeps chasing after you.'

'She's not chasing me. She's just friendly.'

'Do you like her?' asked Sally, deciding to test him.

'What d'you mean? I think she's an attractive girl. But so are many.'

'What about me?' she said, looking at him closely. 'Do you think I'm attractive?' She felt more confident now. This was the start of a game they'd played many times before.

'I think so,' said James. 'But I can't be sure.' Then he added, with a twinkle in his eye, 'You're always covered up. I wouldn't know what's under the wrapping.'

This was part of their game. He was always trying to get her to undress. It usually annoyed her, but today she felt different. Her mother had been at her about it lately. 'Make sure you cover yourself up,' she'd nagged. 'Now you're a grown woman you can't run around half naked like a little girl any more.' Sally had asked her why not. Her mother had said it was wrong. If she didn't cover up, there could be terrible 'consequences'.

Despite persistent questioning from Sally, her mother wouldn't tell her what these 'consequences' would be. Sally wasn't satisfied with this lack of explanation. In the end, Mrs McNeill had fallen back on the Bible.

'It's wrong for women to be immodest. It's in the Bible,' her mother had said. At that point, Sally had given up. She knew she'd be in real trouble if she started to question what was in the Bible. It might have to come to that one day, but Sally sensed it wasn't that time yet.

As for the 'consequences,' Sally couldn't see what all the fuss was about. What could happen, anyway? She always had been headstrong. She decided she'd put it to the test with James.

'All right, then,' she said. 'I'll show you.' It was an impulse. Today she'd play the game differently – according to her rules. She was confident James wouldn't do anything bad. She'd prove there needn't be any bad 'consequences'. She didn't care what other people might think. Today she wanted James to remember her as special – now that he was going away.

'Stand there and turn round,' she ordered.

He looked at her curiously, but stood up.

'Now turn round,' she said firmly.

He did as she asked.

'You're not to look till I say so. All right?'

'All right,' he replied.

Sally stood on top of the flat rock where they'd been sitting. James wondered what she was up to. He was fully alert. He was tempted to turn and look.

Sally noticed the beginning of a movement. 'No looking,' she said sternly.

He stopped.

She liked the feeling of power she had over him when they played games. This time she would take it further. She turned her back on him and began to undress. She took off her boots first. Then she carefully folded her clothes as she took them off, placing them in a neat pile on the far side of the rock. Every now and then, she looked over her shoulder, to make sure he wasn't watching. 'No looking,' she said.

'I won't,' he answered. He kept his word. Now he had an idea of what might be happening. He could feel his heart pounding.

When Sally was completely naked, she turned to face him. 'You can look now,' she said. As he turned round, she stood in the middle of the rock, facing him, with her arms instinctively folded across her breasts.

He felt a rush of blood at the sight. His heart thumped. He'd never seen a woman fully naked before. He didn't know what to think – or do. He devoured the sight. It etched a permanent picture in his memory. He looked at her soft white skin, at her smooth round curves, at the brown triangle between her legs, and at the swelling of her half hidden breasts. Unsteadily, he put a foot forward.

'Stay right there,' she quickly ordered.

He stepped back.

She sensed her control and relaxed slightly. 'This is how you can remember me,' she said. She let her arms drop to her sides. Slowly, she pivoted full circle in front of him, till she was facing him again.

He watched as if in a dream. Then she turned away to pick up her clothes.

He fought to control his animal instinct and half started towards her. 'Sally – ' The tone of his voice betrayed him.

'Stop!' she said, turning quickly and facing him – this time holding her clothes in front of her. 'Don't say anything,' she ordered. She sensed she'd pushed right to the limit. He stood still.

'Now turn round again,' she said. 'I'm going to get dressed. It's not proper to watch a lady dressing.'

He did as she ordered.

When she was fully dressed, she told him he could look again. 'Now you've seen what I look like,' she said, smiling cheekily, 'you needn't ask again.' She knew she'd had an impact. More importantly, she'd been in full command of the situation – and there hadn't been any dire 'consequences'. She felt strangely confident. Let Maggie do her worst, she thought.

Sally was completely innocent as far as matters with men were concerned. She was fortunate that James, too, was not much more worldly wise. Later, she'd look back and wonder in amazement at her boldness in doing such a thing. But she never regretted it.

*

The day James came to say goodbye to Sally, she was much less composed. She did her best to put on a brave front. He rode over to the forge all kitted up, with his swag, his tools and even a tent. She had trouble hiding her emotion. His sadness at their parting was mixed. He was excited at his prospects at the diggings. They had a long hug and he promised he'd write. Sally didn't want to let him go. She had to eventually. Wheeling his horse, he waved goodbye to her and was gone.

The track to the diggings was a muddy highway now. Every few miles, James overtook parties on their way to the diggings. Many were travelling by foot, some pushing barrows, others humping swags. There were bullock drays with their whip cracking, loud swearing bullockies, and, just before Cosgrove's, a spring cart loaded high with provisions pulled by a long-suffering hack. Cosgrove's was a main staging post on the way. Many of the station outbuildings now doubled as sleeping accommodation. An enterprising trader had erected a store tent, and work was in progress nearby on the foundations and walls for more substantial buildings.

James pressed on to Russell's. As he got closer, the wheel ruts deepened and the condition of the track got worse. He passed a bullock team stuck in the mud at a boggy creek crossing. Not long afterwards, he caught up with a party of three riders. He rode with them. They'd come from Sydney, they told him, by steamer down the coast to Merimbula, then by horse through Cathcart and over the Monaro plains. It had taken five days. They were most interested to learn that he was a local, and that he'd already been at the diggings. He agreed to show them the way, though it wasn't hard to see where the crowds had gone before them.

They told him that the most memorable part of their journey had been their stay at Bobundara, two nights back from Cosgrove's. There they'd received warm hospitality from the station owner, who was known to one of their party. They'd been most impressed by his daughter, Tricia, who was visiting after finishing her schooling in Sydney. She had entertained them with her stories and her piano playing. They'd stayed up late into the night conversing, helped by the pick of their host's store of wine.

'Such a talented and strikingly handsome young lady,' said Phillip, the oldest of the riders. 'If only we could find such civilised people at the diggings.'

'My sentiments too,' said Darval, the youngest. 'I only wish we could have stayed longer. I'll admit to being totally smitten. Perhaps I'll have the chance to return one day – when we've made our fortune.'

Russell's was packed with travellers. William Russell had plans for a substantial hotel, with a licence. A contract had been signed, John said. Even so, there was no shortage of spirituous liquor – for those with a ken for it. At meal time, talk about gold alternated with arguments over the best route to the diggings. Each party had strong views about the merits of their own choice. The Goulburn-Queanbeyan-Cooma route was the most popular, but others swore by the coastal route, by steamer to Bateman's Bay, Merimbula or Eden.

'We almost came by Yass,' said one man, a Sydney bookkeeper.

James thought he looked like one, and wondered how he'd go in the mud and slush of the diggings.

'Yes,' said the man. 'We received letters which gave the strongest of recommendations in favour of a journey via Yass. They said we could get all of our needs for the diggings at Yass. Mind you, that advice was from some of the storekeepers of that town.'

'But that's miles away,' said a florid-faced man, who'd been putting away large quantities of liquid refreshment. 'That's the other side of the mountains. What bunkum! Imagine carrying all your stores from there!'

'We came the coast route, and we had the best journey,' said Phillip. 'That's after we got over the bar at the river. We nearly ended at the bottom of the sea!'

'There is a way through the mountains from Yass,' said John. 'Through Goodradigbee, but I wouldn't recommend it. It certainly wouldn't be suitable for drays. You can also go by way of the McKeahnies' – through Gudgenby.'

By this time no one was listening.

'Will there be any women on the diggings?' asked a voice.

'No chance. You've seen the last one tonight,' said the florid-faced man, pointing towards the serving maid. 'Why d'you ask? You can have all the women you need when you've found your gold!'

As the night went on, the stories got taller and the tellers more argumentative. James was becoming quite canny. When asked about his experience at the diggings, he only said he'd managed to wash a little colour, and that he hoped to do better this time.

The next day's journey to the diggings was slow, on account of the poor condition of the track, but there was no sign of bushrangers.

By all reports, there were now over a thousand men on the field. As the diggings came into sight, James thought it looked much the same, except there was more of it. The haphazard sprinkling of tents, huts, pits, trenches and mounds now stretched up the sides of the hills and over both sides of the river – spreading as if it were a fungal disease, pockmarking the face of the land. In the middle of the diggings, carpenters had begun work on the frame for a substantial hotel.

James was ready to stake his claim. He'd bought a miner's right in Cooma, and had his own copy of the goldfields regulations. But it was late in the day, and finding an unclaimed plot didn't look easy.

In the end, he pitched his tent just below the tree line, away from the diggings. Phillip and his party pitched theirs nearby. James was careful to put all his tools inside the tent, and used his saddle as a pillow. He advised the others to do the same. They shared a camp fire that evening. All turned in early so they could get up first thing in the morning to go digging.

When James woke, his horse was gone. For a stockman, losing his horse was like losing his right arm. In a desperate panic, he ran around, looking in all directions. There was no sign of Susie anywhere.

A sinking, empty feeling hit him – like a blow to the pit of his stomach. He collapsed onto the ground beside his tent, completely dispirited, holding his head between his hands.

5

Adelong Diggings
January 1860

Adelong nestles in rolling hills near Tumut, on the western side of the Snowy Mountains. Gold was first discovered there in 1852, although the big rush didn't start until after 1857, when Gold Dust Williams struck payable reef gold on Charcoal Hill.

By 1859, when news broke of the big finds at Kiandra, Adelong was a well established goldfield, with numbers of deep shafts and noisy steam-driven stamping batteries – crushing the white reef quartz. Even so, there was still plenty of gold in the creeks and gullies for parties to make wages from panning and cradling.

In 1860, the Gold Commissioner's quarters at Adelong overlooked Golden Gully and Adelong Creek. It was a damn noisy place, thought the man in charge of the field, Commissioner Stevens – dry, dusty, and dirty too. He was a reluctant appointee, forced to call in a favour to obtain the post when his East Indies trading enterprises failed. It wasn't how he'd hoped to end his time in the colonies. He'd anticipated a comfortable retirement in England. Instead, he'd lost all his property and had been forced to take up this lowly paid post.

The conditions on the field were a sore point. His wife had taken one look at the rough-hewn accommodation and immediately returned to Sydney

'Excuse me, sir,' said Sergeant Ballard, knocking on the commissioner's door. His bulky frame filled the doorway. He had his cap in his hand but his foot was half inside the room.

'What is it now?' asked the commissioner, irritated at being disturbed. He didn't like the man, who was interrupting his quiet smoke after lunch. There was little enough of civilisation on the field.

'Sir, don't you think you should do something about that flag?'

'What flag?' asked the commissioner, looking up from his chair and resting his pipe on the table.

'That Eureka flag, sir,' said the sergeant. 'It's an affront. You should make them take it down.'

'What's all this about? Where is it?' said the commissioner irritably. 'There's lots of flags on the diggings. I can't be taking them all down.'

'That flag stands for revolt. It's the one the rebels flew at the Eureka. I know it,' said the sergeant forcibly. 'I was there. I fought with the 40th Regiment.'

The commissioner didn't care what regiment the sergeant had fought with. He had never liked military men, especially those from the ranks. 'I did hear tell of a rebellion,' he said, scratching his temple with his pipe stem. 'When I was in India. I remember seeing it in the paper. But that was five years ago. That's all over now, isn't it? What does this flag look like?'

'It's a white cross – on a blue background – with stars.'

'Where is it?'

'Near those Victorians. The ones that arrived the other day.'

'But they'd just put up another one, wouldn't they? Then I'd look silly.' The commissioner knitted his bushy eyebrows. 'Is it a crime to fly a flag? What law can I invoke?'

'It's a sign of rebellion, sir.'

'Is there any sign these men are rebelling?'

'No, but…'

'Well, then? It's only a flag.'

'It's not right, sir. We shouldn't allow it.'

'Well, you go and take it down. But don't expect me to get involved. There's enough trouble on this field without me causing more of it.'

The sergeant was annoyed. He'd hoped for a stronger response from the commissioner. It confirmed his opinion about the man – and his decisions. This commissioner's approach to solving disputes was to give the diggers all they wanted. If he, the sergeant, had his way, he'd show this motley crowd who was in charge. He clicked his boot heels, turned and left.

When the sergeant had gone, the commissioner returned to smoking his pipe. Damn these colonials, he thought. And damn those Victorians. They were nothing but trouble. He wished they could be stopped at the border. All they did was send their gold back to Melbourne. He'd have a word to the Secretary of the Lands Department. Perhaps a special tax could be levied on them. That would deter them.

As for Sergeant Ballard, the man would do better to spend his energy closing down the sly grog tents. In the commissioner's view, drink was the cause of half of the disputes on the field. He had a strong suspicion the sergeant might be benefiting in some way from their operation instead of controlling them – though he had no firm proof. The quality of police on the goldfields was a problem. The previous sergeant lasted only a month before joining the diggers. It was hard to get honest and capable men to enlist as police, when the pay was so poor and the digger in the creek could make a fortune in front of their eyes – and often did.

He found it difficult enough himself when unkempt miners from the lower orders struck it rich and lorded it up with their new-found wealth. It was particularly galling to a man of his station, who had recently been in possession of the means to live well. Now he was reduced to a level not greatly above that of the working miners in this Godforsaken colonial outpost.

*

Tents were standard accommodation for the miners on the Adelong goldfield.

Jack Bendigo's tent was a simple canvas awning stretched between two poles in Golden Gully. Jack had just arrived from the Ovens diggings. He was a wiry, unkempt old miner, who looked like he'd never done anything else in the rest of his life. The miners at Ovens called him Jack Bendigo because of where he'd come from, and on account of his reluctance to mention his second name. He was known as a hatter, a man who works alone. It was also rumoured he was a former government man, who'd done a runner from his ticket of leave. On the Ovens diggings, he'd kept very much to himself and never bothered anyone.

The Eureka flag that so disturbed Sergeant Ballard was tied to a pole at the front of Jack's tent. The Hughes brothers, Davy and Alex, had pitched their tent next to it. They'd met Jack on the road from Beechworth and struck up a friendship with him – as much of one as they could, with a man of Jack's reticence.

Leaving the commissioner's quarters, Sergeant Ballard strode though the diggings – past tents, pits and mullock heaps – to where the flag was hanging. It was late in the afternoon. Diggers were returning to their camps, stoking their fires ready for the evening meal. The smell of cooking, wood smoke and hot billy tea drifted through the air. In the background, the dull thud of the stamping batteries reverberated methodically, shaking the ground in waves.

The flag hung limply in the still, hot air. Jack was sitting on a log, poking at his fire with a stick. Davy and Alex were seated in front of their tent on boxes that made do for chairs.

'Whose flag is that?' demanded Sergeant Ballard loudly.

Jack looked up slowly, and adjusted his hat. He eyed the sergeant, then spat into the fire. 'Why do you want to know?' he said.

'Is it yours?' boomed the sergeant, ignoring the question.

Jack thought for a while before answering. 'Yes,' he replied, slowly and deliberately. 'It could be.'

'Take it down immediately!' ordered the sergeant.

Jack looked at him, and scratched his ear. 'Why?'

'Do as I say!' ordered the sergeant.

By now a small crowd had gathered. Diggers were an inquisitive lot. Any disturbance on the field quickly drew a crowd. They kept a respectable distance, given that the law was involved, and whispered among themselves while they waited to see what would happen.

Davy walked across to where Jack was sitting. He stood beside him, in front of the flag. 'Why do you want the flag taken down?' he asked the sergeant, calmly and quietly, but firmly. Davy was tall, young and lightly built, but his voice had the sound of authority. His dark curly hair framed an open face. As he spoke, he looked straight at the sergeant with his piercing brown eyes. His bearing gave no suggestion of deference.

'Do you know what that flag stands for?' the sergeant demanded.

'You tell me,' said Davy.

'It's a flag of rebellion.'

'How so?'

'It's the flag the mutineers flew at Eureka.'

'So? Were you there?' asked Davy.

'Yes, I was,' said the sergeant. 'And proud of it. I fought with the 40th Regiment.'

'Do you know what happened after that?' asked Davy.

'Yes. We crushed the rebels. We stormed their feeble barricades. And we cut them down.' He said the last words with relish.

'But what happened after that?' said Davy.

'The ringleaders were brought to justice – and rightly so,' said the sergeant.

'Exactly,' said Davy. 'And all those charged were acquitted. Isn't that so?'

The sergeant looked uncomfortable. He hadn't anticipated any resistance. The crowd of bystanders made him feel uneasy. He wasn't happy at the way the affair was turning and regretted not bringing reinforcements.

'That may be so,' he said. 'What happened in the courts isn't my business. They were rebels what took up arms at Eureka. And they deserved what they got.'

'But what about the diggers' demands?' said Davy.

'They had no right to make any demands,' replied the sergeant curtly.

'The government listened to the diggers, didn't they?' said Davy. 'They got rid of the licence fee, didn't they? Now we've got a miner's right instead. Isn't that so?'

'That's still too much,' said a voice from amongst the diggers.

'Eureka made the government listen to the diggers, didn't it?' said Davy, addressing the crowd as much as the sergeant. 'Now when the diggers speak, the government listens. Isn't that so? Without Eureka, ordinary people wouldn't have the vote, would they? The diggers here on this field wouldn't have the vote. There wouldn't be a member for the Southern Goldfields, would there?'

The sergeant looked uncomfortable.

'A lot of good that does us!' said a digger. 'They've still got a tax on gold.'

'We won't go into that now,' said Davy. 'But remember, we're not finished with democracy yet. What this flag stands for is democracy. Democracy – and freedom.'

'You're talking rubbish,' said the sergeant. His patience was at an end. 'That flag means rebellion. Nothing less. And it's coming down.' He stepped forward and roughly pushed Davy aside.

As he reached towards the flag, Jack leapt at him like a tiger – bowling him clean over. Jumping up quickly, Jack stood defiantly in front of the flag.

The sergeant was completely taken by surprise. He lay in the dust for a moment, looking up at Jack in amazement. Then a furious scowl came over his face. 'I'll show you!' he said, gritting his teeth. Clambering to his feet, he drew his pistol. 'You're under arrest!' he growled. Keeping his pistol trained on Jack, he tore down the flag.

The crowd booed.

'What's he charged with?' asked Davy.

'None of your business,' said the sergeant.

'Yes. What's yer charge? Yer big clodwalloper,' said Jack.

'Resisting police in the carriage of their duty,' said the sergeant. He suddenly remembered he would need to account for his actions.

'And what duty was that?' asked Davy. 'The man's done no wrong.'

'He can tell that to the magistrate,' the sergeant said curtly. 'Now, move it!' He motioned to Jack with the pistol.

The crowd parted as the sergeant marched Jack off to the lockup.

The following morning, Jack was brought before Commissioner Stevens. It was one of the commissioner's complaints that he had to double as police magistrate, as well as carry out his duties as commissioner. He didn't relish the work of the police magistrate. He much preferred settling disputes by means that didn't involve invoking the penalties of the law. He'd even written to the Secretary of the Lands Department to complain. A junior official had replied, advising that his concerns would be considered. Nothing had been done. It was easy to be ignored here, so far from Sydney, on the far edge of the Southern Goldfields district.

Jack looked even more dishevelled than usual after his night in the lockup. Sergeant Ballard pushed him roughly into place in front of the wooden bench that did duty as a bar in the slab courtroom. Commissioner Stevens was sitting behind the bench. Apart from the accused, the sergeant and the commissioner, a crumpled-looking clerk of the court was seated at a rough-hewn table ready to take notes.

Just as the proceedings were about to begin, Davy strode into the courtroom. He stepped past Sergeant Ballard and stood in front of the bench. 'Your honour, my name is David Hughes. Might I be granted leave to represent this man?' he asked.

'Hold still, young man,' said the commissioner. 'We haven't heard the charge yet. On what grounds do you act?'

'There has been a miscarriage of justice,' said Davy. 'This man was wrongfully arrested. I'm seeking your assistance to have him released.'

'That's not so,' interrupted Sergeant Ballard.

'Order in the court,' said the commissioner, frowning at the sergeant. 'Wait till you're asked to speak.' He enjoyed the opportunity to reprimand the sergeant, who was clearly annoyed by it. Then he turned his attention to Davy. 'It's somewhat irregular,' he said. 'But I suppose you can represent him – that is, if he agrees. Do you agree to this man representing you?' he asked Jack.

'Yes, 'e can,' said Jack. Though he barely knew Davy, he knew he didn't have the gift of the gab himself.

'Right,' said the commissioner. 'Proceed to read the charge.'

The charge was duly read, evidence taken from the sergeant, and the flag tabled as evidence.

'Now, Mr Hughes, what do you have to say?' asked the commissioner.

'I don't deny the accused used physical force against the sergeant,' said Davy. 'But the force was not greatly extreme. It was certainly never likely to do the policeman any harm. You only have to look at the disparity between the parties. Here on the one side we have a well built policeman, and I use that word advisedly.' He paused.

The commissioner couldn't help smiling.

'On the other side we have a small, elderly miner. Hardly an even match, I would think.'

The commissioner was still smiling. 'But what is your point?' he asked.

'The reason I mention the disparity is to point to the inconsequential effect of the accused man's action. But that is not my main point. There might never have been any action by the accused if it were not for the unlawful action of the policeman in the first place. Let me explain.'

The commissioner nodded his agreement.

'Prior to the action by the accused, the policeman in question had sought to unlawfully seize the rightful private property of the accused. This property happened to be a flag – the one you see here on this bench. The particular character of this flag is of no importance. There are many flags on these diggings. Indeed all of the store tents, without exception, have flags of various descriptions.'

'That's true,' said the commissioner.

'I'm not aware of any law that prohibits the flying of flags,' said Davy. 'Nor of one which prescribes the designs that may or may not be displayed. Even if there were a prohibition on flying flags, it would be discriminatory, and quite unfair, to single out the accused for attention, when so many others are allowed to go free – would that not be so?'

The commissioner nodded.

The sergeant shifted uneasily on his feet.

'Clearly, the accused has been treated in an unjust and discriminatory manner by this policeman,' said Davy, looking at the sergeant. 'Imagine the scene. This elderly miner has been quietly enjoying his evening repast. Suddenly his quiet enjoyment is rudely shattered by an uncalled-for intrusion. In response to this extreme, and totally undeserved provocation, he has acted instantaneously to protect his property. It is no more than any reasonable man would do. Surely, to judge him harshly for this would be most unjust.'

Davy paused – to allow the point to be absorbed. 'In short,' he continued. 'The accused has only acted reasonably, given the circumstances, and, returning to my first point, has never risked causing any real harm to the policeman in question.'

Jack grinned at Sergeant Ballard.

'As to the character of the accused,' said Davy. 'I can vouch for him personally from the short time I have known him, but, if you wish, I can call other witnesses to whom he is known. These can attest to his honesty and to his soundness. However, in the circumstances of this case, I'm not sure this should be necessary.'

He paused again. 'In conclusion, I put to you that the charge against the accused should be dismissed. And the accused should be released from custody forthwith. It is most unfortunate that the accused has already been unfairly penalised by detention in custody overnight.'

He paused, and turned to the sergeant. 'I further recommend that you consider taking action to temper the zealousness of the policeman involved in this affair, in relation to such matters in future.'

When Davy had finished, there was silence.

Commissioner Stevens tugged at his side-whiskers before responding. 'Yes,' he said, nodding. 'I think you have put a persuasive case. Case dismissed. Release the accused, and return the flag.'

Sergeant Ballard looked furious. Jack gave Davy a big gap-toothed smile.

This case marked the beginning of the bad blood between Davy and Sergeant Ballard.

Within minutes of Jack's return to his tent, the flag was flying again. Davy boiled a billy to celebrate their victory.

'Can I ask you a question?' said Davy. 'Why were you flying the flag? I've heard about Eureka, but I didn't know there was a flag.'

'Not many do, these days,' said Jack.

'So why fly the flag?'

'I was there,' said Jack.

'Really?' said Davy. He was impressed. He thought for a minute. 'On that account, you've got to be Eureka Jack.'

Davy was last to turn in that evening. He sat by the fire as the coals died, watching the stars overhead. On the far side of the glowing embers, he could see the dark outline of the Eureka flag – a symbol of hope and independence for the future, for the people of this young old land. Beyond, and high above it, the stars of the Southern Cross twinkled strongly and brightly in the clear night sky.

The Eureka design and what it stood for became well known amongst the miners at Adelong as news of the flag incident spread. No one on the diggings liked Sergeant Ballard. He was known for his arrogance, and for his inflexible application of the law. After Jack's acquittal, Davy became as popular on the field as Sergeant Ballard was unpopular. Diggers would recognise him as he walked by, and wave. 'That's the cove what put Sergeant Ballard in his place,' they'd say, with undisguised admiration.

From this time on, whenever diggers needed help in a dispute, or ran foul of the law, they'd turn to Davy. Soon he was regularly acting as an advocate, both on the field and in the courtroom.

Alex resented the attention his older brother was getting. He felt the burden of work on their claim was falling unfairly to him. He was as different in character to Davy as he was in looks. He was shorter and stockier, with straight hair – and had a sulky demeanour. Alex wasn't one to keep a grievance quiet. 'It's not fair,' he complained to Davy. 'I'm doing all the work and you get to keep all the gold.'

'Don't you remember what we promised Father when we left London?' said Davy. 'Are you forgetting why we're here? Don't you remember what we said to Uncle Peter at Beechworth – when the shaft collapsed?'

'None of them's here now,' said Alex. 'There's only us. I don't believe all that stuff any more. Why can't we just look out for ourselves? Everyone else does.'

'That's not why we're here,' said Davy. 'We're not here just for the gold. It's only a means to an end. Anyway, the gold isn't just for us. We're doing this so we can support the cause. Don't you remember?'

'I know all that. You keep saying it. But just saying it doesn't make it true. Father and Uncle Peter might've got it all wrong. They're dead anyway.'

'That's why it's important. It's up to us now.'

'It's all right for you. You believe in the cause.'

'Are you worried about money? Don't you remember we've got all the money we need? It's in the bank. Uncle Peter left it to us. You've only got to wait till you're eighteen. It's only a few years' time.'

'That's ages. It's not fair. You've already got your share.'

'Yes, but look what I'm doing with it. What I'm doing is making a difference.'

'Not to me, it isn't. Why do we still have to send money back home, anyway?

'You keep forgetting – they paid our fares.'

'We must've paid them back many times over. Can't we keep the money for ourselves, now?'

'You've got to stop being so selfish,' said Davy, feeling exasperated and losing his patience.

'You're the selfish one,' said Alex, raising his voice. 'All you ever think of is yourself. You never let me have any fun. You won't even let me have a drink.' This was a prime grievance with Alex. 'You're not my father. I've had enough of you bossing me round. From now on, I'm going to keep all the gold I find. You can do your own damn digging.' He stormed off.

Davy sighed. He had known this was coming. It had been brewing ever since they'd left Beechworth. He wished Uncle Peter was still alive.

Alex didn't return that day. Davy was left to work the claim himself. In the afternoon, he was called to help resolve a dispute two miles down the creek.

By evening, there was still no sign of Alex. He stayed up later than usual, smoking by the fire, before he finally turned in by himself.

A loud crash in the middle of the night woke him up. Something had smashed against the side of the tent, almost knocking it down. In his half asleep state, Davy thought he was being attacked. He reached for the old bayonet he kept under his stretcher. Clutching it tightly, he crawled out of the collapsing tent barefooted. Instinctively, he left by the rear, in case there was a trap.

Outside, it was pitch dark. Vaguely, he made out the shape of a person floundering against the side of the tent. It was Alex. He was drunk. Not just a little drunk – totally incoherently drunk, fall-about drunk, the drunkenness of the young who don't yet know about drink. Davy tried helping him – as best as he could, in the dark. In no time, he ended up joining him in a tangle on top of the tent. After a struggle, he eventually managed to get them both clear of the pile of collapsed canvas.

Davy tried talking to Alex. It did no good. All he could get out of him were some jumbled words about a shanty. Then Alex threw up.

The general commotion woke Eureka Jack. He quickly grasped what was going on and offered to help. Between Davy and Jack, the two of them managed to straighten the tent and get Alex onto his stretcher – but not before he'd knocked over the water bucket, kicked the billy into the fire, and generally created a disturbance.

'Thought yer'd bin mobbed by Vandemonians,' said Jack, as they raked up the fire and put things back in order. 'Takes me back to the early days at Bendigo.'

'What's that?' asked Davy.

'Them convicts from Van Diemen's Land. They'd do yer fer yer gold. Slit yer throat in the night, they would – soon as look at yer.' He spoke with a tone of fear and respect.

They must've been bad, thought Davy, for Jack to be scared of them.

'Now don't yer go bein' too hard on the young fella in the morrow,' said Jack. ''E's only a youngster. The lad's gotta learn.'

Alex didn't remember anything in the morning. He was late to rise, shaky on his feet and complained about his head hurting. He was also very thirsty. Davy wasn't sympathetic. After quizzing him, he discovered Alex had 'borrowed' their week's gold takings and had spent the afternoon at Mad Mary's Shanty, on the far side of the creek, on the road to Victoria. Davy guessed Alex must have found a sly grog shop. He would never have been served in one of the licensed public houses.

Alex was in a sorry state that morning – such as encourages remorse. He promised Davy he would never do anything like it again. For the next few days, he was true to his word and worked the claim without complaint.

Davy was called in to help when Old Cornwallis refused to pay his men at the Strike It Lucky mine. This was a major dispute. An angry mob of miners gathered at the poppet head above the shaft. They demanded the foreman bring Cornwallis to talk to them.

'You bring him 'ere or we'll stave the shaft in!' threatened one.

'We should never have taken wages,' said another. 'We should've stuck with panning.'

'We ain't had no money for two weeks now,' said Mick, their self-appointed leader. 'That mongrel bastard said we was getting paid last week. Remember? He stood right here and said it would only be a day before we'd have the cash!'

'What does he take us for?' said a miner. 'Does he think we can live on air?'

The foreman tried explaining that he hadn't been paid either. This did nothing to calm the miners. The hotheads were all for smashing in the poppet head immediately. Davy did his best to argue for moderation. In the end, the miners gave the foreman an ultimatum. Cornwallis must appear within the hour – or they'd take action.

While they were waiting, Davy addressed the crowd. 'What's happened here proves the failure of the capital method of mining,' he said.

'Something sure as hell's gone wrong,' said a miner, 'when a man can work for weeks and not have bread to eat.'

'If you listen, I can tell you what's wrong,' said Davy. 'Then I'll tell you what you've got to do. Do you want to listen?'

'Yes, go on,' said a miner.

At this stage, the crowd were willing to listen to anything.

'Private property is the cause of all your problems,' said Davy. 'It's the ownership of private property that's wrong.'

'What do you mean?' asked a miner.

Davy remembered how his father had told him about Proudhon, and the Frenchman's famous saying, 'Property is theft.' He decided this audience wouldn't understand. He would need to keep his message simple. 'It's the property owners – the men of capital – who have taken what belongs to everyone,' he said. 'There's no reason why one particular class of persons should be entitled to all the wealth of this land.'

'Hear, hear,' said a digger.

'But where is the wealth in this colony?' continued Davy. It's in the land. And who controls the land? It's the property owners – the men of capital. Is it right that some men should own large tracts of land, and others none? What have they done to earn it? Here, in New South Wales, squatters control vast expanses of land, while miners can hardly afford a few acres.'

'That's right,' said a miner. 'Why should they have all the land?'

'Exactly,' said Davy. 'But it's more than land that's wrong. It's unjust for some people to have capital and never need to work, while others have to slave for wages. That's unfair.'

'When we don't get paid, it is!' said a miner.

'If all the rich people were to share their wealth with all the poor people, there'd be more than enough to go around,' said Davy.

'Not damn likely,' said a miner.

'So what are we to do? What are you saying?' asked another.

'What we need is democracy – true democracy. Take this goldfield. Why couldn't the diggers on this field decide how the wealth is divided up? There'd be no need for a commissioner. There'd be no need for the police. No one would need to steal from anyone else. Where does all the wealth go now? After paying the wages of ordinary diggers, most of it ends in the hands of a few wealthy men of capital – like Cornwallis.'

'The bastard,' said a miner.

'Let me tell you where the wealth of this field goes,' said Davy. 'Some of it goes in taxes. There's a gold tax. There's a miner's right – that's a tax. Then there's licence fees for the public houses – that's another tax. As well as taxes, there's profits. Look at what the storekeepers are charging for goods. Where does that money go to? It goes to a few rich men of capital – to a few speculators.'

'He's right about that,' said Mick. 'The price of tools is a disgrace. They're five times the cost of the same in Sydney.'

'Exactly. But who does the work?' said Davy. 'You do. You're the workers. Who gets the money? The men of capital, and the government.'

'Are you against the government?' asked a burly miner, sounding suspicious.

'No,' said Davy. 'Don't misunderstand me. I'm not a revolutionary. I'm not advocating revolution. What I'm advocating is democracy. If there were true democracy, there'd be no need for government. But that can't happen straight away.'

'Can it ever happen?'

'Yes it can,' said Davy. 'I believe it can happen – in our lifetime – if we want it badly enough. Don't get me wrong. I'm not advocating force. Some advocate force. I don't. I believe in moral suasion. That's what the Chartists used in England – ten years ago. Six million of them. They acted, and the government had to listen. We need to act now. We need to make this government listen too. I believe it's possible. We have to use our votes to make change. Remember that, next time you get a chance to vote. Don't waste it – make sure your vote counts.'

At this point, the foreman returned, accompanied by Mr Cornwallis and Commissioner Stevens. All eyes turned to them.

The commissioner spoke first. 'Mr Cornwallis has asked me to talk to you,' he said. 'It's a very unfortunate situation we have here. Mr Cornwallis would dearly love to pay you.'

'Then why doesn't he?' shouted a miner angrily.

'He has no money,' replied the commissioner. 'I can assure you, if he had the money, he'd pay you. In short, he wants to pay you but he can't.'

'What about us? We've got nothing to eat!' shouted a voice.

'Give me a chance to explain the problem, so you can understand it,' continued the commissioner. 'The situation is simple. There's no payable gold yet been struck in this shaft. You've invested your labour. Mr Cornwallis has invested his capital. But at present, the project isn't making a return.'

'So why can't we be paid?'

'Mr Cornwallis tells me he's sunk hundreds of pounds into the venture himself. And there are other creditors, too.'

'We don't care about them. They haven't been digging the shaft.'

'Let me put it another way,' said the commissioner. 'What are the choices? The project could be abandoned. In this case, you would lose, and Mr Cornwallis would lose. No one would gain anything.'

'What about his other shaft?' asked a miner.

'Which one is that?' asked Commissioner Stevens.

'The Victoria Reef shaft.'

'What can you tell us about that shaft?' asked the commissioner, turning to Cornwallis.

'I don't own it,' said Cornwallis.

'Who does, then?' asked Davy.

'It belongs to Symonds and partners,' said Cornwallis.

'Since when?' asked Davy.

'That's not true,' said Mick, angrily. 'Symonds told me you owned it.'

'That couldn't have been recently,' said Cornwallis. 'I sold it a fortnight ago.'

'So where'd the money go?' asked Mick. 'Why can't we have some of that?'

'There's none left,' said Cornwallis. 'I had to sell it for a pittance. It wasn't producing. I had outstanding debts.'

'It's making plenty now!' said a miner.

'That doesn't help with the problem here,' said the commissioner. 'Mr Cornwallis has told you he doesn't own it any more. You have a simple decision. Either you keep digging – in the hope the shaft will hit payable gold – or you can decide to abandon the project and cut your losses. Either way, you and Mr Cornwallis will be sharing the risks – and the possible rewards.'

'But that's not fair. He'll get more reward than us if we strike gold.'

'You can look at it another way,' said the commissioner. 'Mr Cornwallis has now lost more than any of you. He has lost hundreds of pounds. It's quite simple. Neither you nor he have any money now, but both of you have a chance to get some if you keep digging.'

'We'll sue him,' said a miner.

'That's true. You could take legal action against Mr Cornwallis. You could seek wages owing. But that would only cause him to become bankrupt. What would you have achieved then? You'd never see your money then. It's your choice. Either you call a halt to mining now – and end up with nothing – or you work for a longer period, in the hope of striking a lead.'

The miners started to talk noisily amongst themselves.

'It's your choice,' said the commissioner loudly. 'I've said enough now. I'll leave you to come to your own decision.'

The commissioner and his party withdrew, leaving the miners to decide their course of action.

After a brief discussion, the miners realised they had little alternative. Mick told the commissioner they'd decided to give it another week without pay. If nothing was found by then, they'd abandon the claim and cut their losses.

'We should try Gibson's Plains,' said a miner. 'They say there's gold for the taking up there.'

'You can't believe everything you hear about a new diggings,' said another. 'A bird in the hand, I say. At least we know there's gold on this field. It's just a matter of getting at it.'

Davy listened to the discussion but didn't try to influence the outcome. He told them it was their decision.

Later that day, he made some inquiries. He found out the other partners with Mr Symonds in the Victoria Reef shaft were a Mr and Mrs Spence and a Mr Bolton. He'd heard rumours that Cornwallis was a sly old devil, and he smelt a rat. He made some further inquiries and discovered that Mrs Spence was Cornwallis's sister and Mr Bolton was his cousin.

Sergeant Ballard was also making inquiries. He might be unpopular but he had his informants on the diggings. There were always people with a grudge, or those who could see a personal interest in passing information to the police. That evening, armed with information from an informant, he approached the commissioner.

'What is it now, sergeant?' said the commissioner testily. As usual, the sergeant was disturbing him when he'd rather be alone.

'It's about that Davy Hughes,' said the sergeant.

'Yes, what about him?'

'He's stirring up feeling against the government.'

'How so?'

'He's saying the miners should be in charge of the diggings. He's saying there's no need for the government or the police. He's dangerous. They're listening to him. I've found out more about him, too.'

'What's all this?'

'His father was a Chartist ringleader. He was gaoled in '48.' The sergeant made the last statement as if it proved his case. 'The Hughes' are well known where they come from. They're dangerous radicals. We should see them off this field before they start a rebellion. It'll be Eureka all over again.'

'Really, sergeant. You must be exaggerating. I haven't seen any evidence of rebellion. Where's all this happening?'

'That flag is a rallying point.'

'You're not on about that flag again.' The commissioner sounded exasperated. 'Listen – if you give a man a grievance he'll nurture it. Why would we do that – when there's no need? Grievances are like plants – they thrive when you feed them.'

'But this Hughes is spreading dangerous ideas.'

'What dangerous ideas?'

'He's talking about the diggers taking over. He's talking about direct democracy. He's saying the wealth of the field should be shared equally amongst the diggers.'

'Is he really saying that?'

'Yes.'

'Then I'm not worried.' The commissioner stood up, as if to dismiss the sergeant.

'Why not?' asked the sergeant.

'It'll never happen,' said the commissioner. 'Greed is part of human nature. Why else do people come here looking for gold? It's certainly not because they want to share it. Now, if you'll leave me, I have some reading to do.'

The sergeant left, muttering under his breath.

Alex didn't come home that evening. Davy was disappointed, but hardly surprised. He ate dinner by himself then walked down to Mad Mary's. The shanty was a roughly built slab hut, with a bark roof, constructed with a dangerous-looking tilt. A noisy crowd of drinkers were standing around the building, some leaning against it, unconcerned they might assist its collapse. There was no sign of Alex. Davy noticed that Sergeant Ballard and one of his men were amongst the patrons.

Davy asked one of the drinkers if he'd seen Alex. The man told him Alex had been there earlier but had left. He asked Davy why the police were getting their drinks for free while everyone else had to pay a shilling a nobbler.

Davy returned to his tent. Later a policeman came by with a message.

Alex was in the lock up. He'd been arrested for being drunk and disorderly. The policeman told Davy he could bail him out in the morning.

Next morning, Sergeant Ballard was enjoying himself. 'Pity it's your brother,' he said to Davy. 'It'd be better if it was you in there.'

Davy bailed Alex to appear before the commissioner that afternoon. After he'd signed the bail papers, Davy and Sergeant Ballard were alone in the guardhouse.

'Listen here,' said the sergeant, as he blocked the exit. 'Let me give you some advice. Scum like you aren't wanted here. If I was you, I'd be moving on. There's lots of dangerous shafts around on these diggings. Plenty of accidents happen. Get my drift? If you stay on these diggings, it's certain something bad is going to happen – to you.'

'Let me pass,' said Davy.

The sergeant stood aside. 'I'd move on quickly if I was you,' he said as Davy left. 'The lock-up could be the safest place for you.'

Davy didn't take kindly to threats. After leaving the guardhouse, he went straight to the commissioner's quarters. He caught the commissioner just as he was leaving. 'I'd like to make a complaint,' he said.

'What is it now?' asked the commissioner wearily.

'How is it that sly grog shops can operate openly on these diggings?'

'What do you mean?'

'You know about Mad Mary's shanty, don't you?' said Davy. 'That doesn't have a licence, does it?'

'Is that still operating?' The commissioner tried to sound surprised. He would have preferred not to know.

'It certainly is,' said Davy. 'Not only that – but Sergeant Ballard and his police are being provided with free drinks.'

'Is that so?' The commissioner looked closely at Davy. 'Do you have evidence?'

'Not sworn evidence,' said Davy, 'but you can talk to any of the drinkers there. They were complaining about the police getting free drinks. I suggest you make some inquiries.'

'Thank you. I guess I'd better.' The commissioner wasn't enthusiastic. But now the matter had been raised, he'd have to act.

Commissioner Stevens' inquiries proved unproductive. All the miners he spoke to had very poor memories.

Sergeant Ballard denied the allegations outright. He said Davy had made it up – to try and discredit the rightful authority of the police. 'That's what those radicals do. They spread lies. It's part of their plan. They want to usurp control.'

The sergeant scowled darkly and muttered to himself as he left the commissioner's quarters.

6

To the Snowy River Diggings
January 1860

Stories of the amazing finds at Gibson's Plains were sweeping through the Adelong diggings.

'Here, read this,' said Davy. He passed a copy of the *Sydney Morning Herald* to Eureka Jack. 'It's just come in. It's got the latest on the Snowy River diggings.'

Jack took the paper, but held it upside down. He looked sheepish.

'Go on,' said Davy. 'It's on page three.'

Jack looked at him blankly.

'Wait on,' said Davy. 'You *can* read, can't you?'

'A little,' said Jack. 'I know some numbers.'

'How about words?'

'Not really,' said Jack. 'Them words always was a mystery to me.'

'I should've guessed,' said Davy. 'Don't worry – there's plenty others on the diggings don't read. That's one of the things we've got to change. I guess I'd better read it to you, then.'

Jack nodded.

Davy read, "'17th January 1860 – from the paper's Maneroo correspondent. New Goldfield at Gibson's Plain. An extensive goldfield is now breaking out at Gibson's Plain on the Snowy River. I have seen two nuggets value of each six pounds. The men who have been working here for a fortnight have sixty pounds worth of nuggety gold. Men are beginning to flock to the new field, and a dray has just passed loaded with supplies. The gold is nuggetty, and I am assured it exists in paying quantities over a considerable area.'"

'Them nuggets sounds good,' said Jack.

'It also tells of a dead man that was found in the district,' said Davy.

'"A man in charge of the Twofold Bay Company's sheep at Tantangarra, between Cooma and Tumut, while shepherding sheep recently, found the skull of a human being. No other human bones can yet be found. The hair on the skull is dark brown and curly. A saddle, bridle and two pairs of blankets, with all the necessary clothing, were lying near the remains. It is difficult to suppose the cause of this unfortunate man's death, as he had rations, and none of the clothes were injured. No papers were found, excepting a piece of a Goulburn Chronicle bearing date April ninth 1859. The sum of eighteen shillings was found in a purse. The outside leather of the flap of the saddle had been cut away, as if to find money that might have been secreted. It is supposed that some person was travelling with the deceased, and for the sake of his money committed murder." Curious, that,' commented Davy. 'I wonder what really happened.'

'There's plenty of them sorts of mysteries round goldfields,' said Jack.

'I reckon it's time we tried our luck at Gibson's Plain,' said Davy.

'I may be joinin' yer,' said Jack.

Davy and Jack weren't alone. Most of the miners on the Adelong field were thinking the same way. Reef claims were much harder work than the apparently easy surface pickings at Gibson's Plain.

From Adelong to the Snowy River diggings was less than fifty miles as the crow flies. It would have been a good day's ride on a well made bridle track, if one had existed. For most of the diggers, it was a three-to four-day walk. The going was easy from Adelong and Tumut until Talbingo Mountain. There, over a couple of miles, the diggers had to climb over two thousand feet from the lowlands to the high plains. Dry stringy bark forest on the steep lower slopes gave way to towering mountain ash stands on the misty higher ridges, till they reached the marshy plains of the upper Murrumbidgee and Snowy rivers.

An eagle's-eye view at the time would have shown streams of diggers converging on the Snowy diggings from all directions – thousands of men, women, carts and animals, all on the move together. From Sydney, the main route was through Goulburn, Queanbeyan and Cooma, but many caught the steamer to Merimbula and Twofold Bay, climbing the coastal range at Cathcart. Some came through the Brindabella Mountains along the Goodradigbee River, or up the Naas Valley and through Gudgenby and Yiack. The largest numbers came from the south and the Victorian goldfields. Most of them came via Adelong and Tumut. The publican at Albury reported hundreds passing through each day. A more direct but rather rugged route was from the upper Murray to Lob's Hole. Yet another was Ligar's route, also from the upper Murray, across the tops of the mountain ridges through to Happy Jack's Plain.

Davy bought a packhorse, new tools and plenty of provisions. He knew supplies would be costly and scarce on the new field. He also wanted to purchase saddle horses. None were to be had. With the new rush, prices were soaring. Stores were running out of supplies. The price of flour was rising daily as farmers held onto their wheat.

On the road to Tumut, Davy, Jack and Alex fell in with Mick and a party of miners from the Cornwallis mine. The men had decided to cut their losses after hearing the latest news from Gibson's Plains. A well known Adelong miner, who'd returned to collect his belongings after a visit to the Snowy River diggings, told of easy pickings in the creeks and river, but warned about the crowds he'd seen on the track. He said it wouldn't be long before all the best claims were taken. On hearing this, the Cornwallis miners held a quick meeting and decided to immediately abandon work on their shaft.

At Tumut, the local storekeeper, Mr Manderson, a portly gentleman with bushy whiskers, was complaining loudly to a man dressed like a squatter about how difficult it was to get provisions to the new field. 'I've got three dray loads ready to start,' said Manderson, standing outside his store. 'I've ridden the route and there's no way the drays'll get through. It's so damn steep at Talbingo Hill. And there's too much timber in the way. I don't know what to do.'

The Adelong miners stopped and listened. Any information about the route to the diggings could be useful.

'What about pack horses?' suggested the squatter. 'Maybe I could get you some. But I'd need to ride over to Wagga.'

'How long would that take?' said Manderson. 'If I can't get the drays there quickly, the market will be all tied up.'

'Have you thought about mules?' said the squatter. 'They tell me the Pollocks are using mules to bring in supplies on their side of the mountains. They've got the same problem. Their route's near impassable for drays too.'

'That might be all right for them. It's only twelve miles or so from Russell's to Irishtown. It's fifty from here.' Manderson thought for a moment. 'Could you get me some?'

'Not sure,' said the squatter. 'But I should be able to get packhorses.'

Mick had worked on road construction before he took to mining. He was a former government man, though he kept that to himself. 'What's the problem with the road?' he asked.

'There's no way to get the bullock drays through. It's too steep and the bush is too thick,' said Manderson.

'So what's the problem? You can fix the steepness by loading. If there's timber in the way, you just gotta clear it. I've done plenty of road building in me time. It's not so hard.'

'But how am I going to get the timber cleared?' said Manderson. 'The job won't be worth doing if I can't get it cleared soon. I may as well wait for the government to build a road.'

'Can you wait that long?' said the squatter sarcastically.

'Let me get it right,' said Mick. 'You need just enough timber taken out so a bullock dray can pass through?'

'Yes, that's right,' said Manderson. 'But there's no one to do it. All the men have gone to the diggings. There's no one left this side of the mountains – 'cept old codgers.'

'How much clearing is needed?' asked Mick.

'None this side of Talbingo Hill,' said Manderson. 'There's a few trees on the way up the hill, but not many. Further along, there's a dense stand of mountain ash. But it wouldn't be more than half a mile to get through the worst. Up past Yarrangobilly, the bullockies should be able to find a way through.'

'You wouldn't be wanting the trees grubbed, would you?' asked Mick.

'No. They just need to be cut off at ground level, so the drays can go over the stumps if needs be.'

'And you'd pull the fallen timber out of the way with the bullocks, eh?'

'Yes. I'd do that,' said Manderson.

'Tell you what,' said Mick. 'Let me talk to the lads here and I might have a proposition for you.'

Mick quickly gathered his mates around. He put it to them like this: six of their party would cut the timber on their way to the diggings – for a goodly reward. The other two would go ahead and stake out their claims. There would be nothing lost as far as the claims were concerned, as it should only take a few days work to cut the timber, then they'd all be able to join up again. Manderson would need to provide all the tools, and free provisions.

'This way, we'll be able to start on the new diggings with plenty of provisions, and not get caught short like we was at Adelong,' said Mick.

'He's right,' said one of the miners. 'We ain't got a lot of provisions. And they say there's little to be had at the diggings.'

'How much will we ask?' queried a miner.

Forty pounds was agreed. That was five pounds for each of them, for less than a week's work. If they'd been working for wages, they'd probably only get two pounds for the week.

'We'll share out the cash between everyone when we get to Irishtown,' said Mick.

Mick was entrusted with the task of negotiating the deal. Manderson offered thirty pounds. Mick suggested fifty. Forty was settled on. Manderson agreed to supply the tools, and provide a horse and cart to carry their tools and provisions.

'We'll need to make sure what you've told us is true,' said Mick. 'I mean about the amount of clearing,'

'You'll have to trust me,' said Manderson. 'There's no time. The drays'll be following you as you clear. I'll come with you and show you the way. I've been out four days already and blazed the trail.'

'In that case, we'll need an advance payment,' said Mick.

Manderson wouldn't agree to that. Instead, he offered a week's free rations, but only if the job was finished in ten days.

'Ten days!' said Mick. 'There's a good two weeks' work in the job!'

'The deal's off, then,' said Manderson. 'Two weeks and it'll be too late.'

'All right, then, we'll give it a go at ten days,' said Mick. 'If we do long hours, we should just be able to make it, I reckon. But it'll cost more. We couldn't do it short of fifty pounds.'

The deal was settled at fifty pounds. First thing next morning, the cart was loaded and ready. Mick insisted on carrying Davy and Jack's gear as well.

They pitched camp at the foot of Talbingo Hill that night, along with a number of other parties on their way to the diggings. More arrived during the night. The next morning, Davy, Alex and Jack left the timber cutters to their work and set off up the hill. The initial climb was fearful. It would certainly be a challenge for the drays, thought Davy.

Along the way, there were almost as many travellers returning as going. All gave good reports of the diggings but warned of the scarcity of provisions. Most were returning with packhorses to pick up supplies, or bringing news of the field to their mates.

After a day's travel, they arrived at Yarrangobilly Creek. An enterprising businessman had already established a makeshift public house. It wasn't raining, so Davy's party camped out.

They were joined at their camp fire by a gentleman on his way back from the diggings. He warned them about bushrangers. There'd been some robberies on the road, he told them. 'It's those Victorian riffraff from Omeo,' he said as the billy boiled. He didn't realise he was addressing a group of Victorians. 'Those Omeo diggings are well known. They're the refuge for the worst scum of the colonies – escaped criminals and such like, even Vandemonians. It's the whiff of gold that draws them.'

Davy did most of the talking when they met other parties. Alex said little. He would have preferred to be travelling by himself. Davy's friendliness annoyed him. He couldn't see why Davy needed to be friends with everyone. He wouldn't have spent time with any of these stupid strangers.

Setting off from Yarrangobilly, they walked through mist and rain. Clusters of snow gums grew thick on the ridges, their ghostly forms appearing and disappearing eerily as the mist rolled in and out.

Despite the fog, it was easy to find the way. They only had to follow the muddy trampled tracks. These led them across grassy clearings, through innumerable boggy creek crossings, and up and down marshy gullies, till at last they came to a wide saddle, where a horseman told them it was only six or so miles to the diggings.

*

It took James more than a day to get over the loss of his horse. He spent the first morning trudging around the diggings, searching and making a pest of himself, asking diggers if they'd seen a mountain-bred bay mare.

'Why would you want a horse on the diggings?' was the general response.

'Horses are a nuisance here. You're well rid of it. You can buy a dozen nags if you strike it rich,' said one miner.

James gave up. He decided he'd better select a claim. This wasn't straightforward, as he had little knowledge of what to look for. In the end, he staked his claim in a gully near the river, though without river frontage. All the riverside claims were taken. It wasn't ideal, as he'd have to cart water. Without a horse to worry about, he decided he'd move his tent to his claim. That took the best part of the next day.

James got a pleasant surprise when he started digging. He opened up a small spring. It was in the middle of the gully, only a foot or so below the surface. The water seeped out beautifully clear. Not only that, but he collected over an ounce of gold on his first day of panning. The gold was dark, weather-worn and nuggety. In his excitement, he showed it to the neighbouring diggers. Most of them were doing just as well or better, they told him. The Scully brothers, with two others, had been at the diggings since early in the rush. Dan Scully told James they'd washed a hundred and twenty-five ounces in one week. John Mobbs said he'd been the third person on the field, and his party had washed thirty-four ounces in three days. John Moody alone washed nineteen ounces in a day! With gold fetching over three pounds an ounce, that was some fortune.

Sheedy's party were the only neighbours who weren't doing well. They had the claim next to James. Despite digging three holes, each six feet deep, their wash dirt was yielding less than an ounce a day.

There were three in Sheedy's party. Their principal, who went by the nickname of Shady, had shifty eyes, a whining voice and walked with a limp. His partners, Steve and Brian, looked as though life had dealt them a hard hand. None of the party spent much time at the claim. When present, they worked fitfully, spending as much time looking at what others were doing as working themselves.

'What you got there?' asked Sheedy. He'd wandered over to where James was digging.

James noticed he was unsteady on his feet. 'Nothing much,' said James. He would have preferred to be left alone.

Sheedy pulled a bottle out of his coat pocket, took a swig and held it out to James. 'Want a drop?' he offered.

'No, thanks,' said James. It was mid-morning. 'How's your claim going?' he asked, in between shovelling.

'Not too good,' replied Sheedy. 'Think we've got a duffer.'

James wished the man would go away. He didn't know what to say to get rid of him without being rude. He kept working. Sheedy stood watching him, then tried unsuccessfully to light his pipe in the breeze. James finished shovelling and started panning. As luck would have it, he turned up a small nugget in the first wash. It must have been nearly an ounce.

'How about that,' said Sheedy.

The bitter tone in his voice made James glance up. He didn't like what he saw. The look of envy in the other man's eyes made him feel uneasy. He quickly put the nugget in his pocket, stopped panning and went back to shovelling. He didn't offer any more conversation, and tried to behave as if there was no one there.

Sheedy eventually found something else to take his attention and wandered off, much as he'd come. The alternative didn't involve working on his claim.

*

Sally waited hopefully in Cooma for news from James. She knew she was being optimistic to expect anything yet. He'd been gone barely two weeks, and there was no established mail run from the diggings. In the absence of a letter, she keenly read the *Sydney Morning Herald* for news from the Snowy River diggings. She'd convinced her father to buy the paper on a regular basis to help with her reading practice. He'd agreed, mostly to humour his headstrong daughter. He wasn't a big reader himself, especially now he was getting older.

'Look, there's another report in today's paper,' said Sally, bursting into the room as her parents were eating lunch.

'Gold, gold, gold. That's all they talk about now,' said Mr McNeill. 'They all want tools made, horses shod, an' all in a hurry. Every man an' 'is dog in Cooma's off to the diggings. Then there's the travellers coming through. They all wants it done yesterday.'

'It must be good for business,' said Mrs McNeill.

'Maybe so,' said Mr McNeill. 'I'll still be damn glad when this here rush quietens down.'

'But it won't,' said Sally. 'Haven't you read the paper? Didn't you read that page I left you the other day?'

'I've been busy. Y'know how it is.'

'Dad! Did you read any of it?'

'My eyes got tired. Must've got some dirt in them.'

'All right,' said Sally. She understood. 'Would you like me to read it for you?'

'Yes, if it makes you happy.' said her father.

'I'd like to hear it too,' said her mother. She had never learnt to read properly. It was one of the reasons she'd been keen for Sally to have an education. Her own family had fallen on bad times after the death of her father, and schooling was the first thing that had to be dropped.

'All right,' said Sally. 'The first report is dated Saturday 28th January – from Wednesday's Goulburn *Chronicle*. "New Diggings at the Snowy River. The discovery of gold lately made at Gibson's Plain, near the source of the Snowy River, is beginning to attract considerable attention; and from intelligence that has reached us from various sources, we are inclined

to believe that in this instance a really payable goldfield has been struck."
I'll skip the next bit. It warns not to go to there till the field is fully proven.
"Gibson's Plain extends fourteen miles and is not far from the source of
the Snowy River. It is about sixty miles from Cooma and about fifty miles
from Tumut, but the route from Tumut is unpracticable for drays. The
best route is by way of Cooma."'

'It wasn't a Tumut correspondent wrote that, eh?' said Mr McNeill.

Sally continued, skipping bits. '"The new goldfield can be approached
by drays only within twelve miles, the remaining distance, goods have to
be conveyed by pack horse…already three slaughter houses erected…only
workable November to May, say seven months of the year, the remaining
five months the place is covered with snow to a depth variously stated as
from four to five to twenty feet. Mr Maurice Harnett, who resides near
Cooma, passed Saturday last with sixteen ounces of gold from the new
field which is intended for assay by the mint. The gold is nuggetty, bright
and clean."'

'I saw that,' said Mr McNeill. 'He came through the other day. It
caused quite a stir at the Lord Raglan.'

'What were you doing there?' asked Mrs McNeill.

'Keep reading,' said Mr McNeill.

Sally continued. '"We hear the first party at work have obtained four
pounds weight, and that twelve men, one of whom is named Russell,
obtained in part of two days no less than four ounces. The sinking at
present is from three to six feet. The diggers at last account were sluicing
in the river and tributary creeks, and no shafts had yet been sunk. We
understand an official report from the nearest magistrate, Mr W. Graham,
went down on Saturday night, with a view to proclamation of the new
gold-field, which will no doubt take place at once."'

'That William Russell's done well, hasn't he?' said Mr McNeill.

'Will I keep going?' asked Sally.

'Yes, go on,' said Mr McNeill. He pushed back from the table and
started to drink his tea.

'I'll just read you the main bits,' said Sally. '"…diggers are leaving
Adelong reef in hundreds for the new gold-field at Gibson's Plains…may

be reached on horseback from Tumut in about fifty miles and many are going that way, but drays cannot take that route, as they cannot cross Talbingo Hill… Some Adelong people have visited the new field, and returned, reporting it very good…the workings are reported to be easy and the gold so widely diffused as to almost ensure a reward to persevering miners. Seven to eight hundred men are there…more flocking…receive all glowing reports with great caution. It is a bleak place…it requires some nuggets to pay for tent life. For those who are hardened to all weathers there may be no danger, but city-bred folks, and those who have any delicacy of constitution should beware how they tempt the rigours of the Maneroo Plains and valleys."'

'Must be a Sydney cove what wrote that,' said Mr McNeill. 'He oughta spend a winter here in Cooma.'

'Last is a letter from the Snowy River diggings, dated 24th January,' said Sally. 'It says there's "seven to eight hundred men extending a distance of seven miles along the river. The sinking is shallow – about four feet. I saw one prospect this morning from a tin dish about one ounce. From the different accounts I heard, and what I saw, these will be the richest diggings yet discovered in New South Wales, but they have the drawback of not being able to be worked during the winter months, from the snow that lays very deep, and the first of which may be expected in the month of April…best route is by Twofold Bay…meat is plentiful, but other provisions scarce."' She put the paper down. 'That's it,' she said. 'I do hope James is all right.'

'I'm sure he will be,' said her mother.

'Of course he will be,' said Mr McNeill. 'He's a big lad now. He can look after 'is self.'

*

James worked steadily on his claim for two days. Then he took a break to buy provisions. Although he wasn't out of anything, he thought it would be wise to keep up supplies. It hadn't rained for a few days and the ruts in the tracks had hardened, making walking difficult. Everywhere, the black mud was turning to dust – a black, windblown, fine-grained dust that dirtied everything it settled on, leaving tents, clothes and faces blackened and grimy.

Scores of miners and would-be miners milled around, crowding the insides and outsides of the stores that lined what passed for a street. You could tell the new arrivals – they were the clean ones. There was plenty of grumbling about prices. The sly grog shops were doing a roaring trade, even though it was only the middle of the day. Construction of Adam Kidd's Exchange Hotel was well advanced. A big canvas sign boldly announced, 'Hotel Opening Soon'. Everyone was talking about it. Adam Kidd was a spirited Yankee, with a sharp eye for business and a talent for self-promotion. He was already well known amongst the diggers for his hotel at Albury that catered for the miners' trade.

The two main stores were Pollocks' and Chippendale's. Pollocks' store was a big tent, consisting of no more than a few rough saplings for uprights, to which common grey calico had been nailed. On entering the store, James was shocked at the cost of goods. Twenty-five shillings for a long-handled shovel! He walked across to Chippendale's – prices were just as high. He bought a little flour and some fresh meat. At least the meat was affordable.

As he returned to his claim with his supplies, he saw a large crowd of diggers standing on Sheedy's claim. Then he heard a shout.

'Thief! Thief! There's the thief!' Sheedy was shouting and pointing in his direction.

James turned to see if there was someone behind him. There was no one.

'Don't let him get away!' shouted Sheedy. He ran towards James.

The crowd of diggers were close behind. James didn't try to escape. It all happened so quickly. He was caught completely by surprise and was too confused. He struggled briefly as two burly miners grabbed him, but it was useless, and he soon stopped. They held him pinned, with his arms twisted behind his back. It hurt.

'What have I done?' he asked, squirming to try and ease the pain.

'What's 'e done?' said Sheedy, in mock surprise. ''E nicked our gold. The dirty thief!'

'Shave 'im!' 'Cut off 'is ears!' came shouts from the crowd.

'Hold on,' said Mick Bourke, out of breath as he arrived. 'Let's do this by the rules.' Mick was a thickset, pasty-faced man, with wispy hair and a nose that looked as if it had seen its share of fights. When he spoke, the miners listened. He had authority. He was the chairman of the Goldfields Vigilance Committee. 'Set up the court. Now, who's bringing the charge?' he demanded in a commanding voice.

'We are,' said Sheedy. 'Brian saw that thieving mongrel take our gold.'

'Any other witnesses?' asked Bourke, looking around.

No one spoke.

'But I never – ' started James.

'Quiet! said Bourke. 'I'll tell you when you can speak. You'll get your chance later.'

'Search 'is tent. I bet it's in there,' said Brian, pointing at James's tent. 'I saw 'im take it in there.'

James didn't understand what he meant.

'Wait on,' said Bourke. 'What does this gold look like? All gold's much the same here. How can we know it's yours – and not his?'

'It was in a leather pouch – with a draw cord on top,' said Brian.

'Do you have one of those?' Bourke asked James.

'No, but…'

'Search the tent,' ordered Bourke.

Bourke's helpers hardly needed encouragement. There were plenty of volunteers to do the work of the Vigilance Committee. Over a hundred had been sworn in as special constables. No questions were asked, and there was no qualification required, other than a keenness to see miners' justice be done.

'Is this it?' said a man emerging from James's tent. He held up a small leather bag.

James had a sinking feeling. He had no idea how it came to be in his tent.

'That's it!' said Sheedy.

'What you got to say for yourself now?' demanded Bourke.

'Let's get him!' shouted an eager onlooker.

The crowd sensed a punishment. They were keen to get involved, and surged forward.

'Wait a minute,' said Bourke.

'I never saw it before – honest,' said James quickly. 'Someone must've put it there.' He felt tears coming to his eyes. Not from the pain, but because of the gross unfairness of what was happening.

'Are you accusing us of planting it?' said Brian. ''E's a liar as well as a thief. Punish 'im!'

Things were looking very bad for James.

Just then, a tall man pushed his way to the front of the crowd. 'What's going on here? Why are you holding this man?' he said in a commanding voice, as if used to giving orders. It was Walter, one of the men James had untied on the road from Russell's.

The crowd stopped moving forward and looked at him.

'This is a Vigilance Committee court,' said Bourke. 'This man's been caught stealing.'

'I never did,' said James.

'I don't believe it,' said Walter. 'This man rescued us from bushrangers a few weeks back. We owe our lives to him. We'd been set upon by ruffians and left to die. I don't believe he's a thief.'

'Yes 'e is,' said Brian.

'An' 'e's a liar too,' said Sheedy.

Just then, another man pushed to the front of the crowd. It was Davy, closely followed by Jack.

'What's going on?' said Davy.

'Quiet in the court,' said Bourke loudly. 'I'm in charge here.'

'What authority do you hold?' demanded Davy. He'd quickly assessed what was going on. He'd heard tales of the Vigilance Committee – and its so-called justice.

'None of your business,' said Bourke.

'But it is my business,' said Davy. Then he stopped.

Jack pulled him by the coat sleeve and whispered something in his ear.

'That's Davy from Adelong,' said a voice from the crowd. 'He's done good for the miners at Adelong.'

'I don't care what he's done,' said Bourke. 'I'm in charge here. It's my job to make sure justice is done.'

'Let the man go,' said Walter. 'There must be a mistake.'

'There's no mistake,' said Bourke.

Davy walked over to where Bourke was standing. He stood in front of him and faced the crowd. 'See this man,' said Davy, pointing at Sheedy. 'This man's made false accusations before.'

The crowd fell silent.

Sheedy looked sideways furtively, as if checking for an escape route. Brian started to move away.

'Don't let those men get away,' said Davy. 'Come forward, you two. Now tell us about Ballarat and what happened in '57.'

The two former accusers remained quiet. They hung their heads, shifted on their feet and looked decidedly uncomfortable.

'Well, if they won't tell you, I will,' said Davy. 'In '57, these men falsely accused a miner of taking their gold – so as to get his claim. I have a witness who was there. What store do you put on their testimony now?'

The two miners holding James let go of his arms.

'How were we to know that?' said Bourke.

'You weren't to. But you need to be careful when you act in the name of justice,' said Davy. 'I'm not a great supporter of the legal system, but taking the law into your own hands isn't always the answer.'

'OK, fellas,' said Bourke, trying to reassert his control. 'Take those two away and show them some miners' justice. It mightn't have the force of law, but it'll do for this field.'

The crowd needed little encouragement. They quickly turned their attention to Brian and Sheedy, and marched them off to the river. This was the sport they'd been waiting for.

When the crowd had moved away, Bourke walked back up the hill to his store tent. He'd left it in the care of his wife while he dispensed justice. He took the 'evidence' with him.

James was left alone with Davy, Jack, and Walter. Alex was nowhere to be seen. He'd disappeared as soon as Davy and Jack joined the crowd, leaving their packhorse tied to a tent peg.

James said he didn't know how he could thank them all. He felt quite shaky. Walter said not to worry, he was only returning a favour. He offered James a sip from his flask, which James kindly accepted. He said James was lucky. By chance, he was on his way to his claim, further up the river. He couldn't stay, as he didn't want to leave it unattended for too long.

James offered to boil a billy for Davy and Jack. When Davy returned with the packhorse, they swapped stories about how each came to be at the diggings.

'It's not good to be on your own with a claim,' said Davy.

'I'm not too keen being on my own any more,' said James. 'Not after what's happened. I wouldn't mind finding a partner. I've got a good paying claim here.'

'I won't take orders from no man,' said Jack. 'I'll tell no man what to do. An' no man tells me what to do.'

'That might be all right for you, Jack,' said Davy. 'I'd prefer to be in with a partner. Tell you what,' he said to James. 'How about we join together, if you don't mind. We could register an extended claim. That part of the hill's not taken, is it? My brother Alex could come in too.'

'Sounds good to me,' said James.

'It's a deal, then,' said Davy.

'I'll stake that other part of the hill for meself,' said Jack.

That's how James and Davy came to be partners in a river claim. When they measured the boundaries, they discovered the miners on the adjacent river claim had pegged more than the allowed distance, so their new claim ended up with river frontage. Over-claiming had become rife without a commissioner on the field.

'Remember,' said Davy, 'the pegs must stand one foot above the ground, like it says in the regulations. We don't want some smart bush lawyer trying something out on us.'

'Is that likely?' asked James.

'Could be,' said Davy. 'I've seen all manner of excuses used to jump claims. Some scoundrels stop at nothing.'

While they were hammering in their pegs, Alex returned. Davy knew where he'd been – from his flushed face, and from the smell. Alex said he didn't want to do any more digging. Davy wasn't surprised. He suggested Alex take the packhorse and make wages carting supplies to the field. That was agreeable to Alex.

The next day, Assistant Gold Commissioner Lynch and a party of troopers arrived from Tumut. News of the value of the new diggings, and the prospect of large supplies of gold going to Melbourne, had finally galvanised the New South Wales government to order a commissioner to the field.

The commissioner's party rode onto the field to assert the government's authority. That involved making sure all the diggers had bought miner's rights. The troopers didn't seem too concerned with the sly grog tents, or the occasional fight. Their other main objective was to make arrangements for a gold escort, so the gold could be taken to Sydney, where tax could be levied.

Davy and James registered their joint claim with the commissioner. Jack also registered his.

Davy noticed that Sergeant Ballard had arrived with the commissioner's party. He saw him hobnobbing with Mick Bourke.

7

Kiandra Goldfield
February 1860

From the moment he saw him, James liked Davy. It wasn't only gratitude at being saved from the mob. The more they talked, the more James had a good feeling about their partnership. Davy was so confident. He had answers to everything.

'We need to work as a team,' said Davy. 'Best we get a cradle. It's a mug's game not using machinery.'

James had wondered about using a cradle, but hadn't acquired one, partly on account of the cost. It was worth more than a week's wages. He'd looked at a new one in the store to see how it was made. It was built like a baby's cradle. An oblong wooden box, the size of a large trunk, sat on rounded pieces of wood. It had what looked like a broom handle sticking up, so you could rock it from side to side. Wash dirt was shovelled into the tray at the top and water poured over it. As it was rocked, the material passed through a coarse sieve in the tray. This caught any large pieces of rock. The mixture then drained across tin ridges on the bottom, before escaping over a rim at one end. The storeman explained that the tin ridges were called riffles. The riffles, and the canvas lining on the bottom, were designed to catch the gold as the water and mud drained off, he said.

James asked Davy whether there was a big advantage working with a cradle.

'Certainly is. You really need two to work it best – one to rock and the other to load. It's even better if you have a few more winning the wash dirt.'

'I'll rock, you load,' said James, with a grin.

'We'll take turns,' replied Davy, laughing.

'How are we going to afford one?'

'No need to worry,' said Davy. 'I've got one on the way. Some of the Adelong diggers are carting mine up. They offered to bring it for me. Our packhorse was fully loaded. I think they wanted to do something for me. I'd got them out of a bit of bother with the commissioner.'

Now that they had two tents, they could use one as a living tent and the other as a store. They had just finished putting up Davy's tent when it started to rain. All afternoon, the clouds had hovered in the south, dark and threatening. As the sun disappeared, the air chilled. James shivered. For a brief moment, it was calm. Then the wind started to blow. It came from the south-east, an unusual direction. Driving rain stung their faces. It was soon followed by sleet.

'Get some rocks,' shouted Davy.

He and James weighted down the sides of their tents with as many rocks as they could find. There was a good store to hand that James had just dug up. They saw Jack was doing the same.

'Doesn't matter if it squashes the canvas,' said Davy. 'That's better than being blown away in the night.'

They tried to protect their fire, but failed. The wind was too strong and the rain too heavy. Throwing some firewood into the store tent, they retreated to their other tent to see out the storm. From its shelter, they watched as two tents on the far side of the river were blown six feet into the air and out of sight over the hill. There was no sign of their occupants.

It was horrific that night. Sheets of rain constantly blew against the walls of the tent. Water came in everywhere. James and Davy huddled in the middle of the tent, wrapping themselves in blankets. It wasn't enough to keep warm. A small river poured through the tent. They couldn't see it in the dark. But they kept putting their feet in it. There was nowhere to escape.

The wind blew a gale all through the night, dangerously flapping the tent walls. At times, they heard shouts and screams carried on the gusts. It was frightening. They looked outside, but it was pitch-dark. There was nothing they could do. The freezing, driving rain quickly forced them back inside.

In the morning, the rain eased. It was a sorry sight when they surveyed what was left of the goldfield settlement. They counted more than a third of the tents and shanties flattened, or in tatters. Higher up the hill, the damage was worst. The rocks on their own tents had saved the day for them. Amazingly, Jack's Eureka flag was still flying, though one of its corners was frayed.

James and Davy spent most of the day helping others less fortunate than themselves undertake makeshift repairs. The rain kept falling, but not as violently. It stayed bitterly cold. There was no relief that evening. They spent another night in misery and wetness, in between fitful attempts at sleeping.

When the cost of the storm was finally counted, it was found that over a dozen horses had perished. Their carcasses lay strewn about the field, testament to the ferocity of the storm and to the lack of stables. Amazingly, there were no human deaths – at least none that were reported.

'If this is summer, I don't know how we'd handle winter,' said James.

'It's only a case of being prepared,' said Davy. 'There's a lot of rubbish talked about the winter here. It couldn't be any worse than Scotland.'

'Have you been there?' asked James.

'Yes,' said Davy. 'Parts of this country remind me of it. I thought as much as we came over from Tumut – through those dour, mist-shrouded plains, with their low heathy scrub, rocks and marshes.'

'Do you come from Scotland?'

'No, Wales. But recently Manchester, and London. My father was in the political business, so we moved around a bit.'

'What business was that?'

'He was a Chartist. The government gaoled him. I'll never forgive them for that. All he wanted was justice for the common man.'

'I'm sorry,' said James. He didn't know what else to say. He'd never heard of the Chartists before.

'It's all right,' said Davy. 'Many of the things he fought for have now been achieved. Some working men even have the vote, at least in these colonies. But there's still a long way to go.'

James knew very little about politics. It didn't greatly interest him.

Davy warmed to his subject regardless. 'Men with capital and property still control the government,' he said. 'Here on the goldfields, we can make a life for ourselves, if only the miners could see it. We could all be in charge of our own destiny. When I've got more time, I'll tell you why property is evil.'

'Fair enough,' said James. He didn't encourage Davy.

*

On 10th February 1860, the governor, Sir William Denison, proclaimed the Kiandra goldfield as being 'on Crown Lands at or in the vicinity of Giandrara, or Gibson's Plains, and on the sources of the Snowy and Murrumbidgee Rivers'. The proclamation made little difference to the diggers on the field. It allowed the commissioner to administer the field, and to grant liquor licences, thus providing revenue. It did nothing to increase the supply of gold, or to ensure the success or failure of the diggings.

The reports in the papers varied widely over how many were at the diggings. The *Sydney Morning Herald* could now be purchased on the field – though nearly a week late. The diggers found it good sport to read what the rest of the colony thought was going on at Kiandra. Sometimes it was pretty wide of the mark.

Success and failure went side by side on the field. One party could make a fortune, while a neighbour could fail to cover costs. James and Davy's claim paid good wages, but it was no El Dorado. Jack's claim yielded enough to cover his modest needs. Don McDonald, a friend of Walter's from further up the river, had no success at all. He and Walter dropped by for a yarn. It was an opportunity to boil a billy and have a smoke. James pulled out some packing cases to sit on while they waited. The sun was out and the breeze was light.

'Don here's decided to leave the diggings,' said Walter.

'Sorry to hear it. How about yourselves?' asked James.

'We'll give it a bit longer. I hear there's a rush to Four Mile Creek. There's talk of some good finds at Nine Mile Creek, too. We might try our luck up there. We're only doing so-so down here.'

'That sounds a long way to travel, just on an off chance,' said James. 'We'll probably stick with it here for a bit longer, so long as we keep making wages.'

Davy nodded.

'Its all right for you lads,' said Don McDonald. 'I don't believe this field's got a future. It'll be a second Port Curtis, mark my words.' He was a sour-looking Scotsman, who could see rain coming when the sun was out. Port Curtis was a failed rush that had brought much misery to its prospectors.

'I reckon there's eighteen hundred on the field and no more than a hundred and fifty doing well,' he said. 'It's make or break here, and mostly break. Either you strike it rich, or it's a schicer. Take me. I've been here three weeks. In that time, I've earned ten shillings and my costs have been six pounds.'

'Spoken like a true Scotsman,' said Davy, teasing.

McDonald ignored him. 'That freezing weather the other day was the last straw. There must've been forty horses died.'

'It wasn't that many,' said James.

'I'm going to write to the paper. I'll tell them the truth about this Godforsaken place.' Nothing they said could alter his opinion of the field.

After he'd gone, Davy said it was for the best. 'It wouldn't hurt to discourage people from coming. The field's already too crowded. I'd reckon there's more than two thousand on the diggings now. From what I hear, with the numbers heading this way, it's frightening. There's few enough provisions to go round already.'

*

Sally kept following progress at the diggings in the newspapers.

'Dad,' she asked. 'Can I read you the latest from the diggings?' She had Wednesday's and Saturday's papers in her hand. 'I never did read you Saturday's paper. There's lots about the diggings in it, as well as in today's paper.'

'All right,' said her father. 'But make it quick – just the important bits. I need to get back to the forge straight away. I've got lots of work to do.'

'Here's what it says on Saturday,' began Sally, '"Excitement at Gibson's Plains or "Kiandra" daily increasing. There remains little doubt we are on the eve of a new era in the history of gold mining in the Southern Districts, and that one of the richest fields in New South Wales is in the course of being opened up. Favourable reports reach us from so many quarters, and from authorities so reliable that we can come to no other conclusion than that a genuine discovery has been hit upon at last."

'There's a letter dated 3rd February: "Mr Wilson saw one thousand, eight hundred on the diggings… Commissioner Lynch has arrived with fourteen troopers…diggings worked seven miles along the river…mostly surface. Hall and party averaging thirty ounces per week …a nugget found near Chippendale's store, one ounce…fossicking giving one pound per man per day…plenty of gold waiting to be sent by escort."

'Then there's a letter from Wednesday last: "Two thousand persons, not more than half at work as not, had time to settle in – two thirds at work doing well – working three miles of the river. Those there first marked out claims double the size allowed, consequently a great deal of jumping going on – the strongest party keeping possession – now two Commissioners on the spot. It will be the most extensive goldfield – for twenty miles around gold has been found, but all want to crowd the one spot where so much is doing. Very cold on Wednesday and Thursday."

'Then another letter, from a "less recent but authentic source." This man says it's merely a summer diggings, with inhabitance out of the question after the month of May, on account of the snowstorms. But there's a letter from a party of "experienced" Yankee diggers who say the diggings are likely to prove the equal of Ballarat.

'It's not all good news. Listen to this: "Some haven't tasted bread for five days – there's no flour on the diggings. Meat and tea are the chief food. Cattle and sheep are driven in, cut into steaks and chops, and, before actually cold, put in the pan, cooked and eaten. This must ere long bring on disease."'

'That's rubbish,' said Mr McNeill. 'What Sydney idiot wrote that? The fresher the meat, the better. All you've got to do is cook it properly. Haven't they tasted anything but salted meat?'

'I'm only reading what it says,' Sally protested.

'It's like everything,' said her father. 'You can only believe half of what you hear. An' you never know what half's right. I'm off. Make sure you pay those accounts. If I'm going to have a daughter at home, at least she can be useful.'

'That's not fair,' said Mrs McNeill. 'It's not her fault she's still at home. She's very helpful to me.'

Her words fell on deaf ears. Mr McNeill had already left.

*

The weather eased after the cold snap. Davy's cradle turned up and he and James attacked the hillside with vigour, averaging an ounce a day for the next week. Alex visited them on a new horse, decked out in new clothes. He'd missed the bad weather, being at Russell's. He said he'd struck a good deal with the carrying business. When Davy asked him for details of the deal, he wouldn't discuss them. He said he was independent now and wasn't going to share his business secrets with anyone else.

After Alex had left, James told Davy he'd seen Alex at Mad Mary's grog shop.

'I could have guessed,' said Davy. 'She used to be at Adelong. But I can't stop him now. He's chosen to go his own way.'

'It's not that. It was the company he was keeping,' said James. 'He was in with a bad crowd. I know one of them – a fella called Sweeney.'

James explained how Sweeney had stolen cattle from them when they'd been droving for Cosgrove. He also told Davy how, before this, he and Sweeney had come across the Mulligans' hideout at The Hollow, as Lob's Hole was then called.

'That's interesting,' said Davy. 'Everyone at Adelong knew about the Mulligans at Lob's Hole. When news of the rush to Kiandra broke, they had to abandon it. It's now on a main route for the diggers coming through from Victoria. I've never been there, but they tell me drays can't get through. It's so steep coming down Brandy Mary Spur, the horses have to sit on their haunches.'

'I heard a man was shot the other day at Lob's Hole,' said James. 'Maybe the Mulligans are still active round there.'

'Could be them. Or it could be any number of the other ruffians from Victoria,' said Davy. 'It's a pity gold attracts the worst of humanity, as well as honest men.' He paused. 'What you've told me about Alex worries me,' he said, shaking his head. Then he snapped out of it. 'Come on, we'd better keep going. We can't be chatting all day.'

Two men turned up at the adjacent claim late that evening, just as James and Davy were knocking off for the day. The claim hadn't been worked since the debacle of the false accusations against James, though they'd heard a friend of Mick Bourke's had bought it. The men had a barrow load of what looked like wash dirt, and busied themselves around the claim, straightening the corner stakes. By the time they left, the barrow was empty. Neither James nor Davy noticed what they did with its contents.

'You know,' said Davy. 'Given that claim hasn't been worked for more than forty eight hours, technically it's no longer in anyone's possession. That's what's prescribed in the regulations.'

The following day, a party of three new chums arrived at the claim, accompanied by Mr Alexander, an auction agent. James and Davy didn't pay much attention to what was happening. They were busy repairing the dam that held their water supply. The would-be diggers and the agent busied themselves around one of the old pits on the claim, then the agent left.

When the agent had gone, the new chums walked over to where Davy and James were working.

'Good day there,' said one of them. 'We've just bought the claim next to you, so we thought we'd better introduce ourselves. I'm John. This is Brian. And this is Ian.'

Davy and James put down their tools and shook hands.

'How about we boil a billy?' said James.

The newcomers took up the offer, promising to return the favour as soon as they got themselves established. Introductions continued over mugs of tea. The newcomers were all young and had never been mining before. John was a strongly built farm lad from the Yass district. Ian was a carpenter by trade, with red hair and freckles. Brian, a tall, dark Irishman, described himself as a bush engineer. He'd learnt his trade the Irish way – by practical experience. They'd teamed up on the road to the diggings.

'We worked out that between us we've got all the skills to be successful at the diggings,' said John.

'What you need to be successful at the diggings is a good claim,' said Davy.

'We should have that,' said John. 'We've just washed some dirt and it's come up gold in the first pan.'

'Wait a minute,' said Davy. 'Where did the dirt come from?'

'That pit over there,' said Ian.

'I don't want to tell you this,' said James. 'The previous owners said that pit was a schicer. They reckoned the claim was a duffer.'

'What do you mean?' asked John.

'I should've guessed,' said Davy. 'I know what's happened now. You've been tricked. The claim's been salted.'

'What's happened?' asked John.

'That wash dirt. It was put there yesterday,' said Davy. 'We saw the men doing it.'

'The agent said it was freshly dug,' said John. 'He said the owners had to leave in a hurry. They would've stayed if they could. They had urgent business to attend to.'

'They certainly did, but that's another story,' said Davy. 'I hope you didn't pay too much for the claim.'

'Thirty pounds,' said Brian.

'Really!' exclaimed James.

'The agent said it was a reduced price. On account of it being an urgent sale,' said Ian.

'You've been badly tricked,' said Davy. 'I wonder, maybe you could get the money back. It could be false pretences. Let's go and look at the wash dirt. If we could prove it didn't come from here, we might have a chance.'

The wash dirt looked like any other wash dirt. There was no way of proving it had been imported. Neither James nor Davy had actually seen the men place the dirt. John's party decided to give the claim a go anyway, and got busy. In no time, they'd pitched camp and had a fire going.

*

Surface Hill and Whipstick Gully were now the main sites for mining activity on the diggings. Both lay further up the slope from where James and Davy had their claim. Surface Hill, adjacent to Pollock's Creek, had been rushed soon after the river claims. Whipstick Gully, beside it, was named for the large number of cross trees – long poles with a weight on one end and a bucket on the other, used over the mining pits.

The difficulty for these claims on the hillside, distant from the river, was access to a reliable water supply. To overcome this problem, enterprising miners built water races to divert the local creeks. Once the water was captured, it was used to sluice, or wash, the hillside. The operators of these sluicing claims became known as ground sluicers.

Construction of water races and associated holding dams required considerable investment of labour. Only those with substantial capital could afford to build long races. Many of the sluicing claims ended up being owned by businessmen – storekeepers, auctioneers, publicans and others – who had access to capital from their profits, due to the scarcity of supplies on the diggings. A one hundred per cent profit margin on sale of goods was not unusual.

As newcomers flooded onto the diggings, speculation in claims developed. Claims supplied by water races fetched high prices. Under the goldfields regulations, permits were required for creek diversion, and limits were specified in the regulations on how much water could be taken. A commissioner's permit to construct a water race became a valuable commodity. Not surprisingly, the business community showed a marked interest in keeping on the right side of the commissioners, and in cultivating their friendship. Commissioners were never short of offers of hospitality, or of invitations to functions.

The diversion of the local creeks by the ground sluicers deprived miners lower down the creeks of a reliable water supply. Overflow flooding from the sluicing claims also interfered with the river claims. Feelings ran high and tempers frayed between the ground sluicers and the river men. The commissioners quickly became involved.

The Adelong miners believed the commissioners were biased against them, as a result of previous disputes on the Adelong diggings. Their viewpoint was reinforced every time a commissioner's decision favoured a Kiandra businessman over an Adelong miner. This added to the tensions between the ground sluicers and the river men, many of whom were former Adelong miners.

To work the sluicing claims, and construct races, men were employed on wages. Very quickly, different classes of miners developed on the field. At the top were the capitalist claim-owners. In the middle were independent diggers, who worked their claims either alone or, more often, in partnership. At the bottom were the miners employed on wages.

Davy watched all this with disappointment. He saw it developing just like the Adelong field. Here again was the system of property, capital and labour that had so blighted relations between working people elsewhere.

Brian looked at what was going on up the hill from a very different perspective. At meal time, he reported what he'd seen. 'There's no thought been put into the design of that work going on above us. All the river claims along here, and those on the hill beside us – we're all at risk.'

'Why's that?' asked James. He was stirring a big pot of stew.

The two parties had agreed to share cooking and tent keeping. Today, it was James's turn to cook. They'd invited Jack as well, but he'd declined. He'd said he would be happy enough to share a billy, but that'd be all.

'Those dam walls above us won't hold in a storm,' said Brian. 'And the diversion channels are too shallow. It's all right now, with a trickle of water. But you wait. Next heavy rain, and you'll see. We'll be lucky if we're not all washed away.'

'What can we do?' asked John.

'We need to put up bund walls,' said Brian.

'What are they?' asked James.

'They're earth banks that'll divert the water round the tents,' said Brian.

'So what do we do?' asked Ian.

'We need to build them on the hillside above us,' said Brian. 'They'll need to be solid. And we'll need to dig trenches on the high side.'

'Sounds like fortifications,' said Davy.

'It's the same principle,' said Brian. 'We'll need to protect our wash dirt, too.' He turned to James. 'I wouldn't leave yours in the gully. You might wake up one morning and find it's all disappeared down the river.'

'Can it wait till tomorrow?' asked John.

Brian looked at the sky. 'Probably. Though you never know, with this mountain weather. They reckon you can have four seasons in a day. From what I've seen, that could be true.'

'We'll take the risk,' said Davy. 'I'd better warn Jack. We can help him with his defences.'

After dinner, they sat around the fire and smoked. This was the best part of the day. So long as the weather was fine.

'All those men working for wages up the hill,' said Davy. 'That proves what's wrong with the system of capital and property.' He turned to James. 'Remember the other day? How I said I'd tell you what was wrong with property? I've got the proof right here. It's in the *Sydney Morning Herald.*' He held out the paper in the flickering light of the hurricane lamp hanging from the tent pole.

'What's that about property?' asked John. 'I haven't got any. I'm interested.'

'Listen to this,' said Davy, reading from the paper. '"Where property is not properly guaranteed, men must look on each other as enemies, rather than as friends. The idle and improvident are always desirous of seizing on the wealth of the laborious and frugal. The security of property is, in fact, the source from whence all the arts of civilisation proceed. The right of property is a rampart raised by society against its common enemies – against rapine and violence, plunder and oppression. Without its protection the rich would become poor, and the poor would totally be unable to become rich – all would sink to the same bottomless abyss of barbarism and poverty."'

'So what?' said Brian.

'That's from an article by McCulloch on the right of property,' said

Davy. 'If that isn't self-interested Toryism, I don't know what is. It goes on to quote Bentham. "To enjoy immediately, to enjoy without labour, is the natural inclination of every man – the law that restrains this inclination is the most splendid achievement of legislative wisdom – the noblest triumph of which humanity can boast. The security of property has overcome the natural aversion of man from labour."'

'I don't understand,' said Ian.

'It's all about the men of capital and property protecting their monopoly. And why do you think they wrote this? It's all because a gold commissioner on the Shoalhaven diggings found in favour of the diggers against a property owner,' said Davy.

'What happened?' asked John.

'A landowner wouldn't let the diggers prospect. He said he owned part of the river, even though it belonged to a declared goldfield. There was a big dispute. The diggers held a mass meeting and put their case to the gold commissioners. It took time, but in the end one of the commissioners made the right decision. He allowed the diggers to work the river flats.'

'So what's the problem?' asked John.

'This paper says the commissioner's decision was wrong – that he shouldn't have given in to the mob of diggers. It wants the preservation of property rights against mining. It says the digging interest of this country is attacking the rights of property. Imagine that! It says that compensation for property owners should be sacred. I'll read you some more. "The most desirable thing which can happen for this country is the concentration of mining industry, so as to assure permanent occupation and formation of settled society. We see what has been the result at Ballarat. They have a city there rivalling in its resources and attractions the metropolis itself, and thus bringing under restraining and civilising influences the gold mining population. However desirable it may seem to some that men should march and counter march and carry all their treasures on their shoulders, we are sure that the sober people of these colonies will estimate the immense advantage of concentrated labour."'

'See what these people with property and capital want?' said Davy triumphantly. 'They want to restrain and civilise the gold mining population. They want labour to be concentrated – so they can exploit it!' He threw the paper onto the ground in disgust. 'This rubbish has been written to protect the monopoly on property. You can see it happening on this field too. The rich men with capital are buying up the best claims – and leaving diggers to work for wages.'

'But what can we do?' asked Ian.

'Ordinary miners have to join together. We've got to stand firm and demand our rights. If all the ordinary people had the vote – and if they used it wisely – we could never be ruled by tyrants. Then the rich resources of this land could be shared out fairly.'

'That'd be asking a lot,' said Brian.

'That's what I believe in,' said Davy. 'That's what the Charter's about. That's my cause. Full suffrage and equal justice for every man. It was my father's cause. And I'll keep fighting for it. It may take more than my lifetime to achieve it. But I'll never give up.'

James sensed the others didn't share Davy's passion. He felt a little uncomfortable himself – though he knew Davy meant well.

Davy was true to his beliefs. Whenever pursuing what he believed was a just cause, he never let fear of power or authority get in his way. He took up the claim-salting case with the auctioneer, Mr Alexander, on behalf of John, Ian and Brian. Mr Alexander denied all responsibility. He said he'd only acted on instructions from the owner. He wouldn't divulge the owner's name to Davy.

Davy approached Commissioner Lynch. At first, the commissioner was reluctant to get involved. Davy pestered him to the point of annoyance, until finally the commissioner agreed to convene a meeting between the parties. It was held on site on the claim. At the meeting were the commissioner, the auctioneer, the claimants – John, Ian and Brian – and Davy. The claim owner didn't attend. James was called as a witness.

Davy set out the facts. He explained how the claim came to be vacant, and how it remained so, as was verified by James. He described how two men were seen by witnesses, namely James and himself, bringing wash dirt to the unworked claim. 'A fair-minded man would have to wonder why two strangers would visit a claim and put wash dirt down a hole.'

'It does seem curious,' said the commissioner.

'I only make this as an observation, for the information of the commissioner, so as to alert you to this strange practice,' said Davy. 'As commissioner, you may be interested in such goings on. But let me turn to the main issue.'

'There's no proof these men did anything wrong,' interrupted Mr Alexander. 'They were never directed by me, and the owner denies any knowledge of the matter.'

'That may be so,' said the commissioner tartly. 'But it would have assisted greatly if the owner could have attended.'

'Regrettably he had another appointment,' said Alexander. 'He asked me to represent his interests.'

'Might I address the main issue now?' asked Davy.

'Yes, go on,' said the commissioner.

'The main issue is the time the claim was unattended. You have heard from a witness here that the claim lay idle for nearly a week. I put it to you, Mr Commissioner, that the claim was in fact forfeit to the Crown, as it had lain unworked for over forty-eight hours. This supposed owner had no rights to it. He did nothing to claim it and did no work on it. Thus it must be unclaimed Crown land, and therefore not available for sale.'

'Let me consider that point,' said the commissioner. He thought for a minute. 'When did the owner last work this claim?' he asked, directing his question at the auctioneer.

Mr Alexander looked uncomfortable. 'I'm afraid I don't know.'

'The two men seen on the claim couldn't have been working it for him,' said Davy. 'The supposed owner has denied all knowledge of them.'

'True,' said the commissioner.

'This is the key fact in law,' said Davy. 'If you accept this fact – and all the evidence supports it – then these parties now present,' he said, gesturing towards John, Ian and Brian, 'they can proceed to stake and register a claim over this unclaimed Crown land.'

The commissioner thought for a while. 'Yes,' he said. 'I believe you are right. On the evidence before me, this land must be unclaimed.'

'Then I'll claim it for the owner,' said the auctioneer.

'No, your principal would need to do that,' said the commissioner. 'It's a pity he didn't attend,' he added, pointedly.

'Can we register the claim now?' asked John.

Ian and Brian were already re-hammering in the pegs as he spoke.

'Yes,' said the commissioner.

'What about the money we paid for the claim? Can we get it back?' asked John.

'That's not something I can rule on,' said the commissioner. 'You'll need to take that up with the man you paid it to.'

'What if he doesn't pay it back?' asked Ian.

'That would be a matter for the debtor's court. Now, if you'll excuse me, I have other matters to attend to.'

'Thank you, commissioner,' said Davy.

'We want our money back,' said John.

'I'll tell the owner,' the auctioneer replied.

'You do that,' said John. 'We'll be round first thing tomorrow to collect it from you. Otherwise we'll see the pair of you in the debtor's court.' He sounded as though he meant it.

The auctioneer scowled and hurried off with his head down.

John's party did get their money back. But their victory came at a cost. Davy and his friends became very unpopular amongst certain parties on the diggings, who were allied with Mr Alexander and the 'owner' he had represented. These included Mick Bourke and his mates, The Boys, who drank at Kidd's Exchange Hotel and who fancied themselves as the local push.

*

The Exchange Hotel was finished before the end of February. Others weren't far behind. They included John Carmichael's Empire Hotel, Luke Reilly's Union Hotel and Landers' Hotel. These were the first substantial, weatherboard, shingle-roofed buildings constructed at Kiandra. Other buildings quickly followed. Soon, numbers of shops, stables and houses lined the main street of the new township. The speed of construction was remarkable, as all the building materials still had to be brought in by packhorse. The road to Russell's was getting worse each day.

In February 1860, gold from Kiandra was exhibited in Sydney shopfronts. The *Sydney Morning Herald* fanned the excitement:

> We have unquestionably entered a new era in the history of gold mining in the Southern Districts. So widespread and so deep-seated an excitement has not possessed the minds of our people since the early days of gold mining.

March saw the height of the rush. That was when the world came to Kiandra: Europeans of all sorts – Germans, Italians, French, Portuguese and Scandinavians – Californians and Yankees, and new chums from all parts of the British Isles. There were diggers everywhere. They jammed the access roads in all directions, crowded the new township and swarmed across the creeks and flats. There were rushes to Four Mile, Nine Mile and Tantangara creeks; to Jackass Flat and to Rocky Plains. There was hardly a creek or flat for twenty miles around that didn't have diggers prospecting it. The reports in the papers claimed that ten thousand were in the region. One even said there were fifteen thousand. There was no reliable way of counting them, so it was anyone's guess.

James finally remembered to write to Sally.

Kiandra Diggings
2nd March 1860

Dear Sally

It has been quite some experience to be on these diggings. I cannot start to tell you all of the things that have happened to me. I have been to the lowest of depths and to the greatest of heights. My horse was stolen and all seemed lost. It almost snowed – and this, in summer! Then I found new friends, and we have been washing gold like it will never end.

I hope to visit you before too long, but we cannot leave the claim now for fear of it being jumped. There are so many disreputable characters here you would not believe it.

On the bright side, there is a proper little village developing and in due course I am sure we will be supplied with all we could want. There are now a number of women on the diggings, as the place was previously an all male affair. This has improved the tone a great deal.

Give my love to all in Cooma. Please pass the news in this note to my family as it will have to do for them as well.

Yours affectionately

James.

Sally received the letter three days later. She was disappointed at its brevity. She wished he'd said something more personal.

With March came the rain. Brian was right – the dams didn't hold. The river claims were badly flooded. Thousands of gallons of mud and sludge from the sluicing claims poured down the side of the hill, taking all before them – tents, wash dirt, fireplaces, chimneys. The sludge filled pits and channels, clogged holding ponds and contaminated all it came into contact with. Some claims were more badly affected than others. Fortunately, Brian's defensive fortifications worked well.

By this time, Davy and James had joined with John, Ian and Brian in a combined claim. All they lost between them were their latest workings. Jack's claim also escaped relatively unscathed.

The river men held an angry meeting. They resolved to take their case to the commissioner. They demanded compensation. Davy helped represent them. The ground sluicers denied all responsibility. They claimed the storm was unpredictable. They said they'd be all but ruined by the cost of repairs.

The commissioner ruled that the storm was an act of God, thus there were no grounds for compensation. The outcome was totally unsatisfactory to the river men. They said they'd been warning for weeks about the poor construction standards of the ground sluicers. They called for a ban on any more dam construction above them. This wasn't granted.

Davy's involvement with the river men greatly increased his unpopularity with certain parties on the diggings.

Not long after the storm, James took a short cut behind the buildings at the township. It was night time, but not so dark that shapes couldn't be made out. Suddenly he was surrounded by a group of men. There was a strong smell of alcohol in the air. His heart raced. He tried to keep walking but a rough shove in the chest stopped him abruptly. Despite the dark, he thought he recognised some of the men. He was sure some of them were from The Boys.

'Where yer goin' so fast?' said a dark shape.

'Back to my claim,' said James.

'Why the rush?' said the shape. 'We'd like a word with yer.'

James said nothing. He looked desperately past the dark shapes to see if there was anyone he could turn to for help. There was no one.

'We knows yer's mates with that Davy fella – what's making a nuisance of 'is self round these diggings,' said the shape.

'That Davy's gotta get teached a lesson,' said another voice.

Suddenly a big, dirty-smelling hand grabbed James by the front of his clothes, twisting his shirt up under his nose. The hand smelt strongly of tobacco and putrid meat. James felt his heart race even faster.

'Listen here, fella,' said the hand's owner. 'We don't need your sort on these diggings. Best you and that Davy fella leave these diggings.' The point was emphasised by a further twist upwards under James's nose, half lifting him off the ground. 'Yer days are numbered if yer stays here.'

'Get the point!' snarled another shape.

'That should do,' said a voice from the dark. 'No need to scare the little fella unnecessary, like. Just make sure yer take that back to yer mate. That Davy's riding for a fall if 'e keeps on like 'e's been doin'.'

The hand let go, and James was roughly pushed in the direction of the street. He stumbled, falling over some boxes with a clatter. The mob in the shadows laughed. James scrambled to his feet and made it to the street, where the flickering lamps outside the shops gave enough light to show the ground. His heart was still racing.

When he told Davy what had happened, Davy said he wasn't afraid of threats. He'd never give in to bullies.

'Should we tell the police?' James asked.

'Don't be silly,' said Davy. 'The traps and The Boys drink together. They're as thick as thieves.'

8

Jackass Flat
Autumn 1860

Jackass Flat was a pretty place before the miners came. It lay tucked into the side of a hill, less than a mile distant from Kiandra township. Bullock Head Creek bubbled past, just before joining the Snowy River. The lightly treed hillside rose steeply behind, dome-like in shape. The area was sheltered from the west and close to a good supply of timber. Its prospecting value was yet to be proven, but initial claims around the creek were encouraging.

This was where James and his partners staked their new claim. After the storm, they had decided to move away from the risk of sluicing floods. Their old claim fetched a good price, even though they were honest about its problems. Three parties competed to purchase it, bidding up the price. They called their new venture the Second Chance claim.

The partners now had three tents – two for living and one for stores. Ian and Brian immediately started discussing plans for more substantial accommodation.

'Hadn't we better see if it pays here, first?' cautioned Davy.

'Plenty of others seem convinced,' said Ian, pointing to the claims nearby. 'Every day there's a new tent or so.'

That evening, yet another party of new chums camped close by.

John had a chuckle as they busied themselves. 'Don't they look pale? Not long in the antipodes,' he said, mimicking their accent. 'Just arrived from Great Britain, eh what?' He'd quickly forgotten how recently he'd been new to mining himself.

In the morning, the newcomers walked over to ask for advice. They admitted to being completely inexperienced at mining.

A digger from a nearby claim was passing by and overheard them.

'You want some advice on mining?' he said, stopping and leaning on his shovel.

They turned towards him. 'Yes, we're new chums. Can you tell us where the best spot'd be to look for gold?'

'It's a well kept secret,' said the miner. 'But start and drive a tunnel into that hill yonder.' He pointed to the steep hill behind them. 'You'll need to bring the wash dirt down to the creek to pan it when you're done, but it should be worth it.'

'Really? Thanks. We'll give it a go,' said one of the new chums, a ruddy-faced youth.

'No trouble. Glad to be of assistance,' said the digger. As he walked away, he gave James and his partners a big wink.

'The larrikin,' said James. 'We should tell them.'

It was too late. With the enthusiasm of the inexperienced, the new chums were already off to the hill with their tools. The digger who'd given the advice returned to his claim and gathered his mates round. They cheered, clapped and whistled at the new chums as they watched them dig.

'The poor beggars,' said Davy. 'Still, you never know.'

Even though they suspected they'd been tricked, the new chums persevered. With dogged determination they dug at their tunnel for the next few days. Then they struck gold! It was an amazingly rich seam. All around were amazed – none more so than the miner who'd told them where to dig. Did he come in for some ribbing from his mates.

That's how the rush to New Chum Hill started. News of the find spread through the diggings like wildfire. In no time, the hill was covered with claims, as hordes of miners set about ripping the heart out of the mountain. James and his partners quickly extended their claim up the hill.

'Seems we can't get away from the crowds,' said John.

Brian was busy thinking. 'You know,' he said. 'The trouble with these hill claims is the lack of water. There's no streams up there, and you don't want to be carting wash dirt any distance if you can help it.'

'So?' asked Ian. 'You got another of your bright ideas?'

'Fact I do,' said Brian. 'I've been thinking. I know it's a long way, but if you took the water from Three Mile Creek – from up above the waterfall – you could run it in a race all the way round the side of the hill to New Chum here.'

'But that's miles,' said Ian. 'Would it be worth it? How could you do it?'

'It'd depend on how rich the hill proves in the long run,' said Brian. 'As for how it could be done – I've got a few ideas about a trenching plough. If someone'll lend me a bullock team, I'd like to test them out.'

'I think you're before your time,' said John. 'How about you stop dreaming and give us a hand with digging what's needed on this claim.'

The Second Chance claim paid handsomely. The partners averaged more than twenty ounces a week.

'Hope this keeps up,' said James. He and Davy were sitting outside their store tent, tallying the week's proceeds before divvying it out. 'Reckon that brother of yours made a mistake not coming in with us.'

'That's not the only mistake he's made,' said Davy.

'Yes?' said James.

'I don't want to talk about it,' said Davy.

James could see he'd hit a raw nerve, so decided he'd better leave it at that. It was unlike Davy to be so concerned – he was usually the calm and sensible one.

*

Kidd's Hotel was the diggers' choice. Apart from being the first built, of all the hotels, it was closest to the main diggings, being situated halfway down the hill towards the river – on the Broadway, as it came to be called. No one was ever turned away, no matter how dirty. Adam Kidd knew his business, and who his clientele were. He never pandered to snappy dressers or government officials. The only exception he made was for the police, who of course always found him a most generous host.

Trade in the late afternoon was brisk. As diggers knocked off for the day, they came to the hotel to celebrate what they'd found, or to drown their bad luck.

This day in March was no exception. The rough-hewn tables inside were crowded with drinkers. Outside, beyond the wide open doors, drinkers sat on benches or stood around, leaning against any convenient post or rail they could find. Stray dogs foraged around the feet of the drinkers, mindful of the risk of a swift kick. The noisy presence of the men, shouting, talking and disputing, could be heard from over half a mile away. You could smell it too, depending on the direction of the wind – the smell of stale alcohol and whiffs of pipe smoke.

Much of the conversation went to matters of prospecting – what had been found, where it was found, the method used and by whom. A constant topic of interest was news of the latest rush. New Chum was the most recent.

Betting was a favourite pastime. It filled a need. For a digger who suddenly found himself rich, there wasn't much else to spend large amounts of money on. Men with easy money will always find a use for it, and a goldfield produced plenty – for the lucky.

Bets on Sunday's prize fight were being taken. The purse was twenty pounds. Jackson, a hardbitten bruiser, a well known pugilist on the Victorian diggings, was pitted against Pudgey, a plump New South Welshman. Although it was billed as the battle of the colonies, colonial loyalty meant little when it came to putting down money. Jackson was heavily backed by colonists from both camps, giving Pudgey very good odds.

'That Pudgey's got no chance,' said a drinker to his mate. 'You'd be doin' yer money to bet on 'im.'

'That's not what I 'ear,' said his mate. 'He's so big an' fat nothing can 'urt 'im. Anyways, that Jackson's gettin' on now. Yer can't rely on a record in the fighting game.'

Oddly enough, those with connections to the fight organisers were backing Pudgey.

Alex and Sweeney were sitting at one of the outside benches. They had become occasional business partners. Alex had a talent for finding horses. He helped return 'strayed' horses to their owners, for the advertised reward. Sweeney looked after the financial arrangements. Sweeney had connections. He knew the horse trade – who to talk to, what was saleable and for how much. He also had friends among the police.

'You'll get to learn,' he said to Alex. 'Not all traps can be trusted.'

'How can you tell?' asked Alex.

'It's 'ere,' said Sweeney, tapping the side of his nose.

Alex admired Sweeney. He thought he was so cool-headed. And he seemed to know so much. They often had a drink together. Sweeney was flattered at the attention Alex gave him, and how he was always asking him questions.

'You seem like a fair enough lad,' said Sweeney. 'Not like that brother of yours. He's causin' no end of trouble round 'ere. I wouldn't like 'is chances if he keeps it up. There's some very powerful people he's gone an' upset.'

'Nothin' to do with me,' said Alex, taking a swig from his nobbler.

'What's with 'im, anyway?' asked Sweeney. He spat on the ground beside the bench.

'I dunno. I never agreed with 'im. He's always on about justice an' all that stuff. He reckons property is theft.'

'Did he say that?' said Sweeney, looking interested.

'Some Frenchman said it. Davy's always on about it. Like it's unfair that men with capital own all the property,' said Alex.

'I'd agree with that,' said Sweeney. 'There's not enough sharing of property. The rich don't need it.' He grinned as he pulled out his pipe and started to fill it.

'That's what I think, too,' said Alex. 'Davy says stealing's wrong but, if those men shouldn't have it in the first place, then what's wrong with taking some of it from 'em? They got plenty. I can't see the difference.'

'Better not tell that to the traps,' said Sweeney. 'They act like it's their property what's got thieved. At least some of 'em do. Just as well there's others what understand – with a bit of help. It's amazing what a little cash can do.'

Sweeney put his nobbler down among the collection of other glasses, bottles and drinking pots on the slab. 'I hear Big Jack's found another nugget. He should be here soon,' he said. 'It'll be good to watch.'

They didn't have long to wait. Big Jack soon came into view, surrounded by a group of friends. Nugget-finders always had 'friends'. He was an impressive sight, all six feet and fourteen stone of him. He strode towards the hotel, nugget in one hand and riding crop in the other.

'Roll up! Roll up!' he bellowed, as he approached the assembled drinkers. 'The shout's on me! Clear the tables!' As he walked past, he swept each of the benches clean with his riding crop.

Spilt drinks, mugs and broken glasses went crashing everywhere. Dogs scurried for cover, tails between their legs.

'Let's make this shout worthwhile!' he boomed.

The serving staff rushed about, rescuing what they could, replenishing the tables with full glasses and bottles as the drinkers clamoured for supplies. Adam Kidd was a happy man. On a day like this, he would double his takings.

*

As the numbers on the diggings swelled, so did the incidence of robberies. Horse stealing was rife. Bush ranging on the road from Russell's was particularly frequent. Kiandra's reputation was so notorious it became known as Mount Rascal.

The police numbers on the Kiandra field fluctuated. When the gold escort left for Tumut, most of the troopers went with it. That left only one or two policemen to deal with thousands of miners. To the storekeepers, this was a cause for concern. They pressed Commissioner Lynch to provide a more substantial police presence.

The commissioner took up the case. He wrote to his superiors recommending the immediate appointment of a police magistrate. He told them larceny and robbery from the person were rife, and of daily as well as nightly occurrence, requiring and urgently demanding not only such an officer, but a considerable accession of police force, both mounted and dismounted.

In the meantime, the diggers did their own policing. Thieves caught in the act were given rough treatment – shaved and doused in the river. Mick Bourke's special constables had plenty of sport to keep them amused.

Because of the delay in organising the gold escort, diggers held onto their gold. It was estimated that up to five thousand ounces of gold was held by diggers, secreted away in tents, bags and other belongings. This provided rich pickings for both career thieves and opportunists.

'Did you hear about Harry?' James asked, as he took a break from swinging his pick into the hill. He and John were working their extended claim on the side of New Chum Hill. James was glad he'd teamed up with John. John was as strong as a bullock. He did the work of two men, and never complained.

'No,' replied John, in between heaving shovelfuls of dirt into a barrow.

'You know where the silly old beggar hid his gold?' said James.

'No.' John kept shovelling. He knew Harry had a claim up the slope past Jack's claim on Surface Hill.

'He kept it hidden in his dog kennel.'

'I didn't know that,' said John. He stopped and wiped his forehead, then rested on his shovel. The barrow was full.

'He reckoned the dog'd protect it.'

'It would that, too,' said John. 'It was a fierce beast, I remember. He kept it on a short lead. The mongrel wouldn't stop barking and snarling all the time.'

'Well, someone must've seen him putting his gold there,' said James. 'Anyway, off he goes to check out Four Mile, taking the dog with him. When he comes back, the gold's gone.'

'The silly old beggar. What'd he lose?'

'Over forty ounces.'

'By Hell! Bet that got him mad. He's got a fair temper,' said John.

'He made one Hell of a fuss,' said James. 'He was running round accusing everyone of taking it. He wanted to search all the tents. I got the story from Jack. Jack said it was something to see. I reckon he enjoyed watching it. Jack never did like Harry. It goes back to something in Victoria.'

'I can tell you a story too,' said John. 'You know the party next door, behind the new chums?'

'Yes.'

'Someone slit the back of their tent the other night. They were looking for gold. They never found it, but. The fella what told me, he wouldn't say where they had it hid. And I don't blame 'im.'

'Did they tell the police?' asked James.

'Why bother? The traps wouldn't do anything.'

'I heard there's more troopers on the way,' said James.

'Won't make any difference to us. It's just the storekeepers they'll be protecting.'

Eventually the government paid attention to the commissioner's pleas. In March, Chief Commissioner Cloete and Captain Henry Zouch were ordered to travel to Kiandra with a supplementary party of police troopers. These were important officials. Mr Cloete was Chief Commissioner for the Southern Goldfields. Captain Zouch held appointment as Superintendent of Mounted Patrol and Gold Escorts for the Southern Districts.

Captain Zouch turned heads when he rode onto the diggings, mounted on Lucifer, his magnificent black charger. Horses of Lucifer's quality were rarely seen on the goldfield. The proud stallion had to be nearly eighteen hands, with every inch of his glossy coat stamped with breeding. Even miners without any interest or acquaintance with horses stood and stared.

Alex was among the onlookers. The crowd from the Exchange Hotel came out to watch as the captain's party rode through town. Captain Zouch and Commissioner Cloete led the column of prancing troopers, the captain resplendent in his braided uniform. The crowd cheered, clapped and whistled as the column rode by.

'Where's the war?' shouted an over-excited digger.

He was quickly quietened by his mates. It wasn't prudent to be too provocative in front of such a show of armed force.

The captain's horse was the subject of much discussion, including speculation as to what it would fetch at a sale.

'Could you use a horse like that?' Alex asked Sweeney.

'Sure could,' replied Sweeney.

After the official party had ridden past, Alex watched as they followed the track to the commissioner's camp – around the hillside, half a mile distant. Later, he walked over in that direction and pretended to be fossicking in the nearby gully. He could see the captain's stallion was tethered in the commissioner's camp horse yards. He didn't get too close. It wasn't his habit to draw himself to the attention of policemen.

Early next morning, there was a terrible commotion on the field. Mounted troopers galloped through the diggings in all directions, scattering everything before them. Jack's flag was knocked down. Diggers looked up in surprise. Clearly something was up. Soon the news flashed through the diggings – Captain Zouch's horse had been stolen.

The atmosphere on the field remained tense all day. Relations between troopers and diggers were strained. Minor transgressors were unceremoniously locked up. Diggers found without their miner's rights were arrested on the spot.

That afternoon, Alex caught up with Sweeney at the Exchange Hotel. 'I need to talk to you,' he said.

'Go on,' said Sweeney.

'Not here,' said Alex, looking from side to side. 'We need to be private. Can you come with me?'

They took a walk down towards the river.

When they were out of earshot of everyone Alex whispered, 'I've got the captain's stallion. What will you give me for him?'

'You've what!' said Sweeney.

'I've got Lucifer,' replied Alex.

'You idiot! Why would you have done that?'

'But you said. You said you could use a horse like him.'

'I wasn't serious! God damn it! How on earth could I unload 'im? Every trooper in the land'll be on the lookout. There's only one like 'im. 'E's a marked beast.'

'You won't take him, then?' asked Alex, in a worried voice.

'I might,' said Sweeney. 'But I'd 'ave to take 'im to Victoria. That'd cost. I couldn't give yer much for 'im. A few pounds at best. I dunno – it's a big risk I'd be takin'.'

Alex was crestfallen. He'd heard the horse was worth more than two hundred pounds. After some more discussion, he agreed to a deal. He had no choice. Sweeney said he'd take the horse for ten pounds. Alex then took Sweeney and a friend to where he'd hidden the stallion, in thick bush on the top of a hill, well away from any prospectors. Sweeney's friend was Dan Mulligan. Dan seemed very pleased with Sweeney.

Secrets were hard to keep on the diggings. Word soon got around in certain circles that Sweeney and Alex had been involved in the disappearance of Lucifer. Sweeney didn't contradict the version that had him as the mastermind of the operation. He said he wouldn't divulge details. He wouldn't comment on how they'd managed to take the most valuable horse in the colony – from under the eyes of fourteen heavily armed crack troopers.

'That fella what used to own Lucifer – if it's good enough for 'im to be Captain Henry, then it's good enough for me to be Captain Bill,' he said jokingly.

Oddly, the joke stuck. From this time on, Sweeney became known as Captain Bill, the man behind the disappearance of Zouch's charger. He took to wearing a fancy hat and walking with a swagger. Men who used to look down on him now treated him with respect. Others, who hadn't bothered to notice him before, offered him drinks.

At the same time, Alex became known as Alex the Kid. Captain Bill and Alex the Kid became goldfields folklore on the Kiandra diggings. They were pointed out in whispers to newcomers to the field.

*

In their third week at Jackass Flat, the Second Chance partners found a two pound nugget. With the claim doing so well, they decided to build a more permanent hut. Ian took charge. He quickly had them felling timber, splitting logs and preparing a site. He also had them pulling up and stacking grass tussocks.

'What the hell do you want all this damn grass for?' asked John. 'It wasn't a good idea for the little piggy to use straw. Didn't the big bad wolf come along and blow it down?'

They all laughed.

Ian smiled. 'Don't you worry,' he said. 'Just keep working. If you're so smart, you'll work it out.'

In no time, a sturdy sapling framework was standing, and solid slab walls were in place. There were foundations for a stone chimney in the centre of the rear wall. The hut had a steeply pitched roof frame. 'To shed the snow,' said Ian. Brian made sure the site was well drained.

Where it differed from other huts was in the roof covering. Ian made the roof out of two layers of calico, stuffed with dry grass. He finished it off by laying battens every few feet along the top. These were tied down by thick greenhide thongs. He used a similar double layer of calico stuffed with grass to line the inside of the slab walls. The other unusual feature was a separate entry room.

When it was finished, their hut didn't look so different from many of the other shanties on the field. Many others had calico roofs. The difference was inside, where it looked like the inside of a tent, except that it was amazingly warm, and quiet.

'All right,' John said grudgingly, when it was finished. 'You've done well. It's warm as toast in here – and windproof, too.'

'The doors are only made of hides,' said Ian. 'But the entry traps the air. We can use it to store boots, wet coats and suchlike. That's what they do in the north of Europe.'

'So where'd you get the idea from?' asked Brian.

'I was wondering how they keep warm in Scandinavia,' said Ian. 'They get lots of snow, so I asked Bjorn – he comes from there – and he told me a few things. They use bags filled with feathers on their beds. I thought, why not do the same sort of thing with the roof and walls of a hut? It seems to work.'

'Sure does,' said James.

'But is it going to be rat-proof?' asked John. 'We need something to stop this plague of rats. I reckon they're getting worse. They give me the creeps, how they run over your face at night.'

'They're harmless,' said James. 'They're only bush rats – short-tailed bush rats. They've always been here. Haven't you seen their burrows? We had them when I was droving. You've just got to make sure you hang your food up high.'

'The other thing we'll need if we're staying for winter is plenty of firewood,' said Brian. 'We'd better start stockpiling now.'

'Let's celebrate first,' said John. 'I could do with a drink to wet the whistle.'

They agreed to have dinner at Carmichael's new hotel that evening. Davy led them as they set off into the dusk. Along the way, John and Brian got talking to an old digger mate. When Davy, James and Ian approached the township with its jumble of buildings and flickering lights, the others were a few hundred yards behind.

Suddenly, the three of them weren't alone. A crowd of men surrounded them in the half-dark. There had to be at least a dozen of them, thought James, as his heart jumped.

'Fancy that,' said one of the men, sarcastically. 'Three fine young lads, out for a stroll.'

James recognised his voice – he was the leader of the mob that had threatened him previously.

The men stepped in front of them, barring their way.

'Let's see what stuff yer made of,' said the leader.

From the faint flicker of the lamps, James could see that he was a thickset man. He was hatless and had his sleeves rolled up ready for business.

A thin youth joined in, flushed with the bravery of the crowd. 'Yeah, put 'em up, yer pipsqueaks,' he said, in an excited, high-pitched voice.

At this point, the leader pushed Davy in the chest with two hands. Davy fell back against James, who only just managed to stop them both from falling.

'Come on,' yelled one of the mob. 'Let's get 'em now.'

Just as the serious action was about to begin, one of the surrounding crowd fell flat on his face in front of them. He'd been bowled over by John as he and Brian arrived in the nick of time.

'Let's even up the numbers,' said John as he faced the mob.

'He wants to fight us,' said James, pointing at the leader.

'Does he?' said John.

Without a second's hesitation, he stepped forward and swung an almighty blow at the thug. It collected him on the side of his head and knocked him flat. The man hit the ground with a dull thud, like a bag of flour, and didn't move.

'Any more takers?' said John, turning to the crowd.

Brian stood beside him. They looked a formidable pair. Ian and the others backed up beside them.

The mob suddenly lost their enthusiasm for fighting and stepped back. The man on the ground moaned.

'Let's have dinner, then,' said John. 'You lot aren't invited.' He led the partners forward, stepping round the leader of the mob, still lying on the ground, and now holding his head.

'That was just an appetiser,' said John, as he passed. 'You can have the full meal next time.'

The Second Chance partners didn't let the incident spoil their dinner. Even so, they went easy on the alcohol. They were very alert on the way back to their claim, though there was no further sign of the ruffians.

Accounts of the confrontation started circulating around the diggings in the following days. From these stories, the partners learned that retribution was being sworn. Davy was the main target for vengeance. According to the gossip, he'd deliberately set a trap for The Boys.

9

Kiandra Diggings
Autumn 1860

The big rush in March convinced the government that the Kiandra diggings had a future. The storekeepers in the township certainly had faith. Construction of timber buildings continued apace. This sort of activity was out of character for a goldfield, which usually remained a tent and shanty town in its early years until its longevity was proven. Perhaps the cause was the mountain weather, which required robust shelter even in summer.

All the signs were good. Nuggets continued to be found, and new areas were continually rushed. Despite dire predictions about ice and snow, many diggers started making preparations to stay on through the winter, putting up slab huts and stockpiling firewood. Faced with the evident resolution of the miners, Commissioner Cloete moved to the diggings permanently. Soon he, too, was making plans to stay for the winter.

There was a brief setback in April, when the diggings were blasted by a sudden cold snap, and snow began to fall. This thinned numbers on the field – but thousands stayed.

Smarting from the loss of his horse, Captain Zouch ordered the disposition of a large permanent force of mounted and dismounted police, both at Kiandra and at strategic points along its access roads. He commissioned construction of accommodation and facilities in Kiandra for an inspector and seven foot patrol. Three mounted and three dismounted men were to be quartered at Russell's, three mounted men at Cooma and three mounted men at Queanbeyan. On the Tumut side, the construction of quarters at Yarrangobilly was commissioned – for the placement of a detachment of three mounted men in the spring. A further three mounted men were committed to gold escort duty between Kiandra and Cooma. He even gave consideration to stationing a trooper at Lob's Hole.

The announcement of these measures prompted unkind comments in the Sydney press, which had earlier reported the loss of the captain's horse. It was suggested that the decision to send such large numbers of police was influenced by the captain's personal experience rather than by any real danger from lawlessness. These words were written from armchairs in Sydney, by men who'd never travelled the road from Russell's.

The Second Chance partners were doing well at New Chum Hill. Some of their neighbours were doing even better. The new chums who started the rush to the hill now named after them made such a fortune they were able to sail for home after only a couple of months – well before winter – wealthy beyond their wildest dreams. To top it off, they sold their claim for a tidy sum.

Further along the hill, a party of Cornish Cousin Jacks took to burrowing as only they knew how. Tunnelling was a way of life for these men, who came from generations of miners. In no time, they had torn the entrails out of the mountain, leaving them scattered all over the hillside below. The Cornishman's claim proved to be one of the richest on the field. Other claims nearby included French Joe's and the Homeward Bound claim.

'It's a damned untidy business, this mining,' said John, as he scanned the scarred hillside. 'Just as well we don't plan on staying round. I'd hate to have to clean up this mess.' John was an orderly person who even kept his part of the hut tidy.

'I guess so,' said James. He hadn't thought about it. He had other things on his mind. He was off to Cooma to see Sally. He had promised he'd visit her before winter, and it was now after Easter.

On his way, he dropped in on Eureka Jack to see how he was doing. He suggested that Jack join them over at New Chum Hill for the winter.

'I might do that,' said Jack. 'Some of them louts've been botherin' me.'

James hired a saddle horse from the Telegraph Street horse tailing yards. Being well known, he didn't need to put down a deposit.

'It's ten pounds if you don't bring the nag back,' said the manager. 'That's on account of the saddle and bridle.'

When James reached Denison, he was surprised at how it had grown. The collection of buildings was almost a village now. Russell's new public house, the Gold Diggers' Arms, was open for business. James had a yarn with John Russell as he stabled his horse for the night.

'I'll tell you something, since you're a friend,' said John. 'If I was you, I wouldn't leave your nag outside tonight. It ain't safe. Father told me there's certain parties busy round here what's in the second-hand horse trade.' He winked at James. 'There's plenty of room in the stables.'

James ate in the dining room at the new hotel. Just as he was finishing, a trooper threw open the door with a bang. He was breathing heavily and oozing sweat.

'Bring me a meal,' he barked, throwing his saddlebag against the wall and easing his large frame onto a bench. 'Get me a drink first,' he demanded.

The serving maid quickly brought him a drink.

'Are you the publican?' he said to William Russell, who had just walked into the room.

'Yes,' said Russell. 'What can I do for you?' He spoke politely despite the trooper's rude manner. Russell was a congenial host, well known for his hospitality amongst his friends – though they didn't usually include troopers.

'I need stabling for my horse,' said the trooper.

'I'm sorry, sir, but that won't be possible,' said Russell. 'All the stables are full. You'll have to leave your horse in the yard.'

'That's not good enough!' spluttered the trooper, almost spilling his drink. 'Is that how you treat the Queen's men! You wouldn't be Irish, would you?' He looked at Russell with narrowed eyes.

'That's nothing to do with it,' said Russell. 'I suppose you could bring your horse over by the homestead, near the station stables.'

'All right, that'll do,' replied the trooper gruffly. 'Show me when I've eaten.' The trooper bolted his meal and threw down a few drinks. Then he pushed back from the table, belched, and demanded to be shown where his horse was to be tethered overnight. 'Make sure he gets plenty of oats,' he ordered.

James had to share a room with the trooper that night. He didn't get a good night's sleep. The trooper stank strongly of stale sweat, and snored loudly.

Early in the morning, James was woken by the squawking of a family of magpies having a noisy dispute in the yard outside. This was followed by a loud banging on the door.

'Wake up! Wake up!' shouted a voice outside. The speaker kept banging on the door. The trooper had bolted it.

'What's up?' asked James, as he unbolted the door.

'The trooper's horse – it's gone,' said William Russell, who'd been banging on the door.

'What's the problem?' said the trooper dozily, half rolling over in his bed and looking at them.

'Your horse. It's not outside the stable. It's gone. It must've been stolen in the night,' said Russell.

The trooper blinked at him sleepily. James couldn't understand why he didn't jump out of bed. If it'd been his horse, he'd have been up like a shot.

'Its all right,' said the trooper. 'Mine's in the stable. I put one of yours outside.' He shut his eyes and rolled over.

James would always remember the look on William Russell's face. For once, Russell was absolutely speechless. And that was saying something.

Luckily, Russell had a good sense of humour. It was the gift of the Irish. For years afterwards, he told the story of how the trooper had got one up on him.

James made good time on the road to Cooma, even though his mount was an old hack, and the track was a muddy quagmire.

Sally was very glad to see him. 'I was worried something had happened to you,' she said. 'Why didn't you write more often?'

James didn't have a satisfactory explanation. 'It's not easy, now we're over at New Chum Hill,' he lied.

'I keep reading about all the robberies and stickings-up,' said Sally. 'Is it very dangerous at the diggings?'

'Not really – not where we are,' said James.

'Do you get the papers?'

'Yes, sometimes,' said James. 'They're a week late, mostly. They come in from Tumut.'

'Did you read about the three dead men? The ones that starved to death?'

'No.' said James.

'The report in the paper said they were found in the bush not far from the road to Russell's. They'd left a note scratched on a tin. They must've lost their way.'

'Maybe they got caught in a storm,' said James. 'We've had a few. Lots come to the diggings without a clue. Some don't even bring warm clothes.'

'These ones starved to death, the paper said.'

'It's a wonder more don't die.'

'I keep worrying something'll happen to you,' said Sally. 'Tell me you're going to be safe.' She looked at him with a worried expression. 'Do you really have to go back for the winter?'

'I'll be fine,' said James. Sally's concern reminded him of his mother's fussing. 'I'm with a good mob of mates. And we've built a snug place for the winter.'

He felt a little awkward with Sally. So much had happened since he'd last seen her. He couldn't begin to tell her how it was at the diggings. It was so different from life in Cooma.

'Couldn't you stay here for winter?' Sally asked. 'I'm sure Father could use your help. We've been so busy. I've been helping him with the books. We're now employing four men. It's so busy. Business is growing all the time. We're selling tools as well as making them, now.'

'No. I've made a commitment to stay on at the claim,' said James. 'I couldn't let my partners down. Anyway, we're still making good wages. We'll be in the box seat for the spring rush. Lots of miners are making plans to leave for winter, so costs are coming down. We replaced all our tools for a song the other day. Some parties are practically giving things away.'

Sally was disappointed, but tried to reconcile herself. 'Let's enjoy ourselves while you're here,' she said, trying to sound positive.

James was treated by his parents like the prodigal son returned home. His mother greeted him with tears of happiness in her eyes. His father was pleased to hear that he'd been doing well. This time, his younger brothers and sisters were all ears about the diggings. They kept asking him to show them his gold. It was nice to feel welcome but, with his family, it was like returning to an old world he'd left behind.

'It's so different at the diggings. You really can't understand a goldfield unless you've been there,' he said to his mother.

'It must be exciting,' she said. 'I'm so glad you're doing well.' Then she started to fuss about his wellbeing, as mothers do – worrying about whether he had enough warm clothes, asking if he was eating the right things, and so on.

He was glad to escape to Sally.

Now that he was a successful miner, he took Sally out to dinner at the Lord Raglan Inn. The expense was worth it. Sally was very proud of him.

She spent much of the following morning telling her friends about the meal, and how the maids had been so keen to serve them. 'I never thought I'd be eating alongside gentlefolks. We even had a glass of wine, though I didn't much like the taste,' she said, wrinkling her nose.

New buildings were going up all over Cooma. The place was hardly recognisable from the sleepy village of before the rush. Many of the paddocks where James had once played now had buildings on them. There were lots of strangers in town. James didn't recognise most of the people in the streets. Those he did know were keen to talk to him, especially the storekeepers. Maggie was still at her father's store. She gave him a knowing smile, but there was no opportunity to talk to her alone – Sally quickly steered him away.

During the day, James and Sally often found themselves sitting on their favourite log. James enjoyed the warm feeling of her body beside him again. They seemed to fit so well together. Sally enjoyed snuggling up to him, and encouraged him to put his arm around her. They laughed and played games a lot.

'Careful,' she'd say with a coy smile when he tickled her. 'Watch those wandering hands.'

He could tell she liked it. But even though she tingled every time he touched her, she made sure she stayed firmly in control.

James was just starting to get used to being with Sally again when it was time for him to leave.

'You will write to me?' she said, trying not to sound too pleading.

'I'll try,' said James. 'But it can't be often – the mail's so unreliable. If you saw the road, you'd understand. Anyway, we might get snowed in.' He pointed at the dark mass of clouds towering over the western horizon. 'See. Look at those clouds. It could even be snowing now.'

When they said their farewells, Sally put a brave face on it. She gave him a smile that she hoped he'd remember her by.

James was right about the weather. As he left Russell's later that afternoon, it started snowing. Light, gentle flakes at first, fluttering to the ground and disappearing, leaving a damp patch where they'd melted. Gradually, a white coating appeared on the tops of the fallen logs and the leaves of the bushes and trees, as if a magic wand had been waved over them. The air chilled. James pulled his coat around him and hunched under his hat. He was glad of the new woollen mittens his mother had insisted on giving him.

The snow reduced the risk of ambush from bushrangers. Bailing up a party in these conditions wasn't ideal – it slowed escape and, unless it kept snowing heavily, it made it easier for troopers to follow the tracks in the snow.

The higher James rode, the more the snowstorm thickened. By the time he reached Rocky Plains, he was engulfed by dense eddies of white flakes. He could hardly see fifty yards ahead. In places, the track completely disappeared under the windblown drift. It was fortunate he knew the way.

Inexplicably, by the time he reached Kiandra, the storm had cleared. It went as quickly as it had come. Ahead, the valley was painted white and beautiful. The scars of mining were now invisible, hidden under the soft whiteness that covered the land.

He rode quietly across the white carpet. Beside him, the lower branches of the tousled, white-dusted snow gums drooped under their load. A fluffy white blanket covered the low-growing shrubs. The snow grass flats were a field of smooth white bumps. The scene reminded him of the peacefulness of the mountains before the miners came. He took in the view and breathed in the cold fresh air. He knew this would always be his country.

*

The early snow put an end to the surge of newcomers. But it did nothing to stop the flurry of building activity in the township. The business community was convinced that spring would bring a new influx of miners. They were making sure they'd be well prepared. Construction of the telegraph line from Tumut had begun, and the main township thoroughfare, now called Telegraph Street, was lined with weatherboard buildings. Camp Street, which crossed it and led past Kidd's Hotel to the river, was now known as the Broadway – a permanent town had to have proper names for its streets.

The hundreds of diggers who stayed to brave the winter did what mining they could, in between the weather. Many of their huts now had stone and sod walls and incorporated chimneys. When the ground was frozen and the races filled with ice, there was good money to be made from carting firewood. A man could make more than two pounds a day, as wood was fetching five pounds a load.

James and John tried their hand at cutting firewood. They felled trees on the hilltops above the town, then slipped the logs down the hill. As there was a risk that small logs might be attractive to others, they only left the big ones overnight. It was best to cut the timber one day, then take advantage of the overnight freeze to slide the logs down the icy slope first thing in the morning.

'It's a good way to keep warm,' said John, as they worked the crosscut saw. 'Beats sitting in a hut using up firewood – and we get paid for it. Can't see why more don't do it – instead of sitting round and complaining about the weather.'

'We should make a sled,' said James. 'Like they're using in the town. It'd beat a dray in this weather.'

'That'd be all well and good if we had a horse,' said John. 'But I ain't about to lug a sled up this hill without one.'

On second thoughts, James decided it wasn't such a good idea. It certainly wasn't worth getting a horse, given the exorbitant prices being charged for feed and stabling.

For Ian and Brian, there was good money to be made in building. They started by helping out on one of the stores being constructed in Telegraph Street. They also did some work on the new buildings at the commissioner's camp.

'The place is starting to look like a proper town,' said Ian. 'They've let a contract for the Bank of New South Wales too, so the young fella there was telling me. His name's Preshaw. He's a bit of a toff, but friendly enough. He's staying at Kidd's till the new bank building's finished. He invited me over to play cards. They have a regular session at Mollarde's most nights.'

'What'd you say?' asked Brian.

'I declined,' said Ian. 'I'm not about to hand over my earnings to a mob of card sharps. I don't trust that lot at Mollarde's. They're a bit flash for me.'

'I reckon you're right,' said Brian, smiling. 'You must've been listening to that preacher, eh?'

The day before, a preacher had stood on a rock and tried to bring the word of the Lord to a crowd of diggers. A fight had started across the road, and all the diggers had left to watch it. They laughed at the memory.

'That young fella gave a good account of himself, though, didn't he?' said John.

For reasons no one could fathom, new parties started arriving at the diggings again in June. They were mostly from Victoria. Among them were the first Chinese, led into the township in single file by their headman. The arrival of the Celestials caused quite a stir among the European miners.

Ian brought the news to the Second Chance partners. 'They reckon the diggings'll soon be overrun with Chinamen,' he said, catching his breath after running back to the claim.

'Why so?' asked John.

'A party of eighty turned up today,' said Ian. 'They were over at Benjamin's Argyle Store – getting supplies. I was listening to their headman. He wanted to know the best place to find gold. They told him to go down the river – you know, where all the claims have been worked out. They said he'd be sure to strike it rich down there.'

'You mean where the sluicing run-off goes?' said Brian, laughing.

'Exactly,' said Ian. 'Anyway, this headman said there were hundreds of his countrymen on their way. They told me later that he'd said there'd be twenty thousand Chinamen here in the next six months.'

'Is that true?' asked James. 'He'd hardly seen more than half a dozen Chinamen in his life, before.'

'I don't believe it,' said Davy.

'It'll be a rum show with that many Mongolians,' said John. 'I don't like 'em. We should run 'em off the field.'

'I don't agree,' said Davy. 'They've as much right to be here as we have. So long as they don't bother us, we should let them be.'

'I still don't trust 'em,' said John. 'Why are they coming here anyhow? I can't see how anyone expects to make a living now it's winter. It's all right for parties like us that's got claims already. I wouldn't want to be starting out now – what with the ice three inches thick in the bucket each morning.'

'You might be right,' said Davy. 'I guess we'll have to wait and see.'

The headman may have been over-optimistic about the total number of his compatriots, but his party was quickly followed by many others – some from the diggings in Victoria, others from New South Wales. Within a month, there were hundreds of Chinese on the field, settled in camps at a number of places along the river, including at the first river crossing on the way to Russell's.

John wasn't the only digger who didn't like the Chinese. Antagonism against the Celestials ran high in the mining population. Commissioner Cloete directed them to make their camps well away from the main township, so as to reduce the chance of conflict.

It was hard not to notice the industriousness of the Chinese. They were up early, and always looked busy, working in disciplined teams under the close supervision of their foremen. They seemed to be able to find gold in claims abandoned by other miners. Their success caused resentment, particularly among the lazier European diggers, and those who spent more of their day at the public house than on their claims. Hotel patrons swapped stories about John Chinaman's vices and his dirty habits. Drunks complained you couldn't trust a Chinaman. John Chinaman didn't drink. And he sent all his gold back to China. They didn't have any women with them, either. Parties of miners called for the Celestials to be expelled from the diggings.

The storekeepers were much less antagonistic. They urged the commissioner to keep order. They supported the location of the Chinese camps at a reasonable distance from the township, but they didn't want the Chinese to leave. With the depleted winter population on the diggings, the Chinese were welcome customers.

Few of the Chinese were fluent in English. Mostly they communicated through their headmen, or through an interpreter. Despite their limited English, in their financial dealings they showed a good understanding of the value of money, and they quickly gained a reputation for driving a hard bargain.

Although James no longer owned a horse, he liked to spend time at the horse sale and tailing yards in Telegraph Street. The manager, Mr Shadforth, realised James was experienced with horses. He asked him if he'd help out at the stables during the winter months. For a small payment, James agreed to come by in the evenings to help feed the horses and keep an eye on them.

'I'm sure I can trust you,' said Shadforth. 'That's more than I can with most. The last lad what helped out here rode off on one of my best nags.'

Not long after the arrival of the first Chinese, a young Chinese boy turned up at the tailing yards. He'd been sent by his headman to collect a horse. James was surprised to see him. Most of the Chinese were much older. He was even more surprised when the youngster spoke reasonable English.

As soon as young Tommy walked into the yards, James could tell he'd spent time around horses. He knew the animal he wanted, and had him saddled in no time.

'You've done this before,' said James.

'Yes,' said Tommy. 'At the Shoalhaven. I looked after the horses there.'

Over the next few weeks, Tommy often visited the tailing yards. James liked the youngster. Tommy told James and Davy about the troubles they were having with some of the diggers near their camp. Davy offered to help out if they wanted someone to put their case to the commissioner.

Two days later, Tommy came running across the mullock heaps to the Second Chance claim. Tommy said he had to see Davy. 'Quick as possible!' He looked very worried.

James downed his tools and they went looking for Davy. They found him digging in a ditch.

'Mr Davy,' said Tommy. 'Can you please help. Mr Lee sends me.'

'What's happening?' asked Davy.

Tommy told him the Chinese had been accused of stealing wash dirt and that an angry mob of diggers were threatening to burn down the Chinese camp. Davy said he'd come straight away. James went with him. They told John where they were going.

As they rounded the hillside, they saw a large crowd of diggers in front of the Chinese camp. In the middle of the crowd, a group of Chinese were arguing heatedly with a party of angry-looking diggers. They also saw Commissioner Cloete and a foot patrol of four men coming from the other direction.

Tommy led Davy straight to Mr Lee. 'This is Mr Davy,' Tommy said. 'He can help.'

Mr Lee bowed. He was dressed in traditional flowing Chinese garments and wore his hair in a long pigtail, as did his compatriots. In broken English, he said he was pleased to meet Davy.

While Davy was being introduced, Commissioner Cloete stood on a box and called for order. Cloete had a reputation among the diggers as a fair and reasonable man. Unlike some of the other commissioners, he was known for not taking sides in disputes. The crowd quietened when he spoke. Cloete said he would listen to the facts first, and only one person was to speak at a time.

While he was talking, James noticed more men arriving, including some he recognised as members of The Boys. Mick Bourke was among them.

The diggers at the centre of the dispute put their case first. They had a claim next to the Chinese camp. For the last two days, they'd been digging wash dirt, ready for sluicing. This morning, when they arrived at their claim, they saw a quantity of the material was missing. They accused the Chinese, who were next to their claim, of thieving it. Who else could have taken it in the night? they said. When they'd approached a Chinese digger, he'd tried to run away. If that wasn't proof, then what was? That's why they'd grabbed hold of him.

The commissioner asked to hear the Chinese side. Mr Lee's English wasn't good, so he asked Davy to speak for him, with the help of Tommy as interpreter.

Davy said the case against the Chinese was entirely circumstantial. There was no proof whatsoever that they were at fault. Stealing wash dirt was common. It was a growing problem on the diggings. And it had been happening long before the Chinese arrived.

The diggers pointed to three of the Chinese who'd been working near the claim. They said those men had been acting suspiciously. Davy clarified the accusation. It meant they'd walked away when the diggers had tried to talk to them. With help from Tommy, Davy got each of these Chinese to swear the truth, by their own beliefs, that they hadn't taken any wash dirt. They said they'd been scared of the men shouting at them.

'We can't believe them,' said one of the diggers who'd lost the wash dirt. 'They're not Christians. Why can't they swear on the Bible?'

'We couldn't believe them anyway,' said his mate.

The crowd was unhappy at the way proceedings were going, and started to show it.

'Throw them off the field!' a voice shouted. 'Cut off their pigtails!' The comments came from where The Boys were standing.

The commissioner called for order. He was eventually obeyed. Then he said he was ready to announce his decision. He called for calm. 'It's clear that a crime has been committed,' he began. 'Material has been stolen. I can understand the anger of those who've lost it. But on the evidence before me, there's simply no proof the material was taken by the Chinese.'

The crowd booed.

'This isn't the first time wash dirt has been stolen, and it won't be the last,' he continued. 'All I can suggest is that parties keep a watchful eye on their claims. If parties are particularly concerned, they can mount a guard. We live by the rule of law in this colony. That's our right as true British subjects. I call on all of you to uphold the law, and to not take it into your own hands. To do so would simply reduce us to the level of savages. We live as free British subjects in a state of civilisation. Our rule of law protects the rights of liberty and property. Of this, we can be proud. Let us continue to uphold it. I now ask that all of you return to your claims. This hearing is over.'

With much grumbling amongst the diggers, the crowd began to disperse slowly. The presence of the foot police, who kept their weapons at the ready, made sure there was no further trouble.

James and Davy were jostled on the way back to their claim.

'Why defend the leprosy? You're as yellow as they are,' said one of The Boys as he pushed Davy.

'Don't worry, your time'll come,' said another.

Davy ignored them.

Nothing further happened – probably due to the proximity of the police.

Trouble involving the Chinese continued. The following week, there was a great disturbance within the Chinese camp. The police were called. Five Chinamen were arrested for stealing from their own countrymen. They were sent to prison in Cooma. It was fortunate that the police intervened. Without the protection of the police, they would have been dealt with much more severely than by the British legal system. The merciless way the Chinese treated their own transgressors came as a surprise to many of the diggers who witnessed the fracas.

A week later, two Chinese were caught red-handed stealing from a sluice. This sparked renewed agitation against the Celestials. The hot-headed were all for taking the law into their own hands. Commissioner Cloete found it necessary to move the Chinese camp to a more distant location, half a mile down the river. The *Sydney Morning Herald* reported the incident:

This will, it is hoped, effectually separate them from the Europeans, whose jealousy or distaste of John Chinaman is often carried to unnecessary lengths.

Life for the Chinese on the diggings was very hard. They were bound by a strict indenture system of contract labour, in which their headmen exercised close control over their earnings and the work they could do. In the harsh winter conditions, with the streams and ground frozen solid, their earnings from gold were insufficient to purchase enough food for all of them. The sympathy of the storekeepers for the Celestials didn't extend to offering them credit.

Tommy came less frequently to the horse yards and, when he did, he often hadn't eaten that day. On these occasions, James insisted on bringing him back to their hut and feeding him a meal. He also gave him food to take back to his own camp.

*

In July, it snowed heavily. The first falls melted in a few days, but then the storms set in. It snowed for days on end. There'd be a break for an hour or two, then it'd snow again. All work on the diggings stopped. The overall depth of the cover was only about three feet, but the windblown drifts were four or five times deeper. Diggers were trapped in their huts and tents. Many were nearly buried alive under windblown drifts. For the well prepared, like the Second Chance partners, it was an adventure. For the ill prepared, it was misery – even a matter of life or death. John came back from a visit to the township with news that a youngster had got lost on his way home and nearly perished. He only had to travel a few hundred yards, but the snow was so deep, and falling so thickly, that he had no idea where he was. He also heard that a drunk who'd spent the night outside in the snow had lost his feet to frostbite.

During a break in the storms, James and Davy decided they'd better check on Eureka Jack. The other partners decided to join them. First they had to tunnel through the snow to escape from their own hut. This took some time. When they emerged, the scene that greeted them was straight out of a Christmas in Europe. Everything was totally white.

It took them nearly an hour to walk the short distance over the hill to Jack's claim. Their feet kept disappearing below them as they fell through the soft snow. It was hard to see where the creek flowed. When they crossed it, they did so on a snow bridge, not without some apprehension. By the time they reached Jack's claim, they were wet through from falling in the snow, and quite puffed.

They could see the smoke from Jack's chimney from a distance. Jack's hut was on a slight rise, and he had a good supply of firewood. He'd built up the walls with stones and sods and had strengthened the roof with timber poles. When they reached him, he was busy clearing the snow away from his entrance on the far side of his hut. He told them so much snow had come down his chimney in the storm that his fire had nearly gone out.

'You should've come over with us,' said James. 'Davy told me you were going to.'

'I'm fine 'ere,' he said.

As they were talking, they saw a man further down the slope. He looked as though he was climbing out of a snowdrift. At first James thought he must have been buried under it. That didn't make sense. As he appeared to be struggling, they walked down the hill to help him.

It turned out that his tent had been totally covered under drift snow, and he was climbing out of the chimney. His young wife followed. She was quite distressed. The young digger told them he'd erected his tent in a hollow to protect it from the wind. He'd never imagined there'd be so much snow.

Some other diggers came to the rescue with the offer of a spare tent. Then all hands pitched in to rescue the couple's belongings and carry them to a new tent site, higher up the hill, among the trees. It was hard work tramping through the deep snow loaded up with household goods. They even moved the bedding.

Brian and Ian took charge of constructing the new tent on the hill. They made sure it had a strong frame, and constructed a sturdy stone and sod chimney in the middle of it. By the afternoon they had a roaring fire going. All through this time the weather held out. It stayed clear long enough for James and his friends to make it back to their own hut before nightfall. The following day, another fearful storm blew through the diggings.

The snow storms cut Kiandra off from the rest of the world. There was no mail. The drays bringing supplies to the diggings were all stopped. Many of the trapped bullocks died. Even after the storms had eased packhorses had difficulty getting through. Building work came to a stop. Provisions in the stores started to run low. There was no fresh meat, as stock couldn't be driven in. Firewood was at a premium.

The difficulty of getting supplies to Kiandra briefly created a common interest amongst the merchants of the town. They held meetings to discuss the problem. Knowing the Chinese were desperate to supplement their meagre earnings, William Templeton came up with a solution.

Templeton was a resourceful businessman. He'd always had a shrewd eye for a business opportunity – too shrewd an eye perhaps. In partnership with Shadforth he ran the Kiandra Bazaar sale rooms, where they sold goods, mostly on commission. A successful business it was too – horses, tools, tents, anything you could name, they would sell it, no questions asked. In a pioneer town, documented proof of ownership wasn't always possible. Templeton had a good relationship with the police on this issue. Any problems were quickly sorted out with Sergeant Ballard.

Along with much of the Kiandra population Templeton had watched as the Chinese moved their camp down the river to where the commissioner had decreed. He'd seen them winding their way around the hillside, bowed under huge loads, and wondered at their strength and endurance. The Celestials moved their whole camp without using a cart or horse. This gave him the idea for the Celestial Transport Company. After some quick discussion with Shadforth, and with Messrs Cook and Wilson, he approached the main Chinese headman, Mr Lee, with a proposal.

The principals of the Celestial Transport Company were Messrs Templeton, Shadforth, Cook and Wilson. The Chinese were to be hired to carry goods through the snow from Russell's. Templeton would arrange the contracts. All the Chinese had to do was carry the goods. Mr Lee would act as recruiting agent and would guarantee the reliability of the men he provided. The charge for carriage was set at two pounds per ton, the same as for drayloads. The amount of the payment to Mr Lee and the carriers was not disclosed. Any loss or damage to goods was to be taken out of the payment. Mr Lee wasn't entirely happy with the details of the arrangement but, in the circumstances, he had little choice.

The first goods brought in by the Chinese arrived within days, to the cheers of the townsfolk. Soon there were over a hundred Chinese porters plying the road from Russell's. They carried everything, slung on poles across their shoulders, even shingles, palings and timber. With the help of the Chinese carriers, the storekeepers were able to keep up supplies to the diggings. Soon packhorses were also getting through, both from Denison and from Tumut, and the crisis was over.

Amongst the first loads to arrive on packhorse from Tumut was a consignment of fowls. This was followed by a load of cats, slung in cases either side of a packhorse. An enterprising trader hoped to sell them to storekeepers to rid the town of its plague of bush rats.

Another early load carried by the Chinese were the parts of a printing press. On 14th July, a notice appeared in the *Sydney Morning Herald* announcing that *The Alpine Pioneer and Kiandra Advertiser* would soon be published by Thomas Garrett at Kiandra and Russell's. Garrett had made his arrangements before the July snow storms. He purchased a building in the township and engaged a dray to bring up the printing machinery. When the storms stranded the dray in the snow on the far side of Russell's, Templeton came to the rescue. Fifty Chinamen carried the machinery the fourteen miles to Kiandra – all four thousand four hundred pounds of it. They did this over a period of ten hours, to the amazement of the Kiandra diggers, who stood and watched, mining being impossible on account of the snow.

With the village snowbound, the diggers turned to other amusements. These included the usual diversions of drinking, boxing matches and card playing, with the addition of snowball matches in the middle of the main street. The publicans did a roaring trade. The Second Chance partners wisely stayed away from the hotels. They bought a few bottles and had a drink at their hut in front of the fire.

'You've gotta hear what happened at Benjamin's Inn last night,' said John, after returning from a trip to the township to get supplies. 'You know Mick Roan?'

'Isn't he one of Bourke's mates,' said Ian.

'Yes, that's the one,' said John. 'Well, he was drunk as a lord last night and wanted to fight everyone.'

'What's new,' said Ian.

'Hadkins, the manager, tried to throw him out,' said John, 'on account of his quarrelling. Roan's mates took up the cause. They knocked Hadkins down and kicked him senseless. After that, all The Boys got involved. Like you'd expect.'

'The mongrels,' said Ian. 'Not that I'm a special friend of Hadkins.'

'That wasn't the end of it,' said John. 'The traps were called in. They tried to take Roan into custody. The Boys attacked the traps. There must've been one hell of a brawl, from what I hear.'

'Beauty,' said Brian, starting to get excited.

'I saw some of the traps,' said John. 'They look a bit damaged today. Anyway, in the end they managed to put Roan into the lock up. He should go down for a while.'

'Terrific!' said Brian. 'It's always good to see your enemies fighting each other.' He had a chuckle.

'Why don't we try our hand at snow shoeing?' said Ian.

'What's that?' said John.

'I was talking to Bjorn,' said Ian. 'I was complaining about how hard it was to walk in the snow. He told me that in his country they slide across the snow on long wooden skates. They're a bit like fence palings, with the ends turned up, he said. They call it snow shoeing, or something like that. I didn't understand his lingo.'

'How do they work?' asked Brian.

'I don't know. You'd have to tie the wood to your boots, I s'pose,' said Ian. 'A bit of greenhide should do the trick.'

'Where can we get some palings?' asked Brian.

'I saw a pile of them over by the side of Telegraph Street,' said Ian. 'They were using them to make a fence. Most of them got taken for firewood.'

'Let's find Bjorn and see what we can do,' said Brian.

On their way, they collected half a dozen palings and took them to Bjorn's hut, high on the hill overlooking the town. Bjorn agreed to help. With his help, they fashioned a couple of rough bindings.

'The ends need bending up,' said Bjorn. 'We need steam.'

'We could boil a billy,' suggested Brian.

They boiled the billy and did what they could to turn up the ends by holding them in the steam. It wasn't very successful. By the time they'd finished their handiwork, it was getting late. Ian was keen to try them out.

No one stayed upright for more than ten yards, not even Bjorn. There was a lot of laughing at the spills.

'These not very good,' said Bjorn. 'Not like at my home.'

The sun was getting low in the sky.

'We'll come back tomorrow and make a better pair,' said Ian.

They leant the palings against the side of the hut, next to the wood pile, and hurried home in the half dark. The sun had set and it was bitterly cold. James could barely feel his fingers by the time they reached their hut.

The next morning, Bjorn met them with bad news. Someone had stolen the palings in the night, and half his wood pile. When they went looking for replacements from the pile in Telegraph Street, they too had all disappeared.

'Damn those blasted firewood thieves,' said John. 'They'll take anything that's not nailed down.'

'Even that don't stop them,' said Brian. 'They've taken the wall boards off that new store we were building in Telegraph Street.'

The weather improved in early August. The mail resumed, and so did the influx of diggers. The storekeepers hoped this was the start of the spring rush they'd been waiting for. It was fuelled by news of a twenty-seven-pound nugget found only six inches from the surface.

Agitation by 'the better class of storekeepers', as the *Sydney Morning Herald* described them, brought an end to Sunday trading. Building work continued apace. Large weatherboard buildings were completed for Mollarde's and Robinson's stores.

The diggings were a dangerous place at night, and not just because of the risk of robbery. In one week, there were two deaths from intoxication. A Scotsman was found dead in a prospecting hole near the town, and a well known publican from Sydney, James Smith, was found head downwards with his neck broken in a deep race on Scully's claim, behind Wallace's store on Surface Hill.

With the thaw came the mud. Davy tramped through it on his way to collect his regular supply of newspapers, sinking up to his calves in places. The papers were his link to the outside world. He valued them more than the other Second Chance partners, whose views he thought were far too parochial. 'Here, I've got to read you this,' he said, waving a paper. The other partners were sitting in front of the fire smoking.

'Not more of your politicking,' said John.

'It's just what I've been telling you,' said Davy.

'What is?' asked Ian.

'This proves it. This article quotes Lord Macaulay on the People's Charter. He says it plain. He doesn't want ordinary people to have the vote. You've got to listen to this: "Universal suffrage is incompatible with all forms of government, incompatible with property and therefore with civilisation. Civilisation depends on property. Universal suffrage would produce a destructive revolution. It would give working men absolute and irresistible power. Working men will be the irresistible majority and capital placed at the feet of labour. Knowledge would be borne down by ignorance, by the millions who've so long and so loudly said that land is their estate and is wrongfully kept from them. Fences will be torn down etc. Institutions democratic will destroy liberty and civilisation."'

'What does all that mean?' asked Ian.

'It shows what we're up against. It shows that men with capital and property don't want to share power with the ordinary people. It shows them in their true colours. Here, it goes on to say that property is needed as a qualification for men in the upper house of this colony – "or what hope for liberty, civilisation, property or public credit". What rubbish!'

But how does that affect us?' asked John. 'Who's this Macaulay anyway?'

'These are the men that make the laws. That's how it affects you,' said Davy.

'You mean like the goldfields regulations?' said Ian.

'What's wrong with them?' asked John.

'There's plenty wrong,' said Davy. 'They allow the appointment of commissioners with arbitrary powers, who can act without redress. Then there's licence fees, and gold taxes.'

'But Commissioner Cloete's all right,' said John. 'His decisions are fair.'

'Commissioner Cloete might be,' replied Davy. 'We're lucky we've got him. We could have a bad commissioner. Then we'd be in trouble.'

'I guess I'd worry about that if it happened,' said John.

Davy felt he wasn't making much progress. 'I'm going to write a reply to this rubbish. I can't let it go,' he said.

'A lot of good that'll do,' said Brian. 'You'll only upset people and make enemies for yourself.'

'They need to be upset,' said Davy. 'Everyone has a right to vote, not just those with property.'

'Good luck,' said John. 'Next you'll be talking about women having the vote.'

'Why not?' replied Davy.

John laughed. He didn't take the comment seriously.

10

The Spring Rush
1860

Despite the unreliable weather in August, the spring rush continued. Thousands of hopefuls rode and trudged their way along the boggy tracks to the Kiandra high plains. Almost as many hoped to make a living out of the diggers as were serious prospectors. The government sent more officials – policemen, post and telegraph staff, surveyors and commissioners. The business community swelled. There was a multitude of professions: bankers, jewellers, gold merchants, storekeepers, butchers, blacksmiths, auctioneers, doctors, dentists and even more publicans. Builders and carpenters were in keen demand. Hotels, stores, stables and houses were thrown up to accommodate the new arrivals. The township bustled with activity.

On the goldfields, tunnelling and shaft sinking were pursued with vigour by the more experienced diggers, while hundreds of Chinese concentrated on reworking previously mined ground, mostly along the river. Hordes of prospecting parties scoured the surrounding creeks and rivers looking for a new El Dorado.

The rest of the colony was hungry for news from the diggings. The *Sydney Morning Herald* chronicled the daily events – nightly brawls, deaths from intoxication and other causes, robberies and court cases, and most importantly the latest gold news. The *Alpine Pioneer* was now published twice weekly in Kiandra. Its focus was very much local. Grained leather american pegged boots and Goodyear's patent gum thigh boots could be bought at Kennedy and Dent's on Broadway. Carmichael advertised his Empire Hotel dining room, where diggers could get 'Ham and Eggs and Welsh Rabbit at the Shortest Notice'. Benjamin took out large advertisements for his Old Argyle Stores in Broadway while Robinson and Tebbatt were offering a 'Splendid Stock of Drapery' at their new store in Telegraph Street. Not to be outdone, J.J. Wright's Commercial Store advertised its 'Most Extensive Stock of First Class Goods', ranging from all kinds of provisions, wines, spirits and beers to boots, shoes and furniture. These included carpenters' and miners' tools, ironmongery, locks, camp ovens, horse and bullock bells, hobbles, shovels, rope and pack saddles. In short, there was nothing a miner could need that wasn't now able to be bought in the town.

Benjamin's Store was packed with diggers and new arrivals. James was elbowing his way to the counter when he saw Maggie. His heart jumped. Customers surrounded her, all talking at once. Her face was flushed under her bonnet. He squeezed forward to catch her attention.

'Oh!' she exclaimed, as she saw him. 'I'm so glad to see you. It's so busy and I don't know anyone.' Her voice was trembling. A muddy digger demanded service. She quickly took his payment for tea and tobacco.

'I never expected it to be like this,' she said, turning back to James with a helpless look, her eyes reaching out to him for help. 'It's so nice to see a familiar face. They're so rude. I'm quite run off my feet. I'm so happy to see you.'

'Me too,' said James. 'What brings you here?'

'I only arrived today. The journey was awful! I'm just helping out till Father's store gets finished. I can't talk now. We finish at six. You couldn't possibly come by then, could you? I'd really like some company. I don't feel at all comfortable, alone in this place. There's so many strange people.' She looked at him with an imploring expression, like a little girl lost.

'Yes, I'll come by at six,' said James. It made his heart race just talking to her.

'I'll really look forward to seeing you,' she said earnestly, before another demanding digger asked for service.

James was so unsettled he couldn't remember what he'd come to buy. He left the store to clear his head.

He'd forgotten how attractive Maggie was. There weren't many women on the diggings. None were as young and pretty. Maggie aroused an instinct in him. She attracted him with a strength he couldn't resist, even if he'd wanted to. It was overwhelmingly physical. There was no meeting of minds. He didn't give that a thought. For a brief moment, he felt it might be wrong, and he remembered Sally, but he quickly dismissed the thought. It wasn't as though they were married.

Maggie's eagerness to see him gave him a special thrill. He could hardly wait till six.

It wasn't a dream. Maggie really was there – waiting for him. She quickly untied her apron and hurried out the door with him. 'It's very kind of you to come,' she said. 'I was so glad to see you. You've no idea.'

She took hold of his arm as they walked down the street to the Kiandra Hotel. She insisted on showing him her room. 'They said I'd be in a new hotel. Well, here it is.'

The walls of the room were lined with bare timber boards. Her room had two plain beds in it, and a small four-pane window high up in the far wall.

'It's very Spartan,' she said. 'At least it's a reasonable size. I'm all alone till Father comes.'

James wasn't sure what he should do. He stood in the middle of the room and looked around.

'Aren't you going to ask me to dinner?' she said. 'I'm famished.'

'Yes, that'd be a good idea. Where would you like to go?'

'Is there a choice?'

He thought for a minute. 'Not really. We should eat here. Kidd's would be much too rough for a lady.'

'I'm not really a lady,' she said, laughing. 'But you can treat me like one.' Maggie had picked up now she was with company. She had a bubbly way of talking. 'Could we order champagne?' she asked, looking at him winningly. 'I don't often get to drink champagne. It'd be a real treat.'

He ordered a bottle to drink with their meal. The champagne disappeared rather quickly, and she asked if he'd order some more. He did as she suggested. Soon this bottle was also empty. Maggie started giggling. She couldn't stop whispering and laughing at the funny people in the dining room.

James started feeling quite tipsy himself. 'Let's go for a walk,' he said, thinking it might clear his head.

'All right, let's,' said Maggie.

As they opened the door, the cold night air hit them.

'Oh! That's much too cold,' she said, shivering. 'I'm not going out there.' She held onto him and pulled him back inside the hotel. 'Why don't we buy a bottle and have a night cap,' she suggested.

James agreed. He would have done anything she'd asked.

Maggie insisted on more champagne. They took it to her room with two glasses. He lit the lamp and they sat on one of the beds. After a few drinks, Maggie snuggled up against him. He put his arm around her.

'You will look after me, won't you?' she said in a little girl voice, wriggling closer. 'I do need a strong man to look after me.'

James said he would. His feelings for her went well beyond protection. She lifted her face towards him. Soon their lips were touching. She didn't hold back, and neither did he. The kissing developed into something more, and before James knew it they were lying on the bed wrapped in each other's arms.

'Please touch me,' she said, as she undid her blouse.

He fumbled with her clothes. Soon she was mostly undressed.

'Come under the covers,' she said, pulling back his shirt. As she wriggled under the blankets, she took off the last of her clothes.

Almost without thinking, he followed suit. It was a new experience for him, lying naked in bed with a girl. He pressed his body against her soft flesh, and kissed her wet lips.

What happened next he didn't remember very clearly. The drink had taken effect. It was the first time he'd been with a woman. Maggie seemed to know what to do. The climax was explosive in a way he'd never imagined. Immediately afterwards he went asleep.

When he woke, Maggie was asleep beside him. The faintest grey light of dawn was shining into the room from the high window.

Maggie stirred, then opened her eyes. 'You're still here?' she murmured.

He looked at her soft, half-covered breasts.

'What time is it?' she said sleepily. Then she saw the light in the window. 'You've got to go,' she whispered. 'Go quickly. They mustn't find you here.'

James picked his clothes up from the floor and got dressed.

'Off you go,' she hushed. 'But be quiet.' She pulled the covers over herself and turned away.

His head was swimming as he quietly closed the door and tiptoed out of the hotel. Grey clouds greeted him outside. It looked as though it might snow. His head throbbed. He walked back to his hut and sneaked inside. He only managed to get half an hour of sleep before it was time to get up again.

News had travelled ahead of him.

'I hear you got yourself a girl last night,' said John, grinning as he boiled the billy. 'Enjoy yourself, eh? Bit of the old hey ho?'

James kept his head down and didn't reply.

When he'd done his day's work, James returned to the township. Maggie wasn't at the store. He walked down the street to the Kiandra Hotel. There was no sign of her there. He didn't know where else to look.

He was about to return to his hut when one of the counter staff from Benjamin's Store approached him. 'Can I have the payment now,' he asked.

James had never liked the man. He looked like a weasel, and spoke in a whining tone.

'What payment?'

'For the dress. The dress Mistress Maggie bought. She said you'd be happy to pay for it as a present. It's three pounds.'

At first, James didn't know what to think. He paid the man. There had to be a good explanation, he thought. Maggie would be sure to tell him, when he found her.

There was no sign of Maggie at the store, or at the hotel, the next day either. This time, the porter at the Kiandra Hotel told James he'd probably find her at Kidd's. James thought there might be a mistake, but he walked down to the hotel to see.

The usual crowd were carrying on noisily at Kidd's Exchange Hotel, drinking, swearing and quarrelling. He walked past the bar room door and down the corridor to the dining room, suspecting she might be taking a meal. As he opened the door, he saw her. She was sitting at the far side of the room with her back to him. Crowded around the same table were Sergeant Ballard, Mick Bourke and a young gentleman he didn't recognise. He quickly pretended he'd made a mistake and shut the door. Almost choking, he hurried out of the hotel.

Outside in the fresh air, he felt he could breath again. When the significance of what he'd seen sank in, he began to feel angry. Very angry. He was angry with himself. He was angry with Maggie. And he was angry with Bourke and his cronies. He knew Maggie hadn't made any promises. That didn't seem to matter. He felt he'd been used, that he'd been chewed up like an orange, then spat out like the pips.

It was his pride that suffered most. He narrowed his eyes and swore that he'd never let anything like this happen to him again. He'd never give in to his animal instincts. He wouldn't fall into that trap again. He'd use his will power next time. If there ever was one. He also felt guilty. Before he'd seen Maggie, he'd been about to write to Sally. Now he couldn't bring himself to do it.

*

The young man James had seen at the table with Maggie was Frederick Cooper. Cooper had just arrived in Kiandra to take up appointment as sub-commissioner. He had been invited to the Exchange Hotel by Sergeant Ballard, who'd suggested he join him for a drink to meet some of the locals. Frederick Cooper's father, Robert Cooper, of Cooper's Brewery, was one of the richest men in New South Wales. Before arriving in Kiandra, Cooper had been one of the youngest members of the New South Wales Legislative Assembly, following his election as member for the Shoalhaven district when only twenty-five years old. He'd resigned from parliament unexpectedly to take up the Kiandra appointment.

Rumours about Commissioner Cooper started circulating around the diggings as soon as he arrived. It was said he'd been expelled from Sydney University. There was talk of excessive drinking, and of wild behaviour, though no details were given.

Davy soon met Sub-commissioner Cooper. The river men had sought

Davy's help in their dispute with the ground sluicers. The sluicers' water races were running a bunker from the recent rains, overflowing their dams and causing an avalanche of sludge to pour down the hillside. The river claims were buried in it. When the river men sent a deputation to Chief Commissioner Cloete, he asked Sub-commissioner Cooper to investigate the matter on his behalf. Davy and the river men met Commissioner Cooper halfway down the hill, at the place where one of the dams had overflowed.

From Cooper's youthful and unprepossessing appearance, it was hard to imagine he held the important and powerful office of gold commissioner. He was slightly built, with curly brown hair and a sparse beard. What he lacked in presence the miners soon found out he more than made up for in volatile temperament.

'Here's the problem,' said Davy, pointing to the top of the bank they were standing on. 'You can see where the sludge overflowed in the storm.'

Cooper walked along the top of the bank. He kicked a rock on the side of it. 'It seems pretty sound now,' he said.

'It sure is,' said Vince. He was the spokesman for the ground sluicing parties, and a friend of Mick Bourke's. 'There's never been anything wrong with it.'

'That's rubbish,' said Old Clarke. 'We seen you repairing it.' Old Clarke's claim had been one of the main victims of the overflow sludge. Clarke's party were temperance men. There was little love lost between them and Bourke. Bourke and his drinking mates were always making fun of the temperance men.

'Is there more to see?' asked Cooper.

'See that dam down there,' said Clarke, pointing towards the river. 'It's nearly empty now. We had to clean it out. A day ago it was totally filled with sludge. If you come down with us, we can show you.'

'I don't think I need to,' said Cooper. 'I've seen the evidence. Anyway, it looks like it's going to rain. We'd better adjourn to shelter.'

'And where might that be?' asked Clarke. They were a long way from the commissioner's camp.

'Benjamin's Hotel should do,' said Cooper.

'We can't go there,' said Clarke.

'Why not?' asked Cooper.

'We've taken the pledge,' replied Clarke.

'You've what?' said Cooper.

Vince and the ground sluicers laughed loudly. Vince whispered in Cooper's ear.

'We're teetotal,' said Clarke. 'It's not right to hear our case in a place like that.'

'All right then, we'll settle it here,' said Cooper. 'I've seen the evidence. The dam construction appears sound. There's no requirement for any further action. Case closed.'

'What about compensation for our losses?' asked Clarke.

'Yes,' said Davy. 'They have a right to compensation. Shouldn't you order the sluicers to raise and reinforce the banks?'

'Are you telling me what to do?' said Cooper, angrily turning on Davy. 'How dare you!' He started to go red in the face with rage. 'I'm the commissioner here. Who do you think you are!'

'These men have a rightful grievance,' said Davy.

'That's enough,' said Cooper. 'I've given my decision. I've other business to attend to. Good day to you.' With that he turned his back and walked away.

The ground sluicers were smiles all round. They waved cheerily at the river men.

'See you later, lads,' said Vince, grinning from ear to ear.

Clarke and the river men were fuming. There was nothing they could do. Any interference with the dam wall would only put their claims further at risk.

Vince and the ground sluicers hurried after Cooper as he walked up the hill towards the township. They soon caught up to him. Davy told Old Clarke he was sorry he hadn't been able to do more. Then he followed Cooper's party up the hill, in time to see Vince and Cooper disappearing into Benjamin's Hotel together. He vowed to himself he wouldn't let that be the end of it.

Davy mulled it over. He decided eventually he'd raise the matter with Commissioner Cloete. He knew he'd need to be discreet. It was always risky to complain about the rulings of a commissioner, especially to another commissioner.

On his way to the commissioner's camp, Tommy came running up to him.

'Mr Davy! Mr Davy!' he cried. 'Can you come help.' Tommy explained that Mr Templeton was refusing to pay the Chinese porters' wages.

Davy never rejected a request for help. Tommy took him to the Chinese camp to see Mr Lee. With Tommy's help as translator, Mr Lee explained that Templeton said the porters had eaten too much, and that some of goods had disappeared. Mr Lee said it wasn't their fault. The goods had been stolen after the Chinese delivered them. He had tried to talk to the police. Sergeant Ballard wouldn't help. The sergeant said it was Lee's problem, and that he couldn't see how anyone had committed a crime against the Chinese. He said the Chinese should count themselves lucky they were allowed to stay on the goldfield.

'No fair,' said Mr Lee, shaking his head. He told Davy he'd seen Templeton and the sergeant drinking together.

Davy asked if there was a written contract. Mr Lee told him there wasn't, despite Templeton's earlier promises.

'What about the lost goods?' Davy asked. 'Were there witnesses who saw the goods delivered?'

Mr Lee said there were. Davy decided the best course of action was to bypass the police and go straight to the chief commissioner. Mr Lee agreed to come with him.

Sergeant Ballard was at the guard house. He watched as they entered the commissioner's compound, but didn't follow them. Fortunately, the commissioner was in residence, and agreed to give them a hearing.

Davy put the facts before the chief commissioner. He didn't mention Sergeant Ballard. The commissioner said it wasn't a criminal matter, so it needn't involve the police. It was a matter for the civil court and could be heard on Thursday, when the Court of Petty Sessions next met. He told Mr Lee to bring his witnesses, and to make sure he had an interpreter. He said the process would require giving notice to Templeton, who would be able to bring his own witnesses.

'Then we can establish the facts,' said the commissioner. 'Do you understand? That's the way British justice is done. Everyone gets the chance to put their case. While you're in our country, that's the way it must be done.'

Mr Lee said he understood. He bowed many times, and thanked the commissioner profusely.

When Mr Lee had left the room, Davy said he had another matter to raise with the commissioner.

Cloete listened while Davy told him about the problem between the river men and the ground sluicers.

'Unless a solution's found soon, it'll be a constant cause of disputation amongst the diggers,' said Davy.

'I'm aware of the problem,' said the commissioner. 'I've had a number of parties complain to me already. What can you tell me about it?'

'It's a complicated matter,' said Davy. 'There are merits on both sides. It goes back to the decisions by some of your predecessors.' He explained that Commissioner Lockhart had granted ground sluicing claims and permitted races to be cut to supply them. On the basis of those decisions, the ground sluicers invested effort and resources in developing their claims. 'But the men working the river claims have a right to be protected against overflow sludge. Finding a solution won't be easy. The engineering of the races is very complicated. That needs to be understood before a fair remedy can be put in place.'

'Do you have any suggestions?' asked the commissioner.

'In my view, a properly qualified assessor needs to be appointed. He can advise on the technical aspects. Sub-commissioner Cooper inspected the site the other day. I was with him. I don't want to sound too critical, but I don't think he appreciated the extent of the problem. I'm not sure he has a detailed background in mining or mining engineering.'

'There's merit in what you say,' said the commissioner. 'I'll see what I can do. It's not easy finding a qualified assessor on this field. All the qualified men seem to be aligned with one party or another. But thank you for your advice.'

In his turn, Davy thanked the commissioner.

Mr Lee was waiting outside for Davy. He had a lot of questions, which

Davy did his best to answer. While trying to answer them, he decided it would be best for Mr Lee to have a professional lawyer to represent him in court.

'I know just the man for you,' said Davy. 'Mr Redman is now practising in Kiandra. I'll introduce you. He has a very good reputation.'

For a modest sum, Mr Redman agreed to represent the Chinese in their action against the Celestial Carrying Company. The necessary paperwork was quickly completed and a summons served on Templeton the following day.

That evening, John told Davy he'd overheard Sergeant Ballard and Templeton talking. 'Sergeant Ballard said he was going to get you, for dobbing him in to the commissioner,' John said.

'I never mentioned him,' said Davy.

'That's not what he thinks. He reckons you were behind it all. He said he was gonna break all the bones in your body. I didn't like the sound of it at all. You'd better make sure you stay well clear of him.'

'I will, but he doesn't scare me,' said Davy. 'He's just a common bully. I can deal with his kind.'

On Thursday, a small crowd gathered at the commissioner's camp for the court hearings. James, John and Ian came with Davy to watch the action. Brian said he'd stay and make sure their claim was secure. There'd recently been a spate of daytime robberies from claims whose owners were out working.

When Davy and the others arrived at the makeshift courthouse, Mr Redman was busy conferencing with his other clients. He was acting for a number of parties as well as the Chinese. He looked very dapper for the goldfield, dressed in a waistcoat and suit, and sporting a new black felt hat. Mr Lee and the Chinese witnesses were standing in a group by themselves separate from the other parties.

'Did you hear?' John said in a whisper, as they squeezed into the back of the court house. 'Templeton's been arrested on another matter.'

'How's that?' asked Davy.

'All I know is the new detective took him into custody last night. The case is being heard today. We'll soon find out.'

The first of Redman's cases involved another claim for unpaid wages, McNab versus Weir. It was found in the plaintiff's favour for fifteen pounds.

'See. I told you he was good,' Davy whispered to Mr Lee.

The next case was a charge of Sunday grog selling against Luke Reilly. 'I've no idea how this charge came to be laid,' whispered Ian. 'I thought Reilly had an arrangement with the traps. Something must've gone wrong. Maybe it's to do with the new detective.'

'Could be,' said John. 'I've heard he's been making inquiries and he's upset Sergeant Ballard.'

Inspector Saunderson gave evidence in support of the charge against Reilly. He deposed that he passed the defendant's hotel at half past eleven on the day named and saw parties going in and out of the side door. He went into the bar and saw fourteen or fifteen men there, and several glasses on the counter. On cross-examination, he couldn't recall actually seeing liquor being served. Sergeant Ballard confirmed the same. The barman was then called and swore he didn't serve any liquor at the time. The case was dismissed.

'They must have fixed it up,' said Ian.

The next two cases were for sly grog selling. The first was against A.C. Croy, a colourful Yankee veteran of the Californian rushes who had a store at the Nine Mile. He'd learnt there was more to be made from supplying the diggings than from mining. Mr Redman defended him. The charge was dismissed on account of the deposition not stating that Nine Mile was in New South Wales. John gave James a wink as the verdict was read out.

Clara Smith, of Sawpit Hill, was not so fortunate. She wasn't defended by Redman. The charge of sly grog selling on the sixteenth was proved. She was fined thirty pounds, to be paid in one and a half days, or, in default, fourteen days in gaol.

The deposition against the Celestial Carrying Company was read out next. It named Tommy, boss of the Chinese, as suing Templeton and Cook for unpaid wages of five pounds. He was also suing for wages on behalf of a number of his countrymen. In all, a total of seventy-eight pounds.

'How's that?' whispered James.

'Tommy signed the documents,' said Davy. 'It doesn't matter.'

The deposition said the Chinese had been engaged for thirty-five shillings a week and rations.

'But wasn't Templeton charging two pounds a load?' said Ian. 'I heard single loads were charged at twenty-five shillings.'

'That'd be right,' said John. 'We're in the wrong business.'

Mr Cook, one of Templeton's partners, defended the charge. He went on the attack, claiming a set-off for additional rations and time lost by the porters. He argued that only a few pounds were owed. Redman countered with the Chinese witnesses. He summed up masterfully, resting his case on the principles of contract law. The magistrate, Mr Clarke, decided in favour of the Chinese and awarded them the seventy-eight pounds.

'See,' said John. 'You *can* get justice on the goldfield.'

'In this case, we did,' said Davy.

As they were speaking, Templeton was led in, looking dishevelled after a night in the watch-house – nothing like the pillar of the business community he'd recently represented himself to be. There was a buzz in the room as he entered.

'Quiet in the court,' the magistrate ordered.

George Templeton Campbell, alias William Templeton, was charged with being a prisoner of the Crown, illegally at large from his district.

'I'd never have picked him as a ticket of leave man,' said Ian.

'There's plenty more like him at the diggings,' said John, 'except they've the sense to lie low.'

The necessary facts were quickly proved and the magistrate ordered the prisoner to be forwarded to the inspector-general of police in Sydney.

'Serves him right for being so greedy,' said Davy, as Templeton was led away. 'Pity they're not taking Sergeant Ballard away with him.'

'What'll happen to the Quartz Reef subscription now?' asked Ian. 'Wasn't Templeton the driving force behind it?'

'Not from what I hear,' said John. 'All the storekeepers were in it. Anyway, Shadforth can keep their business interests going. I guess they'll dissolve their partnership now. I wouldn't want to be owed any money by Templeton right now.'

'I reckon those claims at Jackass Flat got a better chance than that reef,' said James. 'Shadforth's got a share in one of them anyway.'

'Did you hear about the mails?' asked Ian. 'There's a new contractor. Greytown Carriers won the contract. I saw their man at the post office. He was all decked out in their fancy blue uniform. He's a Scot from Goulburn – Alec McCrae. He's taking orders for small carriage items right now – down at Wright's Commercial Store.'

'He'd want to be more reliable than the last fella what had it,' said John. 'I've been waiting on a letter from home nearly two months now.'

'Don't forget the snow, and the fearful state of the roads,' said Ian. 'We can't expect miracles.'

Mr Lee met Davy outside the courthouse. Tommy translated. Mr Lee thanked Davy, and invited him to visit the Chinese camp. He was welcome there at any time and could have the pick of their store of opium if he wished. Davy politely declined the offer. He said he was only trying to make sure there was justice for all on the diggings.

John suggested they walk back through the township to see if Alec McCrae had brought in any new mail. Ian left them, taking a short cut back to their claim, going high around the hillside to avoid the worst of the diggings. The recent rain had turned all the roads and tracks into a quagmire.

Davy, John and James walked through the mud and the slush into the township. Halfway along Telegraph Street, they reached the Kiandra Reading Rooms, newly established by Messrs Stormer and Montgomery in a shopfront building on the high side of the street. The sign in the window read,

KIANDRA
CIRCULATING LIBRARY
and
READING ROOMS
Cheap Newspapers
MELBOURNE Weeklies 2s each.
The SYDNEY MAIL (a Weekly Edition of the Sydney
Morning Herald), 1s each

Just Arrived, per Jeddo,
The latest English, American, German, French,
and Californian Papers.
Also,
English and American Periodicals.
THE LIBRARY
Just Received, 200 Volumes, comprising
the latest works.
THE READING ROOM
Is open daily. It contains copies of every paper
published in the colonies. Also, English, Continental
and American Journals.

'I'll drop in and see what books they've got,' said Davy.

John and James had less interest in reading. They told him they'd meet him back at the claim.

Davy did his best to scrape the mud off his boots on the wooden steps before he entered. It was well lit inside. Reading tables had been placed underneath the large windows on either side of the room. A young woman was sitting reading a newspaper at one of them. No one else was in the room. She looked up as Davy entered. The light from the window caught her golden russet hair. Davy thought he'd seen a vision. She was the most beautiful girl he'd ever seen. She had hazel eyes, soft skin and a light sprinkling of freckles across her nose. She looked at him and smiled brightly, with the open confidence of youth.

Davy introduced himself.

'I'm Kitty McCrae,' she said. 'We've just arrived at the diggings. My father's taken up the mail contract. I was amazed to find this library. I'd no idea there'd be something like this on a goldfield.'

'What were you expecting?'

'I don't know. I've heard many stories.'

'And what might they be?'

'Oh, all about snow – and tents – and gold nuggets – and robbers. You're not a robber, are you?' she asked, in mock concern.

'No,' said Davy.

'I really don't know anything about you,' she continued. 'Perhaps I shouldn't be sharing confidences. You could be a bushranger, for all I know. You're not a bushranger, are you?'

'No,' said Davy, laughing. 'I'm not a bushranger. Do I look like one?'

'I don't know,' said Kitty, open-eyed. 'I've never seen one.' But her look told him she didn't think so. 'Some are dashing young men, I hear.'

'Not the ones I know,' said Davy. 'I'm afraid I'll have to disillusion you. All the bushrangers I've known have been men of nasty habits and violent temperaments.'

'That's a pity. Just as well we've got the police to protect us then.'

'I'm afraid I'll have to disillusion you again. The police are generally of the same class as the robbers. They have similar characteristics, except they wear a uniform. In an ideal world, we'd have none of either of them. But that's a story I can tell you at some other time.'

'I'd be interested,' she replied.

They continued talking for a few minutes more, until Kitty suddenly said, 'I'd better go. Father'll be waiting for me. It was nice meeting you.'

'Will I see you again?' asked Davy.

'I'd like to. We're staying at the Empire Hotel.' Kitty hoped she hadn't been too forward. She thought Davy was terribly handsome. She had little enough experience with men, especially young and attractive ones. It was such a change here from the sheltered world of her recent schooling. She did hope he hadn't thought she was too silly and foolish.

Mr Stormer, who'd been going over his accounts in the back room, heard the door close and came out to see if there were any new customers. Davy arranged a subscription to the *Sydney Mail*. He glanced at the book titles but didn't immediately see one that caught his fancy. His mind was elsewhere.

Meanwhile, James and John had found Alec McCrae at the horse rails beside Wright's store. They waited while he finished loading his saddlebags. He was a gruff, no-nonsense Scotsman, with a bristling sandy beard and bushy eyebrows. McCrae wasn't given to idle chatter so their conversation was brief. There was no incoming mail.

'Aye, laddie,' he said to John. 'If there's a letter, ye can collect it Tuesday.'

As they walked back along Telegraph Street, Kitty came walking towards them. She was stepping carefully along the planks that made do for a footpath, looking down at the ground. Her boots and ankles were showing as she lifted her dress to keep it clear of the puddles. James jumped off the boards into the mud to let her pass.

She looked up at him briefly, smiled sweetly and said, 'Thank you.'

He stopped in his tracks. As she walked away, he turned round and stared.

'Psst,' said John. 'It's rude to stare.' He was laughing.

James ignored him. He couldn't take his eyes off Kitty. He watched till she disappeared from view around the corner of the yards beside Wright's Store.

'Looks like you've been smitten,' said John.

'Who was she?' said James, in awe. 'She was beautiful, wasn't she?'

'Not bad,' said John. 'Not really my type, though. Needs more development in the chest department. Just as well. It'd be a rum world if we all liked the same women.'

'What do you like, then?' asked James, finding it hard to believe John hadn't been equally smitten.

'My Lyn'll do me. Nice an' shapely, long legs and golden hair – what more could a man want? Soon as I've got my pile of gold, I'll be off these mountains to see her again.'

'What'll you do then?' asked James.

'Select a bit of land – if free selection gets passed. Clear the bush, build a home, run a few sheep and cattle. Whatever pays. I'm not afraid of hard work – so long as it's working for meself.'

'Sounds good,' said James. 'I don't know what I want to do.'

'Except with women,' said John, smiling.

James didn't reply.

Dinner at the hut was mutton stew – again.

Davy told the others he hadn't found any interesting books at the library. 'But I did meet the most beautiful girl I've ever seen,' he said. 'She's the new mail contractor's daughter – her name's Kitty McCrae. We talked a while. I'll be seeing her again.' Kitty must have made an impact on him. He wasn't usually so candid, even with his friends.

'We must've seen her too,' said John, quickly putting two and two together. 'James thought she was attractive. She's not really my kind, though.'

James had a strange feeling in his chest. He decided not to say anything.

The conversation moved on. Later, James went for a walk by himself.

*

Captain Bill was having an afternoon drink at Turner's newly licensed Camp Inn. This was strategically located in Camp Town, at the centre of the old tent settlement, beside Pollocks' Gully. The clientele were mostly from the lower social classes, even for the diggings. Captain Bill's group included Dan and Pat Mulligan, Alex the Kid, and various other parties involved in the illegal second-hand horse and cattle trade.

'Hey, Capt'n, yer hear the traps got Bricky again?' said Pat.

'No? What happened?' said Captain Bill, alias Sweeney.

'They got 'im on the 'Bidgee, near Hay. 'E's on 'is way back to Cooma gaol now.'

'Poor beggar,' said Dan. 'Reckon we should make a raid?'

'No. They'll 'ave 'im too well guarded. 'He's already done a bolt before,' said Pat.

The bar manager replaced the bottles of drink on the table.

'They tell me Frankie Gardiner's headed this way,' said Dan. 'They've given 'im a ticket of leave.'

'Who's he?' asked Alex.

'Yer dunno?' said Dan. 'Yer dunno Darkie Gardiner!'

'Frankie's one top bushranger,' said Pat. 'He's got class. Even the traps are 'fraid of 'im. Yer never want to cross 'im, but,' said Pat, shaking his head. 'Got a real nasty temper. Shoot a man dead soon as look at 'im, he would.'

Alex left the room to relieve himself out the back. The bar room next door was crowded. On his way back, he bumped into a man standing beside the bar. The man spun round. Alex felt a sharp pain in the ribs. Looking down, he saw a pistol barrel shoved hard into his chest.

'Don't move!' the man hissed.

Alex suddenly felt very sober. His ribs were hurting. He could smell the man's breath.

'Give me all your gold!' the man hissed. There was a mad look in his eyes.

'I – I – I haven't got any,' Alex stuttered.

The man looked at him strangely for a moment, then he gave a nasty laugh. 'Just joking,' he said. He removed the pistol from Alex's ribs.

Alex quickly returned to his table.

A few minutes later, the bar manager came into the room. He whispered to Dan and Sweeney. 'There's a man 'ere what says 'e's lookin' fer Captain Bill and the Mulligans. Do I tell 'im yer 'ere?'

'What's he look like?' said Dan.

'About average height and size. Swarthy-lookin', dark curly hair and beard, olive skin. Dressed a bit dandy. Wearin' a waistcoat an' red silk scarf.'

'Sounds like Frankie Gardiner,' said Dan. 'Where is he? Bring 'im in.'

The manager returned. With him was the man who'd just threatened Alex.

Dan was like a fawning puppy. 'Good to see yer, Frankie. What can we do for yer? Would yer like champagne?' he grovelled.

Gardiner quickly cut him off. 'Don't call me Frankie,' he said curtly. 'Frankie Gardiner ain't here. I'm Mr Christie. Can you remember that?' He looked around the group. 'These your lads?' he asked Dan. 'They up to a big job? Where's Captain Bill and Alex the Kid. Are they here?'

'That's Captain Bill, and this is Alex,' said Dan, pointing to Alex.

'So that's Alex,' said Gardiner, squinting at him. 'We just met.'

Alex was uncertain what he meant. He didn't like the man's snaky eyes.

'We'd better not stay 'ere too long,' said Dan. 'There's too many traps about. Best we're not seen together. They might twig that somethin's goin' on.'

The party removed themselves to a hut on the hillside, some distance from the township, and the commissioner's camp. There, Gardiner asked them how their trade was going. He said little about his recent stint in prison on Cockatoo Island – except that he was going to make sure some of the guards had short life expectancies. He said he was visiting Kiandra to check it out before going to Lambing Flat. His first impression of the place was there were too many traps to operate freely. 'Don't know why there'd be so many,' he said. 'Looks like half the traps in the colony are here.'

Gardiner told them he had some big jobs in mind and could be needing some help. He'd consider taking on men, but he told them anyone who joined him would have to swear total loyalty. Sweeney said he was interested.

Alex didn't volunteer. He wasn't sure he could trust the man.

'This horse and cattle thieving,' Gardiner said. 'It's child's play. It'll never pay more than wages. And you've got to keep paying off the traps. The real money's in highway robbery. That's where the big rewards are. There's no other parties to fix up there.'

Frankie Gardiner had an eye for women. When bailing up parties, he had as much a reputation for his courteous treatment of the fairer sex as for his ruthless treatment of any resistance. After they'd finished discussing business, he asked where he could find a lady on the diggings.

'A lady?' said Sweeney. 'There's Mad Mary's.'

'That's a whorehouse!' said Dan. 'Might be good enough for the likes of you.' He turned to Gardiner. 'Come to think of it, I know a lady what'd be interested to meet yer. I'll introduce yer tomorrow.'

Gardiner was introduced to Maggie the next day. He invited her to join him for dinner at the Kiandra Hotel. Maggie was flattered to receive attention from such a wealthy Sydney gentleman. No doubt, her judgement was coloured by the champagne he so obligingly provided. 'Mr Christie' was a generous tipper. The management of the hotel were most keen to see that he and his lady friend were provided with all they might require.

The following morning, as befitting a wealthy Sydney gentleman, Mr Christie took the air, telling the hotel manager he would be back shortly after his stroll. As he walked past Wright's store, he saw Kitty McCrae. She was struggling to steady her father's horse while she loaded its saddlebags.

Gardiner couldn't resist an attractive girl. 'Here, allow me to help,' he said.

Kitty looked at him. 'No, thank you,' she said. She didn't like the look of him.

'But I insist,' he said, taking a step forward and reaching for the bridle.

'Please,' she said firmly. 'I'd prefer to do it myself.'

'You look as if you could do with some help,' he said, moving closer.

Kitty resented the implication that she couldn't cope. She felt uncomfortable with him so close. She didn't like the way he smelt. His face reminded her of a lizard, or a snake.

'Is this man intruding on you?' asked Davy, who'd just arrived.

'Yes, he is,' she said. 'I'm quite able to do this myself.'

'It's none of your business,' said Gardiner, looking darkly at Davy.

'I suggest you leave forthwith,' said Davy. 'Or do you want me to call that trooper?'

Gardiner let go of the bridle and stepped back. He glanced at the trooper riding by. He looked at Davy. Then, without a word, he turned and left.

'Thank you so much,' said Kitty. She admired the masterful way Davy had dealt with the man. He'd been so brave and strong. Her first impressions had been right. Davy *was* the man for her.

'Who was he?' asked Davy.

'I don't know,' said Kitty. 'I only know I'm glad you came.'

Sweeney had been outside Wright's store and saw the exchange. Gardiner strode straight past Sweeney, without acknowledging him.

Later, Sweeney told Alex what he'd seen. 'There was a murderous look in his eyes,' said Sweeney, shaking his head. 'I wouldn't want to be that brother of yours, not for all the gold on these diggings. They say Frankie never forgets a grudge.'

This information strangely disturbed Alex. It made him realise he didn't think so ill of his brother as to wish him dead.

Meanwhile, the owner of the Kiandra Hotel, Mr Benjamin, was livid. 'Mr Christie' had disappeared without settling his account. Mr Benjamin threatened to take every last penny of his loss out of the personal wages of his manager. With 'Mr Christie' had also disappeared the best horse in the hotel's stables, a roan mare belonging to Dr Ashley.

11

Troubles on the Diggings
Spring 1860

Davy's representations on behalf of the river men produced results. Commissioner Cloete appointed an assessor, Mr McGregor, to investigate the matter. His report recommended re-engineering the races that brought water to the ground sluicing claims, including construction of a six-foot-high dam to collect their sludge. McGregor also recommended strengthening the banks of the main race line, as well as those of the tail race that returned water to the creek. His report concluded,

'It is my considered opinion that, until such time as the proposed works are completed, viz., construction of the dam and the strengthened banks of the water races, the river claims will continue to be at risk of contamination by sludge should there be any significant rainfall.'

Commissioner Cloete acted on McGregor's findings. He ordered the return of the water to its natural channel until such time as the recommended works were undertaken.

On 27th August, Commissioner Scott called on each of the ground sluicing claims to read out the chief commissioner's order. He knew feelings were running high, so he took a contingent of foot police with him. Scott was stout jolly gentleman and this mission was not to his liking.

'That's ridiculous, what you've just ordered!' said Vince. 'How can we work without water? We can't do it. We have a right to the water. It was granted by Commissioner Lockhart. This is outrageous! Only a few weeks back, Commissioner Cloete stood here – right here!' he pointed at the ground angrily. 'He promised we could have water till November. What sort of duplicity is that?'

'Be careful with your words,' said Scott.

'It must be a joke. You're asking us to cut off our living. You can't be serious.'

'I can only warn you,' said the commissioner. 'If you don't comply, you'll be liable for a fine of twenty-five pounds – or, in lieu, three months in gaol.'

'Are you threatening us?' said Vince.

'No. I'm ordering you,' said Scott.

'But the order is manifestly unfair,' said Vince.

'Worse than that. It's stupid!' said an angry miner. 'A six-foot dam will flood half our claim. Can't you see? There's no six feet of fall. The water'll back right up the hill. What's the reasoning behind that decision? What idiot came up with that idea?'

'Yes,' said Vince. 'Explain how that's supposed to work.'

'I'm not at liberty to discuss details,' said Scott.

'Then get us someone who is,' said a miner.

'Why isn't Commissioner Cooper here?' said Vince. 'He understood our situation.'

'The chief commissioner has charged me with implementing his decision,' said Scott. 'I expect the water to be cut off by midday. If you don't comply, you do so at your own risk. You've been warned of the consequences. That's all I have to say.' He turned his back and began walking along the embankment to the next claim.

The ground sluicers called a meeting when Commissioner Scott had finished his round. The men in the field were joined by storekeepers and others who had a share in the claims. The crowd numbered upwards of fifty men and included a sprinkling of publicans, including Luke Bond. Their mood was angry. Vince stood on the race embankment to address them. He was joined by Mick Bourke.

'How did this happen?' asked a miner. 'I thought we had an understanding with Commissioner Cooper?'

'So did we,' said Vince.

'We invested good money in these claims,' said one of the storekeepers. 'You told us not to worry. You said everything was squared away. I'd never have paid so much if I'd known this was going to happen.'

'We're all in the same boat,' said a miner. 'Don't complain. You don't even get your hands dirty.'

'I'm acting for Mr Cornwallis,' said a storekeeper. 'He'll be very upset if this isn't fixed.'

'We'll all be upset if it doesn't get fixed,' said Vince.

'What's made Cloete change his mind?' asked a miner.

'I'll bet that Davy Hughes is behind this,' said the man next to him. 'I seen 'im an' the river men talking to Cloete. They were up to no good, I'm sure.'

'How come McGregor got picked as assessor?' asked a miner. 'Didn't he use to have a river claim? What happened to Skinner? Weren't they going to use our man? I thought we'd fixed it up.'

'We should take it up with Commissioner Cooper,' said Luke Bond. 'We've been looking after him just so this sort of thing wouldn't happen.'

'He can't do anything, now Cloete's got involved,' said Bourke.

'Quiet!' shouted Vince. 'Order! We need a course of action. Who's got suggestions? I say we leave the water the way it is. They can't make us build anything. The river men can go hang!'

'I'd better not see any of 'em at Kidd's,' said a miner. 'Can't answer what I'd do to 'em.'

'Fat chance of that,' said another. 'Most of them are God damn temperance men.'

'Why should we have to build anything?' complained a miner. 'There's nothing wrong with our claims. If the river men want something built, let them do it themselves – on their claims. Why should we have to carry the cost of protecting them?'

'That's right!' shouted another. 'Let's stand firm. Let's not budge. Let them do their worst.'

This position was universally endorsed. After more of the same line of discussion, the meeting voted unanimously to stand firm.

'Let them fine us!' said Vince. 'That'll be the end of this goldfield. Our claims are the most productive on the diggings. We've been producing more gold than anywhere else on this damn field.'

Commissioner Scott had arranged for a spy to attend the meeting.

In exchange for a small reward, he reported what he'd heard to the commissioners at their camp.

'It's no good,' said Commissioner Scott.

'What's the problem?' asked Commissioner Cloete.

'We can't make them build anything,' said Scott. 'All we can do is punish them if they don't. That won't get the result you want.'

Commissioner Scott had never agreed with Cloete's decision in the first place, but he'd learnt it didn't pay to argue. He knew the chief commissioner could be very stubborn once he set his mind on something. Cloete was one of those men who believed in acting on principle. In Scott's view, this was dangerous. Principles needed to be tempered with pragmatism. There were sound business reasons for favouring the more successful and productive on a goldfield. After all, they were where the wealth came from.

'If the miners won't do it, I'll order the police to do it,' said Cloete.

'Is that wise?' asked Scott. 'What if the police are resisted? That could provoke unrest.'

'We have a duty here,' said Cloete. 'We have to protect the men in the river.'

'But their claims are nearly finished,' said Scott. 'Cutting off water to the sluicers will stop them working, and theirs are some of the best claims on the field.'

'As soon as they construct the new dam, they can have water again,' said Cloete.

'But the output of the field will be affected. The sluicing claims are very productive,' said Scott.

'We have to put aside questions of wealth,' said Cloete. 'This is a case of protecting the more vulnerable. As chief commissioner, I need to be scrupulously fair. You wouldn't be suggesting otherwise, would you?'

'Certainly not,' said Scott.

'Then carry out my order. If the races are still flowing after midday, you are to use such numbers of police as are necessary to implement my decision.'

Commissioner Scott knew there was no point in further discussion.

That afternoon, he assembled a contingent of policemen, as many as he could muster at short notice, and instructed them on their mission. The police were very unhappy when they learned of their assignment.

Groups of miners stood and stared as the police contingent marched across the diggings, armed with picks and shovels. The stares quickly turned to laughter. The police were led by Inspector Saunderson. Commissioner Scott was not in attendance. Neither was Sergeant Ballard, who was unable to be found.

The ground sluicing miners were waiting for them. They jeered at the police.

'Watch how you handle that pick – it might go off!'

'Yer gotta swing it, not point it!'

'Don't worry, the dirt'll wash off!' they jibed.

It was hard to imagine a less happy-looking group than the police party. Under instruction from the inspector, they attempted to change the course of the water by damming its flow into the race. Their first attempt failed, breaking the bank and sending a torrent of mud down the hillside, to the mirth of the watching crowd.

'Now we know why yer not miners,' said a bystander.

'I wouldn't pay yer to work my claim,' yelled another.

By late afternoon, the job had been completed. The police party assembled as a troop and marched back to the commissioner's camp. They were a bedraggled and sorry-looking group. As soon as they were out of sight, the miners jumped into the race and demolished the temporary dam. In next to no time, water was flowing freely in the race again.

The following morning, Commissioner Scott reported the problem to Cloete. 'I never thought it'd work,' he said. 'I asked the police to make inquiries. They couldn't find anyone who saw the temporary dam being destroyed.'

'All right,' said Cloete. 'We'll have to proceed another way. Call all the parties to a conference at the courthouse on Wednesday.'

The Wednesday conference produced a compromise – and an uneasy truce between the sluicers and the river men. Davy helped broker the deal on behalf of the river men. The flow of water to the sluicing claims would be allowed to continue, but it would be carefully watched. The construction of a new dam would begin and, to prepare for the possibility of a flood, a new emergency overflow channel would be constructed. The river men agreed to help dig the overflow channel.

Davy's role in the dispute reinforced his unpopularity amongst various parties on the diggings. This antipathy naturally extended to his associates. As a result Eureka Jack and the Second Chance partners were the butt of some negative attention from The Boys and others. Davy was unconcerned. It didn't bother John either. He was happy to deal with any provocation – and give it back threefold. James believed he even enjoyed it. Ian was more cautious. As for Brian, he didn't care. He said he could look after himself. Having once seen him pushed, James agreed.

*

Jack was the first to move camp. It wasn't because of harassment from the sluicers, who'd threatened to light his tent.

'Do that an' yer won't live to skite about it,' Jack told them.

The way he said it made them stop. They quickly said it was only a joke. Jack was an unknown quantity. The tone of his voice and the look in his eyes made his tormenters nervous. It was rumoured he'd done time for murder.

Jack made up his own mind to move. It was never productive to ask his motivation. There was unworked ground within his claim, so it wasn't for lack of wash dirt. The only person he told before he left was Davy. 'Movin' ter Four Mile t'morrow,' he said.

Davy told the other Second Chance partners.

'Why don't we try Nine Mile?' said Ian. 'There's some good finds up that way.'

'There's more down on the Tumut River,' said Brian.

'We're still making good wages at New Chum,' said John. 'I say we give it a bit longer here.'

The consensus was in favour of staying – so long as the yield stayed high.

After Kitty's arrival, James couldn't stop thinking about her. In his heart, he knew she had eyes for Davy. He also knew Sally was waiting for him. Knowing these things didn't stop him. He made excuses to himself to visit the township to try and see her. Whenever they met she was friendly, but he only managed to snatch a few minutes of her company at a time. She was always busy, helping with postal deliveries, doing something or on her way somewhere.

James felt sure that Kitty liked him. After each encounter, he'd go over the clumsy things he'd said, and try and make sense of her responses. He kept turning them over and over, examining them for signs of encouragement. Momentarily, he'd feel positive, then he'd remember how Kitty hung onto Davy's words and how she smiled at Davy. She didn't look at him in the same way.

He knew Davy was spending time with Kitty. He knew, because he watched them together. When he went into town, sometimes Davy was there already. James would wait, then walk past them, as casually as he could, and pretend to be surprised to see them. He felt nervous, and foolish, but he couldn't stop himself.

The more James saw of Kitty, the more he thought about her. He knew it was silly. And that it was pointless. It was as though he wasn't in control of himself. As if he was sitting up high, looking down on himself, watching as he made an idiot of himself. He almost wished he didn't find her attractive. But how couldn't he?

Even before the ground sluicing dispute, Davy had been spending less time than the others at the Second Chance claim. He'd always done a fair amount of coming and going. Now he was often missing for the evening meal, and would come home late in the night. He didn't say what he'd been doing, though James had an idea where he was – some of the time.

One evening, John asked where Davy was. It was Davy's turn to help cook dinner.

'Probably solving a dispute,' said Ian.

'More likely he's chasing that McCrae girl,' said Brian, with a chuckle.

James said nothing.

'I don't mind what he's doing, but we're supposed to be a partnership here,' said John.

'You reckon he's not pulling his weight?' said Brian.

'I didn't say that,' said John. 'But it might be getting close.'

'Don't forget he's helped us out in other ways,' said Ian.

'I vote we have a word with 'im,' said John. 'If he turns up again. He may never come back – if he's found a nest.' He grinned.

James wasn't amused.

Davy arrived shortly after this conversation, carrying a load of supplies and a paper. He handed Ian a bag of onions and threw a copy of the *Alpine Pioneer* onto the bench in the middle of the hut. 'Here,' he said. 'I bought a copy of the *Pioneer* for you. There's some interesting reading in the mining and court reports today.'

'Read us the interesting bits while the stew's cooking,' said Ian. 'Save us straining our eyes.' Ian didn't see as well as the others in the flickering lamplight.

'All right,' said Davy. 'I'll start with the Mining Report. It says the only parties working are the deep sinkers on the New Chum Hill, who haven't reached bottom.'

'They have now,' said Brian.

'This was written on Friday,' said Davy. '"The ground sluicers seem to be going on as usual…a party's gone out to the back of New Chum Hill in search of a reef… The tunnelling party on Surface Hill are run out of funds, and are endeavouring to induce the storekeepers to subscribe to enable them to proceed with their shaft."

'It also says there's a rush to some payable ground between Big Boojong and Happy Jack's Plains. They've sent their reporter and hope to be able to give reliable and full particulars in their next issue. Listen to this: "On Jackass Flat, Shadforth's claim has produced nearly thirty ounces for four men in three days… On the other side of the Flat a party are engaged sluicing all before them, and though the ground has been worked over once, and in some parts twice, they are obtaining good payable wages. There is a party engaged in cutting a flood race close to the right side of the Flat, so as to drain the river and work its bed.

'"We have been informed that a number of diggers have set in to work the Tumut River, about four miles from Nine Mile. Those who visit the Nine Mile for provisions, etc, report having obtained good prospects."'

'I told you we should check out the Nine Mile,' said Brian. 'Sounds like there might be some good prospects up that way.'

'What's in the court reports,' asked Ian.

'There's a report about a Chinaman laying a charge against two of his countrymen – for stealing six boxes of opium from his store,' said Davy. 'It says the charge was sustained, and the accused were committed for trial at the Goulburn Quarter Sessions.'

'I s'pose opium for them is like grog for us,' said John.

'It's not quite the same,' said Davy. 'Opium gives them stamina. How else do you think they carried those loads through the snow from Russell's?'

'Anything else?' asked Ian.

'Danial Nunan was found guilty of stealing two pounds ten shillings and sixpence, in Benjamin's Hotel, and sentenced to four months imprisonment in Goulburn Gaol.'

'Good riddance,' said Brian. 'Wasn't he one of that mob that tried to fight us the other day?'

'Then there's a complaint against Thomas Moriarty for having illegally jumped one of the water races running past the front of the Exchange Hotel. Mr Redman appeared for the defence, and took so many objections the case was dismissed.'

'That Redman's a clever fella,' said John.

'Here's an interesting report,' said Davy. '"Gambling – On Wednesday, two men, one being the notorious Joseph Walker, alias 'Bristol Joe' and James Addison, a packer, were charged by Inspector Carnes of the Detective Department, with the above offence. Detective Lyons proved that on the previous day he apprehended the two prisoners in an unfinished building in Kiandra, in the act of playing pitch and toss. Two pounds seventeen shillings was on the ground when he entered, and on Joe was found a 'grey' or a farthing piece with two heads on it. Mr Redman having raised a technical objection, the accused were discharged – giving Joe another run for it."'

'That's another reason to avoid gambling,' said Ian.

'It's never been different,' said Brian. 'Gambling's a mug's game.'

'Then there's a bit about the Kiandra weather, and how frequent, sudden and extreme the changes can be,' said Davy.

'Is there anything about the four men that were hit by lightning?' asked John.

'No.'

'Strange,' said John. 'There was a big crowd at the burial. The commissioner gave the service. One of the stupid storekeepers was full of hindsight. He kept saying they should have all lied down when the lightning came. It might be fine for them. But diggers aren't going to lie flat on their faces in the mud every time there's a storm.'

'There's a detailed report about Carmichael's free dinner at the Empire Hotel,' said Davy, holding up the paper. 'The one he hosted to celebrate the opening of his new ballroom.'

'Don't read us that,' said Brian. 'I heard the speeches went on forever.'

'Maybe we should've gone,' said Ian. 'It was free.'

'You wouldn't, when I tell you who was there,' said Davy.

'What does it say about the food?' asked Ian.

'I'll read it,' said Davy. 'So you'll see what you missed. "There were not only delicacies which are not always to be found on the table at public dinners in the more settled parts of the colony, but there was such a variety of the more substantial class of edibles as we have seldom seen on such occasions down country. Indeed, one and all as they entered the spacious room for the first time, and viewed the spread in its perfect state, could not refrain exclamations of surprise, and asked themselves, is it possible that this is on Kiandra, which but a few short months ago was a bleak, desolate, and almost unknown and untrodden part of the colony."'

'It does go on a bit,' said Brian. 'Sounds like advertising. Was it really that good?'

'Kitty tells me it wasn't bad,' said Davy. 'She went with her father.'

'That girl of yours was there, too, I heard,' said John, looking at James.

'What girl?' said James.

'The good-looking one what likes a drink,' said John, grinning. 'She was having a great time they tell me.'

'She's no girl of mine,' said James. Sometimes John annoyed him.

'The rest of the report is a blow-by-blow account of the speeches,' said Davy. 'I'll skip them and just tell you who was there. The chairman was Chas Cowper Junior, Esq. JP. He said, "the ministry were desirous of opening up the lands of the country (hear, hear) so that those miners who were fortunate might obtain homes for themselves and their families (loud cheers)."'

'That'd be right,' said John. 'He'd be looking for all the limelight he can get. Isn't he angling to follow his father into parliament?'

'It's what you'd expect from a politician,' said Brian. 'But can he deliver? He's not even in parliament yet.'

'His father is,' said John. 'I'd vote for him. Any politician who supports free selection is getting my vote.'

'The rest of the report's about the toasts and the speeches,' said Davy. 'Here's the toast to the miners: "Mr Kennedy proposed 'The Miners of Kiandra.' He said the miners of Kiandra as a body possessed amongst their ranks more enterprise and determination than any other body in the colonies – men of the highest character and intelligence from the son of the peer down to the son of the iremonger (loud cheers and laughter). Indeed the diggers were like the battlefield – they levelled all distinctions."'

'He must've had a few before saying that,' commented John.

'Then they toasted everyone and everything else, even the ladies,' said Davy. 'And dancing continued till one o'clock.'

'See what we missed,' said Ian.

'There'll be another. When the next hotel's extended,' said Davy. 'You can go to that, if you want. This one wasn't for me. I had a few run-ins with Carmichael when he was in Adelong.'

'He must be making good money now, if he can afford to give that much food away,' said James.

'He sure is,' said Brian. 'There's more money to be made off the diggers than there is to be made out of the ground. That's why the storekeepers are so keen to spread the news whenever there's a good find. They win whichever way it goes.'

'I think I'll stick to digging,' said Ian. 'It'll sit easier with my conscience.'

'Unless you find the big one, you'll never be rich,' said John.

'There's more to life than wealth,' said Davy. 'There's something I've been meaning to say. It's not fair on you others, now that I'm being asked to help out with disputes so much. I've decided it'd be for the best if I was to leave the partnership. Or maybe just become a part-time shareholder.'

'We'd like you to stay,' said Ian. 'At least I would,' he added, looking quickly round at the others.

The other partners agreed. It was settled – Davy was to become a part-time shareholder – and be rewarded accordingly. He would still live at the hut, but he could come and go as he pleased.

Over the next week, Davy had little time for digging. At the weekend, Tommy came to see him. He told Davy the police had just arrested a Chinese doctor. Tommy asked if Davy could defend him.

'Why bother?' said John.

Davy ignored the comment.

Tommy took Davy to visit Mu Chiu in the lock up. He was due to appear in court later that morning. The elderly Chinaman was most glad to see Davy. He looked very frail as he squatted on the dirty lock up room bench, surrounded by puddles of muddy water, his wispy grey beard between his knees.

With a display of excessive zeal, the duty guard insisted on locking the door. It was hard to see the threat the small Chinese man posed. The heavy wooden door slammed shut with a thud, followed by a loud metallic clang as the key was turned in the lock. For a moment, Davy imagined he was the prisoner being locked up. It sent a shiver down his spine.

Mu Chiu explained the circumstances of his predicament in remarkably good English. He'd been charged with trying to sell spurious gold. It was all a mistake, he said. He'd believed the gold was genuine. It had been given to him as payment for opium by one of his compatriots when he was in Tumbarumba. Apparently, the gold had now been judged to be false. He wouldn't know himself. He wasn't a miner.

Mu Chiu explained he was a qualified Chinese doctor. He'd been sent to the colony to attend to his countrymen, who were finding great difficulty in obtaining treatment for their illnesses from European medical men. Also, his countrymen preferred to be treated by one of their own as they didn't trust European medical methods. These differed greatly from traditional Chinese medicine.

Davy agreed to defend him, but explained it might not be easy. He told him there was much feeling against the Chinese on the diggings.

The case was heard by Commissioner Scott. Davy was relieved it was not being held before Commissioner Cooper. The police guard made a disparaging remark about 'The Leprosy' as he shoved the prisoner forward, jabbing him in the back with his rifle butt.

A small wooden box with Chinese writing on it was tabled as evidence. John Pascoe was called. He gave evidence that he was in the employ of Mr Limbert, storekeeper, of Kiandra. On the fourth instant, the prisoner had come into Mr Limbert's store and offered the contents of the box for sale. At first glance, it had looked like gold, so he had exchanged twenty-two shillings for it, at the going rate of seventy-one shillings an ounce. The prisoner had then purchased goods to the value of four shillings and sixpence, which he had left, saying he would return.

After the Chinaman's departure, he suspected the gold was not genuine and applied the test used by Mr Limbert in cases of suspect gold. He had put it on a shovel and heated it on the fire. The metal immediately turned black and had remained so since. He then took it to Mr Horton of the Oriental Bank, and to Mr Moses, the jeweller, and they both confirmed that it wasn't genuine. He then went down the street to Benjamin's, where he found the prisoner and asked him to return to the store. As they did so, they met Sergeant Ballard, who was apprised of the situation. The sergeant immediately arrested the prisoner.

Davy sought permission to ask some questions about the circumstances of the arrest. As Sergeant Ballard wasn't present, Davy directed them at Pascoe. Pascoe said neither the prisoner nor his companion had been given a chance to explain. He admitted the sergeant had made a joke about taking the 'dirty yellow chink to the clink'. The onlookers in the gallery laughed.

The commissioner ordered the case to be remanded until Monday, so the contents of the box could be assayed by a chemist. Bail was refused. The commissioner did not give a reason.

On Monday, Davy had to wait while earlier listed cases were heard. They were the usual. Mary Anne Patterson was convicted of continued drunkenness – sentenced to a fine of two pounds or forty-eight hours in the cells. She swore at the magistrate and was returned to serve out her time. Owen Ryan was convicted of drunkenness – fined five shillings, or six hours in the cells. He was released, as he'd already served the six hours.

James Smith was convicted of throwing a clod. It had hit Constable Murphy on Sunday afternoon when the constable had tried to put a stop to a wrestling match. He was fined four pounds, or fourteen days imprisonment. Daniel McLaughlin was convicted of obstructing Constable Murphy while trying to put a stop to the same match – also fined four pounds, or fourteen days imprisonment. Constable Murphy's conduct in these two cases was highly commended by the Bench.

Davy had heard about the incident. Constable Murphy had been called in by an aggrieved party who believed the match was fixed and who stood to lose a considerable sum of money.

Mu Chiu was brought in next. He stood quietly with his head bowed. Inspector Saunderson reported on the test he'd arranged on the spurious gold. He'd watched as the suspect gold and some genuine gold were heated. Only the genuine gold had kept its colour. No further chemical test was deemed necessary. Davy brought forward a Chinaman as a witness. He was sworn in by blowing out a match. Tommy translated. The witness said he'd been present when the defendant, who was an eminently regarded Chinese doctor, had exchanged six boxes of opium for the contents of the box from a countryman in Tumbarumba.

Davy called the driver of the coach in which the defendant had travelled from Beechworth to Albury. The man stated that the defendant had a box of Chinese medicines with him in the coach, and that while on the way to Albury he had obtained money from another Chinese doctor at Spring Creek, which had since been repaid.

Davy summed up by drawing attention to the circumstances of the case and called for leniency. By leaving his purchases at Limbert's and by not attempting to leave town, it was clear the defendant had no intention of cheating Limbert. He was a Chinese doctor, and had been duped by one of his own countrymen in Tumbarumba, who had given him the material in exchange for opium.

The commissioner agreed with this view of the matter, and dismissed the case. He ordered the defendant to repay the twenty-two shillings to Mr Limbert.

A small group of Chinese was waiting outside the courthouse. They had been afraid to enter the building. They greeted Mu Chiu with the utmost deference, bowing many times. Then they bowed many times to Davy. The miners standing around laughed and pointed at them.

Davy was pressed to join the Chinese at their camp for a meal. Mu Chiu was most insistent. Sensing that refusal would be judged as rude, Davy agreed.

On reaching the Chinese camp, they were ushered into the headman's hut, the largest and best constructed in the camp. There, they were waited on with deference. Unusually, young Tommy kept well in the background. Even he treated the doctor with a degree of respect bordering on reverence.

They were served green tea and a series of interesting dishes made with ingredients Davy was unfamiliar with but which were very tasty.

Mu Chiu thanked Davy for his timely intervention. He was clearly a well educated man in his own country. He talked about the sad events in his homeland, where the Imperial City had been occupied by foreigners, and how there was no respect for China and its people. He also talked about Chinese medicine. Davy didn't understand everything he said, but he politely nodded and smiled.

Mu Chiu said China was very old, and China was very wise. China had patience. Britain had an empire now, but China would have an empire again. 'Your country like a young man. Britain in a hurry. Young man need patience.' Mu Chiu nodded. 'China have much patience.'

Davy knew he wasn't expected to reply. Earlier, he had thought he might explain the benefits of democracy. But he quickly realised it wasn't the right place or time. After the last dish was served, he made his excuses, politely declining the drink that was proffered.

As Davy walked back through the untidy collection of tents and miner's rubble, he was left with an uncomfortable feeling. The Chinese view of life wasn't so different from that of the European diggers who belittled them. They both looked at the world from within their own fortresses. There would be much to overcome before the two peoples could live together in peace and harmony.

That evening Davy had a visit from Mr Gillespie. Gillespie was a principal in one of the river claims. His claim had been badly affected by sludge from the ground sluicers.

The compromise Davy had helped broker between the river men and the ground sluicers had started coming undone as soon as Commissioner Cloete left the scene. He'd delegated its implementation to Sub Commissioner Cooper. Cooper's approach involved calling meetings at short notice, usually in a public house. The temperance men said he did it deliberately – to slight them.

The ground sluicers and their allies managed to convince Cooper they needed more time to complete the new dam and water race modifications. Cooper gave them a month's extension. He also agreed to changes to the specifications for the works, including reducing the size of the overflow dam and changing the route for the overflow tail race. To the minds of the river men, these changes took away much of what Cloete had ordered.

Cooper's actions absolutely incensed Mr Gillespie. He was a self-made man and chief shareholder in one of the largest river claims. Solidly built and hard-working, Gillespie had no truck with fools. He'd applied to Cooper for an extended river claim. Cooper rejected it – without adequate consideration, in Gillespie's view. Gillespie tried appealing to Cloete to intervene but his appeal was intercepted by Cooper. Cooper told Gillespie in no uncertain terms that he, Cooper, and he alone, was now dealing with this matter. Gillespie could forget about appealing to the chief commissioner. It would do him no good.

Gillespie was fuming when he came to see Davy. 'Where do I go now?' he asked angrily. 'Who can I appeal to if the chief commissioner can't be involved?'

'There's no appeal in law past a commissioner on a goldfield,' said Davy. 'That's what's wrong with the legislation.'

'That's outrageous!' said Gillespie. 'I've been a pioneer in developing this field. Now you're telling me I've got no rights.'

'About all you can do is petition the government,' said Davy.

'A lot of good that'd do. They're all tied up on the free selection issue. They wouldn't be interested in what's happening on a far-flung goldfield.'

'That's probably true,' said Davy.

'I'm not going to let this pass. I'll write a letter to the *Alpine Pioneer*. I'll tell everyone what's wrong with these stupid regulations. I'll tell them the mistakes the government is making in its administration of the goldfield, and what an ignorant fool this upstart Cooper is.'

'You'd better be careful,' said Davy. 'There's heavy penalties for defamation, you know.'

'I don't care,' said Gillespie.

When Gillespie had written the letter, he showed it to Davy.

Davy advised him against sending it. 'I'm not sure it'll help solve the problem,' he said. 'It may well inflame it.' He suggested a few changes if Gillespie was insistent on proceeding.

Gillespie was resolute about sending the letter. In the end, he agreed to make some changes to the language – to reduce the vitriol. Even so, it was a very strongly worded letter. It appeared in the *Alpine Pioneer* on 12th October 1860.

Mining Matters on Kiandra (To the Editor of the Alpine Pioneer). Sir – I request the favour of insertion for this letter in your journal. I desire to draw attention to the manner in which the miners are restricted by illiberal and injudicious regulations, and the imperfect way in which the same are carried out.

The peculiar character of the country, and the shallowness of the river beds, demand an altogether larger area than is at present allowed for claims. With regard to hill sinking, the difficulty of striking the lead, and the improved and expensive methods which might profitably be employed, should also entitle that class to larger claims than allowed by the present regulations.

Another crying evil connected with the goldfields is the appointment, by the Government, of Commissioners whose incapacity is the subject of general remark among the miners. It must indeed be a source of consolation for the miner of long experience, whose knowledge extends to every phase of mining, to see, year by year, in rapid succession, men appointed to offices of emolument, trust and responsibility over mining matters, whose capacity, compared to his own, would bear no comparison. Who more qualified to adjudicate on mining difficulties, or of bringing them to a proper solution, than one of that body, whose mining experience should qualify him for that position?

Experience seems to be regarded by the Government as of no weight or authority in selecting Commissioners, while in all other pursuits followed by man knowledge is regarded as the principle qualification. Perhaps, in no portion of Australia is greater ignorance shown by officials than in Kiandra. They appear to have been selected by the Government without any test of ability for this situation. Except Mr Cloete and Mr Lockhart – whose removal from the district was at the time, and has ever since been, a source of regret – none of the other Commissioners are able to grapple with the most trivial case that may require their attention.

If ex-members, or men of influence with those in authority, must have their sons and relations in sinecures of the state, let them by all means choose situations in which at least they can do no harm. The Government must have some inkling of the deficiency, as they endeavour to make up in quantity what the officials lack in quality – the term of office of any ministry is of short duration, and it would be well if those now in power watched the interest of that body that is one of the principle producers – in fact the chief pillar of that pedestal on which their eminence rests. It would not be an unpleasing retrospect for them to look back when their offices shall have passed into other hands, and be able to say that 'while we held the sceptre, our appointments were created in justice, having in view the well-being and good government of the people.' J.E.G."

After Davy had read it out to the Second Chance partners, he said, 'What do you think of that!'

'He's asking for trouble,' said Ian. 'Cooper'll be after his blood.'

'I tried to get him to tone it down,' said Davy.

'I love it!' said Brian. 'I can't wait to see the fireworks.'

The letter became a hot topic of conversation on the diggings. Gillespie didn't hide the fact he'd written it. He was more than happy to talk to people about it. He even mentioned he'd discussed writing it with Davy.

Cooper was summoned by the chief commissioner. 'It's most

unfortunate this letter has been published,' said Cloete. 'This kind of controversy undermines the authority and good reputation of our administration. Why is this man so aggrieved? The way this letter's been written singles you out for special mention. It puts you in a most invidious position. '

Cooper had been expecting something like this to happen. 'I'm told it's that radical, Davy Hughes, that's behind it, sir. He had a hand in writing the letter – so Sergeant Ballard said. The sergeant tells me the man's a troublemaker. He says he's stirring up trouble just like he did at Adelong.'

'What's this about Adelong?' said Cloete, frowning.

'Hughes tried to get the miners to take over the diggings at Adelong,' replied Cooper.

'Mm,' said Cloete. 'I never heard of any trouble there. It couldn't have been very serious. I'm not sure I'd trust the word of that sergeant, from what I hear.'

'I don't know, I'm only repeating what I heard,' said Cooper. 'Mr Carmichael also told me the man was a trouble maker.'

'He probably objected to being overcharged,' said Cloete, with a smile.

'What do you mean?'

'It doesn't matter. It was only a joke,' said Cloete, frowning. 'Now let me give you some advice. You're young, and your responsibilities are weighty. Many men on the diggings are very experienced in mining matters. You need to be particularly scrupulous and fair in order to gain their confidence. True authority can only be won, not forced, on a goldfield. Bear that in mind. You may go now.'

Cooper stood silently while the commissioner spoke. He took it as a dressing down, and felt humiliated. He was especially disturbed at the equivocal nature of Cloete's reaction to the information about Davy. Clearly he couldn't rely on Cloete's support against these people.

As he walked down the muddy track to the diggings, away from the commissioner's camp, Cooper swore to himself he wouldn't forget what had been done to him.

12

Off to Nine Mile
November 1860

James felt guilty. He'd only written two short letters to Sally since he returned to Kiandra for the winter. They were both brief, and mentioned mostly the weather.

Sally treasured his letters. She put them in a safe place. On nights when she was feeling lonely, she took them out and reread them to herself. In his letters, James told her she needn't reply. He had no firm address, so he couldn't be sure of receiving correspondence. Sally was disappointed but initially she complied. In October, when she hadn't received word from him for nearly two months, the last of his letters being dated 29th August, she decided to write to him.

Cooma

20th October 1860

Dear James

I hope you don't mind my writing to you and that you receive this letter without difficulty. In your last letter to me you wrote that it was very cold and the snow had been feet deep on the roof of your hut. We have been reading with interest the accounts of the Snowy River goldfield in the Alpine Pioneer which is now regularly delivered to Cooma and which I also read to my family. They all ask about you. Some of the reports make me wonder if all is well with you. There was mention a few weeks past of the robbery of a Frenchman on New Chum Hill, a storekeeper, by two men. As you told me your claim was on this same Hill I imagine this must have happened near to you, if you are still there. Each issue there are reports from the Courts of robberies and drunkenness and fighting such as to make me wonder over the character of society on the goldfields, and whether it is a suitable place to be. But I also read of ballrooms, bands and dancing, wedding cakes, and talented vocalists entertaining so it cannot all be bad!

We find the advertisements in the paper of much interest with numbers of establishments offering accommodation and amusements – billiards, dancing, bowling – an American Bowling Saloon no less – and a Circus even! By the range and variety of goods for sale there must be a bustling township now grown up. You must be very well entertained if you attend all the amusements on offer, though this would no doubt be somewhat costly and not a good thing to do if you were trying to save money. It is hard to imagine what could not be purchased at Kiandra. Doctors and a dentist are advertising too, I hope you have no need of their services. Did you see the American covered wagons? Two passed through here on Thursday last bound for Kiandra on the new road. You would be interested I am sure as the horses, four for each wagon, were said to be the equal of any in the colony, and I know that you would be able to confirm or deny that claim. They were indeed magnificent to watch and I took the children I am now instructing to see them.

One thing I do not understand are the large number of notices offering rewards for horses – stolen or strayed – as much as five pounds if strayed and ten pounds if stolen. People must be very careless with their horses. I have gone on too long so I will finish now. I am thinking of you and would like to hear from you again if you can find the time to write. I am entrusting this letter to a friend of Father's, Mr McCrae, who now has the mail contract to Kiandra, so I can be sure at least it will get to Kiandra.

Your (most) affectionate friend,

Sally

'A pretty lass in Cooma asked me to deliver this to you,' said Mr McCrae, smiling as he handed the letter to James. 'I didn't realise it'd be so easy.'

James had dropped by the mail room on the off chance of seeing Kitty. She was sitting at a table sorting letters. As her father spoke, she looked up briefly. James felt himself blushing. Kitty didn't say anything. She looked down again and busied herself sorting, but James noticed she was smiling.

Embarrassed, he said thank you to Mr McCrae and quickly found an excuse to be moving on.

Later, when he read Sally's letter at his hut, he had mixed emotions. He still liked Sally, perhaps he even loved her. He certainly didn't want to do anything to hurt her. He could see her face as he read the words, and her pretty smile. But she wasn't here, and Kitty was. He put the letter aside.

For the next two weeks, he struggled with his attraction for Kitty. During that time, Davy and Kitty were seeing a lot of each other. James decided he had to get a hold of himself. He had to stop this silly business of thinking about her all the time and trying to see her. It was unhealthy, and it was demeaning. It would be better if he didn't try to see her at all. If he met her by chance, he'd still be friendly, of course. But he had to stop seeking her out. In fact, he would try to avoid meeting her. Having taken this decision, he sat down and wrote to Sally.

Kiandra

6th November 1860

Dear Sally

I do apologise for being such a poor correspondent. I have no real excuse and will not try to make one up. I hope you will forgive me. I do think of you too.

Life on the diggings is not as exciting as you suggest. Certainly there are a lot of persons trying to interest diggers and others in parting with their hard won earnings. I am not in the habit of attending the various dances, functions and other amusements as these are mostly patronised by those who have spent a deal of preparation in a public house.

The big rush expected by the storekeepers after winter has not now come to pass and many are trying to recover their investments from the working population. You may think I sound cynical but at times there are almost as many persons hoping to make a living out of the diggers as there are diggers on the field. Some come, take a look and leave – now that it requires hard work to get down to the hidden treasures. The weather is also a shock to many, with snow and frost even in the spring and summer.

Without the discovery of a gold bearing reef, which has yet to be located if it exists at all, the future is not assured for this field. That is why the storekeepers are taking up subscriptions for tunnelling parties, here and at Nine Mile. They have as much if not more at stake as the diggers. Diggers are always rushing to new places where they believe El Dorado may be found. It is in the nature of being a digger. There is much excitement amongst the mining population now about Lambing Flat while closer at hand there is the talk of a rush to Crack-em-back, which some say could be another Kiandra. It is often wise to wait for better particulars as early reports can be exaggerated.

The robbery of the Joe the Frenchman happened next to us. We think we know the parties who did it. There are some very bad characters at the diggings, but you need not worry about us as we keep clear of them and can look after ourselves.

Yes I did see the American covered wagons when they arrived, and yes the horses were equal to any we have here. The notices about lost or strayed horses are due to the large number of thefts of these animals. There are a number of parties that make their living in this way. It is strange that so few cases reach the courts. Either the police are powerless to act or they must have an understanding with the parties involved (I believe it is often the latter). If your horse is stolen you only have to place an advertisement like the ones you have seen and a man will quickly 'find it' for you.

Even here the defeat of the Ministry on the Land Bill has caused great agitation and there is much talk of it and the impending election. Chas Cowper is standing for Parliament for Tumut on the position of Free Selection and is taking every opportunity to make his voice known, not that he needs any assistance. The proprietor of the Alpine Pioneer, Thomas Garrett is of similar views as you will be left in no doubt. It is said that he will stand for Monaro so you may hear more of him. Although I support the measure I am heartily sick of it as a main topic of discussion. One of my partners is a strong advocate – John who wants to select land and settle with his girl.

I am not certain when I will be able to find time to visit Cooma again, hopefully at Christmas. I will try to write more frequently.

Your (also most) affectionate friend

James

When he'd finished copying it out, he reread it to himself to check for mistakes. He got John to post it so he could avoid seeing Kitty.

Despite the lower than expected number of new arrivals, hotels continued to be extended and more and varied wares and services were offered. Luke Reilly contracted J. Small, the renowned Irish comedian and vocalist, for an extended season to entertain his clientele at the Union Hotel. William Kidd opened a California bakery. No sooner had Luke Bond opened the Royal George Hotel than he announced plans to extend it. It was to be the biggest in Kiandra, even larger than John Carmichael's Empire Hotel, including its ballroom.

Plenty of gold was still being found, even without the discovery of the elusive reef. More thorough working of the ground and an increased use of sluicing were providing good returns for experienced miners. Four Mile and Nine Mile diggings were now established outposts, with their own stores and hotels and settled parties of miners. The main difficulty for both those diggings, particularly Four Mile, was the lack of water. This was due to their higher elevation. In winter, it wasn't such a problem. Then, their drawback was an excess of snow.

*

When Jack moved to Four Mile, he pitched his camp at the edge of the tree line, just above the waterfall. He fortified his tent with sod walls and hung his Eureka flag on a pole at the front. There, away from the main crowds he was left in peace. That was the way he liked it. All he needed was within a short walk. There was adequate water for mining and personal needs, there was more than enough timber behind him on the ridge, and provisions were available at the local stores.

He had no difficulty in staking out a claim near the creek. The early excitement had died down. There were still plenty of returns to be made but they were steady rather than spectacular. Now, there were only serious mining parties at this outpost. His nearest neighbours were Klaus and his two partners. This German party had set about their task with a thoroughness you might expect. They had constructed a puddling machine on their claim and brought in a draught horse to operate its boom.

Puddling machines made use of a horse-drawn boom to swirl material around in a circular pond, thereby removing the clay and dirt, and enabling large quantities of wash dirt to be worked. The concentrated material was then collected for further processing. It was an efficient way of working the initial part of the mining process. Klaus and his partners were being well repaid for their effort. Two other parties had copied the Germans, so there were three of the machines in operation when Jack arrived.

By the time James and Ian came to visit him, Jack was well settled. They were on their way to Nine Mile, to investigate prospects. The track from Kiandra to Nine Mile passed close by Jack's claim after crossing Four Mile Creek. They brought Jack the latest news.

'The Pollocks are back,' said James. 'They're reopening their store with a new consignment from Sydney.

'Nine Mile's all the go,' said Ian. 'There's lots happening up there, we've been told. We're going to have a look. There's a rush to the Tumut River too.'

'There's reports of gold all over the place,' said James. 'But you never know till you go there. And even then you can't be sure. Some's even been found at Lob's Hole – and there's crowds been going through there for nigh on a year.'

'Wouldn't have anything to do with the new hotel what's been built there, I wonder?' said Ian wryly.

'There's another new doctor in town,' said James. 'Dr Biermann – late physician and surgeon in the Hanoverian army. I guess he'll do all right. There's a fair few Germans on the field.'

'You're next to some here, aren't you?' said Ian. 'One was found drowned in the Tumut River the other day. Scully found the body.'

'There's a German party prospecting for a reef at Three Mile, up the Snowy River,' added James. 'They say the prospects are good. Remember Luke Bond's wife and how she'd carry on?'

Jack nodded.

'There was a terrible to do the other day. It's the talk of the town. All the details were in the paper last week. It ended in court with her charging Campbell with assault.'

'What happened?' asked Jack.

'Campbell said she and Luke owed him money – for taking over the hotel – so Campbell told her to leave,' said James. 'When she wouldn't, he and his mates tried to throw her out. They jumped over the bar. She said they grabbed her by the hair. She wouldn't go.'

'I'll bet she squealed something loud,' said Ian. 'She ain't a quiet one at the best of times.'

'How'd it end?' asked Jack.

'Some of Luke's mates stopped her being thrown out till Luke arrived,' said James. 'In the end, the magistrate found for Mrs Bond and fined Campbell, Hay and O'Connor three pounds each.'

'Would've been worth every penny of it,' said Ian.

'There's lots of Chinese leaving for Lambing Flat,' said James. 'But that still leaves hundreds of them down by the river.'

'Wash dirt keeps going missing,' said Ian. 'It's a bit quieter here, so I s'pose it wouldn't be such a problem. The Chinese are always blamed. I reckon that's just a cover.'

Ian and James were impressed with what they saw at the Nine Mile diggings. On their return, they convinced John it was time to try their luck there. Brian didn't want to move. He'd become involved with race construction works for a number of parties at New Chum Hill, where he was putting his race engineering ideas into practice. The partners held a meeting. They decided to sell their claim but keep the hut. Davy and Brian would stay in it.

Their departure for Nine Mile was delayed by a late fall of snow as a cold southerly swept in. It deposited so much snow that a large public house in course of erection at Four Mile collapsed in the night. Ian said he wasn't surprised. He knew the builder and had a poor opinion of his ability. The *Sydney Morning Herald* made much of the event, mentioning also that several horses died during the night and commenting that it could be November in England. Tell your friends in Sydney, the correspondent wrote, how truly jolly we are, for I feel they must envy the delightful advantages this place possesses over Sydney in the summer season for in place of having to pay for ice creams we can amuse ourselves with snowballs and brandy hot.

John borrowed a packhorse to carry their store tent to Nine Mile. In the end they didn't need it. Numbers of diggers were leaving for Lambing Flat. They were able to purchase a substantially fortified hut, with sod walls and a central fireplace, from a party in a hurry to leave. Ian had a flair for bargaining and obtained it for a low price. They planned on making this their base while they investigated the best place to stake a claim, and did a bit of prospecting in the district. The Second Chance claim sold for a good price so they had cash enough to see them through for the next few months.

James wrote to Sally soon after they arrived at Nine Mile.

Nine Mile Diggings
24th November 1860

Dear Sally

You will see by the address that I have now moved to the Nine Mile. John and Ian are with me. We are well set up with sturdy accommodation and there is plenty of timber for firewood. Even in summer it can be bitterly cold here on the top of the mountains, especially when the wind blows as it seems to do every day.

Nine Mile is a busy place with plenty of stores and hotels to supply the diggings here and on the Tumut River, which is the cause of much current excitement, but yet to be proven. Donald McGilvray has just opened the Caledonian Hotel, the third hotel at this place, which does seem more than enough. The Caledonian has a ballroom, or so the owner calls it that, with dancing nightly at seven o'clock. We already have Croy's Star, which also has a 'ballroom', with a brass band performing nightly at seven o'clock. I think the plan with the construction of so many ballrooms at these diggings is not so much to meet a need, but to hope a need will arise if one is constructed. I haven't seen too many women among the patrons as there are few up here, although there is a party from Maitland at Four Mile who have a girl as a partner. She is as good a worker as any of the men.

We will see how it pans out (a goldfields term!) in this district before trying our luck at Crack-em-back if reports from that locality are still favourable in the New Year. I hope to visit Cooma before then but cannot tell you the time since this will depend on our success or otherwise. It would be best if you do not try to write to me as I cannot be sure of receiving mail now I am away from the township. I will write again as soon as my plans are more settled.

Your affectionate friend

James

On his way back from Kiandra after posting the letter, James paid Jack a visit. He found him knee-deep in the creek trying to repair his water channel. James gave him a hand. When the job was done, Jack boiled a billy and they sat in front of the campfire.

'You know that river claim opposite Black Nat's,' said James, waving the wood smoke away. 'It's for sale for sixty pounds, including the water pump.'

Jack looked surprised and nodded.

'And Cooper, the manager of the Bank of New South Wales,' said James. 'You'd remember him. He got called back to Sydney at short notice. They organised a big farewell dinner for him but he didn't attend. It went ahead anyway. I reckon something fishy's happened. He gave out some big loans, I heard.'

James lit his pipe and drew a few puffs. Jack lit his own. He looked like a little gnome, with his battered hat and bushy beard, as he hunched over his pipe, with his elbows on his knees.

'Did you hear about Dawes and Sergeant Ballard?' said James. 'You'd remember Dawes – that old ticket of leave man from down the river?'

'No,' said Jack. 'What happened?'

'He got beaten by Sergeant Ballard the other day and came to Davy for help. Davy helped him file a charge of assault against the sergeant. The paper here's got all the details. Here, I'll read it to you,' said James, unfolding the paper. '"Court of Petty Sessions, Kiandra, November 23 1860. James Dawes v. Sergeant Ballard, for assault.

'"Dawes said that on Wednesday week, while standing at the bar of Luke Bond's public house, the defendant came in with Mr Mollarde. I was talking to Mr Bond when Ballard knocked another rather roughly against me; on my turning round, and making enquiry as to the meaning of it, Ballard threatened to put me out. He caught hold of me, and struck me repeatedly with a whip. He laid hold of me by the neck and tried to throttle me, and in the scuffle we both fell to the ground. While on the floor he tried to grasp something behind his back. I put my hand in the same direction, and felt as I imagined a revolver. I could not swear it was a revolver. While I was outside he struck me again, but not with his hand.

'"Cross examined by the defendant: I was a ticket of leave man for the district of Goulburn, and was once taken in charge by you. I did not attempt to snatch the revolver from your pouch.

'"Luke Bond, publican: I remember last Wednesday night week. I was talking to the defendant at the bar when the plaintiff came up and interrupted the conversation, when Ballard told him to mind his own business or something to that effect. I did not see Ballard strike the plaintiff, or take him by the neck any more than the plaintiff did to the defendant. Had Ballard struck him with the whip as he says I must have seen it, and I think it would have left some marks on the plaintiff. I am aware that the defendant is a police officer."

'Apparently, Dawes didn't know the sergeant and Bond were mates.'

'How'd it end?'

'How you'd expect,' said James. 'The charge was dismissed. Davy said Dawes got a big surprise when he heard Bond's evidence. The silly old beggar thought Bond would support him. The idiot! That's why he hadn't arranged witnesses. Davy blames himself. He says Dawes only got beaten 'cause Ballard knew we'd been friends with him.'

'That dirty rat Ballard!' said Jack. He spat into the fire.

James relit his pipe. 'Shows you can't trust the courts if you want justice,' he said. 'Maybe Davy's right. Maybe we do need to change things.'

He puffed on his pipe and thought some more. 'Might've been

different if Redman had taken the case,' he said. 'He's too busy trying to get himself elected to parliament. He's standing for Queanbeyan on the free selection issue. That's three of them from these goldfields what's looking to get elected – Cowper, Garrett and now Redman – all free selection supporters. But who isn't these days?'

James looked around at the diggings, with its scattered untidy piles of rocky tailings and uprooted vegetation. The clouds skimmed low over the trees on the ridge, the wind was up and there was the smell of rain in the air.

'Do you really think they care about us here?' he said, talking to himself as much as Jack. 'I know free selection's a good cause, but I can't help thinking these men have more interest in putting themselves forward, and being self-important, than trying to represent the interests of you and me.'

Jack nodded. 'They're all mongrels,' he said. 'All gov'ments are mongrels.' He spat into the fire again.

'Best I make a move before the rain sets in,' said James, looking at the clouds. He said goodbye to Jack, swung his swag over his shoulder and set off for Nine Mile.

He managed to beat the worst of the rain. It set in heavily just before he reached his tent. John and Ian were sitting in front of the fire, having knocked off for the day.

James unpacked his swag and took out the copy of the *Alpine Pioneer*. 'I've brought the paper,' he said. 'It's got all the facts about Crack-em-back.'

'Read it to us,' said Ian. 'Before it gets dark.'

The rain was drumming on the canvas roof and threatening to put out the fire.

'We'd better stoke that up first,' he added.

John sat smoking his pipe while Ian fixed the fire and James read the article. "'Kiandra, Tuesday November 27, 1860. The rush to Crack-em-back has fairly commenced. Within the last few days numbers have left here, and many are preparing to follow. There are many reports in circulation with reference to the population there now, and the amount of gold being obtained; but as yet we are not able to trace them to any reliable sources. As usual at all rushes great excitement prevails amongst all classes, but with miners in particular. Many to our knowledge earning from eight pounds to twelve pounds per week, have sold off and gone there; others are putting on as many hired men as they possibly can for the purpose of working out quickly and following the rush. There seems to be a mania at the present, and yet nothing is known as to the extent of ground to be worked or the gold obtained, farther than the prospectors have stated, and, until some reliable information is received we would advise all miners to look before they leap. That it may be a rich and extensive Goldfield is very probable, but, for men who at present are in good claims to sacrifice them for the purpose of going there is sheer madness. Let them wait patiently for a few days until such information as can be relied on is received, and then they can better judge whether to go or to remain."

'That's the editorial. There's more under Latest Information,' said James. 'It says there's only forty on the field and the only party at work is Grice's. The distance from Kiandra is sixty-two miles. The road is very bad but well marked. Mr Garrett is leaving for Crack-em-back today and there'll be a full report in Friday's paper.'

'We'd do well to wait,' said John. 'Sounds like it's mostly profiting the storekeepers at present.'

'You're right,' said James. 'They're all jumping on the bandwagon. There's big notices from Benjamin and Joseph saying they'll be opening stores at Crack-em-back soon. There's one from Tresse saying he'll be delivering goods there on Thursday.'

'Bet they'll cost,' said John.

'There's also great complaints being made, it says, about the tardiness of the commissioner not sending over police and not having proclaimed it as a goldfield, so that spirits can be sold,' added James.

'Who writes this stuff?' said John. 'That's just a whinge from a publican missing out on making money. Bet there's no shortage of sly grog for the ones that want it.'

'I reckon the jury's still out on Crack-em-back,' said Ian, looking serious. 'Like the paper says, there's plenty of parties leaving perfectly good claims at Nine and Four Mile to go there. I was talking to one what's come back. He said it was just like any other rush. Some got lucky early but most haven't found anything much. You never know, it could be a schicer.'

'That's done then,' said John. 'We'll stay put till there's better particulars. I'd hate to go to a schicer.' He grinned. 'We'd never live it down from Ian!'

*

Sally opened the *Sydney Mail*. There was a long article on Kiandra, headed 'A Summer's Day Ramble Through Kiandra'. It was written in a humorous manner and started,

> Reader, have you a great-coat, a good muffler, and a pair of thigh boots? If you have, and feel disposed to enjoy a good walk on a summer's day about Kiandra, just arrange your fixings and come with me.

Sally was amused by the article, which went into great detail about the wet, muddy and freezing conditions in the half-built township. But she suspected the author may have stretched the truth for effect. If conditions were so hard for the storekeepers, how much harder must it be for the miners, she thought.

The weather in Cooma had been quite different. It had been overcast, but that had not stopped her taking her pupils for their nature study walks down by the creek.

Reading the article reminded her she hadn't received a letter from James for quite some time. She wished he'd write more frequently.

13

Christmas at the Diggings
December 1860

Sally received James's letter of 24th November at the end of the first week in December. She ignored his advice not to reply.

Cooma

8th December 1860

Dear James

I hope you receive this letter in time, and that you forgive me for my boldness, the cause of which you will know when you have read what follows.

I have made arrangements to visit Kiandra at Christmas. I will be accompanying Father, who has business in Kiandra, as he is now in partnership with a supplier of materials to a number of the blacksmiths working in Kiandra and the surrounding district.

We will be staying with Mr McCrae, who I believe I told you earlier is a friend of Father's, and his daughter Kitty. I am informed they have comfortable quarters at Rocky Plains on the road to Kiandra. Have you met Kitty? She is an attractive girl and I am sure I would be jealous if you were to like her. I know you must have met Mr McCrae as he has delivered my earlier letters.

We plan on arriving in the week before Christmas and leaving in the week after, Father's business commitments permitting. I hope you will be able to find time to see me and perhaps to show me something of gold mining and its methods. Kitty tells me it is most interesting to watch how the material is obtained and that it is not as simple as many of us at a distance might assume.

Now that Kiandra is a settled township I am sure it must be a more suitable place for a woman than your earlier information suggested.

Father certainly thinks so, as he was not previously willing to allow me to visit with him. From Kitty's account a number of respectable women now inhabit the township, although she also told me there are some women of ill repute and bad habits, as it would not be surprising to find on a goldfield.

I do hope you are able to spare the time to provide me with company for some of my stay in Kiandra. I am sorry for the short notice as the opportunity of accompanying Father only arose after Mr McCrae made a kind offer to accommodate us when he and Kitty recently visited.

Your (still very) affectionate friend

Sally

Sally wasn't entirely honest about how she came to be visiting Kiandra. When Mr McCrae and Kitty visited the McNeills in Cooma, it was Sally who raised the possibility of a return visit. She asked Kitty if the McCraes would have room at Rocky Plains to accommodate her and her father. Kitty said she thought they would. Mr McNeill only agreed after persistent pestering from Sally. It was against his better judgement, as he still had reservations about taking his daughter to the diggings. In the end, he gave in with a sigh, noting that she usually did get her way. He found it hard to resist his strong-willed daughter.

Sally was unapologetic about pressing to see James. It was all very well for women to wait for men to make arrangements. But sometimes a girl had to take the initiative, or nothing would happen. If James didn't want to see her, then that was all very well. It would bring the matter to a conclusion.

*

James met Davy at their old New Chum Hill hut with the documents to finalise the sale of the Second Chance claim.

'Looks like we'll be entertaining the women over Christmas,' said Davy, after the purchasers had left.

'What's that?' queried James.

'Haven't you heard? Your Sally's coming to stay with Kitty over Christmas,' said Davy. 'Didn't you get her letter?'

'No,' said James, puzzled.

'You'd better go and see Old Man McCrae. He'll have it for you,' said Davy. 'The girls have cooked it up between them. Kitty's been at me about going to the Boxing Day sports too.'

'What sports?' asked James, now even more puzzled.

'Haven't you seen Friday's paper?' said Davy. 'Benjamin's got a big notice in it. Here, have a read.' Davy threw James a copy of the *Alpine Pioneer*. It was open at the page.

Boxing Day. Boxing Day

SPORT SPORT SPORT

B BENJAMIN

Kiandra Hotel

Being desirous of affording to the inhabitants of Kiandra

some amusement on the above day, has determined

to offer the following prizes for competition.

Foot Race

100 yards; heats. Prize 8 pounds.

Climbing a Greasy Pole.

Prize – New Cabbage Tree Hat, and 2 pounds.

Jumping in Sacks.

Prize 2 pounds

Wrestling.

Prize 4 pounds

And several other prizes for the usual out-doors amusements.

A Band will be in attendance during the day.

Dinner will be provided FREE

GRAND BALL IN THE EVENING

God Save the Queen

'Look on the next page,' said Davy. 'See the notice from Turner and Quail. It's next to Benjamin's one about the new rush to Thredbo and Crack-em-back.'

James read that too.

BOXING DAY!!!
Camp Town
Sports for Christmas!
Messrs Turner and Quail
Give notice that they intend giving the following prizes for Sports &c.
Climbing a Greasy Pole.
Prize – Cabbage Tree Hat and 2 pounds.
Running, Foot, Wheelbarrow & Blindfolded Races.
Prize 2 pounds each.
Jumping in Sacks.
Race between two Women,
For 5 pounds, 100 yards.

'Who are the women in the race?' asked James, shaking his head in surprise.

'I don't know,' said Davy. 'That's what Kitty asked too. I told her the sports mightn't be a suitable place for women. She said she'd like to go. She said it'd be a lark, and that if two women could race in sacks she'd like to go and see it. She also wants to go to the ball at Benjamin's.'

'Does Sally know about all this?' asked James.

'I don't know,' said Davy. 'You'd better read her letter. Kitty says she'll be arriving next week.'

John and Ian were more than agreeable for James to have time off with Sally at Christmas. They suggested he move back to the old hut with Davy and Brian for the duration of her visit.

Brian had just settled a major contract for race construction. 'Maxwell and Hawkins have bought the Homeward Bound Claim next to us,' he said. 'You met Maxwell. He's the old bloke with the white hair – the one with the walking stick. He'd injured his foot or something. Remember him?'

'Yes, I do now,' said James.

'He brought Sam Hawkins round to see me, one of his partners, and we talked about water races and such like.'

'You didn't encourage them, I suppose?' said James with a grin.

Brian ignored the jibe. 'Sam's new on these diggings. He's an

Englishman, though I won't hold that against him. He's done a fair bit of mining elsewhere and he certainly knows the business. He and Maxwell have great plans for the Homeward Bound claim. They want to bring water to the top of the claim so they can use it to sluice the slope. You know, that promising one above the rocks. They've already applied to Cloete and he's given them permission.'

'How will they get the water there?' asked James.

'It'll have to come in a race round the side of the hill,' said Brian. 'I reckon something like nine miles or so of race'll need constructing. It'll take some doing. Anyway, they've given me the contract for the works. It's worth nearly two thousand pounds.'

'What!' said James. 'Did I hear right? Two thousand pounds?'

'That's right,' said Brian. 'That's the total, of course. I won't be getting that much. There's bullocks to hire, and some places we'll need to blast the rock. It'll take months to build.'

'Sounds like an old scheme of yours to me,' said James laughing. 'You sure you didn't give them the idea? You'll have fun, though.'

'I sure will,' said Brian. 'So long as they pay me. Seems like they've got plenty of cash, though. They never blinked at paying for all that sluicing gear from French Joe's claim. Gave him the price he wanted without a quibble.'

Brian tipped the dregs of his tea onto the ground. 'Too many leaves,' he said. 'Didn't you lose your horse a while back?'

'I don't want to talk about it,' said James.

'It was a bay, wasn't it? There's been some mentioned in the *Pioneer* lately. There's a notice about one they've found running with the mail horses at Bredbo. There's also a notice about a bay that's running with some man's horses at the top of Talbingo Hill. You might want to check them out. You never know.' Brian laughed.

James didn't. The loss of his horse was still a sore point. Brian didn't mind taking the rise out of James occasionally. He thought James took life a bit too seriously.

*

James was waiting to meet Sally when she arrived in Kiandra. Kitty was there too. The coach was a basic affair, not much more than a covered spring cart. James helped Sally step down onto the planks in front of the mail room. He thought she looked pretty and radiant despite her windblown hair.

'Hello, there, young fella,' said Mr McNeill as he jumped down after Sally. He seized James's hand and gave it a bone-crunching squeeze. 'I've got to make arrangements,' he said. 'I'll leave Sal in your care. I'm sure she'll be right with you and Kitty, won't you, little Sal?'

'Of course I will,' said Sally, in a mildly annoyed tone.

Kitty watched the exchange with a smile.

James looked at Sally and Kitty as they stood beside the coach. Seeing them together for the first time invited comparison. They were both very attractive girls. Kitty was beautiful. Sally was pretty in a more homely way. He watched as they spoke to each other. He was fascinated by the way they moved, their little gestures and the way they smiled.

'What have you arranged for us?' asked Sally, interrupting his train of thought.

He was momentarily caught off guard. Sally noticed. She had been watching the way he looked at Kitty.

'We'll meet Davy down at the horse tailing yards,' said James. 'We've arranged to hire horses for all of us over Christmas.'

'What a good idea,' said Kitty. 'Davy never told me.'

'Have you done much riding?' Sally asked Kitty. 'I'm not terribly good myself.'

'Father taught me when I was little. I used to live on horses when we were at Uncle's farm. Uncle breeds them. That's what I miss here, not having a horse of my own. Mail horses aren't the same.'

'Sally's not such a bad rider herself,' said James. 'Despite what she says.' He sensed a need to get himself back into Sally's good books.

Davy met them at the tailing yards. Sally was immediately struck by his dark good looks. Despite that, she immediately knew he wasn't her type. Kitty need have no worry there, she thought. As he greeted her politely, she noticed the slight trace of an English accent. The way Kitty looked up at him made her feel more comfortable about herself and James.

It was lunchtime by the time the hire arrangements for the horses had been settled. They ate at Benjamin's Hotel, after leaving their horses in the care of the stable hand at the rear of the hotel. It was a service the hotel offered its customers.

As they left the dining room after their meal, they met Maggie as she walked into the hotel, leaning on the arm of a well-dressed gentleman.

'My, my,' said Maggie, disengaging herself from the man and stepping towards them. 'If it isn't James. Fancy meeting you here.' Under her powdered face, her cheeks were flushed, and she spoke with an exaggerated emphasis. 'And if it isn't Sally! It's been so long, *so* long. My goodness, you do look different!' Then she noticed Davy and Kitty, who were standing behind James. 'And who is this handsome man? Tell me, James, where have you been hiding him?'

James was embarrassed. He didn't know what to do. He was nervous at what Maggie might say next.

'Aren't you going to tell me, you naughty boy?' said Maggie. 'Well, I'll tell you who *my* friend is. Come here, Stephen,' she said, turning to the gentleman beside her. 'This is Stephen, Stephen Saunders. Mr Saunders has just arrived from Sydney. Stephen's such a nice man, aren't you, Stephen?'

The gentleman looked sheepish.

'I can call you Stephen, can't I?' said Maggie.

Saunders took a step forward and bowed stiffly towards James.

Maggie swayed unsteadily but caught herself. 'These are my friends – from Cooma,' she said. 'At least, James is. Sally too. The others I don't know. Now, do tell me your names.'

Davy was always polite. 'I'm David Hughes, and this is Kitty McCrae.'

'Haven't I seen you before?' asked Maggie, moving close to Davy.

James watched Kitty's expression as Maggie approached him. He hadn't seen her eyes flash like that before. 'We'd best be going,' he said, coming to the rescue. 'We have an appointment to keep. It was nice meeting you.'

'Do you really have to go?' said Maggie, petulantly. 'It's only early. Why don't you join us? I'm sure Stephen wouldn't mind, would you?'

'No, we really must go,' said James. He was almost certain Stephen *would* mind.

'Your appointment can wait,' said Maggie. 'It can't be that important. Come and join us for a drink.'

'No, I'm afraid we must go,' said James. 'It was nice to meet you, Mr Saunders.' He ushered his friends to the door. 'Nice to see you again, Maggie.'

Once outside, he felt a sense of relief. They were at the front of the hotel. Their horses were in the stables at the back.

'Let's get those horses quickly,' he said, 'and get out of here.'

'Thanks for the rescue,' said Davy.

'Who *was* that woman?' asked Kitty, frowning.

'That's Maggie,' said Sally. 'She wasn't always like that. How she's changed. Did you see how she'd painted her face? She looks like a common tart now.'

'Bit early to be under the weather,' said Davy. 'Imagine what she'll be like by evening. It's a shame to see a pretty girl like her going that way.'

'You found her attractive, did you?' said Kitty, raising her eyebrows.

'Not really. Not when she's like that,' said Davy.

'So she's pretty when she's sober?' asked Sally. 'Is that what you think too, James?'

'Come on, girls,' said Davy. 'You know what we mean. We feel sorry for her, don't we. James? But we're not about to have anything to do with her.'

James shook his head. 'No way,' he said. And he really meant it.

'We've already got the most attractive girls on the goldfield,' said Davy, smiling coyly. 'Now let that be the end of it.'

For the moment it was. Davy and James took the girls on a ride. It was a guided tour of the goldfield – to show Sally the main areas of the diggings. Starting from The Broadway, they rode across Surface Hill and Whipstick Gully, past the ground sluicing claims – explaining the way the water races worked – down to the river claims with their dams, water wheels, diversion channels and flumes (raised water races) – then on to the Chinese camp. Sally was impressed by the extensive trestlework that supported the flumes.

From the Chinese camp, they followed a miner's track beside the river to Jackass Flat and New Chum Hill. At New Chum Hill, after inspecting the work of one of the tunnelling parties, they stopped at the Second Chance claim to show Sally their hut. Brian was in residence, so they boiled a billy for afternoon tea.

'I had no idea it'd be so messy,' said Sally. 'Everything's been dug up, all the hills, even the river. There's so many dams and channels. There's water everywhere. It must get awfully muddy when it rains.'

'It sure as hell does,' said Brian.

'I still can't get over how people live in the middle of all this – in all those tents and huts we saw,' said Sally. 'Most of them aren't even proper buildings – no wonder there's not many women here. I don't know how they could survive the winter.'

'Some didn't,' said James. 'Some were found frozen in the snow.'

'But not many,' said Davy. 'And mostly on account of too much drink.'

'More died of influenza,' said Brian. 'It came from the diggings in Victoria, remember.'

'That's true,' said James.

After hot mugs of tea all round, the men showed the girls how to cradle and pan for gold. Sally and Kitty both got some colour in the dish. This made for great excitement. Kitty jumped up and down when she found hers. Sally so forgot her inhibitions she gave James a big hug, even though she'd been splashed with mud and water. Kitty wasn't any cleaner.

'What'll we tell your fathers?' said Davy. 'They'll think we've been dousing you in the creek.'

'Just tell them we're miners now,' said Sally, laughing.

It was strangely exciting for James, the thought of these two pretty girls as miners.

Neither Mr McCrae nor Mr McNeill seemed too concerned about the condition of their daughters when the girls rejoined them that afternoon.

'Make sure you look after those horses,' shouted James, as the girls cantered off towards Rocky Plains behind their fathers.

The McCraes' hut at Rocky Plains was well away from the main diggings. He'd chosen this location as it was safer, and it gave him room to yard his horses when they weren't on the mail run. His intention was for Mrs McCrae and their younger children to join him when he was properly established. Kitty insisted on coming with him, promising to help him with the mail and with the housekeeping. He was glad she did, as she was a hard worker and a great help.

Sally got to know Kitty over the next few days. Kitty was down to earth, and not at all standoffish. She had a good sense of humour, often at her own expense, and she never tried to trade on her good looks, as sometimes is the case with pretty girls. Sally liked her.

Davy and James met the girls each day and took them riding.

Sally could see that James found Kitty attractive. She didn't blame Kitty, as Kitty did nothing to encourage him. It was something she'd have to live with, she decided. Because of Kitty's devotion to Davy, it worried her less. When Kitty was with Davy, he was like a magnet to her. She watched his every move and hung on every word he said.

It was clear that Davy liked Kitty too, but he was more reticent. He often had other things on his mind. He'd talk about the injustices on the diggings and what was needed to be done to fix them, about the need for democracy, and how it might be achieved. On these subjects, he was passionate.

Although Kitty was still attentive when he spoke on such matters, Sally sensed she didn't have the same commitment to these causes as did Davy. 'Don't you find all that talk about politics boring?' she asked Kitty as they were preparing dinner.

'I don't mind it,' said Kitty. 'It's good that Davy believes in a cause.'

'James says it'll get him into trouble,' said Sally.

'It does worry me sometimes,' said Kitty. 'I'd hate for anything to happen to him. He's only trying to help people. He means well.'

'What do you think of James?'

'James?' said Kitty. 'Oh, James is nice. I like him. He's a good friend to Davy, isn't he?'

The reply satisfied Sally.

*

Davy and James spent an overcast and windy Christmas Day with the McCraes and the McNeills at Rocky Plains. Kitty and Sally put on a splendid meal.

When it had been accounted for, Kitty's father brought out the whisky. 'We'll just have a wee dram for the occasion,' he said, offering a glass to Sally's father.

Kitty asked for a taste. Mr McCrae wouldn't agree at first. After he and Mr McNeill had drunk a few more tots, he mellowed and let 'the young folks' have a 'wee drink'.

Kitty had first taste. She grimaced as she drank it but with her usual pluck kept going till it was all finished. Sally was next. She hadn't tasted whisky before. Her reaction was a treat to watch. The others had a good laugh. She drank everything in her glass too. She wasn't about to be shown up by Kitty. James and Davy sipped theirs without incident. Neither were especially partial to whisky, but it would have been rude to refuse an offer from Mr McCrae.

Boxing Day started late for most on the diggings. By lunchtime, the crowds had started gathering. They milled round the Kiandra Hotel in readiness for Benjamin's competitions. Others congregated in Camp Town, where Turner and Quail were making arrangements for their sports. The principal preparation undertaken by intending competitors appeared to involve liquid refreshment in the form of nobblers. By afternoon, when the band was in full swing and the competitions were scheduled to start, the crowds were boisterous.

Davy, James and the girls had an early lunch before setting off to ride into town. They could hear the noise of the revellers even before they reached the river crossing, as it drifted over the hill past the commissioner's camp. From a distance, the occasional iron roof glinted in the sun amongst the collection of timber and shingle clad buildings. Telegraph Street was more crowded than James could remember seeing it even in the big autumn rush. Wagons of all sorts – buggies, spring carts and drays of various descriptions – choked the street on both sides. Hitching rails were crowded with horses. Everywhere there were throngs of people. Hats and clothes were all colours, types and descriptions.

'Looks like every man and his dog's come to town,' said Davy.

'And his woman,' added James.

'We'd be stupid to leave our horses unattended,' said Davy.

James agreed. He'd already recognised some faces in the crowd who had form in relation to horse thieving. They decided it was best to leave their mounts at the tailing yards. James settled it with the groom before they walked the short distance to Camp Town.

The heats of the greasy pole competition were in progress when they arrived. These were being personally overseen by Turner, who was there to present the prizes. There was much amusement as well primed diggers had a go, egged on by their mates. The scene threatened to turn nasty as they watched. A drunken digger accused the organisers of over-greasing the pole. When someone suggested he might be a poor loser, he took it as a personal insult and wanted to fight all comers.

As an uneasy peace was being restored, James saw Alex in the distance. 'Isn't that your brother?' he said to Davy. 'I thought he'd gone to Lambing Flat.'

Davy looked across to where James was pointing. 'Yes, that's him.'

'You've never told me much about your brother,' said Kitty. 'You must introduce me. Why don't you talk about him?'

'It's a long story,' said Davy. 'I'll tell you one day.'

Kitty sensed his reluctance so she didn't press him further.

Alex looked in their direction and recognised them. He weaved his way through the crowd to where they were standing. 'G'day, gents,' he said. 'That's a fine lot of sheilas you've got with yer.'

From the roughness of his greeting Kitty immediately understood Davy's earlier reticence. It was obvious the drink in his hand hadn't been his first.

'I heard you'd gone to Lambing Flat,' said Davy in a less than friendly tone.

'Been and gone,' said Alex.

The way he looked at Sally made her feel uneasy. He was swaying on his feet.

'So what's your plans now?' asked Davy.

'Plans? Who needs plans?' said Alex. 'Ter 'ave a good time.' He raised his drink. His presence put a stop to the conversation.

For the next few minutes, they watched the action at the greasy pole.

'I'm off to Lambing Flat when this is done,' said Alex. After a few minutes more, he said, 'Best be getting on. You lot, you're about as much fun as a bag of spiders.'

James watched as he stumbled off. He saw him join Sweeney before they both disappeared into the crowd. He'd heard Sweeney was at Lambing Flat too. No doubt the pair of them had been up to no good. The sooner they both left Kiandra for good, the better.

Alex's visit only temporarily dampened things. Kitty and Sally sensed the problem and worked to lift Davy's spirits. They were helped by the string of diggers who greeted Davy like a long-lost friend. It seemed as though every second person in the crowd had been helped by Davy at some time or other.

After the greasy pole competitions, it was time for the foot races. The heats were well contested. The form of the winners led to a flurry of late-placed bets for the final. Davy knew the race marshals, Henry and George. He'd helped them out over a claim-jumping dispute.

'Roll up, roll up,' shouted Henry, standing on a wagon that made do as an impromptu stage. From there, each race was announced and the prizes were awarded. 'Final! Final! Place your bets for the final. Glasgow Flyer versus Bristol Racer!'

Henry also announced the race between two women. 'Roll up! Roll up! See the race between two women! First time only! Here at Kiandra!'

When nothing more had been announced for a while about the race for women, Kitty pestered Davy until he asked George what was happening with it.

'We've had a late scratching,' said George. 'Looks like we'll have to cancel it.'

'What's happened?' asked Kitty.

'One of the girls, the Maitland lass from Four Mile, she's hurt her foot,' said George. 'A horse stepped on it. We don't have anyone else.'

'I could do it,' said Kitty.

'I'm not sure that would be a good idea,' said Davy.

'And why not?' said Kitty. She wasn't about to be told what to do by anyone, even Davy.

Davy decided not to argue. He'd already experienced Kitty's determination on other matters. 'I suppose, if you want to,' he said lamely.

'That's settled, then,' said Kitty. 'Now explain to me what I have to do,' she said to George.

'It's easy,' said George. 'You just get in the sack – hold it up round your waist – and jump from the start to the finish.'

'It's on the same course as the foot racers we've been watching, I take it?' said Kitty.

'Yes,' said George. He was surprised a pretty girl like Kitty would even consider entering. From the time it had been advertised, this race had been the cause of considerable discussion and amazement amongst the patrons of the public houses on the diggings.

Henry was also surprised to hear Kitty's offer. But he quickly took advantage of the new development. 'Latest! Latest! Hear the latest! Race between two women! New challenge from postal lass!' he shouted.

Davy began to regret he hadn't taken a firmer line with Kitty. He was disturbed at the prospect of Kitty being the centre of attention amongst this increasingly rowdy crowd of diggers.

While the competitors were getting ready for the final of the foot race, George joined Davy and Kitty. He had a worried look on his face. 'We've had another scratching,' he said. 'The other lass what was in the race for women, she can't do it now.'

'What's happened?' asked Davy.

'To tell the truth,' said George, looking sheepish, 'she can't stand up.'

'Why not?' asked Kitty.

'She's had a skinful,' said George. 'She's dead drunk.'

'Looks like the race's off, then,' said Davy. He was relieved.

'Why so?' said Kitty. 'We'll just have to find someone else to race me.'

'That won't be easy,' said George. 'Before you turned up, we couldn't find anyone to replace that Maitland lass.'

'Sally will do it. Won't you, Sally?' said Kitty.

'Yes,' said Sally. 'I will.' She didn't hesitate. She wasn't about to let Kitty show her up, even though she had doubted Kitty's wisdom in offering to race in the first place.

Now it was James's turn to feel uneasy. Sally didn't even ask him first!

The final of the foot race was a disappointment. Henry told them to bet on the Glasgow Flyer. He wouldn't say why. He just said he had inside information.

The favourite, the Bristol Racer, hardly got going. He showed none of the form he'd displayed in winning his heat. The Glasgow Flyer took the prize by nearly ten yards. Those who bet heavily on the Racer lost a lot of money. Surprisingly, the Racer's seconds didn't look too unhappy at the end of the race. Henry gave James a wink.

When it was time to start the race between two women, the jumping sacks couldn't be found. Henry blamed George. George said it wasn't his job to provide them. His job was to look after the finish, not the start. Kitty and Sally stood at the starting post while the men argued. The crowd started to get restless. They booed loudly when Henry announced there'd be a slight delay.

'Bring on the women! We want to see the women!' shouted diggers in the crowd.

Henry looked increasingly uneasy. 'Can't someone find me some sacks?' he asked.

No one volunteered.

'Are we going to run this race or not?' asked Kitty, becoming impatient.

'I hope so,' said Henry.

'Well, I'm not going to stand here and wait forever,' said Kitty. She was beginning to think it hadn't been such a good idea to volunteer. But she wasn't about to back down now. 'If you can't find the sacks, we'll just have to race on foot,' she said. She turned to Sally. 'Would you agree to that?'

'Yes,' said Sally. So long as Kitty was game, she'd be game. She was beginning to feel a little nervous, and was keen for the event to be over.

'I know we're not dressed properly for this,' said Kitty, looking at her long riding skirt and boots. 'We'll just have to hitch up our skirts.'

When, after a few minutes longer, there was still no sign of any sacks, Henry announced the new arrangements. 'Hear ye! Hear ye. Race between two women! Start in five minutes. New format. Now a foot race! Postal Lass versus Cooma Flash!'

The announcement had the desired effect on the crowd. There was a buzz of anticipation. Bets were traded furiously. Kitty told the men to wish them luck.

James and Davy walked to the finish post with George. Course preparation had been limited. The biggest holes had been filled with mining rubble and the rest of the surface roughly graded. Already, one of the earlier competitors had taken a fall. James didn't envy the girls. It would be hard work keeping an even footing, without the added handicap of holding up a skirt.

Henry called the girls to the start. He raised his hand, called, 'Ready,' then fired his pistol in the air.

They were off! Arms flailing, elbows akimbo, legs scurrying and skirts billowing as they flew across the ground. The crowd roared. The pace was fast and furious. The girls were clearly intent on making a race of it. Kitty got an early break. She was a few yards ahead at the halfway post. Both girls had determined looks on their faces. As they came bouncing and bobbing towards the finish line, James could see Sally was giving her utmost. She made a big effort and with twenty yards to go she drew level. Kitty put her head down, dug into her reserves and found an extra sprint. She crossed the line yards clear of Sally.

After they'd passed the finish, both girls nearly collapsed. Davy caught Kitty and held her up. James ran over to Sally. The girls' faces were flushed as they gasped for breath.

Sally was nearly in tears. 'I couldn't…do…any better,' she said between gasps. 'I tried. I just…couldn't go…any faster.'

'You did well,' said James, holding her round the shoulder. 'It was only a race. It doesn't matter.'

When the girls had got some of their breath back, they were offered water. They gulped thirstily from the cups. James wiped Sally's face with a damp cloth. She was still panting in between gulps. It gave him a strangely exciting feeling as he held her round the waist and watched her little chest heaving.

Henry joined them. 'That was some race,' he said to Davy. 'Here's the five pounds prize money. Turner said to tell you – that girl of yours, she's a top sprinter. We should match her against the Glasgow Flyer.'

'I don't think she'll be doing this again in a hurry,' said Davy.

Sally looked up at James like a little girl who needed to be comforted. James put his arm around her. 'Sally certainly won't,' he said firmly. 'This will definitely be the last time she'll be racing.'

'Just as well life's not a short race,' said Davy, quietly. 'Otherwise the sprinters would always win.'

James was left wondering at his meaning.

After the race, the girls were hot and tired. Sensibly, in James's view, they decided to pass up the free dinner and return early to Rocky Plains. As they rode along Telegraph Street, the condition of the patrons lining up outside Benjamin's Hotel suggested it was a wise decision.

The girls' fathers were unimpressed when they heard about the race. Mr McCrae said he'd never have allowed it if he'd been there. Mr McNeill said it was unladylike.

'And who's a lady, then?' said Sally testily. 'I've got no pretensions about being a lady. After all, I'm a blacksmith's daughter, aren't I?' she said pointedly.

James put Sally's grumpiness down to the effect of the race. He made sure he stayed out of the discussion.

Kitty came to Sally's defence. She said the racing was all her idea. She now realised it hadn't been such a good one. Her father said it was a damn fool one. That prompted Kitty to tell him he didn't get everything right himself. He replied by suggesting it would be good if she went to bed early that night.

James and Davy were about to set off for the ride back to their hut when Mr McCrae told them to wait. He said he and Mr McNeill would both be leaving early next morning. Sally's father had business in Tumut and he had a special delivery to collect from Goulburn. After that, he planned on dropping in at his brother's place on the way, where his family were staying. He said they'd both be gone nearly a week.

Mr McCrae and Mr McNeill asked Davy and James to take care of the girls while they were away.

'No more foot races,' said Mr McNeill, with a grin.

'You can count on that!' said Davy.

'You can leave the horses here – they're safer,' said Mr McCrae. 'And I wouldn't worry if you fix yourselves some bedding in the stable. That should be comfy enough. You lads must be used to rougher billets than that. Come to think of it, why don't you stay the night here?'

James and Davy accepted the offer. With the help of some straw and some blankets, they'd made themselves comfortable in no time. Kitty and Sally came to say goodnight. They had a giggle at their new 'guest accommodation' before heading for bed themselves.

*

Next morning, the weather was fine. Kitty suggested they explore the district. She and Sally had never been outside the Kiandra township and were both curious as to what lay beyond.

They started their tour by following the Lob's Hole track beside Bullock Head Creek up past the new horse tailing yards. After crossing Three Mile Creek, they left the track and the diggings and rode towards the mountain ridge with views towards Victoria. Weaving their way between the twisted old snow gums, they soon reached the top. They were close to where James had seen the brumby stallion.

He told them the story, pointing to where he and Sweeney had chased the stallion down the spur. 'It seems so long ago now,' he said. 'Like it was in another lifetime.'

After admiring the view, they found a sheltered clearing. They hobbled the horses and let them graze while they took a leisurely lunch, sitting in the snowgrass amongst the wild flowers. Then they lay down to rest. Lying with her head on James's chest, Sally watched the white clouds scampering across the bright blue sky. It was as near to contentment as she could ever have wanted. Kitty had similar thoughts as she lay in the grass with Davy.

Davy was the first to see the snake slithering between the grass clumps near James's feet. 'Psst – snake!' he hissed.

James looked down. The silvery brown snake was barely two feet away from his feet. Sally and Kitty saw it too.

'Don't move!' said James, urgently but quietly. 'Keep still!'

They all froze, and watched. James held Sally tight. He could feel the tenseness of her body and the pounding of her heart. After what seemed like an age, the snake went on its way, sliding back into the snow grass as silently as it had come.

'That scared me,' said Kitty, breathing quickly.

They all stood up, looking around carefully as they did, unsure if there might be another one nearby.

'We should have killed it,' said Davy.

'No need,' said James. 'As long as you leave them alone, they won't bother you.'

'But aren't they poisonous?' said Sally. She still looked frightened.

'Very,' said James.

'And I was feeling so happy before, with this beautiful weather, the pretty countryside, the flowers and everything,' said Kitty.

'It just shows you,' said James. 'There's always danger where you least expect it. You're never safe in this world.'

'I hope you're wrong,' said Sally. 'I'd hate to have to worry whenever things seem safest.'

Back on their horses, James led them over the saddle to the headwaters of Six Mile Creek. They had a long, refreshing drink from the clear waters of the creek. Being upstream from the diggings, it was running fresh and clean. Then they returned to Kiandra along the Tumut Road. The sun was shining fiercely in the now cloudless sky. The road was shadeless. By the time they reached the McCraes' hut at Rocky Plains, they were hot, sweaty and dusty.

A small creek flowed out of the bush beside the hut. A dam had been constructed across it just below the tree line. This was the McCraes' source of fresh water, for their own needs and for their horses.

As they dismounted at the yards, Kitty looked towards the dam. 'Look at that,' she said as she wiped her forehead with her sleeve. 'Wouldn't it be good to jump in there?'

'Why don't we?' asked Sally. She looked at Kitty.

Kitty looked back. 'All right,' she said decisively. 'We'll go first. You men can make yourselves useful round here. You can wipe down the horses for a start.' She turned to Davy. 'Now, don't you lot go looking at us,' she said, smiling. It wasn't clear from her tone how seriously she meant it.

Davy raised his eyebrows and looked at her quizzically.

Sally smiled at James. He thought he saw her wink, but he couldn't be sure.

James busied himself wiping his horse as the girls walked the fifty yards across the hillside to the dam. Davy did likewise. When they reached the creek bank, the girls stopped and started to undress. They kept their backs to the boys and placed their clothes neatly on the ground beside them. Davy and James stopped pretending and stood watching – motionless. The tension was almost audible. They watched as the soft, rounded curves of these two pretty, shapely girls appeared from under their wrappings. The sight of them, as they stepped out of the last of their clothes, with their backs towards him, was an image James would not quickly forget.

The girls walked to the dam completely naked. Each put a foot into the clear, cool water. Sally turned briefly and looked over her shoulder. She could see the men were watching, and smiled to herself. James was watching Kitty as much as he was watching Sally, but he thought he saw her smile.

'Gosh, it's cold!' said Kitty, gasping and laughing as the water came up to her waist. She splashed Sally.

Sally splashed her back. In no time, they were both completely wet. They ducked in and out of the water.

'It's lovely,' said Sally, resurfacing. 'Isn't it?'

Momentarily, they forgot about the men.

After splashing around some more, kicking their feet in the water, Sally looked over towards the hut. 'You know,' she said, 'the men are watching us.'

'That's naughty. I told them not to,' said Kitty. She didn't seem overly concerned. 'They can't see much, now we're in the water,' she said.

When they'd had enough and decided it was time to come out, Kitty waved towards the boys. 'No watching, now,' she shouted out.

Davy and James turned their backs as asked. Kitty made a dash for her clothes. She almost reached them before the boys turned to look. James saw enough to etch an indelible image in his mind – of her small bouncing breasts and the dark raven thatch between her legs.

Sally wasn't so rushed. She took her time. She smiled to herself as she stepped out of the water. She believed she had just as good a figure as Kitty. Subconsciously, she didn't mind that James knew. It was strangely exciting to know that Davy was watching too – it made her feel naughty – an unusual feeling for her, which she couldn't explain.

Watching Sally as she walked, wet and naked, towards her clothes, had the expected effect on Davy and James. The tension grew. James clenched his teeth. Davy held the rail with white knuckles. Neither said a thing, nor looked at each other, as they fixed their eyes on Sally's gently bouncing movements.

It didn't take long for the girls to dress.

'We're not going to watch while you bathe,' said Kitty pointedly, when she and Sally had joined the men back at the yards. 'Someone's got to cook the dinner.'

Davy and James were left to themselves to clean up in the dam. They spent some time lying in the cold water, cooling their ardour as well as their bodies.

The following day, it rained. For most of it, they stayed at home in front of the fire, apart from a short ride to watch the river in flood.

On Friday, it was warm and sunny again. They rode to Nine Mile, stopping along the way at Four Mile to see Eureka Jack. Kitty had already met him. Sally thought he was a funny-looking little old man. He reminded her of a tramp more than a digger, with his leathery face, his pipe-stained beard and his battered clothes. 'He doesn't say much, does he?' she said later.

'There were too many people,' said James. 'They put him off. That's what a hatter's like.'

At Nine Mile, John and Ian were working their claim. They were glad of the excuse to take a break and boil the billy.

Sitting in front of the campfire, holding her mug of tea, Sally felt like a true bush girl. She wished she could go mining, like the men. It was so much easier being a man, with the freedom to go anywhere and do just as you pleased.

'Will you lot be going to the New Year's Races?' asked John.

'There's all the details in the *Pioneer* today,' said Ian.

'We haven't seen the papers for a while,' said Davy. 'Can you show us'?

Ian ducked into the tent and came out with the paper. 'There it is,' he said, spreading the paper on the ground.

Kiandra New Year's Races

STEWARDS

J A Goulstone	J Yates
M J Bourke	C Dixon
F S Cohen	Jas Conway
A D C Larnach	Thos Horton
J Limbert	Henry Broadie
C Cowper	James D'Arcy

JUDGE

P L Cloete Esq, P.M.

TREASURER

F Cooper, Esq

STARTER

G O M Clarke, Esq

CLERK OF THE COURSE

Geoffrey Phelan, Esq

DIGGERS PURSE

Of 30 sovereigns; mile heats. Entrance 5 per cent;
second horse to receive 5 pounds

LADIES PURSE

Of 20 sovereigns; mile heats. Entrance 5 per cent;
second horse to receive 5 pounds

HURRY SCURRY

Of 15 sovereigns; mile heats. Entrance 5 per cent.

THE CONSOLATION STAKES

Of 10 sovereigns; Mile heats. Entrance 5 per cent added.

RULES

No horse permitted to start that has won an advertised prize

Catch weights for all races

Three entrances or no race

All disputes, objections, and complaints arising out of

the racing to be decided by the majority of the Stewards

in attendance, whose decisions shall be final.

Post entrance

First race at 12 o'clock sharp

W A MACDONOGH

Secretary

'See the notice below,' said John. 'There's a free ball at the Empire Hotel for New Year's Eve.'

NEW YEAR'S EVE

DANCE THE OLD YEAR OUT AND THE NEW YEAR IN

JOHN CARMICHAEL

Intends to give a

Free Ball and Refreshments,

So as his Old Friends can dance with Eclat on this most auspicious

occasion when he invites 'ALL HANDS' to come and

Join in the Merriment of the Evening.

'Come One, Come All.'

'I can imagine what that'll be like!' said Davy.

'There's more,' said John. 'Turn it over. There's a full page on the New Year's Day sports.'

'Benjamin's putting on a free luncheon. There'll be a "monster band" in attendance all day,' said Ian.

'I don't think we'll be doing sports again,' said James.

'You girls might want to give the foot race a go. See, it's for all comers,' said John, with a big smile.

'You must've heard about our race, then,' said Kitty, somewhat apprehensively.

'Who hasn't!' said John. 'You girls are the talk of the diggings. They can't wait to see you in action again.'

Kitty and Sally both blushed.

'What have you heard?' asked Kitty.

'Lots, but not much I can repeat in front of either of you,' said John.

'It was a mistake,' said Kitty, sounding serious. 'We won't be doing it again.'

'I was only joking,' said John. 'You needn't worry. No one's said anything bad. All I've heard said is that you were two very plucky girls.' He turned to Davy. 'Back to my question. Are you going to the races? What say we enter a horse?'

'We wouldn't stand a chance,' said James.

'That doesn't matter,' said John. 'That colt of yours looks like it's a bit of a goer. Ian's the lightest of us. He can be the jockey. Or James can. We'd have no chance in the big races so I say we save ourselves for the Hurry Scurry, or the Consolation, when the other horses are tired. How about it?'

It was agreed.

'We'll meet you at the racecourse at noon,' shouted John as the riders left the Nine Mile. 'See you on the far side of the Tumut bridge.'

The day was warm and sunny. By the time the riders reached Rocky Plains, they were hot and sweaty.

Sally took the initiative this time. 'Let's take a dip in the dam again.'

'All right,' said Kitty. 'But you men must behave this time.'

Sally detected a slight nervousness in Kitty's response. Kitty was usually so confident. For once, she felt she had an advantage. 'Why don't we all do it together this time?' she said, surprising herself. 'If you're game, of course,' she said to Kitty.

Kitty hesitated briefly, then said, 'I'm game. If the men are.'

The men were.

'You let us get ready first,' said Sally, taking charge.

The girls stripped off quickly and ran into the dam, followed closely by the boys. There was much splashing and laughing. Once they were in the water, Kitty regained her confidence. She had as much fun as any of them.

Sally remained in charge. She made the men wait in the water while she and Kitty got out and got dressed. She had an instinct that it was important to stay in control of the situation. She liked it when the men did what she told them. There were few enough occasions in her life when this happened.

14

The New Year
January 1861

As the sun rose over the hilltops on New Year's Day, it cast a golden glow over Kiandra's pockmarked landscape. For a few brief moments, the surface of the diggings was bathed in gold. The symbolism didn't go unnoticed. Some saw it as an auspicious omen for the future of the field. To the less superstitious, it was only on account of the smoke haze from the bushfires in the east.

The hotels were open early and did a brisk trade catering for those whose celebrations from the night before had not yet finished. By late morning, the crowds had moved to the entertainment venues. They started gathering near Benjamin's Hotel in preparation for his New Year's Day sports, and at the makeshift racecourse beyond the Tumut bridge.

James led the party of riders from Rocky Plains along Telegraph Street towards the racecourse. They had to weave their horses through straggling groups of diggers and out-of-towners. As arranged, John, Ian and Brian were waiting for them on the far side of the bridge.

Horses were being ridden everywhere, in amongst the crowd, and sometimes even across the course, making it hard to tell who was racing and when. The course was short and rough, with the corners marked by stakes. In between, it was go as you please. The finish was up a slight rise. The organisation of the first race set the tone for the day.

'Lucky the stewards aren't fighting a war,' said John. 'You'd want to run up the surrender flag now. It's complete chaos over there. Everyone thinks they're in charge. And no one pays attention to anyone else.'

There were two heats for the main race, the Digger's Purse. The final was closely contested and only marred by minor jostling at the last turn. After a protest, J. Preshaw on Banker's Pride was declared the winner. It was one of the few races in which justice prevailed.

'That's the banker's young brother, isn't it?' asked Ian. 'They'd hardly need the money, you'd think.'

As the afternoon progressed, the crowd grew rowdier in direct proportion to the amount of drink consumed. The Boys were out in force, led by Mick Bourke, who was one of the stewards. He made sure The Boys' favourites were given every chance to win, both on and off the course. There were protests in nearly every race. Some of the more reputable stewards went missing. Bourke's faction amongst the stewards didn't make a big effort to look for them. They thought the proceedings were a great joke.

During the final of the Ladies Purse, Bourke was sitting on a hired hack near the winning post. Chas Cowper's horse turned the last corner well clear of the field. The Boys had their money on another horse. As Cowper came galloping towards the finish, Bourke rode onto the track, pretending his horse had bolted. Cowper ploughed head on into him. There was a bone-crunching thud as both riders were thrown clear. Bourke quickly jumped up and put on a great show about how it wasn't his fault. Meanwhile, the horse with The Boys' money on it crossed the line. Luckily, neither of the fallen horses was badly hurt. The steward's decision gave the race to the horse favoured by the Boys – by a narrow majority.

In the Hurry Scurry, one of The Boys raced his horse beside the field and tried to upset the favourite by striking at him with his whip. This caused the favourite, in this case owned by Chas Cowper, to collide with another horse and break its leg. Bourke realised The Boys had gone too far this time. The stewards' decision awarded the race to Cowper's horse.

'I know there was an injustice,' said Ian, who'd been watching the race. 'But how can you give the race to a horse that never even passed the finish line?'

'Beats me,' said John. 'But it shouldn't surprise you. Nothing should today, from what we've seen.'

John's racing strategy proved a sound one. By the time of the Consolation Stakes, any horses with talent had either been injured or pulled up lame. The rules excluded previous prizewinners.

'Are horse races always like this?' asked Kitty. She was feeling distinctly uncomfortable. She and Sally had been receiving an amount of unsolicited and unwelcome attention.

'Not always,' said Davy. 'Don't worry. We'll go as soon as our race is run. Ian's over at the start now.'

Ian won his heat by a couple of lengths. As a result, Davy's horse firmed as favourite for the final. The Boys had entered a worn-out stock horse. It looked to have no chance, so they decided they'd better do something. A mob of them surrounded Ian and Davy at the marshalling area. They suggested Davy withdraw his horse. When Davy wouldn't agree they started to make threats.

'Your nag won't gallop too good when its legs is broke,' said one.

Others in their party started ripping up the posts and rails from a nearby picket fence to put this proposition into action.

John saw the trouble developing. 'Stay right here,' he said to Kitty and Sally. We've got some business to attend to.' He turned to Brian and James. 'Come on, fellas,' he said.

Jumping onto their horses, they galloped over to Ian and Davy. It was like the charge of the cavalry.

John rode straight into the mob, scattering them in all directions. 'We've come to make up the numbers,' he shouted. 'You want trouble, we'll give it you.'

Bourke had also seen what was happening and ran over to the disturbance. He quickly sized up the situation. It was clear John and his friends meant business. Victory for The Boys was far from certain and would undoubtedly come at a cost. He decided to calm his men. They took some convincing. The hotheads were jumping about and were all for a brawl. Bourke told them it wasn't the time or place to settle scores. That could come later.

'Your time'll come,' were his parting words to Davy.

'Idle threats,' said John. 'We'll be waiting for you.'

Ian was a clear winner in the final. Davy accepted the prize, then he and his friends quickly left the racecourse.

'I didn't like those people,' said Kitty. 'Now I know why the diggings mightn't be a good place for a girl.'

'So much for your democracy,' said John. 'You want that lot to decide our fate?'

'Most of them are half decent when they're sober,' said Davy. 'It's the drink that does it. That and the gambling. There's just a few bad ones that lead them on.'

'I don't want to go to any more races,' said Sally. 'I've seen enough.'

The goldfield returned to normal the following day. The out of town visitors left and the diggers returned to mining. It was time for the miners to recoup the money they'd spent on drink or lost on the horses. Kitty's father returned from his visit to Goulburn with a load of fresh provisions. Sally's father returned later the same day.

It was the end of the holiday for Sally. She and James had only one day left together. They spent it alone in the bush, on the top of a mountain, amongst the snow gums, watching the clouds in the sky.

Sally was quieter than usual and a little sad. She needed to be held a lot. 'It's all right for you,' she said. 'You'll be off mining. I've got to go back to Cooma by myself and look after children. How much fun's that?'

James tried to sound positive; he wasn't very successful. It was true, he was looking forward to mining again. The holiday had been long enough. 'We'll get to see each other again,' he said. 'I might come down to Cooma. After we've been to Crack-em-back. It'll depend on what we find. And on the others.' He promised he'd write more often. 'I'll try, anyway,' he said. 'It isn't easy, 'specially if we're in the bush somewhere.'

'I know,' said Sally. 'I shouldn't be so selfish. It's just I really look forward to your letters. It's so dull otherwise. Thank you for spending so much time with me this Christmas. It's been a holiday I'll never forget.'

They said their goodbyes in the morning. After returning their horses to the tailing yards, James set off on foot along the track to Nine Mile. It took him most of the day to get there.

John already had most of the essentials organised for their trip to Crack-em-back. He'd even managed to acquire a packhorse. Recent reports from the new diggings had been favourable, so they started their journey with optimism. They weren't in a hurry, so they allowed three days for the trip.

The new field at Crack-em-back was spread amongst the snow gums and muzzlewood trees in a sheltered valley, overshadowed by steep, brooding mountain slopes. A small tent settlement had sprung up around the junction of the Crack-em-back and Little Thredbo rivers. There were no timber buildings, the largest structures being the stores tents, which lined either side of a rough thoroughfare leading to the river. The main action was in and around the river. It wasn't anything like the size of the Kiandra diggings.

James and his partners pitched camp on the edge of the settled area. Flat ground near the river was at a premium. Most of the river bank had already been claimed. They were standing around debating what to do when a weedy-looking miner came up to them and offered to sell them his claim. He said he had to return to Sydney urgently. The others let Ian take charge of the negotiations. They trusted him to drive a hard bargain.

Ian told the man they'd only do a deal if they had a day's trial first. The man looked uncomfortable. At first, he wouldn't come at this arrangement. Eventually, he changed his mind and agreed. This would give them a day to wash dirt. If the claim produced gold, they'd pay him twenty pounds for it. He wanted fifty at first but Ian beat him down.

'I'm not sure I trust that fella,' said John. 'He's more shifty than I'd like. I reckon he's got something to hide. I'm going to camp down by the claim tonight. I want to make sure there's no funny business.'

'You might be right,' said Ian. 'He did drop his price rather quickly.'

Nothing happened at the claim overnight. The partners panned two ounces of gold the next day. In the evening, the man came round to collect his money.

'It'll have to be tomorrow morning,' said Ian. 'We didn't get a full day's work done. We need some more time digging. Anyway, we don't have the cash with us. We'll need to arrange some credit through Mollarde's Store.'

Ian was lying. He was still worried the claim might have been salted. He thought it best if they dug a bit more extensively. The seller had no choice but to wait. After some grizzling and whining, he slunk away, muttering to himself.

The next morning, they'd been working the claim for less than an hour when two angry diggers appeared on the bank above them. The men demanded to know what they were doing. It was their claim! It took some fast talking to avoid physical violence. Ian explained the situation, omitting to mention how much gold they'd found. The claim owners said they'd been two days away and had asked their former partner to mind the claim while they were gone. It turned out he also owed them money.

'That two timing little bastard. I'll flay 'is bloody hide if I catches 'im!' said one of the diggers.

'Where's a bloody commissioner when you need 'im?' said his partner.

'Cooper'll be here tomorrow,' said the first digger. 'We can tell him.'

'Dunno what good that'll do you,' replied his mate. 'That man's useless from what I 'ear. Unless you're in with 'im.'

James and his friends quickly packed up their tools and left the claim to its rightful owners.

After this false start, Ian spotted a small unclaimed area in a gully away from the river. It didn't look very promising. They staked it out anyway.

'We'll give it a go for a couple of days,' said John. 'If it's a duffer, we'll try something else.'

Commissioner Cooper and his entourage arrived that afternoon. They established their quarters on a small rise, overlooking the main thoroughfare. As John, James and Ian walked back to their tent at the end of the day's work, they saw the commissioner's party entertaining themselves at Rawson's Store. From the amount of noise being made, there had to be a liberal amount of alcohol involved.

'Rawson must be selling them sly grog,' said Ian. 'There's no licences been granted yet. The place hasn't even been declared a goldfield. The storekeepers in Kiandra were complaining about it.'

'That'd be right,' said John. 'Two sets of rules. One for the diggers, another for the toffs. Not that sly grog's hard to come by if you want it.'

'You wouldn't want it at Rawson's price,' said Ian. 'I reckon the stores here don't want licences. They get more for it when it's sly.'

After a yarn and a smoke in front of the fire, John suggested they turn in early, so they could be up before dawn the following day. In this hot weather, it was best to get their digging done before the heat of the day, he said. By midday, they could be panning, which wouldn't be so bad in the heat.

As they dozed off, they could hear occasional shouts and snatches of songs coming from the direction of Rawson's Store, as the commissioner's party extended their carousing into the night.

At midnight or thereabouts, James was woken by a loud clanging. It sounded as though someone was banging pots and pans together. Then someone started shouting, 'Wake up! Wake up! Wake up all!' in a drunken voice.

'What the hell's going on?' said Ian.

'I'll crush that bastard's vital bits if he doesn't stop that noise,' said John.

The noise didn't stop. It was followed by the sound of men shouting and arguing. The commotion was coming from the direction of the main thoroughfare.

They decided they'd better get up and see what was going on. Other miners who'd been woken by the racket joined them as they made their way in the moonlight towards the store tents.

The source of the noise was Commissioner Cooper. He was banging a billy against a frying pan as he lurched past each of the tents on either side of the thoroughfare yelling at everyone to get up.

'The man must be an idiot,' said Ian.

They knew Davy had clashed with Cooper, so they decided not to get too close. Cooper wasn't alone. As they watched, he and a number of his equally drunken mates linked arms and stumbled from side to side down the street. By now, a sizeable crowd had gathered in the half dark. Probably most of the miners on the diggings, thought James.

At the end of the row of tents, Cooper said something that James didn't hear. Then he took off his clothes and threw them away. Linking arms again with his mates on either side he lurched back down the street – totally naked! It was some sight, even in the half dark.

'Well, I'll be blowed,' said John. 'What a goose!'

Cooper disengaged himself from his friends in front of Rawson's Store and climbed onto an upturned case, still completely naked. He needed a couple of attempts. The case was next to a tent pole. He held onto it for balance, swaying the tent backwards and forwards dangerously as he did so, the motion threatening to dislodge the lamp that was hanging in front of the store.

'Listen here,' said Cooper. 'Listen. I've got something to say.' At that point, he nearly fell off the case. He steadied himself in time, but nearly brought down the tent.

Diggers were now gathered round, mostly out of curiosity.

'I'm a generous man,' said Cooper, holding onto the pole. 'I want all of you to know that. I'm a generous man. Some of you here – you'll know – I was member for Shoalhaven. A damn good member too. And a generous one. I want all the miners on this field to know I'm a generous man. You should vote for me.'

Some of his mates started laughing. 'There's no election,' said one.

Cooper paused and asked for a drink. He was handed one.

'It doesn't matter. There's no election. So what! If there is one, you should vote for me. You can ask the voters of Braidwood. Go on. You ask them. Ask them, has anyone been more generous handing out food and grog. Ask Rawson over there.' He pointed at Rawson, who was standing at the side of the tent at risk of demolition.

'You were generous all right,' Rawson shouted back. 'But you haven't paid me. You still owe me thirty-five pounds for champagne.'

'That's rubbish,' said Cooper. 'I don't owe you a thing.'

'You do,' said Rawson. 'I sent you seven baskets of champagne – at five pounds a basket. That's thirty-five pounds.'

'You lousy scrooge,' said Cooper angrily. 'Who do you think you are? I owe you nothing.' He nearly lost his balance. 'How dare you talk like to me that. Do you know who I am? I'm the commissioner for this damn goldfield.'

'Commissioner or no commissioner, you owe me for the champagne,' said Rawson, sounding as angry as Cooper.

James guessed he must have been drinking too.

'You used my grog to get the Braidwood votes, now it's time to pay,' said Rawson. 'I'm fed up with waiting. It's over a year now.'

'You'd better hold your tongue, you jumped-up storekeeper,' said Cooper.

'What about the grog I sold you tonight, then?' demanded Rawson. 'When are you going to pay me for that?'

'Damn you, you swine!' said Cooper. 'I'll have you lagged for sly grog selling. You've got no licence here.'

This leap of logic was too much, even for the commissioner's mates. They urged him to get down from his box and forget the matter. One of them brought him his clothes. In the meantime, others were trying to calm Rawson, telling him it would all be right in the morning.

Cooper was helped by his friends to get dressed. Some of the less intoxicated in his party then shepherded him in the direction of his quarters. With the action over, the crowd dispersed and returned to their tents.

'I'll bet that doesn't get into the papers,' said Ian. 'I can't wait to tell Davy. What a riot!'

'That man's dangerous,' said John. 'Best we stay well clear of him.'

*

James and his partners stayed at Crack-em-back till the end of January. They didn't strike it rich.

While they were still there, news broke that a reef had been found at Jackass Flat. William Wallace mentioned it when Ian collected the paper. William had the contract to carry mail on horseback from Kiandra to Crack-em-back – at a shilling a letter and sixpence a copy for papers.

'They sent seventeen hundredweight of quartz to Adelong and it yielded a hundred and twenty-two ounces,' said Ian, reading from the paper. 'Maybe we should've gone there, instead of wasting our time at these diggings.'

'And how would we crush the rock?' said John. 'Reefs are only for parties with plenty of capital. You need a stamping battery. Or you have to pay through the nose for someone else to crush your rock. Anyway, reef claims end up being worked by men on wages, not diggers like us. Look what happened at Adelong.'

'There's lots of other places we could try,' said Ian. 'We could give Lambing Flat a go. Everyone else is.'

'Not in this weather,' said John. 'I know that country. It'll be dry as a bone now. They say Kiandra's getting dry. Over Yass way, it'll be ten times worse. I vote we go back to Nine Mile for starters. At least we know there's a steady living to be made.'

On the return journey to Kiandra, they stopped at Denison. William Russell was cheerful as ever and brought them up to date with the news. He told them business was booming but most of the traffic was going away from Kiandra. Nearly all the Chinese at Kiandra had left for Lambing Flat. They'd been filing through Denison over the past few weeks, trooping by under the strict control of their headmen. The storekeepers at Kiandra were complaining about the low level of business, on account of the large quantities of stores they were holding. Commissioner Cloete had left for Lambing Flat. There was no problem crossing the river, as it was so low. What was needed now was good soaking rain.

There were few diggers left at Rocky Plains. When they reached Kiandra, it was very quiet. They visited Brian and checked out the Jackass Flat reef with him. It had been extensively staked out, but not a lot of digging was going on. Brian said shares were now being offered. He smelt a rat about the whole project. The news had broken at a very convenient time for the stores, just after Christmas, when they were down on business, and when diggers were leaving in droves for Crack-em-back and Lambing Flat.

They spent the night with Brian at the old hut. Brian said he still had a couple of months of race construction work to go. He told them he might try another rush after that. He said Davy was also thinking of leaving soon, probably for Lambing Flat. Davy turned up later. He said he'd come with them as far as Four Mile the next day, as he hadn't seen Jack for a while.

The four of them, James, John, Ian and Davy, set off early in the morning for the walk to Four and Nine Mile, taking turns to lead their loaded packhorse. They decided it would be as easy to sell the horse at Nine Mile as at Kiandra. If they couldn't get a reasonable price, they might even keep him. The grey sky teased with the promise of rain but the clouds quickly disappeared as the morning wore on.

'It's strange to be wanting rain,' said Ian. 'I never thought I'd wish for it here.'

'You can't wash gold without water,' said John. 'It's just we could do without it falling out of the sky.'

'I don't mind the rain,' said James. 'At least it gets rid of these damn flies.'

When they reached Four Mile, they found Jack sitting in front of his tent, hunched over, with his head between his hands. He didn't see them till the last moment. Davy was the first to notice that the Eureka flag was missing.

'That bastard's taken the flag,' said Jack, as soon as he saw them.

'What bastard?' said John.

'Ballard. That mangy spittle lickin' cur.'

'What's happened?' asked Davy.

'I sees 'im rippin' down the flag from the claim,' said Jack. 'The mongrel! Couldn't do nothin'. Last time 'e put me in the clink.'

'Where's the sergeant now?' asked John.

'Back up there,' said Jack, pointing in the direction of the Four Mile buildings.

'We're goin' that way,' said John. 'We'll see if we can't catch up with him.'

'Was he alone?' asked James.

Jack nodded.

Sergeant Ballard's horse was hitched to a rail outside the public house. The tattered Eureka flag was tied behind the saddle.

'Looks like we're in luck,' said John. 'Keep watch, will you.' He quickly untied the flag.

The sergeant walked out of the public house just as he was finishing. 'What do you think you're doing!' he demanded.

'Returning some property to its rightful owner,' said John.

The sergeant looked at the group facing him. His hand hovered over the pistol in his belt.

'Don't try it,' said John. 'There's four of us. One shot – then you'd be dingo meat!'

The sergeant could see John meant business. 'That flag's police property,' he said. 'Return it immediately. That's an order.'

'What right did you have to take it?' asked Davy. 'Have you got a warrant?'

'I don't need a warrant,' the sergeant said curtly.

'The commissioner wouldn't agree with you on that,' said Davy. 'Remember what happened in Adelong.'

'Commissioner Cooper'll give me a warrant.'

'So you haven't got one now?' said Davy. 'You're admitting you've got no warrant? I've got four witnesses here.'

'I'm admitting nothing to you, you piece of scum. I'll get a warrant and I'll be back. This isn't the end of it. I'll arrest the lot of you if you try to stop me.'

'You can try,' said Davy. 'If you get a warrant I'll appeal against it to Commissioner Cloete, even if I have to ride all the way to Lambing Flat. I've got some other interesting things I can tell him about you.'

The sergeant went visibly white. He grabbed the reins of his horse, jumped into the saddle, and galloped off in the direction of Kiandra.

'You've done it now,' said Ian.

'Did you see the look on his face!' said John. 'Whatever you've got on 'im, it's got 'im dead scared.' He shook his head.

'I was bluffing,' said Davy. 'I've got plenty. But nothing I can prove. They're all too frightened. So frightened none'd be willing to take the stand against him.'

'You'd better come over to Nine Mile and lay low with us for a bit till this passes,' said John. 'We'll take the flag with us. It'll be safest there. Otherwise, old Jack'll end up copping it.'

Davy wasn't inclined to come with them at first. In the end, they talked him into it. Before leaving Four Mile, they told Jack what they were doing. He gave a big whoop when they told him how they'd taken the flag back.

Davy only had to stay one night at Nine Mile. The next day, they learnt that Sergeant Ballard and all the troopers bar three had been ordered to leave immediately for Lambing Flat. They were needed on account of the trouble with the Chinese at those diggings.

Davy returned the flag to Jack on his way back to Kiandra. Soon it was proudly fluttering from Jack's tent again, only slightly the worse for wear. Ian had stitched the torn corner.

15

Winter at the Nine Mile
Autumn 1861

James settled back into the rhythm of work at the Nine Mile with Ian and John. There were few others left, so they had the pick of the claims. Lack of water was their chief difficulty.

James wrote to Sally.

Nine Mile Diggings
5th March 1861

Dear Sally

I hope you got my message from Crack-em-back. We have now been back at Nine Mile for about a month I believe. I lose count of time when we are working in the bush. Crack-em-back was a great disappointment and not only for us as I do not believe there was any party that made much more than costs when you count all the expense of travelling there and setting up in a new diggings. Perhaps only the storekeepers were the exception as they usually are. You can never trust a report of a rush until you have been there yourself. We learnt a lesson the hard way!

Lately there has been great excitement about a reef at Jackass Flat, and then reports of a reef at Four Mile. Of course all of these turned out to be without foundation and of no value except for some of the claim owners who sold out very smartly.

It is reported there are hardly more than a few hundred diggers in the whole Kiandra district now. All have gone to Lambing Flat, including the Chinese. Where there were hundreds of them on the river there could not be more than a few dozen now. At Four Mile and here at Nine Mile we are down to a handful of miners, with a fearful shortage of water for working. I don't know how much longer we will be able to keep going without rain.

We hear many reports of the violence against the Chinese at Lambing Flat, also of robberies and stickings up, with one man knocked down in the main street with a tomahawk and expected to die, all adding to the reasons why we have decided to stay at Nine Mile. It is very quiet here with none of the usual faces in the town, including those who make their living thieving off others. They must all now be at Lambing Flat.

You would hardly recognise Kiandra township. The newspaper I am reading sums it up. 'The town presents an almost deserted appearance. Half the stores and shops are shut and where it was difficult to elbow one's way through the crowd, it is now a matter of wonder to see half a dozen diggers together.' I totally agree. What is amazing is the amount of disputing. This is even greater than when there were thousands on the diggings. Water or the lack of it is behind nearly all the quarrels, as most of the claims now depend on water brought from many miles away in races. Race walls are always being breached and 'accidentally' flooding lower placed claims. Only the river men, those few of them who are left, are not complaining loudly, though even for them water is not plentiful and some of the water wheels in the river have stopped turning.

Davy has now decided to go to Lambing Flat. He leaves tomorrow. Kitty tried to convince him to stay but he is resolute. She of course cannot leave as her father has the mail contract until the end of the year. No doubt she will tell you this when you next meet. Marriage could be a remedy but I am not sure this is in Davy's plans. He has political interests as you know, which he holds most strongly and chooses to put before more personal matters.

I will try to visit you in Cooma before winter. By then I hope to have got back the cash we lost in our ill fated expedition to the Thredbo Diggings. We now call them the Duffer Diggings!

Your affectionate friend

James

Reading the letter, Sally imagined James was in the room with her. It was James talking to her. She could feel his presence. She pictured him, with his cheeky smile and his hair falling across his face, winking as he teased her. But the letter was full of news about events, not feelings. If only he would tell her how he felt.

She wrote back to him within days. He never received the letter. It got lost somewhere between Kiandra and Nine Mile.

In April, James wrote to Sally again.

Nine Mile Diggings
3rd April 1860

Dear Sally

Even though I haven't received a letter from you I thought I would write again to tell you what is happening here. Not a lot in short. The lack of water has continued to such a degree we are only able to work a few days at a time here at Nine Mile, and it is worse at Four Mile. In-between we have been camping down at the Tumut River near Scully's claim and doing some useful panning. Scully's party has been getting good returns. We are not alone as many parties have only been able to work three days in the week. It is quite disheartening, as there is plenty of gold for the getting, if only there was the water to wash for it.

John and Ian are now talking of quitting the field before winter sets in. John is only waiting for the Land Bill to pass so he can take up a selection. Brian has already gone. We have not heard from Davy since he left. Nor has Kitty. The Chinese are back in large numbers (hundreds!), having been thrown off the diggings at Lambing Flat by the Europeans and have taken up most of the claims at Jackass Flat where it's a real Chinatown now. You would not recognise it. The Celestials seem to be able to find gold where others have given up.

Most of the public houses are closed and boarded up and good weatherboard houses that cost over one hundred pounds to build are now on offer for ten pounds. It would be foolish to purchase as prices could go even lower. Eureka Jack is occupying one of the public houses at Four Mile as a caretaker to give the appearance of habitation and so prevent vandals making free. If I stay over winter we may do the same here at Nine Mile. It would be a pity not to make use of the buildings in this way when the winter snows come, as they no doubt will. The weather must break soon. I will try to visit you before the winter sets in.

Your affectionate friend

James

The last day of April was a summer's day. Overnight, there was a sudden change. On the first day of May, the diggers woke to dense fog, followed by heavy rain. This continued during the week, turning to sleet, then snow, which settled six inches deep. After that, the usual winter weather pattern set in: intermittent fine weather, rain, sleet and, occasionally, light snow. The nights were frosty and the mornings icy.

At Nine Mile, the diggings were often blanketed in thick fog till late in the morning. On other days, the wind blew as if it was trying to blast everything and everyone off the face of the mountain. No wonder the old man snow gums were so sturdy and twisted, thought James. From the shelter of his doorway, he watched as the driving sleet and rain whipped the young saplings almost flat to the ground.

In Kiandra township, the early snow falls provided opportunity for sport. The remaining residents took to snowballing. Walking across the junction between Broadway and Telegraph Street was particularly risky after snow had fallen. Although the early falls were only a foot deep on the flat, windblown drifts were up to six and eight feet thick. The road to Russell's was cut and there were heavy falls as low as Denison. After an accident near the Denison bridge, the Russells had to dig a rather chilled man out of a drift. He was lucky to be alive.

Despite the snow, James often found a reason to make the journey to Kiandra. It gave him the opportunity to talk to Kitty. She told him how much she missed Davy. He would have preferred another topic, but any conversation with her was better than none. He enjoyed watching her. She had such pretty eyes.

'I don't know why he hasn't written,' said Kitty. 'I do hope nothing's happened to him.'

'I'm sure he'll be all right,' said James.

'I hope so. I wish he hadn't gone. I don't know why he had to. He thought he could help the Chinese. I don't see what he can do – the way the miners' feelings have been got up against them.'

'I thought he was going to teach the diggers about democracy. That's what he told me,' said James.

'Maybe,' said Kitty. She frowned. 'You know, James, I'm not so sure about that political business. It's not really that I disagree with Davy,' she quickly added. 'I just wish he wouldn't spend so much time on it. The way he goes on it's almost an obsession.' She suddenly smiled. 'I suppose I'm only being selfish. I guess I really want him to spend his time with me.'

'I'm happy enough to keep you company in the meantime,' said James.

'That's nice of you, James.'

He liked it when she said his name. 'If it weren't for others, I'd be happy to spend even more time with you,' he added.

Kitty looked as though a thought had crossed her mind. 'I really like you, James. We can always be the best of friends.' She paused and looked at him intently. 'You do know how much I care for Davy, though, don't you? I made him a promise. I said I'd wait for him, no matter what.'

James nodded. He suddenly worried he might have gone too far. But Kitty smiled so sweetly he felt reassured. Perhaps they truly could be friends.

Before the winter arrived in earnest, James took a week off mining and borrowed a horse to ride to Cooma. Sally was delighted to see him. They visited their old haunts and shared the warmth of their bodies again. They fitted together so comfortably, like a pair of old gloves, it seemed they'd always been intended for each other. Sally's parents thought as much, and said so, to James's annoyance and to Sally's embarrassment. James still felt uncomfortable at the thought of settling down. He insisted on returning to the diggings to see out the winter.

New Providence, a few miles upstream from Denison, was nearly deserted when James made the return journey. Only one public house and one store were still open, a complete reversal from only a few months ago. He'd never seen it so quiet at Denison, with no travellers evident at Russell's.

The real winter came to Kiandra in June. Heavy falls of snow blanketed the diggings. All outdoor mining work was brought to a halt. Only tunnelling could still proceed. The road from Denison to Kiandra was impassable for days due to the deep drifts, and both Four Mile and Nine Mile were cut off from Kiandra. The few miners left on those fields were confined to their huts while the storms blew themselves out. James took the opportunity of the enforced break to write to Sally.

                                                    Nine Mile Diggings
                                                    18th June 1861

Dear Sally

I am writing this to the sound of the howling wind, which outside
is blowing such a gale we dare not open the door for fear of the damage
it might do. I am not sure when I will be able to post this letter as I will
have to wait until the storm has passed and even then it will be a most
arduous journey to reach Kiandra through the snow which already is
piling up in drifts many feet deep.

You need not worry on my account as we are as snug as toast here
with a roaring fire at Nine Mile having taken up occupation in one of
the abandoned buildings and having stockpiled all the necessaries for an
extended winter stay. Not long after I returned John left to take up land at
Mullion Creek in the Yass district and to get married to his sweetheart, Lyn.
I wouldn't be surprised if he doesn't visit the Lambing Flat Diggings before
too long though. It is not so far distant from his new property he told me.

Ian and I decided to stay the winter at Nine Mile where we know
there is plenty of gold to be had if a man is willing to work for it rather
than go to a place unknown and risk all again with no certain prospect
of reward. Aside from the snow, which I am almost becoming used to,
this being my second winter, these diggings now have the benefit of only
being sparsely populated so we can take our choice of where we prospect,
and even where we stay as there are many abandoned buildings we can use
for shelter wherever we chose to work or visit. As an instance our old hut
at New Chum is now empty and Eureka Jack is caretaker in a building at
Four Mile, though I think I told you this before.

Not many days ago Kitty finally received news from Davy at Lambing
Flat. The letter was very brief. To my mind she was disappointed at the
lack of detail he included as to his current occupation and his plans for
the future.

At least the snow has put paid to all the disputing about water. Now
the complaints are about too much of it, or the damage the ice is doing
by preventing all manner of working including sluicing and panning with
many of the races frozen solid each morning. In an old paper I found
these words of wisdom:

'Diggers are always the hardest used individuals on the face of the earth; they have always some standard grievance, besides a host of minor ones and beat the 'honest farmer' all to nothing.'

You only have to listen to any discussion amongst diggers to know this is so true.

I will finish writing now as the wind is easing and we will need to dig out our entrance so as to prevent us becoming trapped in an icy grave (only a joke). I may write again next storm which no doubt will not be so long in coming.

Your absent but affectionate friend

James

James posted the letter a week later and at the same time collected a newspaper. It was the *Sydney Mail* of 15th June. He settled down to read it in front of the fire. 'We were right to stay put,' he said to Ian. 'Listen to this about Lambing Flat: "The ground, though rich enough to repay steady work, is also just poor enough to have the very minimum of attractiveness, and diggers are naturally tempted to be off at the first news of richer ground being struck."'

Ian stoked the fire, sending a shower of sparks up the chimney.

'Remember Bill Archer?' said James.

'Wasn't he working on Scully's first claim, down by the river?'

'He's dead now,' said James.

'How's that?'

James read from the paper. '"The body of William Archer was found dead in a waterhole at Spring Creek. An inquest was held – verdict accidentally drowned. A woman, name unknown, was found dead at Tipperary Gully. An inquest was held – verdict, died from exposure and intemperance."'

'I bet there was some intemperance in Bill's case too,' said Ian. 'He wouldn't have been going for a swim.'

Sally was also reading the papers. There were only occasional references to Kiandra now. The Sydney papers were her only source of information, as the *Alpine Pioneer* had ceased publication in March after the diggers had left Kiandra in droves.

Most of the gold news was about the violence against the Chinese at Lambing Flat. But she read a report about two large nuggets found at Kiandra. She also read that Too Fee, one of the Chinese headmen, had a large gang working on one of the old river claims, and that a Chinaman had paid one hundred and thirty pounds for a large claim in Whipstick Gully. There were very few references to Nine Mile.

In early July, Sally received the letter James had written in June. Despite the failure of her previous letter to reach him at Nine Mile, she decided to write him a reply.

Cooma
9th July 1861

Dear James

Mr McCrae has just handed me your letter. I'm so glad to hear you are securely established despite the fearful weather. We in Cooma have only had some light falls of snow, which barely last a day, unlike the stories I hear from you and others about the conditions at Kiandra. Of course we can have very cold nights here, as you know, and having to break the ice in the bucket more than an inch thick has not been uncommon in the morning lately. Undoubtedly it is much more severe where you are.

Mr McCrae tells me he has been prevented on many recent trips to Kiandra from completing the journey by coach, or even on horseback, the mail having been collected by men wearing snow shoes. Do you know about them? Mr McCrae says they are from Canada and stop your feet sinking into the snow. I cannot quite imagine them.

I don't know how you can do any mining at all if the snow is as many feet deep as I am told. Father could do with your help here if you find it isn't possible to continue. Michael has left home, after a terrible row with Father, and I believe is now at Lambing Flat. It has upset Mother terribly. Otherwise nothing much has changed at home. Your own mother was asking if I had news from you and I was able to tell her the contents of your letter. This put her mind at rest, as she, like me, had been worrying about you. I suppose it is the lot of women to worry in this way. You should write to her more often as she has troubles enough already with the younger children. I hope you don't mind me giving you this advice. It is well intentioned. As you can see there are many here who are thinking of you and will look forward to hearing from you. Of course I miss you.

Sally's letter was handed to James at Nine Mile by the local publican. James and Ian were just about to leave for Kiandra. James quickly skimmed the letter before tucking it into his pack. They'd decided to abandon the high country until the end of winter. The snow was so deep on these mountain ridge-top diggings that it was pointless continuing with any pretence of mining. The exposed nature of the field meant it always bore the brunt of the storms, with the snow lying many feet deep, long after it had melted down at Kiandra.

It took them most of a day, trudging through the snow, often sinking below their knees, before they reached Four Mile. The weather was clear and windy, otherwise the track would have been near impossible to follow. At Four Mile, the drifts were almost as deep as at Nine Mile, in many places exceeding the height of a man. Jack boiled a welcome billy and they spent an hour warming themselves in front of a roaring fire, having a smoke and a yarn.

When they ventured outside again, the sun had disappeared behind dark glowering snow clouds. Jack wouldn't hear of them continuing and insisted they spend the night with him. It was a wise move, as the storm broke within the hour.

They made an early start next morning, which was crisp and clear. Fortunately, not much new snow had fallen overnight and the ground was frozen solid, making for easier walking. Lunchtime saw them in Kiandra. There they stocked up on supplies before heading across to their old hut at New Chum Hill.

There was no escape from the snow, even in Kiandra. With mining activities impossible, once more the locals turned to other amusements. James and Ian joined in. Bjorn tried his hand at making snow skates out of palings again, this time with more success. He made sure he kept them inside his hut when not using them.

Heavy falls of snow took their toll on the less sturdily constructed buildings. The roof on Robinson and Tebbatt's old store fell in from the weight of snow on it. Firewood thieving was even worse than the year before. Stores and stockyards moved off slab by slab, rails and posts disappearing every night. Unoccupied buildings, especially those with storm damage were most at risk. Templeton's stockyard was carried off in the night and heartless thieves even took the palings from around the graves at the Kiandra cemetery.

In August, the *Sydney Morning Herald* included an unusually detailed report on the effect of the winter snows at Kiandra. Sally read it with interest.

THE ALPINE FORESTS – The residents on the Four Mile Creek have been completely snowed out, the snow became so deep that they could not clear it away any longer. Our correspondent's place of business caved in on the nineteenth, and he sold his stock at about one third of the cost to a party who had a strong house, fitted on a pair of snow shoes and took refuge in the Alpine Metropolis. Several of the few remaining storekeepers were about to leave Kiandra and take their goods to Cooma. No idea can be formed except from actual experience of the horrors of a winter in that part of the country. The roads are impassable except with show shoes or the more novel mode of travelling on skates. The skates are constructed of two palings turned up at the front and about four feet long, with straps to put the feet in, and the traveller carries a long stick to balance himself and to assist him up the hill. Down hill they can go as fast as a steamer and on the level, with the aid of the pole, they can make good headway. Some of the buildings at the Four Mile and Nine Mile have fallen in and others were only saved by great exertions. The party above referred to as the purchaser of the goods, had to place supports to the back and front of their house and trice it up with ropes inside to prevent it caving in, and it is a remarkably strong building. It was impossible to get the horse post in; the letters were carried by men on snow shoes and the papers were left behind.

She put it aside to read to her father. It would also make interesting reading for her pupils, who had now grown to six. Her reputation as a teacher was spreading and a number of families had inquired as to whether she could give instruction to their children. She was keen to take on more students but was unable to do so as she did not have a proper classroom. If only James would return. She had some ideas she would like to put to him.

In Kiandra, following Bjorn's example, the locals took to snow shoeing with gusto. Almost daily, races were held down a makeshift course marked out on Township Hill. There were many spills and collisions and fouling was frequent. The control of the racers over their direction and speed was minimal. The long sapling poles the racers used as brake sticks quickly turned into weapons when objection was taken to interference by another competitor.

James and Ian were sitting out a storm at Carmichael's Hotel when news came over the wire that rioters at Lambing Flat had burnt the commissioner's camp. The message said the government had ordered in the troops. They wondered where Davy might be in all these troubles.

'Probably in the middle of them,' said Ian.

James bought a paper. The police report said a mounted patrol had caught up with a gang of bushrangers. In the encounter which took place, a trooper had been killed. He read the report to Ian. It said one of the bushrangers, named Gardiner, had been wounded and captured, but two others had made their escape.

'Wasn't that Gardiner here in Kiandra a while back?' said Ian.

'He sure was,' said James. 'He and the local scoundrels were best of mates. The troopers seem confident they'll catch the others. I wouldn't put my money on it.'

'Nor me,' said Ian.

Nearly three weeks after she'd written to James, Sally received his reply.

New Chum Hill
28th July 1861

Dear Sally

Your letter reached me at Nine Mile just as Ian and I were leaving. We have now moved back to our old hut at New Chum Hill to escape the worst of the winter snows, it being impossible to continue mining in drifts many feet deep.

The snow shoes you mention are a terrific invention and I only wish we had learned about them earlier. We have now made some for ourselves, as best we can, and use them regularly. At first I thought you must have meant the snow skates that Bjorn Bumpstone showed us last winter, which were made from palings and on which great speed can be obtained on a downhill slope. These are also called snow shoes by some and great sport is now being had by many climbing the hill above the township and sliding down with these palings on their feet at the speed of a railway train.

Ian is most skilled at this sport, and has won a number of the races that have been hastily arranged to fill in the time when mining is not possible. Of course some use the opportunity to bet on these races leading inevitably to conflict on occasion. There are still some of 'The Boys' on these diggings who you saw in action at Christmas time whose interest is primarily in arranging the outcome of any race instead of allowing it to run on its merits. Ian and I make sure we keep our distance from them. We haven't forgotten the past, nor have they.

You can tell my mother not to concern herself on my behalf. She has no need.

Kitty has received another letter from Davy in which he says he will be returning to Kiandra soon. He tells her there has been horrific violence against the Chinese by men with whips and by men with dogs. A number of Chinamen have been killed and others badly beaten and all that just because they happen to have been born Chinamen. He hasn't made contact with me or Ian but he is welcome to join us again at New Chum Hill.

The race line Brian was engaged to build to bring water to the Homeward Bound Claim is now finished and is in operation. It is an impressive engineering feat no doubt, but is recently the source of dispute as the claim owners (our closest neighbours) believe others are unfairly using its water. There is no end to the matters that can cause bad blood on a goldfield!

I will try to write to you again to let you know our plans, which are still not settled. I think of you too.

Your affectionate friend

James

Sally was glad to hear that James was well and that he had now moved from Nine Mile. She found it frustrating not being able to do anything except wait for news from him.

16

Trouble at the Homeward Bound Claim
August 1861

Despite the snow and freezing weather, numbers increased again on the Kiandra goldfield in August. They included many Chinese, fleeing from the violence at Lambing Flat.

In early August, with the military now on the field at Lambing Flat, it was judged prudent to release some police to return to Kiandra. The Kiandra storekeepers had been pressing for their return, worried at the possibility of violence on their diggings too. Amongst the troopers who were ordered back was Sergeant Ballard.

Davy returned to Kiandra in August too, arriving the day before Sergeant Ballard. He met Kitty in the township, where she was working at the mail depot. She was shocked to see the condition he was in. She almost didn't recognise him. He was so thin, pale and dishevelled. He said he was on his way to New Chum Hill and wouldn't stop for long as he needed to rest. She could see he was exhausted, so she didn't press him. She wished she could have been free to go with him.

James and Ian were about to knock off for the day when they saw Davy approaching. The faint winter sun had just dropped behind the hill, bringing a sharp chill to the air.

'By hell, you look crook,' said James.

'You're as yellow as a Chinaman,' said Ian. 'We'd better stoke the fire and get some hot broth into you.'

'It's so cold here,' was all Davy could say. He started shivering.

James and Ian helped him into the hut, where he collapsed onto a stretcher. James put a blanket over him while Ian fixed the fire.

After a cup of hot broth and some food, Davy started to look better.

He spent most of the next day sleeping. Ian insisted that he rest, and wouldn't let him get out of bed.

In the afternoon, Kitty came over to visit. Even though the weather was fine, they sat around the fireplace inside the hut to keep Davy company.

'You had me worried yesterday,' said Kitty, still sounding concerned.

'I'll be right now,' said Davy. 'I wasn't used to the cold.'

'You could still do with some improving,' said Ian.

'It's a long way from Lambing Flat,' said Davy. 'It's hard going through the mountains, even with the new road. I never stopped, except for a few hours sleep.'

Davy told them about the troubles at Lambing Flat. He'd been caught in the middle trying to talk reason and had received a beating for his troubles. 'It was a pack of ruffians behind it,' he said. 'They wanted to jump the Chinese claims. They spread lies about the Celestials and stirred up ill feeling. Ordinary diggers were taken in.'

Davy said he'd realised in the end there was nothing he could do. 'When it gets to violence and the troops are sent in there's no place for reason and logic,' he said. 'Sense flies out the window. I only hope it never comes to that on these diggings.'

'Did you know your brother was back in Kiandra?' asked Ian. 'I saw him yesterday.'

'No, I didn't. Was he by himself?'

'No, he was with that Captain Bill and some of their sort.'

'It'd be too much to hope for anything else,' said Davy.

'They'd be up to no good, for sure,' said James. 'I've told you about that Captain Bill before. I knew him when he was a stockman, before he took to thieving and got in with the Mulligan gang.'

'There's someone else unpleasant in town again,' said Kitty.

'Who's that?' asked Ian.

'That horrid man Davy saved me from. Someone told me his name's Gardiner, Frankie Gardiner. They said he's a bushranger.'

'Are you sure it was Gardiner?' asked James.

'Yes, it was the same man,' said Kitty. 'This time I hid so he wouldn't see me.'

'There was a report in one of the papers a while back about how his gang shot a trooper,' said James. 'The report said Gardiner was captured. Looks like he must've got away. They were offering a reward for the capture of his bushranger mates. A hundred pounds, I think.'

'That wouldn't tempt anyone,' said Ian. 'You'd be dead before you'd collect it. You'd never be safe. Not unless the whole gang of them was caught and hanged.'

'I'm surprised he's come back here,' said James.

'It'd be safer here,' said Davy, 'now the troops are at Lambing Flat. With the military taking care of the diggings, the traps over there'd be looking for a bit of sport.'

Ian insisted on walking Kitty back to the township. Davy was still too weak.

It was back to work in the morning for James and Ian. While the weather was fine, it was unwise to waste too much time. They wouldn't let Davy join them. They insisted he sit in the sun on the sheltered side of the hut, where he could see them working down by the river. As they set off, they could see one of the Chinese gangs was already hard at work downstream.

While Davy was sitting smoking his pipe, a well dressed digger came walking up the slope towards him. He was muttering to himself as he came, clambering over the untidy piles of rocks and skirting the icy puddles, where an unwise step could plunge a man ankle deep in slush. It was Sam Hawkins, partner in the Homeward Bound claim.

Hawkins was a stocky Englishman with a sandy beard. 'Good day,' he said, lifting his hat to Davy, an English custom not generally favoured by the locally born diggers. 'You're Davy Hughes, are you?' He fiddled nervously with the brim of his hat. He was clearly agitated.

'Yes,' said Davy.

'I've heard you're a good advocate. I was told you might be able to help me,' said Hawkins.

'What's the problem?' asked Davy.

'It's Cooper,' said Hawkins. 'That damned upstart commissioner. He's just ordered us to give all our water to Shinnick.' He spoke quickly and excitedly. 'It's outrageous! Shinnick's race is nowhere near ours. It's over on the western fork of the creek. It's higher than us. To give our water to him we'd have to make the water flow uphill! How ridiculous is that? I don't know what to do. I'm at my wit's end. This isn't the first time. That commissioner is quite incompetent. Totally incompetent. My party are depending on me and I can't do a thing. Cooper has got a set against us and won't listen to reason. He won't even inspect the site. How can a man make a decision like that?'

'Hold on a moment,' said Davy. 'What do you want from me?'

'I need help,' said Hawkins. 'I don't know where to turn to. I hear you've taken cases before. People told me you've been able to help them.'

'That's true,' said Davy. 'I've been able to help some people. I'm not a qualified lawyer or anything like that,' he added. 'I've just tried to help, where there's been injustice.'

'There's injustice here all right!' said Hawkins. 'I've never seen such injustice. Cooper disregards the law at whim. He's a law unto himself. He aligns himself with parties then finds in their favour, regardless of the merits of the case.'

'You'll need to tell me more about what's happened,' said Davy. 'I'm not promising anything. There may be little I can do. Let's boil a billy first.'

Over a mug of tea, Hawkins filled Davy in on the background to his difficulties. He explained he was wearing his suit because he was on his way back from court. The hearing had been held in Carmichael's Hotel. 'Cooper always holds them there, instead of the commissioner's camp,' said Hawkins. 'That way, he can have an audience of his drinking companions to play to.'

It was a long story. Davy listened patiently. The trouble first started for Hawkins and his Homeward Bound partners when Taggart lodged a complaint on 29th July. Taggart and partners said their race was being deprived of water by the Homeward Bound race. Both parties drew their supply from Bullock Head Creek. Cooper ordered Hawkins to provide water to Taggart. Hawkins said they complied with the order as best they could. Two days later Taggart complained again. This time he said his race was entitled to more water, and that their claim had priority as their water right had been given before the one granted to the Homeward Bound Claim. Cooper appointed two assessors, one of whom was Shinnick, who made a report. On the basis of Shinnick's report, Cooper ordered all of the water out of the Homeward Bound claim race.

'We complied,' said Hawkins, 'even though we believed the decision was grossly wrong. I protested most forcefully. Cooper wouldn't let me finish my speech. I told him we fully intended appealing, by whatever means we could, and to whomsoever we were able.'

'Why would Cooper make such a wrong decision, if the facts are as you say?' asked Davy.

'Taggart and his partner Yates are Cooper's friends,' said Hawkins. 'They play cards together at Carmichael's. But it's worse. I've now found out that Shinnick and Yates are partners in another enterprise. That means Shinnick sat in judgement on his partner's interests. It's no surprise he decided against us and in his partner's favour.'

'What's the situation with the water?' asked Davy, looking puzzled. 'I'm not sure I understand.'

'Taggart never had any right to the water in the first place,' said Hawkins. 'Goldfields regulation number 19 says water shall be measured by a plank sluice head having a sectional area of twelve inches by one inch, with a fall of one in twenty four. That's how his entitlement should have been measured. It was Commissioner Scott who gave Taggart his entitlement last year, so I sent a telegram to Scott asking him to confirm the fact. Scott's reply fully vindicated our position.'

'That means he should be getting much less water than Cooper ordered?' asked Davy.

'Absolutely,' replied Hawkins. 'Our race is practically dry due to Cooper's stupid order. That nincompoop wouldn't know a plank sluice head if he fell over it. He's got no experience in mining, and no apparent interest in finding out. As soon as I got Commissioner Scott's reply, I took it to Cooper.'

'And he didn't accept it?' guessed Davy.

'Worse than that,' said Hawkins. 'There's more to tell you. The day before I got the reply from Scott, we ourselves complained that Speck, another friend of Taggart's, was taking our water. That man had no permit in his name to take any water from anywhere. I proved it to Cooper. Cooper completely ignored me. I got very angry with him. And I let him know it. Mind you, I said nothing but the truth. The next day, Taggart and Yates complained again. This time, they produced a trumped-up charge that we were taking spring water that should have come to them. This was complete nonsense. I believe they deliberately made the complaint for the express purpose of annoying us.'

'It seems to have worked,' said Davy.

'It certainly did,' said Hawkins, ignoring the irony in Davy's remark. 'Cooper fined us eight pounds. But no one delivered the order to us. When the fine wasn't paid, Cooper had Mr Maxwell, my partner, arrested and locked up for non-payment. I believe it was done deliberately. Mr Maxwell is an old man. What they've done to him is unforgivable. He was held overnight in a dirty, freezing lock-up. It's got no fireplace, no beds and no floor, and the icy wind comes straight through the boards. There was even a filthy evacuation in the corner.'

Hawkins became emotional at this point. He shook his head, temporarily lost for words. 'Mr Maxwell is a gentleman,' he said, blowing his nose. 'He doesn't deserve this. Now he's very sick. He's been confined to bed ever since. I'm most worried about him.'

Hawkins stopped for a moment to recover himself. 'Now this stupid, malevolent, ignorant, spitefully motivated commissioner has ordered us to divert all our water uphill to Shinnick!' he said, getting worked up again. 'It completely beggars me. I don't know what to do. Cooper didn't even visit the site when he made that decision. He said the weather was inclement. That was rubbish. It was only drizzling. He just didn't want to interrupt his cosy game of cards in front of the fire.'

'Well,' said Davy. 'I'm not sure how much I can do. You say Commissioner Scott has already supported your case about the water right? If Cooper won't accept that evidence, I'm not sure what I can do.'

'What appeal rights do we have?' asked Hawkins.

'None,' said Davy. 'The regulations give all power to the commissioner on the field.'

'That's ridiculous,' said Hawkins. 'What if a commissioner is corrupt?' He thought for a moment. 'I'm not saying Cooper's corrupt, of course. It's more that he's lazy, ignorant and prejudiced. He's totally unsuited by training and temperament to the position. I've no idea how he got the post – though I hear his family is well connected.'

'I suppose the remedy would be for the government to take away his commission,' said Davy. 'That would probably be a decision for the Secretary of the Lands Department.'

'Then I'll write to him,' said Hawkins. 'I've a mind to write to the paper too.'

'I'm not sure that would be wise,' said Davy. 'Someone else wrote a letter to the *Alpine Pioneer* last year about Cooper – though it didn't mention his name. It didn't do that writer's case a lot of good.'

'I don't care,' said Hawkins. 'We've got connections too. People need to know what's going on. I'll be damned if I'll be fooled around with by this midget colonial upstart. He needs to know he's nothing but a minnow in a very small pond.'

'Sometimes it's best to work quietly behind the scenes,' said Davy. 'If you like, I can help you draft a complaint to the Secretary of the Lands Department. You could also write to the chief commissioner, Mr Cloete. He mightn't have direct power but he's got influence. There's a good chance the secretary would ask his views on the matter.'

'That's useful advice. I'll consider doing just that,' said Hawkins. 'Thank you for your help.' Hawkins took his leave, thanking Davy again for his help.

Not long afterwards, James and Ian returned.

'That was Hawkins from the Homeward Bound Claim you were talking to, was it?' asked Ian.

'Yes. He was asking for help. He told me all about their problems with Cooper.'

'We've heard about them too,' said James. 'That Cooper's a right bastard.'

'Hawkins doesn't help himself,' said Ian. 'I've heard him carrying on. He thinks he knows better than Cooper. And he makes no secret of it. He might be right. But it's no way to get a favourable decision out of Cooper.'

'I guessed as much,' said Davy.

'No one's ever right except Hawkins – if you listen to him,' said Ian. 'He's pretty arrogant. That, and him being so English, would get right up Cooper's nose.'

'Hawkins isn't the sort of person I'd usually help,' said Davy. 'I guess it's a matter of principle. Justice needs to be done – regardless of personal prejudice. What Cooper is doing is wrong. Someone has to try and set it right.'

'You need to watch out you don't get caught in the crossfire,' said Ian.

A day later, Hawkins gave Davy the drafts of two letters. One was addressed to the secretary of the Lands Department. The other was addressed to Commissioner Cloete. Davy reviewed them and returned them to Hawkins with some suggestions for changes.

Hawkins didn't show Davy the letter he wrote to the *Sydney Morning Herald*. It appeared in the paper on 17th August.

JUSTICE ON THE GOLDFIELDS

To the Editor of the Herald

Sir – The manner in which Justice is administered on some of the goldfields, and the arbitrary and overbearing conduct of some of our J.P. Commissioners, would, if it were generally known, somewhat astonish the public, and doubtless exercise a beneficial control over their conduct. Here upon Kiandra, for instance, are some three hundred miners, hemmed in by snow, out of reach of legal assistance, at the absolute mercy of one individual utterly ignorant of mining affairs; his decisions once given are final and irrevocable no matter how glaringly unjust they may be afterwards proved to have been. An admitted wrong is inflicted, and because an official has caused it to be perpetrated, all redress is denied to the injured party. I am a simple Englishman, and have been taught that the Crown can do no wrong, its pygmy representative in these Alpine regions has however inflicted a wrong and, knowing it to be so now, still refuses to redress it. The only resource, therefore is to appeal to the public through the press, and to the Government, through the members of the goldfields. Of both these opportunities I have now availed myself.

The facts to which I alluded are these:- A party of miners have held an official permit, fifteen months old, for a certain specified quantity of water from a small creek. They now discover that double that quantity would be an advantage to them; they therefore apply to Mr Cooper, the Commissioner, for the increased supply, telling him that – although their permit expressly mentions a certain quantity – they originally asked for, and supposed they had obtained, the larger measure. Mr Cooper granted the application from the original date, in the teeth of the written document to the contrary. Now, in order to give these parties the additional supply, it was necessary to deprive some one else of water; and our right being only ten months old, we were ordered to cut off our supply from the head of our race, nine miles in length, constructed at a great outlay of capital and labour, upon the strength of an interpretation of the reading of prior water permits. We protested, but we were forced to comply. Emboldened by success, the same parties complained that their supply was deficient, and that we still retained possession of some springs which, by the way, we were never ordered to resign. Upon this the Commissioner called two assessors, and, between them they fined us eight pounds for retaining springs which, until this day, were never mentioned. We refused to pay the money, knowing the water to be unquestionably our own. We were allowed a week to find the money, and, in default at the expiration of that time, one of our party was to be imprisoned for seven days. In the interim we telegraphed to Mr Scott, the Chief Commissioner for this place, who was absent, we received an answer repudiating the new reading of our opponent's permit, and, consequently, confirmed our right to the whole of the water we had been deprived of, and establishing the injustice of the fine. I also discovered that one of the assessors was a partner of the chief complainant, who was no other than the manager of the Bank of New South Wales. This man, therefore, actually judged in his own cause, and awarded damages to his own partner. This is a fact that requires no proof; it is unblushingly admitted. Now any reasonable man would have supposed that after the confirmation of our right and proof of the damning fact of a community of interest, between the complainant and the assessor, that the case would have been quashed. Nothing of the kind. On the evening of the sixth day after this trial, I waited upon Mr Cooper and called his attention to the subject; he told me that the question was definitely settled, and that I had 'no appeal, not even to the Governor,' I quote his own words.

On the following morning two policemen apprehended one of my partners compelling him to submit to the indignity of the searching of his person, and then thrust him into a filthy lock up, the receptacle of felons, for not paying the fine. We had all determined not to pay this money but when it became known, numbers of people volunteered to advance it, and one more zealous than the rest, actually paid it without our knowledge and released our partner.

One more case even more inconsistent than the foregoing, and I have done. Another party, of whom this same banker is also the chief, complained to the Commissioner of a deficiency of water, and demanded that, as our right was of a later date than theirs, we should supply them. Mr Cooper instantly gave us an order to turn our water out of the head of our race, and let it run into the head of the banker's. Now, neither the banker or the Commissioner knows anything about the natural features of the country at the heads of these races, or they never would have made such a demand upon us, compliance with it being, in point of fact, physically impossible, inasmuch as it would be necessary to make the water run up hill, a feat in hydraulics which has yet to be accomplished. Still, having a wholesome dread of fine and imprisonment, we obeyed the first part of the order, and turned the water out, and afterwards endeavoured to explain to Mr Cooper the real state of the matter, and to request permission to send the water down our race, which was being ruined by the frost and choked by the drifting snow. He positively refused, and stated in his anger that as I had appealed to Mr Cloete, I should wait until that gentleman replied, and that when he did, he would inform him that he had no power over himself, and that the water should remain out of the race. He was deaf to every argument, and I am now actually compelled to turn all water out of the race for the supposed benefit of a man who never can obtain it. I challenge Mr Cooper to gainsay a single statement I have made, or to invalidate or confute any portion of my complaint.

The Press of New South Wales continually bewails the lack of enterprise and energy displayed by her miners. How can it be otherwise? If a man is foolish enough to expend his time and money upon her goldfields, he is soon made aware of the risk he has incurred. In Victoria, his property is secure. No man can deprive him of it, and his undertakings are fostered and encouraged. Here, on the contrary, nothing is secure. One day you procure from the official in power a permit authorising a certain undertaking. Vainly trusting to the delusive document, you carry out your project, and then, as in our case, after ten months solid work, without a penny's return, we find our permit swept from under our feet by the stroke of the pen of another official, 'who knows not Joseph,' and our money and our labour is scattered to the winds.

I trust, Sir, you will do me the favour to publish this statement. I pledge my honour every word of it is true, and both can and will be substantiated on the oaths of numerous witnesses.

I am, Sir, your obedient servant

SAMUEL HAWKINS

New Chum Hill, Kiandra, August 12th.

James was the first to read the letter in the paper. He ran all the way back from the township to New Chum Hill. 'Look what Hawkins has written,' he said, still panting.

Davy took the paper and quickly read the letter. 'Hell and damnation! That's done it.' He gave the paper to Ian.

'When Cooper reads this, he'll hit the roof,' said James. 'Did you see that? He calls Cooper the Crown's pygmy representative! What a lark.'

'Hawkins has no idea,' said Ian. 'The Boys'll be out for his blood. Where is he now? Someone better tell him.'

'I just saw him in town,' said James.

'You're right,' said Davy. 'I'd better warn him.'

'We'll come too,' said James.

The three of them hurried along the muddy track, through misty rain, to the Kiandra township. When they reached the main thoroughfare, they saw Hawkins leaving a store fifty yards down the street. Before they could reach him, three men ran out from behind a building and set upon him, punching and beating him. He fell to the ground and the men started kicking him. His cries turned heads. Davy, James and Ian raced down the street. Davy was the first into the fray, leaping on top of one of the men. Ian and James were right behind. Under a barrage of blows, the surprised assailants turned their attention from the man on the ground. A bystander who'd witnessed the affair helped Hawkins out of the mud. The confrontation quickly developed into a stand-off. Hawkins' attackers weren't so keen on an even contest.

'You miserable cowards,' said Davy, as the two sides eyed each other.

'He's only gettin' 'is just deserts,' said the leader of the assailants, a burly, rough-looking thug. 'The mongrel deserves a thrashin'. He's been writin' lies to the paper.'

At the sight of an approaching trooper, the three men ran off. Hawkins was muddy and sore but no bones had been broken. When he'd recovered his composure, he told them he was on his way back from seeing Commissioner Cooper. Yet another grievance had been lodged against the Homeward Bound claim. Taggart had sold out to Darcy, who'd now filed a fresh complaint claiming deprivation of water. Hawkins said Cooper had promised he wouldn't hear this latest complaint until he had advice from Commissioner Scott.

Davy asked if Cooper had mentioned the letter. Hawkins said he hadn't.

'The paper's only just come in,' said James. 'He mustn't have read it yet.'

'He will have by now,' said Ian. 'Let's get out of here before there's any more trouble.' He looked around nervously.

'I suggest you make yourself scarce,' Davy said to Hawkins. 'I don't think you were wise to write what you did. Cooper will have a real set against you now.'

'He already has,' said Hawkins. 'It couldn't get much worse.'

'Don't bet on it,' said James. He kept looking over his shoulder as they hurried back to New Chum Hill, now through the pouring rain.

Overnight, the rain cleared. In the morning, the pale winter sun glinted on the icy ground. Remnant snow drifts glistened with a myriad of tiny white crystals. There was the hint of spring in the air.

At nine o'clock, Hawkins and Maxwell got news that one of their miners was now in Dr Biermann's invalid home. He had been badly beaten the night before. At eleven o'clock, a trooper rode up and served Hawkins with a summons to attend court. The Homeward Bound Company was charged with stealing water from Darcy's race. The hearing was scheduled for two o'clock that afternoon.

'How will I have time to get my witnesses?' Hawkins asked the trooper.

'That's your problem,' replied the trooper, and rode off.

The court was convened at the Empire Hotel. Davy, James and Ian walked to the hotel with Hawkins. Maxwell was unable to attend, as he was still sick.

The hotel was packed. Darcy and his supporters had received advance notice of the hearing and were gathered in force. Cooper's friends and supporters were also prominent, including a strong representation from what Hawkins described as 'that notorious mob of ruffians, prone to intimidate the peaceful portion of the community' – otherwise known as The Boys.

The hostile crowd jostled Hawkins as he entered the hotel. Seeing Cooper near the reception counter, Hawkins made straight for him. He asked Cooper to defer the trial so he could have time to obtain witnesses. Cooper said it wasn't possible to discuss the matter outside the hearing. Hawkins then asked for protection. He said he'd been assaulted and feared for his safety.

'I don't care tuppence about it,' said Cooper. 'You're brought down here to answer a charge and I can't help it.' He turned away and walked into the room where the court was to be held.

Sergeant Ballard was guarding the doorway to the room. He allowed Hawkins to follow Cooper, but stopped Davy, James and Ian from following. 'There's no room left inside,' he said.

That didn't prevent him allowing more of Darcy's supporters to pass.

The case began with the charge being read out. From outside the room, Davy and the others could hear what was being said, but couldn't see the proceedings.

Cooper appointed two assessors, drawn from the crowd. Hawkins protested. He asked permission to bring expert witnesses from amongst the river men. This was denied. Cooper said the chosen assessors were experienced and unbiased men, sworn to carry out justice. He resented any imputation to the contrary. Evidence was then heard. Hawkins said it was impossible for Darcy to have been deprived of water. All the races were overflowing on account of the recent heavy rain. A long, whispered conversation followed between Cooper and the assessors. Hawkins was then ordered out of the room while the verdict was considered.

The room had two entrances, both leading into a corridor. Hawkins was sent out of the rear one, at the far end of the room from where Sergeant Ballard was keeping guard. A number of ruffians who'd been in the courtroom followed Hawkins into the corridor. The men immediately set to and gave Hawkins a hiding. James and the others could hear what was happening but couldn't do a thing. It was horrible to hear Hawkins' cries and not be able to help. The corridor was blocked by a group of Darcy's supporters. They stood, arms folded, with their backs to the fracas.

'Aren't you going to stop that?' Davy demanded angrily, as he stood in front of Sergeant Ballard.

'Stop what?' said the sergeant. 'I can't see anything.'

'They're beating Hawkins,' said Davy. 'Can't you hear it?'

'No, I can't hear anything,' said the sergeant, slowly shaking his head from side to side. 'Not a thing. What about you, lads?' he said, looking at the men with folded arms. 'Can you hear anything?'

'No,' they said, also shaking their heads.

What Davy didn't know was that Sergeant Ballard was acting on orders. Before the hearing, Cooper had told the sergeant to make sure he slipped out of the way while The Boys gave Hawkins a hiding.

Davy stood fuming. There was nothing he could do but listen. After a few more minutes, the thuds and cries stopped.

'Sounds quiet to me,' said the sergeant.

Hawkins was called back into the court. Cooper read out the judgement. The complaint was found proven. Hawkins, as principal of the Homeward Bound Company, was fined twenty pounds, or in default three months imprisonment in Goulburn gaol. The fine was payable by ten o'clock the next morning.

Hawkins shouted out angrily. He said the decision was unjust. Cooper told him the case was over. Payment of the fine was now a police matter.

'I'll pay the fine,' said Hawkins, 'even though it's grossly unjust. But first I want to make a complaint. I want everyone in this court to know I've just been brutally beaten in the corridor. You all heard the noise.'

The room was suddenly quiet.

'Listen here!' he said, shaking his finger at Cooper. 'If anything else happens to me, I'll hold you personally responsible. I fear for my life. This is the third time I've been set upon murderously in the last twenty-four hours. I demand protection.'

'All right, you can have protection,' said Cooper. He could hardly deny it in the circumstances. 'Sergeant, escort this man safely out of the building.'

It was raining outside as Hawkins left the hotel with Davy and his friends. Hawkins was shaking.

'You'll be next,' shouted one of The Boys at Davy as they left.

Neither Hawkins nor any of the others said anything as they walked disconsolately through the mud and slush back to New Chum Hill.

'With Cooper in charge, there isn't much hope for justice on this goldfield,' said Davy when they reached their hut. 'It might've been a mistake coming back. I think I'll head up to Four Mile and stay with Jack a while. I could even go back to Lambing Flat.'

'It wouldn't be a bad idea if you spent some time at Four Mile,' said Ian. 'Looks like they're out to get you here.'

'I still think it's all because of property,' said Davy. 'It's property ownership that sets men against each other. There'd never be any of these disputes if property rights weren't enshrined in law. We need a different way of organising society, a sharing way. Sometimes I despair we'll ever make such progress.'

When Hawkins went to pay his fine next morning, he asked Davy to come with him. They set off early so as to lessen the chance of meeting thugs, who generally took a while to show themselves in the morning. Hawkins bought a pistol at Gouldstone's Store on the way. After the fine had been paid, Davy stopped at the post office to see Kitty and tell her his plans. He immediately saw she was upset.

'Davy, I'm so sorry,' she said. 'I think I've just caused you some terrible trouble.'

'I'm sure you haven't,' said Davy. 'Here, don't look so sad.' He put his arm around her. 'Tell me what's wrong. It can't be all that bad.'

'You know that horrid man?' she said. 'The one you saved me from, when we first met?'

'Yes,' he replied. 'You mean Gardiner.'

'Yes, Gardiner, the bushranger,' she said, looking tearful. 'He came here yesterday. You were at the court hearing. He kept trying to take advantage of me. He must've known you wouldn't be here. It was beastly. You've no idea. He tried to take hold of me.' She started to sob.

Davy felt his blood beginning to boil. 'The miserable cur!'

'It's all right. I didn't let him,' said Kitty quickly. 'I told him to stop – and that if he didn't leave I'd tell you. I mentioned your name. It just happened. I didn't mean to. I was so frightened.'

'What happened then?' asked Davy, frowning.

'He said he knew you. And that he wasn't scared of you. He said he'd enjoy getting rid of you. He said the traps would do it if he didn't. He said they'd like it if someone else did the job for them. Why would he have said that? I'm so worried for you.'

'You needn't be,' said Davy. 'There's no need at all. Those sort of threats are made all the time.' He tried to sound calm and reassuring, though the information worried him. 'I came to tell you I'll be moving,' he said.

'What?' said Kitty. She sounded panicky. She didn't want to lose him again.

'I'm only going to Four Mile.'

She looked relieved.

'But now I'm worried about leaving you here,' he added.

'I'll be fine,' said Kitty. 'I told Father about the man. Now he won't let me out of his sight. See, he's watching us now. He said he'd deal with Gardiner himself – if he ever saw the man bothering me again.'

'I hope that never happens,' said Davy. He thought for a minute. 'I guess if your father's going to be here, it should be all right for me to go.'

'Of course it will,' said Kitty. 'You must go.'

'I also came to tell you I'll be heading back to Lambing Flat soon.'

'Take me with you,' Kitty quickly replied. She looked into his eyes pleadingly.

'I don't think that would be possible. Anyway, I haven't decided yet.'

'You must take me,' Kitty said firmly.

'I'd better go now,' he said, glancing around.

The hotel doors had opened and miners and others were starting to wander down the street.

Kitty gave him a hug as she held back her tears.

'Don't worry,' he said. 'I'll come and see you again soon.'

By nightfall, Davy was comfortably settled at Four Mile. Despite his solitary inclination, Jack insisted that Davy join him in the building he was caretaking. It had plenty of spare rooms and hadn't been damaged in the snowstorms.

When James visited a few days later, Davy told him the move to Four Mile was the best thing that had happened to him for ages. 'The first day out digging I found a twelve-ounce nugget,' he said. 'Here, take a look at this.' He carefully unwrapped the nugget. 'It looks just like a little boot.'

'You're right,' said James. 'It's a little golden boot.' He grinned. 'They come in pairs, don't they? All you need now is to find the other one.'

Davy laughed.

17

How the Winter Ended
August 1861

In mid-August, anti-Chinese riots broke out on the Kiandra diggings when a party of Chinese were caught red-handed cleaning out McGee's race in Pollocks' Gully. An angry crowd of diggers burnt tents in the Chinese camp and attacked the suspects. A number of Chinese were seriously beaten. Fortunately for the offenders, the police stepped in and made arrests before the crowd could complete its execution of summary justice. To many on the goldfield, this incident confirmed their views about the Chinese. Davy became involved in the dispute and in the process managed to add to the number of his enemies.

Shortly afterwards, there was a great fight inside the Chinese camp. On 21st August, ten Chinese were handed over to the police as thieves and gamblers by their own compatriots. This attempt by the Chinese leaders to clean up their camp failed to change the views of most of the European miners. A petition with three hundred signatures was forwarded to the government asking for the immediate expulsion of the Celestials from the diggings.

With the diggers and the police busy with the Chinese, other law-breakers were free to go about their business unhindered. Frankie Gardiner rode openly down Telegraph Street. Without attempting to disguise his appearance, he had arranged to meet with Captain Bill and the Mulligans in Carmichael's Hotel. Benjamin was no longer in Kiandra, so there was no risk that 'Mr Christie' would be pursued for his unpaid debts.

The patrons in a goldfields hotel were a rough and ready lot. They were noted for their colourful language and for the wide variety of trades, classes and nationalities represented. There were always new faces, and a man's livelihood wasn't obvious. No one could tell whether a drinker made his living from mining, stock riding or bushranging, or whether he might just be passing by. In Kiandra, Gardiner and his mates didn't stand out from any other party of drinkers.

Captain Bill thought he and Gardiner would be discussing plans for joint ventures. Gardiner had a different view. He had come to Kiandra to recruit locals who might be willing to serve under him in his gang. He had ambitions and plans, and he needed men to pursue them.

George Jenkins was standing at the bar of Carmichael's Hotel when Gardiner's party walked in. The bar was doing a brisk trade but was by no means full. Jenkins was a former military man with a strong liking for drink. By the time Gardiner's party arrived, he was well primed, having gone straight to the hotel on his arrival in Kiandra.

Jenkins spotted the newcomers and moved over to join them at their table. 'I'm new on this 'ere diggings,' he said. 'Me name's Jenkins. Plain George Jenkins now. I was Sergeant Jenkins in the Crimea, yer know.' He leaned unsteadily towards Gardiner. 'What's yer name?' he asked.

Gardiner paused. He appeared as if he was in two minds – to humour the man, or to cut him dead. In the end, he told Jenkins his name was Frankie.

'I mean yer other name,' said Jenkins. He looked at Gardiner with steel-blue eyes, deep-set in a broad, weathered soldier's face. He was a big-chested man and had he been standing would have topped six feet.

Gardiner took all this in. 'Christie,' he replied.

'Yer know,' said Jenkins, 'I been 'ere since June. In this 'ere colony. They tells me in Sydney – they says fer gold, yer gotta try Kiandra. Was they pulling me leg?'

'Didn't they tell you 'bout Lambing Flat?' asked Alex.

'They did,' said Jenkins. 'They tells me the place was full of Chinese. Said the army'd been sent in. I got a problem with the army. Didn't want to go there.'

Jenkins stopped to take a drink from his glass, then wiped his mouth with the back of his big leathery hand. 'They told me there'd be gold on the Lachlan. Got as far as Eugowra. Reports was mixed, so I changed me mind and thought I'd come 'ere first. What do I find when I get 'ere? It's full of damn Chinese!' He paused for another drink. 'So, what's the best place to find gold?'

'Depends,' said Alex. 'Easiest way is opening a store.'

The men in earshot laughed.

'That'd be right,' said Jenkins, laughing too. 'But easier still bushrangin', eh? They tell me there's plenty of it goin' on round 'ere.'

'So they say,' said Gardiner. He shook his head in mock seriousness. 'But *I've* never been bailed up yet.'

The party at his table laughed loudly. The joke was lost on Jenkins, who took another long swig from his glass.

'Yer know,' said Jenkins, wiping his moustache. 'I'm a military man. I got thinkin' when I was travellin'. There's plenty of gold gettin' transported on these roads. There'd 'ave ter be good pickings for a well drilled band of thieves.'

'What d'you mean?' asked Gardiner, suddenly paying close attention.

'What's the gold escort worth 'ere?' asked Jenkins.

'Only a few hundred ounces now,' said Alex. 'It's in the papers each week. There's lots more goes from Lambing Flat. There's thousands of ounces goes to Sydney each week from there.'

'I was thinkin' 'bout the Crimea,' said Jenkins. 'The battle's half won if you catch the enemy off guard. Our stupid officers never thought about tactics. They was too stuck-up. Just charged straight at the enemy. Thousands was butchered. Cut down with never a chance. We should've ambushed the Cossacks.' He downed his glass before continuing. 'Good tactics is 'bout surprise. The Americans used the ambush on us. It worked for them.' He paused. 'I been thinkin'. It's not so different from highway robbery. It's the same principles as for war.'

'Tell me more,' said Gardiner. 'Here, get the man a drink. It's on me.'

'A band of bushrangers could use a bit of military strategy,' said Jenkins, 'I seen them escort coaches. They was on the road from Sydney. The guards was half-asleep. With a bit of surprise, at the right place, it'd be dead easy makin' off with a coach load full of bullion.'

Jenkins's drink arrived. Everyone in Gardiner's party was now paying close attention.

'Similar thought's occurred to me,' said Gardiner. 'The guarding's pretty slack. But there's lots of troopers. And they're well armed.'

'Yer gotta pick yer place,' said Jenkins.

'What d'you mean?' asked Gardiner.

'Top of a hill, a creek crossing or somethin' like that,' said Jenkins, 'where the coach'd be goin' slow.' He stopped to hiccup. 'Yer want's a trap. Somewhere to stop the coach going forward and block it going back. Yer wants good cover for the ambush party too.'

'Some rocks – somethin' like that?' suggested Gardiner.

'Yer got me drift,' said Jenkins.

'You got a place in mind?' asked Gardiner. 'What got you thinking this way?'

'I was on the Sydney road,' said Jenkins. 'The gold escort just come the other way. We got stuck behind some bullocks in a creek. There was boulders all round – an' them native pines was growing all thick like.'

'Where was this?' asked Gardiner.

'Just short of Eugowra. I remember, 'cause me nag went lame. 'Ad to buy a new one. Cost an arm an' a leg. That's when I changed me mind and decided to head for 'ere.'

'Dunno if you were right,' said Gardiner.

'Yer'd need the right band of men,' said Jenkins. 'Like me men at the Crimea – till they was mown down by the Cossacks.' He paused while a faraway look came into his eyes.

No one in Gardiner's party spoke as they waited for him to continue.

'Yer'd never do it without discipline,' he continued. 'Yer'd need a well armed party too. Least as many men as troopers. Then yer'd 'ave ter drill 'em. They gotta work with precision. Hardly likely, is it, eh? I mean fer bushrangers.'

'Don't sound like the breed of bushrangers we got in this colony,' said Gardiner.

'No,' said Jenkins. 'It's just an idle speculation. Me men are all dead. If they wasn't, we could've done somethin'. I owe the army nothin'. Not after what it done ter me.'

'An interesting idea, all the same,' said Gardiner.

Jenkins took out a battered pipe and started to fill it with tobacco. 'Now, what can yer tell me 'bout prospectin'?' he asked. 'I been told there's two large nuggets found the other day. They said one of 'em was at Four Mile. Twelve pounds, I 'eard. Where's that from 'ere?'

'Over the hill past the commissioner's camp,' said Captain Bill. 'What did you hear?'

'It was a man named Hughes what found it, they said. Thought I might try a bit of prospectin' there first.'

'Mostly that's mined out,' said Dan Mulligan. 'You'd do better near the township.'

'How about that,' whispered Captain Bill to Gardiner. 'A twelve-pound nugget at the Four Mile, eh?'

*

After the Homeward Bound court hearing, Ian and James were abused by Darcy's men whenever they saw them. Some of The Boys paid a visit to their hut at New Chum Hill one night. Ian and James barricaded themselves inside. The thugs were well primed. They threatened to set the building alight unless Davy came out. Ian shouted out that Davy wasn't there. James told them to get lost. He said Davy was now at Four Mile and that if they wanted him they should go there. It got rid of them. As soon as they'd gone, he regretted telling them where to find Davy.

After this harassment, Ian decided he'd had enough. The returns from prospecting were dwindling. 'Half the time you can't work because of the snow and ice,' he said. 'Then, when you can, it floods and washes everything away. Now we've got these ruffians pestering us.' He said he'd go back to building. 'It's no harder work. At least you know the wages you'll make. It's not as if I haven't given prospecting a fair go. I guess I'm never going to strike it rich.' The next day he left for Tumut.

Davy returned to Kiandra to tell Kitty he'd decided to leave for Lambing Flat.

'Will you take me with you?' she asked pleadingly.

'I can't really,' he said.

'Why not?' she said, with a quiver in her voice.

'I don't have any plans. I don't have a place to stay. And there's sure to be trouble. You must understand.'

'I don't care. I want to be with you.' Then she had a doubt. 'Don't you like me any more? Is that it? Is there someone else?'

'Of course not. Don't be silly. There's no one else. You know I like you.' He frowned. 'You're just being emotional.'

'Well, if you truly liked me, you'd take me with you.'

'I've told you already,' said Davy, feeling exasperated. 'I can't take you. It's not possible. We're not married. What would your father say?'

'We could get married,' said Kitty. As she heard herself saying the words, she suddenly realised their meaning. She felt shocked at what she'd said. It wasn't right for a girl to talk like that.

'Get married?' Davy looked at her in complete surprise. The thought of marriage had never crossed his mind. 'No, I don't think that would be right,' he said. 'That would be a very serious decision. Marriage is a commitment for life. We'd both need more time to think about that.'

'I didn't really mean it,' said Kitty, lying. She was quite disturbed by his reaction. Surely he must have thought of it before? She felt bound to retreat. To mask her disappointment, she decided to make light of it. 'I was only joking,' she said. 'I didn't mean for you to take it seriously. But it could be fun.'

Davy wasn't entirely convinced. He looked at her with new eyes. He was flattered at the thought of her wanting to devote the rest of her life to him. He knew she liked him, but he'd never expected she would want to take it that far.

The thought of settling down with a woman wasn't high amongst Davy's aims. He liked Kitty. He certainly found her attractive, and good company too. Surely that should be enough. But women weren't the main focus of his interests, even one as pretty as Kitty. There were a number of other things he hoped to accomplish before he could think about settling down. 'We don't have to be married to remain friends,' he said. 'I'll keep in touch. I'll write to you.'

'I'll be waiting for you,' said Kitty, trying to keep her voice under control. 'Now you'd better go. Father's waiting for me.' She lied again. She felt terribly upset but didn't want Davy to see it, and wasn't sure how long she could keep her composure. 'When will you be leaving for Lambing Flat?' she asked.

'In a day's time.'

'You will come and say goodbye, won't you?'

'Of course I will.'

Davy left Kitty and walked over to New Chum Hill. James was panning by himself. After a brief greeting, he told James he'd decided to leave for Lambing Flat. 'Where's Ian?' he asked.

'He's gone,' said James grumpily. 'He's had enough. He left for Tumut yesterday.' It hadn't been a good day for James. Everything seemed harder on his own. To top it off, he'd just dropped a rock on his foot.

'Why, what's happened?' asked Davy.

'It's your fault,' said James. 'Some of it, anyway. Those thugs came round looking for you the other night. I'm fed up too. I don't know why you've got to interfere in other people's problems all the time.'

'What do you mean?'

'You're always getting involved in other people's disputes. There's no point. You talk about democracy and how it'll make things better. It's bunkum. I don't believe it. All you do is get your friends into trouble.'

Davy was taken aback. 'I'm sorry to hear you say that. Is it what you really think?'

'I never said anything before, because I didn't think it mattered,' said James. 'If you really want to hear what I think, I'll tell you.'

'Go on.'

'I reckon you've got it all wrong about democracy,' said James. 'You want the people on a goldfield to be in charge. You say they'll make the right decisions. I reckon you're wrong. Most people are selfish, greedy and nasty. Look at what's happening here. We mightn't have democracy but we've got mob rule. The majority on this field support the thugs who've been bullying us. The storekeepers, the traps and half the diggers are all in on it. Look at the turn-up they had for that meeting to support Cooper. Hundreds signed the petition. Where's the benefit of democracy in that?'

'So what do *you* think the answer is?' said Davy coldly.

'We've got to be selfish – and look out for ourselves. We've got to stick together. That's the only way we'll get anything. You've got to stay with your mates. When we had John, Brian and Ian, we were doing fine. On your own, you're at the mercy of the thugs, including the ones in uniform.'

'I guess you've a right to your opinion,' said Davy curtly. 'I'll be off now.'

James watched as he walked away. As soon as he was out of sight, he felt he might have overdone it. He liked Davy and it was sad that he was leaving. They shouldn't be parting other than as friends. But it was all true. Davy had brought it on himself.

James worried about it overnight and decided he'd better visit Davy at Four Mile and say goodbye to him properly. As he set off at midday, he was still turning over in his mind what he'd said the day before. He hoped Davy hadn't taken it too badly.

The sky was an intense clear blue and the path was muddy from snow melt. The glare of the sun on the patches of brilliant white snow hurt his eyes. He pulled his hat down over his face as he trudged up the slushy track towards the trees, away from the commissioner's camp.

After he'd travelled a mile or so, he glimpsed a horsemen galloping towards him through the trees. He stopped before a bend in the track and stepped sideways to let the rider pass. The man splashed past in a hurry and didn't notice him. James was halfway into the bushes behind a tree and had his hat down over his face. He recognised the rider. It was Captain Bill.

A mile further on, James heard another horseman riding towards him. Instinctively, he decided to make himself scarce again. He took a quick detour into the snow and scrub beside the track. Following some animal tracks to disguise his footprints, he crouched in a hollow until the rider had passed. He was glad he'd taken cover. The horseman was Sergeant Ballard.

When James reached the Four Mile diggings, there was no sign of Davy. Nor was there any sign of Jack, either at the creek or at his hut.

The Eureka flag was missing. He stood for a while in front of the hut, wondering what to do. He was about to leave when Jack came into sight, bent double under a load of fire wood.

'Thought I'd missed you,' said James.

'Been up the hill,' said Jack.

'Where's the flag?' asked James.

'Inside. I takes it in when I ain't 'ere, now. Saves trouble.'

'Fair enough,' said James. 'Is Davy round?'

'No. 'E's gone.'

'When did he go?'

'Early this morn.'

'Will he be back?'

'No. Said 'e was goin' prospectin' down the creek then 'e'd be off to Lambing Flat.'

'Pity,' said James. 'I was hoping to see him before he left.'

Jack invited him to share a billy. James told Jack how Ian had now left and he was by himself at New Chum. He also told him about the unwelcome attention they'd been getting. Jack suggested James join him at Four Mile. He could have Davy's room now Davy had gone. Up here, it was out of the way of trouble, and there was good colour to be had below the falls.

James took up Jack's offer and made the round trip the next day to collect his things from New Chum.

When he'd settled in, he wrote to Sally.

Four Mile Diggings

4th September 1861

Dear Sally

I'm now at Four Mile as you can see, staying with Jack, who you should remember from your meeting with him at Christmas time. The thaw has truly set in down in Kiandra with mud and slush everywhere. It is a miracle to walk ten yards without losing your boots to the quagmire, every footstep being almost up to your knees in gripping mud. The horses and bullocks have made a terrible mess of the road.

All my friends have now gone to other places, John as you know before winter, Ian not long ago to Tumut, and now Davy has gone to Lambing Flat. Kitty is quite unhappy at the last, I could tell, when I saw her on my visit to the township, and I tried to cheer her up.

The administration of this goldfield is a joke. The Commissioner (Cooper) sides with his friends and all others can go hang. It's one of the reasons I moved to the Four Mile. Davy tried to change things but all that happened was that attention turned to him. The police are in it too.

I'm not certain I will stay much longer as a digger. When it is properly spring I might return to stock riding instead. I'm finding it lonely without my old friends. Jack is fine but he's old and likes to spend time on his own. I haven't made a great fortune out of this gold mining business.

Your affectionate friend

James

When Sally read James's letter, she wished she could be there with him. She didn't like to think of him being so lonely. She didn't care that he hadn't made his fortune. Why didn't he just come and see her? She was sure they could arrange something now she was earning wages from her teaching. It would be far better than him spending his time trying to cheer up Kitty.

On 9th September 1861, the same day that she received James's letter, the *Monaro Mercury* published an article titled 'Scenes on Kiandra'. The article ridiculed Cooper's conduct as a magistrate and as a commissioner. It didn't pull any punches. No wonder James was thinking of giving up mining, Sally thought, with someone like that in charge of the diggings.

A few evenings later, as Sally was waiting to meet her father outside the Royal Hotel, a trooper rode up to the hotel, hung his horse on the rail and joined a party of men standing under the outside lantern. The men couldn't see her. She was hidden by the shadows of a loaded wagon.

She recognised one of the party as a miner she'd seen at Kiandra. The trooper started to give the men instructions. Sally was shocked at what she heard. He was telling them to watch out for 'Cooper', who would give them a sign. Then they were to give 'Dixon' a hiding. The men addressed the trooper as sergeant.

Worried that she might be in danger from what she'd overheard, she quietly slipped away. Later, she told her father what she'd seen. He said to keep it to herself. What she'd seen was other people's business. She'd do best to stay right out of it. 'There's nothing but trouble to be gained by meddling in other people's business,' he said. The way he said it was an order.

Sally kept thinking about what she'd seen. It didn't take her long to put two and two together. She knew the editor of the *Monaro Mercury* was a Mr Dixon and remembered Cooper was the name of the gold commissioner mentioned in the article she'd just read. She was sure what she'd seen had to be connected with the article, especially after what James had written in his letter. The sooner James left the diggings the better, she thought.

After Davy had left, things quietened down for James and Jack. James kept clear of Cooper and the Hawkins dispute, and The Boys soon turned their attention to other amusements.

Following the 'Scenes on Kiandra' article, interest in Kiandra outside the diggings fell off. It hardly rated a mention in the Sydney newspapers any longer. Hawkins continued to write to officials and to parliamentarians, agitating for an investigation into his grievances, but without any immediate result. The officials concerned had more pressing issues to deal with, including the continuing disturbances at Lambing Flat. On the river, in the gullies and on the hillsides around Kiandra, the remaining diggers busied themselves with mining activities, obtaining some good results.

*

With Davy gone, Kitty turned to James for support. If it hadn't been for Kitty, James would probably have left the diggings straight away.

Davy's sudden departure continued to bother Kitty. 'He should have come and said goodbye to me properly, don't you think?' she asked James.

They were sitting in the building that had once held the library. It was empty now. Kitty had a key and had been charged with keeping an eye on it until business picked up and the shop could be rented again.

'You weren't the only one,' said James. 'He disappeared without me seeing him too.'

'I know it shouldn't, but it makes me upset,' said Kitty. 'I was willing to give him everything, and he goes and disappears just like that. It makes me wonder, did he ever really care for me? What do you think?'

James looked at her sad eyes. He didn't like to see her upset. 'I wish I could do something to cheer you up,' he said. 'Let's not talk about Davy. It only makes you sad.'

'You're right,' said Kitty. 'I shouldn't be burdening you with my thoughts.'

'It's not that,' said James. 'You can talk to me about anything. I just don't want to see you sad.'

'From now on, Davy is dead and gone. Well, he may as well be,' she said. 'I won't mention him again.'

She was true to her word. Though she never mentioned Davy again, secretly she still hoped to hear from him. She imagined receiving a letter. He'd tell her he'd changed his mind. That he was on his way to see her. Her hopes faded as the weeks passed and there was no word from him. Distance and time worked to dull the intensity of her feelings. What started as a burning passion ended as a dull ache in her heart. But it never went away. She knew she could never forget Davy.

Knowing she was the mail man's daughter, sometimes people gave Kitty letters for her father to deliver. This led to a strange experience, which she told James about.

'I was standing outside the post office,' she said. 'It was shut for lunch. All of a sudden, one of the new policemen came running up to the mail room. He saw the door was shut, looked at me, then handed me a letter. He asked me to make sure Mr Bourke got it. He said it was urgent and that it was from the commissioner. Then he said he had an appointment and that he had to run. Before I could ask him any more, he was gone.'

'Why would he do that?' asked James, looking puzzled.

'Perhaps he thought I worked at the post office,' said Kitty. 'Anyway, the letter had 'Mr Bourke' written on the front. Nothing else, just that.'

'Curious,' said James.

'I didn't know which Mr Bourke it might be. I thought it might be the storekeeper, but I didn't know for sure. I opened the letter to see if there was an address. I know I probably shouldn't have, but what else was I to do? Anyway, there was no address, so I read the letter. I remember the words exactly. I'll tell you what it said: "Dear Bourke, Get the boys to beat the old Russian; he has returned from Queanbeyan where he has been consulting a lawyer. Commissioner Cooper."'

James looked astonished. 'Did it really say that?'

'Yes, those were the exact words, I swear to you.'

'Have you told anyone else? Does anyone know you read it?'

'No. It wasn't properly sealed. I folded the letter again and delivered it to Mr Bourke, the storekeeper. I thought it must be him as I know he has a connection with The Boys.'

'Be sure you don't say a word to anyone – even your father. Promise. Otherwise you'll be in real danger. These people are ruthless. They'll stop at nothing. This proves the police are part of it too.'

'Why? What does it all mean?'

'The old Russian, that's Fred Cohen the jeweller. I heard he won a lot of money from the commissioner at cards the other night. Cooper accused him of cheating. It turned nasty. Everyone in the bar room next door heard it. Cohen accused the commissioner of defaming him. I bet that's why he was off to see a lawyer. Now Cooper wants The Boys to beat him.'

'But that's terrible,' said Kitty.

'It is, but there's nothing we can do. Not when it's coming from the top and the police are in on it too. There's no hope of justice here. Davy thought he could change it. You can't. Power goes to people's heads. The only thing you can do is keep your head down. This world is a bad place, run by bad men. If you try and fight them, they'll just crush you.'

'You make it sound so bad. Is it really like that?'

'It will be, so long as Cooper's here. But you don't need to get involved. Just stay right out of it. Say nothing, keep clear of Cooper and his cronies, and you'll be all right.'

Kitty did as James suggested, despite some lingering doubts. She never mentioned the letter to anyone. It gave her some comfort that nothing appeared to happen to Mr Cohen.

When he was visiting Kitty, James never seemed to have other pressing business. Kitty's father noticed that James and Kitty were spending a lot of time together. He didn't say anything, although he knew that Sally was keen on James. He'd learned to be wary of intervention in human relationships, particularly anything involving Kitty, or her mother for that matter. At least James's companionship could make Kitty smile, and a daughter's happiness was something a father could be grateful for.

On a windy day late in September, as James was walking down Telegraph Street on his way to New Chum, holding onto his hat, he saw a familiar-looking horseman riding towards him. It was Clarrie, head stockman from Cosgrove's.

'Why, if it isn't young James,' said Clarrie, pulling his horse up short. 'How'd you be?' He was dusty and travel-worn, but otherwise looked much as James remembered him.

James had always liked Clarrie. 'I'm doing fine,' he said. 'What brings you here?'

'I'm on me way to Cosgrove's. Come up from Tumut. Been a long ride.' Clarrie's horse started fretting.

'The old girl needs a feed. We're nearly there now,' he said, giving her a pat. 'Listen, why don't we have a drink together?'

James agreed. They took Clarrie's horse to the Empire Hotel stables and sat down for a drink in the bar. The room was half-empty and not too noisy. Over a drink and a smoke, they swapped stories about what they'd been doing since they'd last met. Clarrie told James he'd been out west droving cattle – as far north as the Queensland border. James told Clarrie something about his mining experiences around Kiandra, at Crack-em-back and at the Nine Mile and the Four Mile Diggings.

'So what brings you back this way?' James asked.

'I got a message from Cosgrove, by way of Tumut,' said Clarrie. 'He learned I was in town and wired me he was short of stockmen. All his hands had gone to the diggings. He asked if I'd come back and work for him again.'

'And you said yes?' guessed James.

'I did,' said Clarrie. 'He offered me good wages, so I agreed. I done a lot of travellin' the last year, so I'm ready to settle down for a bit. Why don't you join me? He asked if I knew any other hands. Ones with experience, that is.'

'I'll have to think about that,' said James. 'I might be interested.' He didn't need to think long. Before they parted, he told Clarrie he'd take up the offer.

Clarrie said he'd settle the arrangements as soon as he got to Cosgrove's. James told him he could always be contacted through Mr McCrae, who did the mail run.

Three days later, Kitty handed James a letter. It was from Cosgrove, instructing James to go to Russell's, where there'd be a horse waiting for him. He was to join Clarrie and a mob of bullocks Clarrie was droving up through Nine Mile.

James told Kitty what he'd arranged. 'I'll still be nearby in the district,' he said. 'I'll make sure I come and see you.'

'You'd better,' said Kitty.

He gave her a hug goodbye. He noticed that she blushed. It gave him a strange feeling.

After saying goodbye to Kitty, he made fast time on the track to Russell's and arrived before dark. The horse he'd been assigned was being used to muster stock, so he had to stay the night. Clarrie and the mob of bullocks had left earlier in the day. With time on his hands, he remembered he hadn't written to Sally recently. He borrowed some paper and wrote her a letter.

Russell's Station

6th October 1861

Dear Sally

I've now left gold digging for good to take up stock riding again and am presently at Russell's to pick up my horse. Tomorrow I'll be riding up past Nine Mile to meet up with Clarrie (my old boss) and a mob of bullocks from Cosgrove's, which will take me I know not where, other than it will be in the high country beyond Kiandra.

This all came about suddenly when I met Clarrie last week in Kiandra and he offered me the work.

I will try to write to you again when I better know what is happening.

Your affectionate friend

James

John Russell said he'd make sure the letter was safely delivered to Sally in Cooma.

While at Russell's, James heard news that a young boy had come across the body of a miner floating in a creek near the Kiandra township. The man had gone missing months ago in the vicinity of the racecourse water holes during a winter snowstorm. Only when the ground thawed had they found his body. It wouldn't be the first or the last time that happened, William Russell said.

Despite his good intentions, James didn't get away early. He helped John in the stockyards with some brumbies before he left.

With the freedom of his own horse again, James decided to take a short cut up Four Mile Creek. On the way he met Clarke's party at the river. After yarning with them, he crossed the river and followed Four Mile Creek upstream to the lower Four Mile flats. It was there that he found Davy's body poking out of the mullock heap.

18

Davy's Legacy
October 1861

As he rode into the wind and rain, away from the Four Mile diggings, James couldn't get the gory image of Davy's mangled arm out of his mind. He shut his eyes. It didn't help. He kept seeing Davy's ghastly stare – and the sight of his broken body, as it rolled over, crumpled and lifeless. The shocking images wouldn't go away. He felt all knotted inside. He wanted to burst out sobbing. Nothing would come. He stopped riding. Leaning forward he rested his head on his horse's neck.

He was shattered. How could his life ever be the same? He didn't know what to do. What could he tell Kitty? He felt so sad, so empty – and so alone.

It seemed a lifetime before he was able to grit his teeth and face the track again.

He'd been so wrong. Davy hadn't deserted them. He hadn't left without saying goodbye. He'd been murdered. He wished he hadn't been so quick to think badly of Davy. He wished he hadn't argued with him before he left. And he felt so guilty. Maybe it was his fault. He shouldn't have told The Boys that Davy was staying at Four Mile. Maybe they'd had something to do with it.

He started to wonder who could have murdered Davy. Apart from The Boys, there was Sergeant Ballard. The man hated Davy. He remembered seeing the sergeant riding away from Four Mile around the time Davy disappeared. But what about Cooper? Maybe he'd been involved. He hated Davy too. Then there was Frankie Gardiner. Kitty had told him how Davy had upset him.

He rode on mindlessly, not noticing where he was going. His mind felt like the centre of a swirling storm. Thoughts rushed through his head in a jumble. He rode past the sparse, stunted snow gums as they clung to mountain's rocky backbone. He rode past shallow ponds, through sodden flats and across boggy marshes until, almost by surprise, he came upon Clarrie and the mob of bullocks. He'd almost forgotten why he was going to meet them.

Clarrie was riding at the rear of the mob, hunched forward on his horse as he faced the buffeting wind, his coat wrapped tightly round him. Ben, a young stockrider, was at the front.

James shouted as he approached, but the wind blew his voice away. He had to ride alongside Clarrie and yell before he was noticed. He told Clarrie he'd found a dead body. The body of a friend. He had to tell Kitty in Kiandra. She was Davy's girl.

Clarrie told him to go. 'Meet us past Three Mile when you're done,' he shouted.

As James rode down the mountainside to the Kiandra township, the wind and rain eased. Kitty was on her own in the post office. When he banged open the door, windblown and wild-eyed, she immediately knew something was wrong.

'What is it?' she asked, looking worried.

'It's Davy,' James blurted out. 'He's dead. He's been murdered.' It wasn't how he'd planned to tell her. He hadn't wanted to shock her.

'What do you mean?' she said, her voice quivering.

'I found him. His dead body. At the Four Mile.'

Kitty turned white. She looked as though she was about to faint.

James moved towards her.

'Don't touch me,' she said. She steadied herself against a chair. 'What happened? Tell me slowly.' She suddenly felt very weak.

'I was riding to the Four Mile,' said James. 'There was this mullock heap. I found Davy's body. It was half buried in it. He'd been murdered, I'm sure.'

'How? Who did it?'

'I don't know.'

'Are you sure it was Davy? How could you tell?' Kitty didn't want to believe him.

'I saw his face. It was terrible.'

Kitty gave a start, and put her hand over her mouth.

'It's all right. I covered him over. Then I rode straight here.'

'What do you mean, you covered him over?'

'I buried him again.' James nearly mentioned the crows but stopped himself in time.

'You left him buried – there? In a mullock heap?' Kitty frowned and looked at him, half cross, half distraught.

'Yes,' said James. 'Is something wrong? I made sure he was well buried. I put a blanket over him first.'

'He can't stay there,' said Kitty firmly. 'He's got to have a decent burial. He must have a proper Christian burial.' She was most emphatic.

James had learned not to argue with Kitty when she'd set her mind. 'Don't worry. I'll make sure he gets a proper burial,' he said quickly. 'We'll bring him here. We can bury him in the Kiandra cemetery.'

'You must,' she said. 'Promise me you will.' She was now pleading, looking at him with teary eyes. Suddenly she was weak and helpless.

'Of course I will,' said James.

Kitty sat down. 'To think I doubted him,' she said, shaking her head slowly from side to side. She was talking to herself more than to James. 'I should never have been angry with him. I should have trusted him. How can I forgive myself? Now I'll never see him.' She was becoming more distressed with every word. 'He won't ever be able to forgive me. I can't take it. I don't want to live any more.' She burst into tears.

James wanted to comfort her and started to move his hand. An instinct stopped him. He stood there. He felt very uncomfortable, and very unhappy. He didn't know what to do with himself. His sadness about Davy was complicated by his feelings for Kitty.

After a few minutes, Kitty stopped sobbing. She looked upwards at James through her tears. 'I promised Davy I'd wait for him. I promised I'd be true to him,' she said. 'How can I ever keep true to him now? Now we can never get married.' She burst into tears again.

James knew she didn't expect an answer. He felt powerless to help her, to ease her torment. His own sadness seemed so insignificant. Now he realised how deeply she cared for Davy. He should have expected her reaction. Yet he was shocked and disturbed by it, even though he knew he had no right to be.

He waited until Kitty was no longer so visibly upset then explained why he couldn't stay. He said Clarrie was waiting for him to return to help with the bullocks. They were depending on him.

'You're not going to leave Davy where he is, are you?' she said.

'I'll come back as soon as I can. I'll get Jack to help me. I'll only be gone a few days,' said James. 'We'll bury him properly then.'

This response appeared to satisfy Kitty, for the moment.

James said goodbye. As he left, Kitty looked at him blankly, as if she no longer recognised him. She was in another world. It further disturbed and unsettled him.

Once James was riding in the wind and the rain, his own sadness returned. It was a hollow, despairing sadness. He felt so alone. Kitty was so distant. And Davy was dead.

He caught up with Clarrie and the mob of bullocks past Three Mile Creek. It was hard to tell Clarrie what had happened. He didn't want to talk to anyone about it.

Clarrie and Ben went looking for brumbies the following day, leaving James to look after the mob. Clarrie told him to be careful the cattle didn't stray. He'd heard news from Golden Gully the Mulligan gang were back in the Kiandra district. 'Make sure you keep the bullocks up here in the hills. It ain't likely for them bushrangers to be up this way. It's the roads what'll be dangerous now,'

Clarrie and Ben returned two days later with three brumbies in tow, two mares and a young stallion. The wild horses were in surprisingly good condition, considering they'd just spent the winter in the mountains. Clarrie was as pleased as punch. It was arranged that he and James would take them to Kiandra in the morning. They set off early and were at the stockyards before most of the township were awake.

Tommy, the young Chinese horse breaker, was at the yards already. He remembered James and asked him if he'd heard from Mr Davy lately.

James had to tell him what had happened.

Tommy didn't believe him at first. He was very upset when the news sank in. 'Mr Davy very good man,' he said, shaking his head. 'Who could've done this bad thing? Who?'

James had no answer.

When they'd finished their business at the stockyards, James got Clarrie's permission to take the rest of the day off. He rode straight to the post office to see Kitty. She wasn't there. Nor was her father. The post office manager told James Mr McCrae had taken ill the day before. He hadn't seen him since. He said he'd given the mail bags to Kitty the night before.

*

Kitty spent the previous afternoon waiting for her father. Davy was always on her mind, her thoughts feverishly alternating between grief and anger. Her own life seemed so unimportant now. As the day went on, her father's absence began to worry her. He'd never been this late before.

She leant on the gate at the Rocky Plains yards and looked down the road towards Russell's. The western sun skimmed the tree tops on its way home for the day, the last of its rays briefly touching her raven curls and lighting them with a golden amber glow. As he came riding slowly along the track, Mr McCrae caught sight of the tiny glint of gold in the distance. His daughter was worth far more than her weight in precious metal to him.

'The fever's got me agin me gal,' he said, almost collapsing as he slid off his horse. He steadied himself against the rails. 'I canna do it. I canna take the mail. You'll have to do it for me.'

'Of course I'll do it.' Kitty was more concerned about him than herself.

'I wouldn't ask if I did nay have to. I'll lose the contract. Carmichael's been complainin' agin.'

'Don't worry,' said Kitty. 'I've done it before. You go straight to bed. I'll stoke the fire before I go.'

'I left the other nags at the Traveller's Rest, with the coach. Postboy here's the best. He knows the way. He'll get you safely down with the mail.'

'Off to bed with you,' said Kitty.

'You'll need to collect the bags from the post,' said Mr McCrae. 'They'll be waiting for you.'

'I know what to do, Father. Off you go. I can manage well enough.'

The firmness in her voice finally had its effect. Slowly he made his way across to the hut, leaving her to organise the horses. It didn't take her long before she had everything ready. She slipped on the blue-serge postal outfit and buckled it tight around her waist. She almost disappeared in it. It was designed for a man. After making sure the fire was stoked and that her father was comfortably settled in bed, she set off to the Kiandra township to collect the mail bags.

Postboy was tough as nails. There was no expensive blood in the old iron-grey horse, but he was sure-footed on the steepest slope. Bred from a mountain mob, he'd been run in as a colt by Dusty Bob in the days before the rush. Her father could not have given her a better mount.

When Kitty arrived, the post office was shut. She went looking for the manager. She found him at Carmichael's, as she'd expected. He'd heard about the Mulligans and was reluctant to let her take the mail. She told him not to worry on her account. Since Davy's death, she was completely mindless of her own safety.

'It's not the first time I've taken the mail,' she said. 'Anyway, it'll be safer now it's dark. No one'll be expecting me.'

The manager still felt uneasy as he unlocked the safe and handed her the gold consignment. 'I don't know why they ever stopped the gold escort,' he said. 'Penny pinching, I'd say. Instead, they wastes their money employing more officials.'

The night was crisp and clear. The mountain air hung damp and cold above the ground. Overhead, the broad band of the Milky Way sparkled and twinkled in the night sky and a sliver of moon lit up the track

Kitty rode back over the hill to Rocky Plains, through wisps of fog gathering in the gullies and across mountain streamlets gurgling to themselves amongst the marshes. She followed the track over Connor's Hill then rode down through the tall, stately stands of mountain ash, their straight trunks painted silver in the faint moonlight. As the forest shadows receded and the ground opened out, she gave Postboy his head. He knew the track as well as he knew the path to his stable. He was galloping hard as they approached the clearing beside the abandoned hut.

Skulking in the shadows of the hut were the dark forms of three armed men, Captain Bill, Dan Mulligan and Alex.

'Are you sure the post'll come today?' whispered Alex. 'Haven't we waited long enough?'

'Of course it will,' said Captain Bill.

'But what if it doesn't? Are we going to wait all night? I still don't think this is a good spot. It's too open.'

'Shut your mouth,' said the Captain. 'I'm in charge. You'll do as I say.'

'But Gardiner said – ' started Alex.

'I don't give a damn about Gardiner. Keep your mouth shut and do what I tell you. Gardiner thinks he's so fancy. I'll show him a thing or two. Quiet,' he hissed. 'There's a horse coming.'

The men crouched behind the brush fence facing the track. Seconds later, the galloping horse came into sight on the far side of the clearing.

'Stand!' shouted Captain Bill, as they stepped out of their cover.

'Bail up! We want the mail!' shouted Dan.

Kitty had no intention of standing. Her only thought was to save the mail. She was as brave a lass as ever rode a horse. She spurred Postboy forward – straight at the men who blocked the track.

Dan clutched vainly at the bridle as she charged by. He was flattened by one of Postboy's hoofs.

As she galloped away, Kitty heard a sharp crack, then felt a shot whistle past her head. 'You cowards!' was all she could say. She leaned forward, desperately urging Postboy on.

He was galloping at full stretch across the flat. He couldn't go any faster. Another shot rang out. This one found its mark.

Postboy never slackened his pace. The shot hit Kitty in the side. She flinched in pain. Soon, the blood from her wound started to seep down Postboy's flank, turning it wet and sticky. Her grip on the reins weakened. With every stride, she became more and more feeble. She felt herself losing consciousness and slumped forward onto Postboy's neck.

They were now clear of Warrigal Flat and fast approaching the Redbank diggings. There, as Postboy slowed to a trot, Kitty gave a last feeble cry. Then she fell, lifeless, onto the ground.

Postboy stopped. He sniffed at her pale face lying upturned in the dusty track. Kitty made no move. He snorted, then he resumed his journey, trotting along the track that led to the postal change at Denison.

John Russell was amazed to see a riderless horse approaching the postal gate. He ran over to investigate. By the light of a lamp, he recognised it was one of the mail horses. He could see it was covered in blood, sweat and dust. There was no sign of the rider, but the saddlebags appeared untouched. Clearly, there'd been foul play. He rushed over to tell his father.

An armed party was quickly mustered. They set off along the Kiandra road, expecting the worst. John took the lead. He was the first to see Kitty's body, lying in the middle of the dusty moonlit track, like a bundle of discarded rags. He recognised the postal uniform and gave a shout. As he jumped down, he saw Kitty's upturned face and her twisted neck, her motionless gaze fixed upon the silent moon. It gave him a terrible shock. They were fully expecting to find Alec McCrae, and hoped he might only be wounded. John was badly shaken. He felt sick in the stomach and had to steady himself against his horse.

The rest of the party quickly gathered round, looking down at the pathetic little bundle on the ground. All were badly affected by the sight.

After they'd got over their initial shock, they had a hurried conference and decided it would be best to take Kitty's body back to Denison for the night. Then they'd make arrangements to carry her by coach to Kiandra in the morning. It was left to the older men in the party, those more used to the sight of death, to move Kitty's body. Even those hardened men couldn't remain unaffected, seeing the now lifeless form of this beautiful young girl, without an enemy in the world, brutally murdered in the bloom of her youth. It brought tears to their eyes.

*

James stood outside the post office wondering where Kitty might be and what he should do. A horseman came galloping up the road. James recognised him as one of the hands from Russell's.

The man jumped off his horse and rushed over to where James and the manager were standing. 'Kitty McCrae's dead,' he said breathlessly. 'They've taken her to Rocky Plains. The mail got through but they killed her.'

'What?' said the manager in disbelief. 'Kitty's dead?'

'What happened?' said James. He felt as though he had a vice tightening round his temple.

'They found her near the Redbank diggings, just short of Russell's. She'd been shot.'

'What happened? Where is she now?' asked James, in a flustered voice.

'It's just like I said. They've taken her to Rocky Plains, to her father's place. She was shot last night. They must've tried to bail her up. Then they shot her when she didn't stop. Her horse kept going. It turned up at Russell's with the mail.'

'I'm off to Rocky Plains,' said James, jumping onto Jasmin. He still couldn't believe the news. He galloped down the road, heedless of travellers and obstacles. The world was unreal. Kitty couldn't be dead. She mustn't be. He wouldn't believe it until he saw her. Maybe the man was wrong?

James could see a spring cart and a number of horses tied up outside the McCrae's hut. Some men from Russell's were standing beside the cart when he reached the yard. He leapt off his horse and ran to the door. Inside, the hut was crowded. He saw Alec McCrae, wrapped in a blanket and sitting on a stool. He was leaning over Kitty's body, which was laid out on an improvised stretcher.

James saw Kitty's pale, lifeless face, her eyes now permanently closed. The reality sank in. There was no mistake. He felt sick in the stomach and stopped.

Alec McCrae must have heard him come in. He turned his head slowly and looked at James. It was the gaze of a shattered man. He'd aged ten years in a day. His eyes were red and tearful, his skin pale and jaundiced. 'James,' he said, his voice quavering. 'James, laddie, look what they've done.'

James moved forward and put his hand on the old man's shoulder. 'Who could have done this?' James asked. Seeing Kitty's father brought so low gave him the courage to sound firm.

'I canna believe it,' said Alec McCrae, in a weak but determined voice. 'I'll nae rest till the murdering swine is in 'is grave.' He tried to stand, but the effort was too much. 'The fever – it's still got me,' he said, breathing heavily. 'You were Kitty's friend. Here, laddie, take this.' He fumbled under the blanket and handed James a pistol.

James knew how much the weapon meant to Mr McCrae. Kitty had told him her father never let anyone else touch it. With its carved wooden handle, worn smooth from handling, and its delicately etched barrel, James could see it was no ordinary pistol.

'Ye can use it, till I'm well enough,' said Mr McCrae.

'I will,' said James. He didn't hesitate. It wasn't bravery. It was the instinct of the moment. In that instant, he committed himself to avenging Kitty's death.

'I swear by Saint Andrew of Scotland, and by Almighty God,' said Alec McCrae, standing unsteadily. 'I'll nae touch a dram o' whisky agin. Not till the cur what did this deed is dead and gone. May the mongrel rot in hell!' He sank back down after this effort, exhausted.

James and the others helped him to his bed.

They buried Kitty next morning at the Kiandra cemetery. Alec McCrae was so weak he had to be helped from the cart. In the daylight, he looked even more frail. Two friends had to support him during the brief ceremony.

As Kitty's body was lowered into the grave, a lone bagpiper stood on the hillside, playing a mournful Scottish tune. The sad strains of the music tore at James's heart. As he watched the last sods being shovelled onto the grave, the tragedy of Kitty's death overwhelmed him. He'd never see her pretty smile again, nor hear her cheerful laughter. Her bravery had been her downfall. Now she was gone forever. She'd been such a brave girl. He stood looking at the sad little mound of earth and the tears ran down his cheeks.

When the small group of mourners had left the graveside, James approached Alec McCrae as he was about to be helped up into the spring cart. 'I don't know what to say,' he started.

'No need to talk, laddie. Here, I forgot to give ye this.' He handed James a letter.

James put it in his pocket. They exchanged glances.

'You can trust me,' said James. 'I know what needs be done.'

'Aye, ye do. Nae worry. I'll soon be well enough to join ye.'

After the funeral party had driven out of sight, James opened the letter. It was from Sally.

Euecumbene Station

8th October, 1861

Dear James

You can see from my address above I have now left Cooma and am residing at Euecumbene station. Mrs Crow has just been blessed with another child, a beautiful baby girl, and I am helping out with the older children as she is a little out of sorts. Mother made the arrangement as she heard the older children needed a tutor, and we have known the Crows for some time, mother having been friends with Mrs Crow when they were both young.

The Station is well located near the Eucumbene River, with views to the distant hills and mountains. I could not have wished for a more amenable place to spend the next few months until Christmas.

I hope all is well with you, though I have not heard from you for some time.

Still your affectionate friend,

Sally

James folded the letter and put it in his pocket. He didn't have time to think about Sally now. He had things to do. He hadn't forgotten his promise to Kitty. Now he felt an urgency to honour it. He had to give Davy a proper burial.

Quickly unhitching Jasmin, he set off for the Four Mile diggings. This time, he found Jack digging at his claim. James quickly explained the terrible news about Davy and Kitty. He asked Jack for his help to move Davy.

Jack listened quietly. When he heard the circumstances of Kitty's death, all he said was 'Those bastards.' He had come to expect the worst in this world. He'd experienced much of death and unhappiness in his own life, though he kept the details to himself.

They loaded Jasmin with blankets and rope, collected some tools and followed the creek downstream to where Davy was buried. The mound was undisturbed, just as James had left it.

While digging away the earth covering Davy's body, James noticed the stem of a pipe sticking out of the rubble. He pulled it out. It was a hand-carved briar. 'That's a fancy looking smoking piece, don't you reckon?' he said, showing it to Jack. As he brushed the dirt off, he thought it looked familiar. Then it came to him. 'Sergeant Ballard had one like that. I remember. He was smoking it at the Hawkins court case. Do you think? Maybe – '

'You sure it's the same one?' asked Jack.

'Dead certain,' said James. 'You know what this means?' He looked at Jack. 'How else could it have got here? If it was that bastard – '

'That's no proof,' said Jack. 'I seen plenty others like that at Benjamin's Store.'

'It's damn suspicious, all the same,' said James. He put the pipe in his pocket. 'We'd better keep going.'

After carefully scraping away the earth and removing the blanket, they gently lifted Davy's body onto a clean piece of calico. Wrapping and binding it like a swag roll, they loaded the sad bundle onto Jasmin, together with their tools. James spent the journey to Kiandra so absorbed in his thoughts it could've been hailing and he wouldn't have noticed. Jack showed little inclination to talk either.

From the hill above the commissioner's camp, James led them straight to Kitty's grave. Without saying a word, he took a pick and started digging next to it. Jack joined him. The ground was full of rocks, so it took them nearly an hour to get the depth they needed. While they were digging, the weather changed. The sky turned dark grey and the air chilled. By the time they were heaving the last spadefuls onto the grave, snowflakes had started falling. They stood up and leaned on their shovels, easing their backs.

James watched as the little white flakes settled lightly on top of the mound, melting away as they touched it. 'At least they'll be close together now,' he said.

Jack nodded.

They stood silently for a few minutes, each thinking their own thoughts. James felt drained of energy. His arms and shoulders were tired from the digging. But it was more than that. He felt for the pistol in his belt. He still had a commitment. Doubts started to worry him. What if he failed? He didn't want to let anyone down. He owed it to Kitty, and to her father. But what if he couldn't do it? He'd never had to kill a man before.

Jack broke the silence. 'I'm going back to Victoria,' he said suddenly. 'They've found gold in the hills at Walhalla. Could be an El Dorado. I've had enough of this New South Wales. Davy was a good man. Let him rest in peace.'

He crossed himself. James had never seen him do that before.

They packed up the tools. Jack said he'd take them to Four Mile with him, before leaving for Victoria. James helped him roll them up in a blanket and rope them over his back, then they said goodbye.

'Take care, young Jimmy,' said Jack.

'You too,' said James.

James watched as Jack walked purposefully up the hill towards Four Mile and Walhalla, without a backward look. As he disappeared out of sight, the snow started settling on the ground.

*

James stood silently in the gently falling snow. Gradually, it covered the recently scarred earth, leaving a white, peaceful blanket over the two mounds in front of him. Under their soft quilt of snow, Kitty and Davy were now side by side, together in death, forever. In a small way, James felt he'd finally done something right. He'd met Kitty's last wish, though she could never have foreseen how it would end. He desperately wished it hadn't ended like this.

The sight of Jasmin, tied forlornly to the lone cemetery fence post, reminded James that he had other things to do. All the other posts and palings had disappeared for winter firewood. He walked slowly across the fresh snow to where she was tethered. As he was unhitching her, Alex came riding along the track to the cemetery. James had only met Alex a couple of times, and they'd hardly exchanged words.

Alex pulled up his horse beside James. 'You're a friend of my brother's, aren't you?' he said, bending down and whispering.

'Yes,' said James, suspiciously. He knew about Alex's involvement with Captain Bill and the Mulligans.

'I need your help,' said Alex. 'I've got to get a message to Davy. I haven't seen him and don't know where he is. It's about Kitty.'

He kept looking nervously in the direction of the commissioner's camp. The camp was quiet, as it usually was late in the afternoon. By now, its occupants were more likely to be found in a public house.

'All right,' said James. He surreptitiously felt for the pistol under his coat.

'We can't talk here,' said Alex. 'It's too open. Let's get under shelter. How about that hut over there?' He pointed to an abandoned hut further round the hillside.

James nodded. Leading his own horse, he followed Alex to the building.

One of the walls of the hut had fallen in. Planks were missing from others. They tied their horses to the uprights and took shelter under what was left of its shingle roof. Wary of a trap, James kept a careful eye on Alex. He made sure he never turned his back on him.

'I heard you just buried Kitty,' said Alex.

James nodded.

'I know how she died. And I know who killed her,' said Alex. 'I want you to tell Davy.'

James felt a flush of excitement. 'Who was it?' he asked, trying to sound as disinterested as possible.

'First you've got to promise not to mention my name – except to Davy. You've got to leave me out of this if you tell anyone else.'

James hesitated slightly. 'All right,' he said. 'As long as it wasn't you that killed kill her.'

'I didn't,' said Alex. 'It was Captain Bill. I know – I was there. Listen carefully. You've got to tell Davy everything I say.'

James looked Alex in the eyes. Could he trust this man? He decided it would depend on what Alex said next. He kept his right hand free, in case there was a trick.

'It was Captain Bill's plan to rob the mail,' said Alex. 'Dan and me agreed to go along with it. The captain wanted to show how good he was at highway robbery. Frankie kept sayin' the captain was nothin' but a two-bit horse thief. The captain wanted to show him a thing or two. Have you got any baccy?'

'Yes,' said James.

'Can I have some?' said Alex, pulling out a clay pipe.

James stepped back and took a block of tobacco and a knife out of his pocket. He quickly cut some off for Alex. He didn't take out his own pipe. He wanted to keep his hands free.

Alex lit up using a fancy imported match. Then he continued his story, in-between puffs. 'It was the wrong place for a sticking-up. It was wide open. I told the captain. He wouldn't listen. We didn't know it would be Kitty. She should've stopped. She kept galloping when we bailed her up. I saw it was a girl but I never knew it was Kitty – I swear. The captain shot her after she'd passed. He must've known it was a girl. You could see her face, even in the moonlight.'

Alex paused and relit his pipe. His hands were shaking. 'At first we didn't know she'd been killed. I found out later. After she'd gone, the captain and me had a quarrel. I told him he shouldn't have shot the girl. He said he didn't care. We ended up fighting. Dan had to pull us apart. That was the end for me. It woke me up. I don't agree with shooting women. I told 'em I was quitting the bushranging game. I come back here and hid out in the hills.'

Alex stopped and spat into the snow. 'Dan's brother told me about Kitty this morning,' he continued. 'Now she's dead, the troopers'll be after me too. He said the traps caught up with Dan and the captain near Michelago. They thought they had Gardiner. They've been after his gang ever since that trooper got killed.'

'So what happened?' asked James. He now believed Alex was telling the truth.

'There was a shoot-out. The captain got killed. Dan was wounded.

Now he's under escort to Goulburn. I don't think he'll tell on me. But I can't be sure.' Alex stopped talking and looked out at the white landscape. His hands were shaking as he tried to relight his pipe.

'Is that everything you wanted to tell me,' asked James. His head was whirling from what he'd heard. Now, he'd have to tell Alex that Davy was dead.

'Yes,' said Alex. 'Except you can tell Davy I've gone to Victoria. I'll go the back way, by Ligar's route. That should keep me clear of the New South Wales troopers.'

Alex glanced around the side of the hut, like a hunted man. All his youthful bravado had gone. 'You can also tell Davy I'll be taking an honest path from now on. I've had me eyes opened. I never realised what bushranging was really like. You know, Kitty wasn't the first person the captain killed. I had no idea. Dan told me. The captain murdered a digger last winter. He bragged to Dan about it.'

Alex looked at James. He had Davy's eyes. They were full of sorrow and regret. 'I'm not religious,' he said. 'But I know it's wrong to kill a man in cold blood. The captain killed that digger to steal his nugget. Dan said the captain showed it to him. He said it looked like a little boot.'

James felt a rush of blood to his head. He gulped.

Alex noticed. 'What's wrong?' he said suspiciously.

James tried to stay calm. Now he was the one who felt shaky. He took a deep breath. 'I've got something to tell you,' he said. 'Davy's dead. We've just buried him. Over there.' He pointed to the graves. 'Next to Kitty. That boot-shaped nugget – it was Davy's.'

It was Alex's turn to look shocked. He stood there, at first not believing what he'd heard. When he spoke, it was in a very quiet voice. 'So it was the captain that killed them both,' he said. 'I wish I'd known before. I could have saved Kitty.'

He looked at James and their eyes met. An unspoken message passed between them.

'Thank you for telling me,' Alex said. 'I must be off.' Knocking the embers out of his pipe, he untied his horse and swung himself up into the saddle.

James watched as he rode off up the track through the snow – in the direction of Victoria.

*

When Alex had gone, James led Jasmin across to the cemetery again. It was no longer snowing but the sky was darkening as night approached. He stood once more beside the two white mounds and their buried memories. There was nothing more he could do. There was nothing more to say. He looked around at the deserted goldfield, covered in its soft white mantle of snow. In the distance, the dilapidated Kiandra village stood bleakly silent. Mournful wisps of smoke twisted skywards from its few active chimneys. All around him was a dead and frozen world. He shivered as he felt the evening cold descending.

'I'm sorry,' he said, looking at the two sad mounds. 'I'm so sorry. I can't do any more.' He shook his head.

He eased himself up into the saddle. After taking a long last look at the graves, he headed along the road that led away from Kiandra.

When he dismounted at Rocky Plains, he found Alec McCrae sitting in front of the fireplace inside his hut. He still looked very sickly. James told him the man who'd killed his daughter was dead – shot by the traps.

Then he took the pistol out of his belt. 'I won't be needing this any more,' he said. As he handed the weapon back, the reality that he wouldn't need to use it finally sank in. He felt the lifting of an immense burden from his shoulders.

'Just as well they got him before I did,' said Alec McCrae. There was a bite to his voice.

James then told him it was the same man who killed Davy, and that Kitty and Davy were now buried beside each other in the cemetery.

'Pass me that bottle will ye, laddie,' said Alec, pointing to the bottle of whisky on the high shelf. He offered James a drink. After they'd each had a glass, he said, 'I'll be right by meself now. There's some things a man's got to deal with on his own.' There was a faraway look in his eyes.

Outside the hut, the stars were out. The night was cold and clear. By

314

the faint starlight, James could just make out tracks in the snow. He knew now what he had to do. He pointed Jasmin towards the road to Russell's and Adaminimi.

Jasmin's hooves crunched through the soft snow and icy puddles as James urged her on, retracing Kitty's fatal ride. Over Connor's Hill he rode, then down through the tall stands of stately alpine ash, their trunks dappled in the moonlight. Without pausing, he rode past the place where Kitty was shot. On the lower slopes, the snow gave way to slush and mud. Never slackening, he rode over the river at Denison and on to Adaminimi, not even stopping at Russell's. By late in the evening, he'd reached the yards at Euecumbene Station.

Sally was in the parlour when James arrived.

'There's a man to see you on the back veranda,' said Mrs Crow, in a tone of mild disapproval.

At first, Sally wondered who it could be. Her heart gave a jump when she saw it was James.

He was a sight. He looked all the part of a wild man from the bush, as if he'd just stepped out of a shaft at the diggings. His hair was windblown, his face unshaven and weather beaten, and his clothes were spattered with mud. Sally could understand Mrs Crow's reaction.

'I need to talk to you,' he said. 'Can we go for a walk? I can't come in like this.'

'Of course,' said Sally. 'Let me get a coat.' She disappeared inside the house and quickly returned with a warm shawl.

It was a still, cool night on the river flats. Here, the heavens were at peace. At this distance from Kiandra, Euecumbene Station had escaped the stormy weather of the distant mountains. As James and Sally walked down towards the river, the broad band of the Milky Way arched overhead, its tiny stars twinkling their myriad messages.

'Sally,' said James, plucking up courage. 'Do you still have that little gold nugget I gave you last year?'

'Yes,' she replied.

They walked a few paces. Her heart was racing as she waited for his next words. It seemed an eternity to her.

'Sally,' he said. 'Will you marry me?'

'Of course I will,' she replied. She gave him a big hug. 'Sally Boake sounds good, doesn't it? I've always liked the idea of being Mrs Boake.'

'I'm so glad,' he said, holding her tight. 'I was worried. I haven't treated you well. So many things have happened.'

'It doesn't matter now,' she said.

They held hands and faced each other in the silvery light.

'Do you remember,' said James. 'Before I left for the diggings, how I said I wanted excitement in my life? And you said we were just ordinary people. That we can't expect to live more than ordinary lives.'

'I remember,' said Sally.

'You were right,' said James. 'We're just ordinary people. I was wrong. There's so many things I wish I'd done different.'

Sally had heard about Kitty's death and knew how much James had cared about her. She had an idea what must be going through his mind. 'That's all over and done with,' she said. 'We've got each other now. We've got our future. There's no need to dwell on the past.'

Sally didn't want to think about what would never be, either in his life or in her own. She didn't need to know about Kitty. And there was no need for James to know about Duncan. She'd send Duncan a letter, now he'd left the district.

'I guess we'd better turn that little nugget into a ring or two,' said James.

'Yes, we'd better,' said Sally. 'I'm so happy.' She hugged him again, holding him ever so tight.

He buried his head in her hair. He was so glad they had each other.

High above them in the night sky, the stars of the Southern Cross twinkled brightly, as they had for ages, and as they would for ages, in this young old land.

The end
…and the beginning

Appendices

Historical Facts

The Homeward Bound Inquiry

Following his injudicious letter to the *Sydney Morning Herald* in August 1861, Samuel Hawkins continued to pursue his protests against the decisions of Sub-commissioner Frederick Cooper. On 12th November 1861, Commissioner Cloete recommended that Mr James Harrop Griffin, his replacement as Commissioner in Charge of the Southern Goldfields, immediately visit Kiandra to investigate Hawkins' claims. By this time, a number of other grievances against Cooper had been raised.

In his recommendation to the Secretary for Lands, Commissioner Cloete said the matter involving Hawkins was 'so complicated it can only be decided on the spot'. Nevertheless, he acknowledged there was substance in Hawkins' claims. Cloete said that two sluice heads 'cannot mean two ground sluice heads as Mr Cooper would seem to have decided' since a ground sluice was double the quantity and would have been mentioned on the permit. He also said he could not see the utility of Cooper's order to supply Shinnick, as Shinnick's water supply came from a different, higher source than the Homeward Bound claim.

In January 1862, Commissioner Griffin visited Kiandra to conduct the Inquiry into the charges made against Cooper. He refused a request by Mr G.B. Barton, the barrister representing Hawkins, to make attendance by witnesses compulsory. Not surprisingly, many witnesses were not available. Numbers of those who attended swore that Kiandra was an orderly place and that they were unaware of anything untoward in Mr Cooper's behaviour. In particular, Michael Bourke denied being the leader of the 'Irish Mob' and denied saying he would swear anything for Cooper, although he did accept that he was known in the street as 'the Commissioner's tool'.

During the inquiry, a police witness gave evidence that Cooper had told the police to turn a blind eye while Hawkins was given a hiding. Other evidence was heard that Cooper had given orders for Mr Cohen to be beaten and for the editor of the *Monaro Mercury*, Mr Dixon, to be beaten. The inquiry was also told about an incident when Cooper had walked through the diggings at Crack-em-back in a state of drunken nudity.

Despite all this evidence, and statements from three other complainants in addition to Hawkins, Griffin dismissed most of the charges against Cooper's actions as 'mere assertions, without proof'. In only one case did he censure Cooper, that involving the arrest of W.A. MacDonogh and his subsequent imprisonment as a vagrant for not being able to produce his Miner's Right. Griffin said this action was, 'if not entirely illegal – improper, harsh and uncalled for'. He presented the results of his inquiry in a memorandum.

> After carefully considering the evidence taken during the Inquiry held at Kiandra, for the purpose of investigating charges preferred against Mr Cooper, I am of the opinion that Mr Cooper has not been actuated in his proceedings by malicious and corrupt motives, but has erred from inexperience and want of judgement; and this being the first time that his official conduct has been called into question, I would recommend that he be permitted to exchange, and proceed to some other field, with the understanding, that in the event of such an exchange not being effected within a given period, his removal from Kiandra will result.
>
> 31 January 1862
>
> J.H. Griffin, Commissioner in Charge, Southern Goldfields

Hawkins was not satisfied with the outcome of the inquiry and continued to press his grievances. In May 1862, he petitioned the New South Wales Government with a list of charges against Cooper drawn up by Mr Barton, seeking eight hundred pounds in compensation.

After the inquiry, Cooper was moved to a government post at Eden. No further charges were laid against him. Hawkins was never paid any compensation.

The correspondence relating to Cooper, including the inquiry papers, were ordered to be printed by motion in the New South Wales Legislative Assembly. They can be found in Volume 4 of the New South Wales Legislative Assembly *Votes and Proceedings and Papers Ordered to be Printed During the Session of 1862*.

Cooper's later life was more settled. He resigned his Eden post in 1862 and moved to Queensland. In 1864 he was called to the bar in Sydney and Queensland. After practising in Queensland and New Zealand, he was elected to the Queensland Parliament from 1879 until 1883. He then moved to Victoria, where he married and continued to practise until his death in 1908.

Frankie Gardiner

Frankie Gardiner, alias Francis Christie, was one of Australia's most infamous bushrangers. After being released from Cockatoo Island Prison on a ticket of leave in 1859, Gardiner made for the Kiandra and Lambing Flat goldfields, where he quickly became involved in illegal activities ranging from horse and cattle thieving to highway robbery. He was arrested in 1861 but escaped from police custody.

In June 1862, Gardiner masterminded Australia's largest-ever gold robbery. Gardiner and his gang, which included Johnny Gilbert and Ben Hall, ambushed the gold escort at Escort Rock, three miles from Eugowra on the Sydney–Lachlan Goldfields road. After blocking the road with two bullock teams and greeting the troopers with a hail of gunfire, the gang made off with two thousand seven hundred ounces of gold and three thousand seven hundred pounds in cash. Amazingly, only two of the fleeing troopers were wounded. One of the bags from the robbery was recovered within days, but nearly half the bullion was never found. Gardiner escaped capture until 1864, when he was recognised near Rockhampton and arrested. He served ten years in goal before he was pardoned on the condition that he leave Australia. He married a rich widow and ended his life as a saloon keeper in San Francisco.

Later History of Kiandra

After the initial heady rush in 1860, Kiandra continued to produce gold for the next forty years, but only on a relatively small scale. There was a brief revival of activity in the 1880s, when Three Mile Dam was constructed and hydraulic sluicing hoses were used to blast into New Chum Hill. At the time of the Snowy Mountains Scheme in the 1950s, construction workers were based at Three Mile Dam. Material for the hydro dams was quarried from the Kiandra hills, and Telegraph Street became part of the new Snowy Mountains Highway.

In 1968, Kiandra was acquired by the National Parks and Wildlife Service (NPWS). By then, the township had been reduced to a few buildings beside the main road, although a ski tow operated on Township Hill until the 1960s. In the 1970s, in an act that can only be described as heritage vandalism, a number of the remaining buildings in Kiandra were deliberately destroyed by the NPWS in line with its 'regeneration policy'. The ground was even ploughed to ensure that nothing remained. Ironically, the NPWS permitted extensive development in the previously undegraded and more fragile alpine environment around Thredbo and Perisher.

Kiandra is now uninhabited. Over recent years, the NPWS has changed its approach and has made a belated effort to recognise and mark some of the historic sites in what was Australia's unique snow-bound gold rush township.

Chinese at Kiandra

After the riots and anti-Chinese petition in August 1861, relations between the Chinese and European miners quietened down. Hundreds of Chinese continued mining in Kiandra for the next ten years. In 1863, they even briefly outnumbered the European diggers. As late as 1900 there were still seventy-five Chinese residents in Kiandra. The Chinese gradually became an accepted part of the local community, moving from mining into storekeeping, taking part in skiing competitions and in some cases marrying Europeans. Numbers of descendants of the Chinese of Kiandra still live in the Tumut district, perhaps the most notable being the descendants of Tom Ah Yan.

Skiing in Australia

It is claimed that skiing first took place in Australia at Kiandra in the winter of 1861, when a Norwegian called Bumpstone skied down the main street on a pair of hastily constructed snow shoes, as skis were then called. Others immediately copied him, and the slope above Kiandra on Township Hill is where Australia's first organised ski races were held, beginning in the 1860s.

It is hard to believe that not one of the hundreds of miners who braved the first winter in Kiandra in 1860 experimented with skis or snow skates. In *Kiandra Gold* it is assumed that skiing did in fact take place during that first winter.

Brumbies in the Snowy Mountains and Kosciuszko National Park

Wild horses have a long history in the Snowy Mountains, pre-dating even the Kiandra gold rush. From the earliest times of European settlement (in the 1820s and 1830s), wild horses and cattle could be found in the high country, having strayed from the initial herds brought to graze the mountains in summer.

A report in the *Alpine Pioneer* on 28th December 1860 describes how a party of 'enterprising gentlemen' including an American, Mr Inchcliffe, climbed from the Thredbo/Crackenback diggings to the top of the adjacent mountain range. The climb took upwards of three hours and once on top the party found remnant snow drifts three feet thick. The report said, 'On ascending the table land, immense herds of wild horses were seen, which it would be impossible to drive in.'

From the descriptions given in the report, it would appear that the party climbed the Ram's Head Range and looked out across the alpine country in the vicinity of Perisher Valley. Clearly, the horses they saw had been in the area for some time.

The *Alpine Pioneer*

Following its dramatic beginning in August 1860, when its presses were hauled through the snow on the backs of Chinese coolies, the *Alpine Pioneer* was published twice weekly for the next eight months. On 21st March 1861, due to falling numbers on the goldfield, the *Pioneer* announced it was ceasing publication in Kiandra. The presses were moved to Cooma, where it became the *Monaro Mercury*, the predecessor to Cooma's current local newspaper, the *Cooma Monaro Express*.

Only sixteen issues of the *Alpine Pioneer* have survived. These date from the initial issue of 3rd August until the issue of 28th December 1860. Copies are held by the Mitchell Library in Sydney, the National Library in Canberra and on microfilm by the Cooma Monaro Historical Society.

Lob's Hole (The Hollow)

The dramatic scenery in the Lob's Hole/Ravine area, at the junction of the Yarrangobilly and Tumut Rivers, is claimed to have been the inspiration for 'The Hollow' in Australia's premier bushranging novel – Rolf Boldrewood's *Robbery Under Arms* – though others believe it was the Burragorang Valley. The Hollow was the secret place, ringed by mountains, where the bushrangers hid out between forays.

Lob's Hole was located on one of the routes to the Kiandra diggings. The approach to Lob's Hole was so steep that horses had to ride down Brandy Mary Spur on their haunches. For many years after the gold rush, the residents of Kiandra used this sheltered valley to escape the rigours of the Kiandra weather. The river junction is now flooded by the Talbingo Dam, but the mud brick walls of the old hotel at Ravine are still partly standing.

Impact of the Snowy Mountains Hydro-electric Scheme

The Snowy Mountains Hydro-electric Scheme, which involved a massive program of engineering construction from 1949 until 1974, had a dramatic impact on the environment in the mountains and surrounding districts. Roads were cut though previously inaccessible terrain and dams constructed on all the major rivers. The creation of Lake Eucumbene in 1958 flooded Euecumbene Station and Cosgrove's Adaminimi Station. The buildings from the Adaminaby village which had grown up in the vicinity of the Station were moved north to a new Adaminaby township site on the relocated Snowy Mountains Highway.

The new alignment of the Snowy Mountains Highway has diverted the Kiandra road away from Denison and Russell's Station. It no longer crosses the river at the old Denison Bridge. Much of Russell's Station was flooded by Lake Eucumbene, and the station buildings have all been removed.

Kitty McCrae
(by Barcroft Henry Boake, 1866–1892)

The Western sun, ere he sought his lair,
Skimm'd the treetops, and glancing thence,
Rested awhile on the curling hair
Of Kitty McCrae, by the boundary fence;
Her eyes looked anxious, her cheeks were pale,
For father was two hours late with the mail.
Never before had he been so late,
And Kitty wondered and wished him back,
Leaning athwart the big swing gate
That opens out on the bridle-track,
A tortuous path that sidled down
From the single street of a mining town.
With her raven curls and her saucy smile,
Brown eyes that glow with a changeful light,
Tenderly trembling all the while
Like a brace of stars on the breast of night,
Where could you find in the light of day
A bonnier lassie than Kitty McCrae?
Born in the saddle, this girl could ride
Like the fearless queen of the silver bow;
And nothing that ever was lapped in hide
Could frighten Kitty McCrae, I trow.
She would wheel a mob in the hour of need
If the Devil himself were in the lead.
But now, in the shadows' deepening
When the last sun-spark had ceas'd to burn,
Afar she catches the sullen ring
Of horse-hoofs swinging around the turn,
Then painfully down the narrow trail
Comes Alex McCrae with the Greytown mail.
'The fever-and-ague, my girl,' he said,
''Twas all I got on that northern trip,

When it left me then I was well-nigh dead,
Has got me fast in its iron grip;
And I'd rather rot in the nearest gaol
Than ride to-night with the Greytown mail.

'At Golden Gully they heard to-day –
'Twas a common topic about the town –
That the Mulligan gang were around this way,
So they wouldn't despatch the gold-dust down,
And Brown, the manager, said he thought
'Twere wise to wait for a strong escort.
'I rode the leaders, the other nags
I left with the coach at the 'Travellers' Rest'.
Kitty, my lass, you must take the bags –
Postboy, I reckon's about the best;
'Tis dark, I know, but he'll never fail
To take you down with the Greytown mail.'
It needed no further voice to urge
This dutiful daughter to eager haste;
She donned the habit, of rough blue serge,
That hung in folds from her slender waist,
And Postboy stood by the stockyard rail,
While she mounted behind the Greytown mail.
Dark points, the rest of him iron-grey,
Boasting no strain of expensive blood,
Down steepest hill he could pick his way,
And never was baulked by a winter flood -
Strong as a lion, hard as a nail,
Was the horse that carried the Greytown mail;
A nag that really seemed to be
Fit for a hundred miles at a push,
With the old Manaro pedigree,
By 'Furious Rising,' out of 'The Bush,'
Run in when a colt from a mountain mob
By Brian O'Flynn and Dusty Bob.

And Postboy's bosom was filled with pride
As he felt the form of his mistress sway,
In its easy grace, to his swinging stride
As he dashed along down the narrow way.
No prettier Mercury, I'll go bail,
Than Kitty ere carried a Guv'nment mail.
Leaving the edge of O'Connor's Hill,
They merrily scattered the drops of dew
In the spanning of many a tiny rill,
Whose bubbling waters were hid from view:
In quick-step time to the curlew's wail
Rode Kitty McCrae, with the Greytown mail.
Sidling the Range, by a narrow path
Where towering mountain ash-trees grow,
And a slip meant more than an icy bath
In the tumbling waters that foamed below;
Through the white fog, filling each silent vale,
Rode Kitty McCrae, with the Greytown mail.
The forest shadows became less dense,
They fairly flew down the river fall,
As out from the shade of an old brush-fence
Stepped three armed men with a sudden call,
Sharp and stern came the well-known hail:
'Stand! for we want the Greytown mail!'
Postboy swerved with a mighty bound,
As an outlaw clung to his bridle rein,
A hoof-stroke flattened him on the ground
With a curse that was half a cry of pain,
While Kitty, trembling and rather pale,
Rode for life and the Greytown mail.
To save the bags was her only thought
As she bent 'fore the whistle of angry lead
That follow'd the flash and the sharp report;
But, 'Oh, you cowards!' was all she said.
Fast as fast as the leaden hail –

Kitty rode on with the Greytown mail.
Safe? ah, no, for a tiny stream
On Postboy's coat left its crimson mark.
Still she rode on, but t'was in a dream,
Through lands where shadows fell drear and dark,
Like a wounded sea-bird before the gale
Fled Kitty McCrae with the Greytown mail.
And ever the crimson life-stream drips,
For every hoof-stroke a drop of blood,
From feeble fingers the bridle slips
As down the Warrigal Flat they scud,
And just where the Redbank workings lie,
She reels and falls with a feeble cry.
The old horse slacken'd his racing pace
When he found the saddle his only load,
And nervously sniffed at the still, pure face
That lay upturned in the dusty road;
Like a gathered rose in the heat of day,
She droop'd and faded, Kitty McCrae.
Did Postboy stay by the dead girl's side?
Not he. Relieved of her feather-weight,
He woke the echoes with measured stride,
Galloping up to the postal gate –
Blood, dust, and sweat from head to tail,
A riderless horse with the Greytown mail!
And now a river-oak, drooping, weeps
In ceaseless sorrow above the grave
On the lush-green flat where Kitty sleeps,
Hush'd by the river's lapping wave –
That ever tells to the trees the tale
Of how she rode with the Greytown mail.

'Kitty McCrae' was first published in the Sydney *Bulletin* in December 1891. Many of Boake's poems are based on events that occurred in the areas in which he worked and travelled. Barcroft Boake lived in the

Monaro district for two years – from 1886 until 1888. During this time he visited Kiandra, which was still an active gold mining town. Eight of his published poems feature stories from the Snowy Mountains/Monaro area. More of Boake's poems and details about his short and interesting but tragic life can be viewed at www.boake.net.

A Summer's Day Ramble Through Kiandra

(from the *Sydney Mail*, 8th December 1860)

Reader, have you a great-coat, a good muffler, and a pair of thigh boots? If you have, and feel disposed to enjoy a good walk on a summer's day about Kiandra, just arrange your fixings and come with me. I do not pretend to show you the City of Palaces, or the Castles of Gold, at present – they do not exist in these Alpine Regions; but that you may thoroughly appreciate the pleasures and advantages of this Alpha and Omega of New South Wales, we will commence starting from that elegant building called the Exchange Hotel; should you be at all curious to know anything about that wonderful establishment, a reference to our local journal will supply you with the desired information. There you will learn that it was the first hotel ever erected on Kiandra; and, however much you may be disappointed, after reading the very graphic description the advertisement that appears in the said local journal gives of this hotel, which now presents the appearance of some old farm house barn in its last days of rapid decline and fall – yet, reader, not many months ago it was the only comfortable house, in fact the only building, that could lay claim to the name house at all. Could you have been here when numbers of men, struggling in the snow and mud, were engaged in carrying that house into Kiandra, you would not wonder at its present appearance. You seem surprised at my saying 'carrying the house,' but such literally was the case, not only with that house, but with all Kiandra, for no timber fit for building purposes is to be had nearer than three miles. It is only very lately that drays have been enabled to get into this place, so that the city of Kiandra may boast of being shouldered into existence.

Before we commence our tour, let us enter, and (in a colonial phrase) do our beer, which means in the dialect of Kiandra, in this weather, brandy hot. You see that the days of a perforated nail-can, filled with charcoal and placed in the middle of the room, stifling everybody, and causing a chilly dampness to surround all, have passed, and in its place a large fireplace, with a roaring fire. I tell you this, or perhaps you might leave with the idea that there is no fire in the place, for with the mob of diggers standing before it and their steaming glasses of grog, I must admit it is very difficult to see, and to get near it would entitle no persevering individual to a great amount of praise. But let us go outside and commence our ramble; – before you start, let me call your attention to the hill we are now standing upon. This is Surface Hill, from which so large a quantity of gold has been taken – nuggets from five to twenty-eight pounds weight have been some of the prizes that have been drawn from this bank. See, there are two parties endeavouring to work in spite of the snow; should you wish to see what work men will do under the excitement of gold – come here to-night, let it be about ten o'clock, and you will find men working – two or three fires – the reflection from which will show a small white circle on the snow that looks not unlike monster bull's eyes endeavouring to throw a light upon the labours of those moving creatures that you must suppose to be men but cannot possibly distinguish; the falling of the water from various races; the low murmurs and peculiar grating sound that sticks in your ear from the conversation and work that is being carried on at the same time, will, perhaps enable you to appreciate the enjoyments of gold digging. Let us proceed. But what's the matter? I thought you might have known, from that streak of snow that's lower than any other, that it was a race, and would have avoided it; but because you have deposited your precious body in the snow and water do not complain. It's a mere trifle, I assure you, wet though I dare say you are; but you have this consolation to console yourself with – that many in their houses are no better off.

We will now take our course up Broadway. There is more traffic here, so the snow will not mislead you. You would sooner have snow than this mud, would you? Well, if you complain of this, you will complain of anything; you are not yet knee deep in it. Wait till I take you through the bog they call Telegraph Street, and with this drifting snow in your face if you do not wish yourself in Sydney, and give Kiandra your blessing, you desire the title of the patient man. You are mistaken; the roof of that place was not blown off, for a very good reason, it was never on – that is the Royal George Hotel. You could do with a glass of brandy hot, could you? Well, I am not surprised at that, considering the tumbling performance you went through in the race. We will go inside, and you will have the opportunity of seeing it. They have shingled over some fifteen feet of the roof; that long skeleton of a place was intended for a ball-room; but whether they fell short of funds or intend to have an al fresco place of entertainment so that the summer heat should not oppress them, I cannot say; but I did hear that the sign of the hotel is to be altered next licensing day. They are making a great mystery of the name it will receive at the next christening; but from private information I have obtained, as the police say I am in possession of all the facts, and Campbell's Folly vice Royal George, resigned, some say dismissed, will be the next sign that will astonish the native of Kiandra. No, I will not take another glass of brandy hot, for I have business to do – many have taken an active part in the formation of temperance societies in different parts of the world, and in Sydney in particular. It is to be hoped they will never attempt it here, for it is impossible to live on Kiandra without a small portion of that poison called alcohol to keep life and body together, as it is to drive bullocks without swearing, and having heard that even a clergyman could not accomplish the last mentioned feat without committing himself, there cannot be a very great sin in the other.

Now be careful how you slip off the steps as you come down from the Royal, and let us proceed up Broadway – you see we have bowling saloons, stores, butchers and bakers, jewellers, shoemakers and snobs. Should you require to send your friends a full length portrait of your Kiandra appearance? A photographic artist resides there, who for a very moderate sum, will condescend to oblige you. We have now reached Telegraph Street, the grand centre of the town; it crosses the Broadway. On the four corners so formed the most profitable businesses here are conducted; two public houses and two banks – the Oriental and Bank of New South Wales, the Empire and Kiandra hotels. Let us look into one of the banks; there sits a clerk, all alone in his glory, trying to keep himself warm by a fire, about large enough to put into your pipe to light it; but see the rush he makes to the door. He sees what appears to be one of the imps of darkness, wending his way along the street; his black face and clothes contrasting strangely with the snow, as he carries a large bag upon his shoulder, containing wealth most desirable here, charcoal. Notice their countenances; the doleful appearance of the clerk when in reply to his enquiries the man of coal puts on a savage grin, and utters one monosyllable – sold. It is difficult to say which is most decidedly sold, the clerk or the coal.

Looking down Broadway towards Surface Hill you have a fine view of mud larking and dray bogging – with the distant hills covered with snow that you must be a miserable being if you cannot enjoy yourself – just take a glance up Broadway, it will be quite sufficient, for I do not expect on a day like this you would ever attempt to mount that and examine he site where Kiandra proper originally stood. That sign you see about half way up the hill seems to attract your notice – those monster letters are sufficiently plain for you to see that from that building the literary wonder of Kiandra – the Alpine Pioneer is issued – but in case you should mistake the splendid picture in the centre for the sign of the Spread Eagle public house, I may as well inform you that it is supposed to represent a printing press.

We will now go down Telegraph Street – that building – the only one we can boast of is for the post and telegraph offices – they are not yet occupied. Opposite are the Kiandra newsrooms, if you can manage to cross the road we will pay a visit to the temporary telegraph office, in yonder store. You will find the station-master very obliging should you wish to send a message, or make any enquiries; and when you see the accommodation he possesses – that he should answer, much less be civil, to any question you may put, will surprise you; cross that respectable looking ditch, and before you enter read the notice on the board, 'No admittance except on business.' Do not be surprised, there in the corner is the telegraph. These piles of goods are not Government property; the tea and brandy, sugar and shovels, wine and flour, boxes and bales, saddles and casks that are piled up belong to a private individual, who, to oblige the public, puts himself to great inconvenience, and does not even receive their thanks. Step over those long handled shovels, and you are in the office. What does he say? He cannot send a message, for communication is interrupted with Sydney. The line inspector is despatched to see if he can find out the cause; and as you with difficulty make your way out of the office, which is beautifully carpeted an inch in depth in snow and mud, you hear the station-master blowing on his finger-ends for the purpose of imparting a little warmth to them. Look, there is a coloured gentleman with a broad grin upon his face. What does he want? See, he makes his way to the station-master and says, 'I guess you can't send a message to Sydney today?' 'No, Sir; communication is interrupted, I am sorry to say.' 'Interrupted, is it? Well, I kind of guessed it was, and I came to give you a bit of information. I have only just arrived here, but at a distance of some fourteen miles from this place I noticed one of the telegraph poles very much excited, and casting my eye up, observed about a score of messages all close together and sticking to the top of the pole. I suppose you will stand for that information.' Then bursting into a loud ha ha he soon makes tracks.

Before leaving this place, allow me to call your attention to this snug room, about ten feet square. It is the honorable member for Tumut's sleeping quarters (Chas Cowper). Come inside, and you will see that even M.L.A.s are not so comfortable as one would suppose. It is certainly very dark; but look at the bed – did you ever see anything more picturesque; look at the splendid canopy formed over the head of it by sundry great coats, for the purpose of keeping that crystal stream that flows so gracefully through the roof from making it damp; you see that oil cloth at the foot prevents the three inches of snow that lies upon it from penetrating. Just fancy a night's rest in that bed, and the delightful prospect presented to you at early morn. I have it on the authority of the honorable member himself that this morning there was nothing dry in the place except his boots, he having taken the precaution to place them under the stretcher; it's true they were filled with snow, but that's nothing.

We will now resume our journey. You have a slight sideling (slope) to get up before you can get on the road. But how came you to fall, you are now covered with mud. It's a bog is it? Well, then I will not dispute with you, but in a few yards you will get on the only piece of road yet made in Kiandra. See the Government have placed four or five small bridges over the worst bogs, and made a road several hundred yards in length. I imagine it's only the commencement, for there is a bog at either end of it. This leads to Camp Town. We will now proceed to the Police court, but before you enter such aristocratic places, you had better sit down on that large boulder in the creek, and wash a little of the mud off yourself. Yes, that is the camp, but you cannot proceed that way, the snow hides several bogs and quagmires, and, like all Government approaches, it is only to be made by a great amount of circumlocution. We will take the left-hand road – you are again in error; that green wide place without a roof was never a billiard room, neither is that dilapidated tent, the Camp Inn – they are two fugitive signboards that have broken away from their moorings, and have brought up there as you see. Let us now enter the Hall of Justice, but it is vacant, and today is a court day – true it is a cold miserable place – the crow certainly comes through the shingles – there is also a fair quantity of mud – but there is no fireplace – but what has that to do with it – do not the public pay the magistrates, of course they do; then what excuse have they – if they were knee deep in snow, and their ink frozen they are bound to do their duty. What a blessing it is we have a free Press, that we can expose their doings. What does that policeman say? – The court is being held in the sergeant's room? What a pity he should have told us, for he has deprived us of giving the magistrates a little abuse in the newspapers, for we have the same privilege that others have exercised in writing letters for the edification of the public, without making any inquiries or knowing anything about the parties we so charitably abuse, of course, for the public good. We will go and visit the sergeant's room, and see if we cannot get something to write against. Now look around and see what fortunate fellows these officials are, they are assembled doing their public duty, in a room some fifteen feet square, that boasts of a table about four feet long, a fire-place with a small amount of fire, and two or three stretchers; before the fire stands the great lawyer of Kiandra, pouring out his eloquence, and monopolising the fire; at the table sits the magistrate engaged taking the depositions, the inspector of police, a constable, a member of the fourth estate in one corner taking notes under difficulties, a lady giving her evidence, and a few of the public, comprise the company assembled on this occasion.

Let us leave this place and call on the Commissioners, for they are certain, from the very liberal manner in which they are paid, to be in among quarter and enjoying themselves – but you see even commissioners cannot boast of their accommodation – in a room about the size of the one you have just left, without any fire, in consequence of the contractor for the wood being unable to deliver any. One muffled in his great coat is walking up and down to keep up the circulation of the blood, another with a ruler, the tips of his fingers almost frost bitten, endeavouring to make up some official forms, but they are constrained to be very polite to us because we (that is the public) pay them, and should they offend our dignity, we have the privilege of abusing them. You are getting tired, are you? I will not detain you much longer – those horses lying there died last night. In that small building resides the Colonial Architect; come and look at his quarters – you see his desk is covered with snow, the floor also, and his bed forms no exception to the general rule in being wet through; but remember he is another official – he must have no excuses or favours shown him; the public pay him also, so you can abuse him.

It is getting late. I will now take you to an hotel, where you can get a bed. You are afraid it will be damp; not at all; for I have secured two beds under a billiard table, and if there is such a thing as a dry bed on Kiandra, you shall have it tonight.

Reader, since you have favoured me with your company so long, I will now say farewell – should you be in Sydney – you can put on your overlander – your light clothes – your drab boots and sun yourself in George Street – should you find it too oppressive, you can go to the Domain or Botanical Gardens and enjoy the sea breeze, and remember that your visit to Kiandra was towards the end of November, 1860, in the supposed summer season, and you may then have some idea of winter in that favoured quarter, and I think you will agree with a friend of mine, who said that the one thing alone was wanted to make Kiandra perfect, and that was an earthquake.

J.A.H.

Acknowledgements

I would like to acknowledge the kind assistance I have been given in writing this book by many people who share an interest in the history of the Snowy Mountains. In particular I would like to mention Heather Rhodes from the Cooma Monaro Historical Society, John and Roslyn Rudd from Reynella (John is a descendant of William Russell), Paddy and Jan Kerrigan, Neville Locker, Lindsay Smith, Klaus Hueneke and Tom Wiles from Adelong. Dr Peter Hebbard advised on the likely medical condition of Davy's body.

I owe a special debt of gratitude to Lindsay Smith, who kindly lent me his copies of the *Alpine Pioneer* and his own research project thesis, 'The Chinese of Kiandra, New South Wales' (1997).

A number of books and theses proved useful in researching the history of Kiandra. Most prominent among the books were *Historic Kiandra*, edited by D.G. Moye, and Cooma Country, by Lauri Neal, while the Perkins Papers, held by the Cooma Monaro Historical Society, provided a useful pointer to relevant material. Unpublished theses included Alison Tait's extended essay, 'Kiandra, the forgotten town; a study of a gold town' (1977), G. Gregors' 'Kiandra Precinct Plan' (1982) and Rob Warren-Smith's ANU thesis, 'The Rush that Ended: Towards a social reconstruction of Kiandra during the decline of the gold rush in 1860' (1991).

The *Sydney Morning Herald* and the *Sydney Mail* from 1860 to 1862 and the extant issues of the *Alpine Pioneer* were invaluable contemporary records, as were the Frederick Cooper Inquiry papers. The latter can be found in Volume 4 of the New South Wales Legislative Assembly Votes and Proceedings and Papers Ordered to be Printed During the Session of 1862 (pages 65 to 113). The National Library of Australia proved a valuable resource in accessing this contemporaneous material.

I also wish to thank my family for their help and their forbearance. Special thanks are due to Judith and Anne, but I would also like to thank Bronwen, Michael, Peter and James, and Denis McNeill.

Hugh Capel
October 2003